Dedication

In loving memory of my dear mother,
The one who championed my writing journey,
These books stand as a testament to your never-ending belief in me.
As my biggest fan, your encouragement was unwavering throughout
the years I spent writing this book series. Though you're not here to
see the culmination of my efforts, I know you are watching over me,
cheering me on from a place where love transcends all boundaries.
Your absence is deeply felt, but I carry your love and support within
me, inspiring me and giving me the courage to chase my dreams.
You are forever in my heart.

How to Seduce a Rockstar

Arabella Quinn

Copyright © 2023 by Arabella Quinn

All rights reserved.

No part of this publication may be reproduced, distributed, or transmitted in any form or by any means, including photocopying, recording, or other electronic or mechanical methods, without the prior written permission of the publisher, except as permitted by U.S. copyright law.

If you purchased a copy of this eBook, thank you. Also, thank you for not sharing your copy of this book. This purchase allows you one legal copy for your own personal computer or device. You do not have the rights to resell, distribute, print, or transfer this book, in whole or in part, in any format, via methods either currently known or yet to be invented, or upload to a file sharing peer-to-peer program. It may not be re-sold or given away to other people. Such action is illegal and in violation of the U.S. Copyright Law. If you would like to share this book with another person, please purchase an additional copy for each recipient. If you're reading this book and did not purchase it, or it was not purchased for your use only, then please purchase your own copy. Thank you for respecting the hard work of this author.

The story, all names, characters, and incidents portrayed in this production are fictitious. No identification with actual persons (living or deceased), places, buildings, and products is intended or should be inferred.

Contents

Chapter 1	1
Chapter 2	7
Chapter 3	17
Chapter 4	21
Chapter 5	25
Chapter 6	35
Chapter 7	45
Chapter 8	52
Chapter 9	64
Chapter 10	68
Chapter 11	78
Chapter 12	84
Chapter 13	91
Chapter 14	111

Chapter 15	127
Chapter 16	133
Chapter 17	141
Chapter 18	151
Chapter 19	165
Chapter 20	183
Chapter 21	197
Chapter 22	207
Chapter 23	221
Chapter 24	242
Chapter 25	252
Chapter 26	263
Chapter 27	270
Chapter 28	276
Chapter 29	289
Chapter 30	298
Chapter 31	309
Chapter 32	319
Chapter 33	326
Chapter 34	337
Chapter 35	343
Chapter 36	362
Chapter 37	403
Chapter 38	408

Chapter 39	419
Chapter 40	427
Epilogue	433
Next in Series	442
Arabella Quinn Newsletter	444
Bad Boys of Rock Series	445
Also By Arabella Quinn	448
About the Author	450
Excerpt	451

Chapter 1

Talia

Well, that was ... ugly.

My heart sank as I watched Max storm off, angrily pinballing off shoulders as he weaved through the crowded bar, desperate to escape the heated fight that had flared up between us. This wasn't the first time he'd walked out on our bickering. Lately, he'd been sidestepping my nitpicking as much as I waited to pounce on his petty criticisms. It was a vicious cycle.

Suddenly, the music that pounded all around me seemed too hostile and aggressive. My heart was beating wildly in my chest, adrenaline surging in the aftermath of our argument. I knew I should chase after him, but I remained frozen to the spot.

How had we gone from celebrating his birthday to hurling insults back and forth in five minutes flat?

Ignoring the sting of tears that welled in my eyes, I threw back the

Alabama Slammer that was clenched in my hand. I squeezed my body through the crowd, four people deep at the bar, in search of more alcohol. The bartenders were hustling; there was no way they would serve me anytime soon. I left the empty shot glass at the edge of the bar and backed away.

I scanned the crowd for Max. He'd been heading toward the exit. Would he just up and leave? On his birthday?

Yeah, he would.

Feeling sorry for myself, I swallowed down a threat of fresh tears.

My best friend, who was also my roommate, Ellie, was here somewhere. I hadn't seen her in at least an hour; I guess she was trying to make herself inconspicuous while Max and I had been getting along for a change. The last I'd seen her, she'd given me a thumbs up from behind Max's back before retreating to her group of work friends.

I headed toward the tables in the back where I knew she liked to hang out. I found her crammed into a booth that was dangerously exceeding its maximum capacity. I didn't recognize anyone there except for one of her coworkers, Gina, who I'd met a few times before.

The laughter froze on Ellie's face when she spotted me. A tenuous smile skated across my lips, but there was no fooling her. She mouthed, "Where's Max?" I frowned and shook my head in answer.

She began the arduous process of extricating herself from the booth, claiming she urgently needed to use the ladies' room so people would move. I felt bad. Here I was, killing everyone's buzz. First Max's, on his birthday no less, and now Ellie's. If I were a better friend, I'd spare her the ordeal of having to talk me down from another fight with Max, and I'd just go home and wallow by myself. But I needed her calming words of wisdom. I needed someone to tell me that everything was okay.

But, things weren't okay with Max and me. We were drifting apart.

We'd been dating for almost three years. Just this past Christmas, he said he had a big surprise waiting for me. For some dumb reason, I thought it might be an engagement ring. And in those two weeks of waiting and wondering, that little seed of hope had grown into a deep-rooted blossom of obsession. When Christmas finally came around, the punch to my gut was palpable when Max presented me with tickets to a show I'd vaguely mentioned wanting to see instead of a marriage proposal.

Things went downhill after that and a lot of it was my fault. I started noticing all the maddening little things that I'd previously ignored about him. And, to be honest, things hadn't been exactly perfect before that, anyway. Max was beautiful, but he was so darn fragile. Unless I was stroking his ego, he never seemed happy.

He was always telling me how gorgeous I was and how lucky he was to have me. Get beyond the superficial, though, and things just ran off the rails. We hardly agreed on anything. Did he even value me as a person?

I shook my head bitterly. The vicious path of my thoughts astonished me. How the heck could I be questioning my feelings for him after three years together? It was ludicrous. I just needed the reassurance of an engagement ring on my finger.

My frown grew as I waited for Ellie. After several moments of struggle, her foot finally dislodged from the tangle of people in the booth, and she thudded ungracefully at my side. She was lucky she didn't fall flat on her face.

"What happened?" She pawed at me as she regained her balance.

"Uh, the usual." I inhaled shakily, recalling the nasty words we had hurled at each other. "I don't even remember what started it this time. And of course, he blamed me for all of it."

I did, however, clearly remember the angry look of disbelief on his face as he flung his parting words at me. "Couldn't you just leave it alone this once, Tal? It's my birthday, for fuck's sake."

Maybe I had started the fight.

Ellie's eyes swept around the bar. "So, where is he?"

"I think he left."

"On his birthday?" Her eyebrows shot up in surprise.

"I know," I huffed. "How'd I screw this up so bad? I mean, with the whole birthday surprise and all."

Ellie nodded sympathetically, then arched an eyebrow as her hand landed on her hip. "Birthday surprise? Don't you mean Operation Limp Dick?"

I giggled nervously and looked around. "Shh. Someone will hear you."

She rolled her eyes, but continued in a soothing tone, "Don't worry. You didn't totally screw up, Talia. All is not lost because everyone knows makeup sex is the very best sex. You guys will get your sex mojo back tonight with O.L.D. — I'm sure of it. You'll just have to chase after him and hunt him down. And once you find him, don't let him come up for air!"

I laughed for a moment at the visual. Ellie knew exactly what kind of sex was on the agenda. We'd discussed it a few nights before. We had laughed ourselves silly and coined it 'Operation Limp Dick' or O.L.D. as our secret joke. "He won't get any air, believe me, his mouth will be occupied."

She grimaced and held up a hand. "Stop. I don't want to picture it."

Max's sexual fantasy, or at least the one he shared with me, was more like my biggest nightmare. With longing in his eyes, he'd mentioned it to me a few times, and I'd always teasingly told him there was no way it was going to happen. But I'd confessed to Ellie that I was going to make it happen on his birthday. Tonight.

The actual sex he wanted was no big deal. It was the standard sixty-nine position, and I absolutely believed that mutual oral sex was kind of, well — sexy. Very sexy. It was the 'morning' part of the fantasy that I abhorred.

Max was the epitome of a morning person. In fact, he'd probably stormed out on me tonight, in part, because he was overtired. It was only about half past midnight, but knowing him, he'd been getting cranky hours ago. We'd both worked the full Friday, but I was ready to party for another couple of hours. At least.

We were complete opposites.

When Max nudged me at 7 a.m. on a Saturday morning to go a round with him … ugh. The morning breath. Eeew. The ratty bedhead. Yuck. The morning sun shining through the windows. Stab it. The full bladder. No. Thanks.

And, wouldn't you know, he was The. Horniest. Guy. in the morning. After midnight, not so much. But any man would eventually quit trying to get morning sex after getting shut down over and over. Almost every morning he was up by 5:30, out jogging or heading to the gym before work, well before I could even attempt to crack an eyelid open.

It was really no surprise he wanted morning sex. His fantasy involved being woken up while getting his cock sucked. The first thing he'd see when he opened his eyes were my lady parts dangling above his face. That was his fantasy — a surprise sixty-nine.

While I wanted to give him that exact fantasy, it would never happen. Sex in the morning … just no. But sex at 3 a.m.? It's on, baby. And that was how I was going to rock his world tonight. I'd give him another hour, and he'd be fast asleep. He'd awaken to his big birthday surprise.

I spent the next hour and a half partying with Ellie and her friends.

It turned out that I was a lot more relaxed without Max there. I did far too many shots until I was tipping the scales well beyond buzzed. Mixing with the alcohol, a languid anticipation was thrumming in my veins. I hadn't been this excited or nervous about sex in the longest time. It was going down tonight.

And so was I.

Chapter 2

Talia

BY THE TIME I got to Max's apartment, it was close to 3 a.m. I thanked my driver as I stepped out of the car and then dug Max's key out of my handbag. I hadn't used his key in a long time. We spent most weekends at my apartment. My place was cleaner and always had more food stocked. He still lived more like a college kid, even though he was pushing 30 years old.

As I made my way carefully up the sidewalk, I went over Operation Limp Dick in my head. Just thinking of our stealth name for it had me chuckling to myself in the dark. What would Max say if he knew Ellie and I had chatted about his flaccid dick in minute detail? I giggled again. He would kill me.

Ellie and I had discussed the plan over a couple of bottles of wine. We had gone over all the logistics. The plan was for me to get completely naked before I crept into bed with him. Max slept in a T-shirt and boxers, so we both agreed that the boxers would make the mission more doable. If he wore tighty-whities or snug boxer briefs, it definitely would have been more problematic.

Then we spent hours collapsing together in laughter, trying to imagine the next part. We debated how to remove his cock from his boxers. Pull down his boxers, fish his cock through the hole sewn into the front, or slip it out the wide side leg of the boxers? What was the best way to maneuver his cock without waking him?

Of course, that question led to a very mature debate on what the state of said cock would be at the time. We both agreed that if Max was sleeping, his cock would most likely be limp. Through howls of laughter, I admitted I hadn't really noticed Max's cock when limp. Guys got hard at even the tiniest whiff of sex. Anytime I'd seen him naked, he'd been erect. Sure, maybe not completely hard right away, but never completely deflated.

So after two bottles of wine, the conversation degenerated even further to the whole sucking-the-cock part of the plan. Because we both assumed I'd have to suck a limp dick. At least initially. That was so ... unsexy. Hence, we named the whole thing Operation Limp Dick.

After a bit of fumbling, I opened the front door of his building and made my way up to the second floor, where his apartment was. I took a deep breath before I turned the key in his door. I was nervous about my mission but excited too.

We hadn't had sex in about two weeks. I thought that withholding sex might make him realize what he was missing and value me more. It was a passive-aggressive move in that I wasn't outright denying him. It annoyed me to no end that it almost seemed like he didn't even notice. Ugh. How did it come to this?

Did he want to break up with me? Did I want to break up with him? I didn't even know anymore, but this breakup/makeup dance was getting old. I sighed as I allowed my eyes to get used to the dim light in his apartment; keeping the lights off was integral to the plan.

I wasn't quite ready to give up on him. Maybe I wasn't trying hard enough to be a good girlfriend. Well, tonight I'd show him. I'd let all my pent-up sexual frustration out to play. I was ready to rock his world.

After a night of mind-blowing sex, maybe we'd lounge in bed together all morning. Or not lounge, but do other sexy things until we were too hungry. Then we could shower together and then walk hand in hand like lovers to the tiny Italian restaurant down the street for his birthday lunch. A languid, sexy Saturday. A girl could dream.

Stepping inside, my eyes swept through his front room, noticing the typical clutter lying about. I didn't hear any noise from the bedroom, so I assumed he was fast asleep as I tiptoed to his bedroom door and carefully opened it a crack.

It was dark in there. Max didn't have any curtains on his windows, but he had those cheap plastic mini-blinds that were perpetually covered in a layer of dust. He was usually too tired at night to rotate them closed, so the bright sunlight would beam down on the bed in the early morning. He probably preferred it that way. I made a mental note to remember to close them after we had sex tonight.

I could just barely see his form on the bed; his arm was bent and raised, his wrist resting over his forehead. It was such a dramatic pose. I almost giggled. His chest looked bare, which was unusual, and a single sheet snaked around the lower half of his body. My heart tugged a little at the sight of him. He looked the perfect mixture of strong and vulnerable.

I backed my head out of the door, my heart picking up its rhythm. I was ready to do this. Even turned on. That excited me even more. It'd been far too long since the prospect of sex had excited me. Even before

I'd been withholding sex from Max, we'd been in a missionary-style rut.

I tiptoed my way over to the bathroom. I had to pee, and I wanted to clean up. If my pussy was going to hover over his face, it had to be sparkly. I held back another tipsy giggle as I used the bathroom, being as quiet as I could.

I hadn't given Max a blowjob in months. Not that I hated doing it, but it just didn't really seem to be reciprocated that much. Not that I needed some oral attention every single time I gave him a blowie. And maybe not necessarily right after I did it, but maybe the next time? At least keep it kind of even. Right?

Not that I was keeping score of every single blowjob I gave him. Okay, I guess I was keeping score. Because I was at minus 12 right now. Since I started keeping score, that is. I had given him head 12 more times than I'd gotten oral from him. That was a significant gap. And, hell. When I ended up getting tongue sex from him, I usually ended up faking an orgasm, because, after a while when I knew the big "O" would not happen, I would feel bad. It always felt like it was more of a chore for him to go down there. Like he wanted me to orgasm after only 30 seconds or something. So, I'd fake it just to end it.

He never seemed to have any problem getting off. And then he'd seem half-hearted trying to finish me off. Especially when it seemed to take me so darn long to orgasm. At some point, faking it had just become easier. Then I'd end up masturbating in the bathroom while he passed out.

Another ugh.

I finished cleaning up and resolutely shook off the depressing turn my thoughts had taken. Tonight was different. I was already feeling excited about having sex. The alcohol gave me some liquid courage to shake off any inhibitions. I slipped off my shoes and then stripped naked.

I left my clothes in a pile on his couch and then crept back to his door, which I had left cracked open. He hadn't moved a muscle. He looked beautiful lying there in the dark. Messy and rumpled and very masculine.

My hands slid down my body and then I began to play with myself, but I was too impatient to get very far. I wanted Max's mouth on me, not my fingers. It was show time.

♫♫♪♪

Operation Limp Dick was moving along nicely. I'd snuck into Max's bedroom and delicately peeled the sheet from atop his body without waking him. He was out cold. It was so bloody dark in the room; I couldn't see anything.

My eyes focused like a laser toward where I could vaguely make out his cock as I reverse-straddled his body in slow motion, painstakingly making sure not to touch him. I must have looked utterly ridiculous, but I couldn't believe that I was pulling this off. Even in my inebriated state, I hadn't woken him yet. The bigger surprise had been that Max was sleeping in the nude. He'd never gone to bed nude with me, but he'd often not bothered re-dressing after sex. Maybe he slept nude sometimes when he wasn't with me? Ellie and I had spent all that time trying to figure out the boxer problem, and it had magically worked out. Ta-da!

I was kneeling over him and I needed to get my mouth near his cock and my pussy near his mouth. I slowly leaned down on my elbows, coming within inches of his limp dick.

I stopped.

It didn't seem as small as I'd imagined it'd be. It didn't seem entirely limp either. In fact, it looked semi-hard. Maybe he was having a pleasant dream? I was sure he was still asleep. His breathing hadn't changed, his muscles hadn't tensed; he hadn't moved at all. Well, that was fine. I didn't relish sucking a limp dick, anyway.

Somehow, I maneuvered my knees on either side of his face. He had moved a little this time and his arm slid off his forehead to his side, but if I had to bet, I'd bet he was still sleeping. If he opened his eyes now, all he'd see was my pussy, which was the plan. Operation Limp Dick was a go.

Satisfyingly, there was a sweet ache building between my legs. I stifled the urge to mash my pussy right into his mouth and wake him up that way. Patience, Talia.

I lowered my mouth closer to his cock and just breathing on it seemed to bring it to life. It looked even bigger. Ellie had asked me how big Max's cock was and had laughed like crazy when I told her I didn't really know. It was a normal size. I mean, I never got out a measuring tape and studied it. It always seemed just fine.

But now it seemed bigger. Had I really put that whole thing in my mouth before? I gave it a lick with my tongue. Mmmm. How had I never noticed that Max's cock wasn't just average? It seemed bigger. I flicked my tongue over the tip. Wow, it was still getting bigger.

I almost groaned out loud. I was getting pretty turned on. Crazy, but I actually wanted him in my mouth. I gently grabbed his base with my right hand and lifted his cock to my mouth, slowly sliding my lips over it.

I teased him slowly. Lightly. I caressed and sucked and licked until he was as hard as a rock. I spent a good five minutes exploring him this way. Cupping his balls and running my fingers everywhere. Trailing my nails gently across his sensitive flesh as I sucked up and down his length. I was getting hornier by the second.

I focused everything I had on giving him pleasure. His muscles had tensed under me at some point, and I knew he was probably now awake. His awareness made me double down on my surprise seduction.

He smelled so good. Different somehow. Not his usual cologne, but something more woodsy. Or spicy. Just yummy masculine goodness. He tasted even better than he smelled. Off-hand, I never remembered him having a particular taste. He tasted like sex. And his body felt so hard beneath me, humming and vibrating with barely restrained energy. My hard nipples kept dragging back and forth across his abs as I sucked him off, and it felt so good. They felt so tight and achy; I dragged them over him again and again.

My mouth was worshipping his cock like I was sex-starved. He was groaning and growling now. Fighting to keep his hips on the bed. Usually, Max was pretty quiet during sex — maybe he'd grunt when he climaxed. This ... was hot. He was letting go. It was so sexy. I was excited that I could make him feel this way.

I pushed his cock deeper into my mouth, touching the back of my throat and I still couldn't fit all of him. Had I ever really tried before?

Max moaned deep in his throat, and then I felt his hands on my hips. They clasped to me like iron, pulling me down to his mouth. Really, after that, I don't know what I was doing with his cock or my mouth or hands, because my body was igniting. About to combust.

His tongue was on my clit, yes, but so were his teeth and lips. Things happened that I'd never even imagined. There was licking, there was stroking, there was nipping and there was sucking. His mouth worshipped every part of me.

I was about to come. Come hard and fast. For some reason, that panicked me a bit. I didn't want to come right on his face. In his mouth. I tried to pull off, but he locked me in place, his fingers planted like steel traps on my hips. He wasn't letting me go anywhere.

I was about to explode. It was building and building. A sweet, overwhelming torture of immeasurable pleasure. I was moaning uncontrollably, even while my mouth was stuffed full of his cock. My pussy couldn't escape the unbearable tongue-lashing. I might just die.

I didn't die.

I came. Intensely. Too much.

It felt juicy. Like a flood. Oh, God.

I wanted off his mouth. I tried to pull off, but he gripped me firmly. And with a few thrusts of his hips, pushing his cock into my now motionless mouth, he tensed for a moment and then spilled inside me. He spilled and spilled what seemed like an awful lot of cum.

I swallowed over and over until he was spent, while he was still eating me like crazy. Going to town. Like I was his last supper.

What was happening here? Before I could even guess, I felt a finger slide inside me. My whole body twitched, and I squeaked like a mouse. Again, I tried to leave his face. And again, he didn't let me go. Holy smokes.

His finger was doing wicked things to me and his tongue was languidly working on my super-sensitive clit. This was insanity. I might shatter. That crazy feeling was building again. But somehow, it was even more frenetic this time.

What was happening? We both just came. I should be trying to cuddle. He should be about to pass out. Lord, save me. This was too much.

"Oh God, Oh God, Oh God ..."

Was that me doing all the moaning?

His finger slid in and out. It was so amazing. So right.

"Yes! Do that."

His teeth grazed my clit.

"Yes, more!"

Once I had spoken, words kept spilling out. I ground my pussy into his face.

"Omigod. Another finger."

Another finger joined the first. Oh my.

"Press my clit with your thumb and fuck me with your tongue."

Where the hell did that come from?

I didn't have long to wonder, because Max was pretty damn obedient right now. And, oh ...

"Yessss."

I thought I might suffocate him; I was pressing against him so hard.

"Oh! I'm gonna ..."

I came again. Like a flash fire consuming the entire world. I was blinded for a second, and I'm pretty sure I saw stars.

Several moments later, when I flew back to earth, I realized I was completely sitting on Max's face. Upright. All my weight on him. This time, he let me slide off. He probably needed the oxygen. Mindless, my rubbery body collapsed against his.

Max was pulling me in for a kiss, and despite where our mouths had just been, it was sexy as hell. I'd just given him his fantasy and his kiss told me it'd surpassed his wildest dreams. Because kissing Max had never been this intoxicating. He'd never been so hungry. So passionate.

While we were kissing, his hands were stroking me masterfully, down my side, over my hips, skimming over my nipples before caressing a handful of breast. It was like he couldn't get enough of me. Our kiss deepened. So romantic. My head was spinning. Bliss was seeping through my body, even as pleasure spun wildly in circles all around me.

Through all this, something important was trying to niggle at the outskirts of my brain. But, whatever.

Chapter 3

Max

It was a Friday night. The rest of the world (well, maybe not the entire world) was out partying, but all I wanted to do was sleep. I was so damned tired. And after the week from hell that I had, sleep was so comforting. I could forget all the bullshit going on in my little slice of the world for just a bit.

I had to get my act together, figure out what I was gonna do. But that could wait till tomorrow. Saturday was soon enough.

Sleep was doing me good. Really good. I was having a pleasant dream. It involved my cock and a hot, wet mouth. Those were the best dreams.

Everything was white and wispy. I was floating on a cloud. My lips curved into a smile. I thought I was getting blown by an angel. Her lips and tongue were doing incredible things to me. Heavenly things.

Wait! Did I die? What the fuck?

I tried to think. Did the tour bus crash? What town was I even playing in last night?

My angel was touching my balls. Fuck, that felt ... divine.

No, the tour was over; we'd just finished it up. I wasn't dead. Or was I? Getting a blowjob in the afterlife?

She was squeezing my shaft and lavishing my cock with angel love. I was pretty sure I wasn't dead, but it didn't matter. I was just gonna lie here and enjoy the angel on my dick.

Did she just moan? The vibration ... ah, God.

I cracked open an eye and was surprised to see pussy. Right fucking there. If I stuck out my tongue, it would touch it. So that's where that heavenly scent was coming from. Musky sex and what? Vanilla? Something angelic.

I growled as I reached for my angel's hips. I pulled her down right on top of my mouth and dug right in. What do they call that taste? Angel juice? Ambrosia? Delicious. So fucking amazing. I thought I'd write a song about it. The Taste of an Angel. Fuck, that sounded familiar. Did someone already write that?

I'd woken up before, usually drunk as fuck, with some groupie's hand in my pants or getting blown, but I'd never woken up to pussy in my face. I breathed deep, inhaling her essence, as my tongue lapped at my angel's clit.

While I was only getting started, I could tell my angel was gonna orgasm. She was flying high. Spinning way too fast. My tongue hadn't even left her clit yet. I let her ride my face, her thighs straining around my head while I worked her mercilessly.

Her mouth was doing more moaning against my dick than sucking, but I figured that was okay. Just hearing the little noises she was making was taking my breath away. And if her tits rubbed across my abs one more time, I just might blow my load any moment.

When she finally let go, I tasted her release. This wasn't just angel juice; this was the nectar of the gods. I wouldn't last much longer with her coming on my face and tasting this good.

She tried to pull away while her muscles were fluttering against my tongue, but no way was I missing any of this. Sorry, Angel. I pushed my cock a few more times into her mouth until I couldn't hold back any longer while I lapped at her pussy. I think my cum surprised her, but she took it all, milking me good.

Angel was trying to wiggle away again. She wasn't going anywhere. I slid a finger into her soft pussy and she inhaled sharply. I didn't give her time to think before I started devouring her some more.

I was so hot for her I figured if I kept her busy for another ten minutes or so, I'd be ready to fuck her properly. Yeah, my dick was already twitching back to life. Amazing.

Her head was resting on my stomach, but her pussy was still on my face. Grinding. Angel liked what I was doing to her. Her fingernails were digging into my thighs. Scratching my skin. Pleasure ripped through me. Tying me in knots. She was like a sweet, intoxicating drug.

She was half sitting up now. Moaning. Pushing into my face.

Angel was calling out to God. Then telling me how she liked it. Begging for more. She was getting kind of carried away. Making a big fuss. What a wild one!

She fucking turned me on.

Now she was telling me what to do. Bossy angel. More fingers. Harder.

"Press my clit with your thumb and fuck me with your tongue."

Fuck, if that wasn't hot. My angel had a filthy mouth, and she was ordering me about. Yeah, my dick was paying attention.

When she climaxed this time, I felt her convulsing around my tongue. After a few moments of aftershocks, she slid off and collapsed on top of me, her silky hair splayed around her like a halo. I let her go, only because I needed to breathe.

She tried to snuggle into me while I was gulping down air. As soon as I'd caught my breath, I captured her mouth with mine. I kissed her solidly. Couldn't stop touching her. She was like heaven.

A few more minutes and my cock would be ready. I wanted to make her come while I was buried deep inside her. Maybe let her ride me so I could watch her tits bouncing. I'd felt them, but I couldn't see them.

As my sex-hazed brain calmed down a bit, I realized I didn't even know what my angel looked like. Or, for that matter, just who the fuck she was.

Jesus.

Chapter 4

~~Max~~

Ryder

I WASN'T DRUNK. I was stone-cold sober. And there was a warm woman cuddled up in my arms.

I remembered where I was. I'd crashed at Max's place because I didn't want to face my mom and her husband just yet. Still, that didn't explain this angel that had just been sucking on my dick or how my tongue had ended up in her sweet pussy. Ah hell, I should quit thinking. But something about this didn't seem right. Even for a fucking rock star.

Even as my cock was growing harder, she was falling asleep. Cuddled up and tucked in so softly next to me, like a little kitten.

I tugged at her nipple playfully. "Angel?"

Her response was unintelligible. "Quarmph plff."

I fought to keep my hand from sliding between her legs. I wanted her so badly.

"Angel?" A little louder this time.

She burrowed into me deeper.

Shit. I leaned over and just managed to reach the lamp on the nightstand. With a little fumbling, I switched it on.

She was groaning in protest, burying her head into my armpit.

I got my first good look at her. Well, not at her face, because that was hidden. She had a knockout body. Tall and lean, with miles of long leg. Soft feminine curves with just the slightest hint of ass dimples on her lower back. God, my tongue was so going there. Her hair was pretty long, halfway down her back, and the most magnificent color. Kind of dark blonde with other colors mixed in. Highlights, I guess. Bright blondes and coppery red streaks created a subtle mixture of colors that caught the lamplight and shimmered like an angel's hair.

I still hadn't seen her face, but I knew that I'd never met her before. I'd remember.

I untangled her from my armpit. "Angel, wake up."

She turned to me, eyes still closed, and frowned. "How? Why?" Then a few seconds later, "What?"

Her eyes flitted open.

She was beautiful. More beautiful than the angel I'd imagined in my dreams. I locked eyes with her baby blues for a few seconds and I felt my insides seizing up. Fuck, I needed to hold her and protect her, as much as I needed to fuck her senseless. She stirred my blood. And yeah, my cock was ready to go. Hard as a rock. Standing at attention.

She blinked. And then she jolted up so damn fast she smacked her head against the headboard.

"Whoa, Angel. Hold on." I held out my hand to calm her, but that only freaked her out more.

She grabbed a pillow and tried to cover her nakedness with it, crouching up against the headboard. She was looking around the room frantically. Wildly. Her hair was messy and sticking up like crazy. Her eye makeup had smeared a bit and a crazy fire was blazing in her eyes.

My angel with the filthy mouth looked nothing like an angel. She looked like a hellcat. Ready to pounce. With claws flying.

"Where's Max?" She kept glancing at the door like she was planning a getaway.

Fuck. This fiery kitten belonged to Max. Fuck.

"Not here."

I knew I should try to remove the scowl from my face, but fuck, she thought she'd done that with Max? No way. She was too good for Max. Hell, she was too good for me.

"Where'd he go?"

I ran my hand through my hair in agitation and she flinched at the movement. Did she think I was going to hurt her or something? The fuck?

"I haven't seen him since this morning."

Confusion. Her brow wrinkled. "Then ..."

I knew the exact second she figured it out. She had done all that with me.

She started shaking her head. "No." Her eyes widened. "No. No. No. No ... Oh God, no!"

There was my angel, talking to God again.

She batted me away frantically with her hands. She was borderline hysterical. "Get out of here! Now!"

I got off the bed and turned to her, trying to figure out what to say that would calm her down. Her eyes sank to my cock. My very erect cock.

She stopped talking for a moment. A blush crept over her face and across her chest, but she couldn't tear her eyes away from it. Damn, I almost stroked it right then while she watched. She probably would have keeled over on the spot.

"Go!" she gurgled. "And bring me my clothes. They're on the couch."

There was bossy angel again.

I left the bedroom and stumbled around until I found a light switch. I flipped on the lights and then found her clothes, neatly folded in a pile on the side of the couch.

So tidy. By the time I brought them back to her, she was wrapped from neck to toe in a sheet from the bed and peeking out from behind the door. She grabbed the clothes from me and then immediately slammed the door in my face.

I was still buck-naked and there was no way this girl would talk to me unless I covered up. But my duffel bag was still in Max's room. I didn't have much time to think about what to do, because she came storming out soon after. She marched out of the bedroom and went to collect her purse.

"Angel, hold on a minute ..."

She wouldn't listen. She was waving her hands frantically around, I guess trying to ward me off or something, while doing everything not to look anywhere in my direction. She scooped up her purse and flew straight to the door.

"Angel, wait..."

But she was already gone.

Chapter 5

Talia

I WAS STILL SMILING when I woke up. Remnants of my dream flashed in my head. It was some kind of crazy sex dream about the perfect man; the mythical, perfect man that didn't really exist.

As reality interrupted, I wiped off the sleep drool that had collected on the back of my hand. Yuck. I had slept on the couch. Had I been too wasted to make it to my bed?

The first thing my aching head reluctantly remembered was partying at the bar with Ellie and the all too many shots I'd done. No wonder my head hurt so badly. Then I remembered the fight with Max. On his birthday. I cringed.

Not even a second later, I remembered.

It.

The crazy good sex.

With Not Max.

Oh. My. God.

I sat up. Did that happen? Or was it all a dream? Think Talia!

Scenes worthy of a low-budget porn movie flitted through my mind. I felt my body flushing wildly just reliving them in my head. God, I think it really happened, but how?

Had I gotten so smashed that I picked up some random dude at the bar? No, I remembered leaving by myself. I'd gotten a taxi to Max's place.

For Operation Limp Dick.

Yeah, I remembered being in Max's apartment and then stripping in his bathroom. It was definitely the right apartment.

And, holy cow, I'd surprise sixty-nined someone. Who wasn't Max. My toes started curling at the memory. It had been good. Smoking hot. I'd orgasmed. A lot.

Oh, My God, I had to fast-forward that part in my mind. I needed to put that away for now, because who the hell was this guy?

One of the last things I remembered before coming back here was running out of Max's apartment in shock. The guy I got dirty with was every synonym of sex that I could come up with. He was absurdly gorgeous.

Another flash of memory materialized from when I was bolting from Max's apartment like my hair was on fire. The mystery dude called me Angel. Jeez, I'd conducted Operation Limp Dick on some random dude who thought my name was Angel.

I stewed on that for a few minutes. My brain was sluggish. Nothing made sense. I finally got up and headed to my bedroom. I needed more sleep. About to collapse on top of the unmade bed, I noticed a note lying on my pillow.

```
Tal,
Sorry about last night. I shouldn't
have left you at the bar. I was an
ass.

You didn't have to sleep on the
couch. I'll make it up to you
tonight.

Heading to the gym. Didn't want
to wake you-you looked comfy lying
there. Don't forget my birthday
lunch. I'll meet you there.
Love ya,
Max
```

I stared at the note. So Max slept here last night? And he thought I did too. Well, I did. Except for the kinky pit stop at his apartment where I had sex with some beautiful stranger that was mysteriously sleeping in his bed.

Thank goodness I didn't have to face him just yet. I needed time to figure this thing out.

I tried to lie down and close my eyes, but it was no use. All I kept thinking about was this guy. And his mouth. And his tongue ...

I checked my phone. It was only 10:23, a little early to wake up Ellie, but this was an emergency.

It took me a while to shake her awake. When she finally shook off some of the grogginess, she frowned. "You're back already? I thought you were going to hang out in bed with Max until your lunch? Did that bastard leave you and go to the gym after O.L.D.?"

I loved that Ellie was always in my corner. "Actually, he did go to the gym."

She scrunched up her nose. "Oh no. Not after ... wait! You didn't chicken out? Talia, tell me. Did Operation Limp Dick go down?"

"Oh, it went down."

She pulled at her lip contemplatively. "Aaand? Wait. Hold that thought. Find me something for this splitting headache and start a pot of coffee. I'll be there in a minute."

I set about making coffee and some toast in our tiny kitchen while I waited for Ellie. She came out of the bathroom a few minutes later. "I'm ready for the debriefing. Spill it all. Every last detail."

"It's all a bit fuzzy. But it's starting to come back to me in pieces."

She started fixing her coffee. "Yeah, you were doing a lot of shots. I knew I should have cut you off sooner. So what happened? Did Max wake up before O.L.D. fully commenced? No wait. First tell me, did you slide down his boxers or did you fish his dick out the hole? Because that other thing we were talking about was just never gonna work."

"He was naked. No boxers."

"Oooh. That was convenient. Lucky break! But now we'll never know about the whole boxers thing." Ellie thrust out her bottom lip like she was sad about it.

I started buttering the toast while Ellie watched me expectantly. "Well, stop being so coy. Give me the deets. How limp was it? And did it get hard pretty quickly? Because, if not, that would be so—"

I cut her off. "Hold on a sec. Take a breath. I'll give you all the dirty details. First off, his dick wasn't limp at all. Even in his sleep, it was pretty big. And once it got some loving, it got huge. It seemed awfully different from how I remembered it being. It was bigger. His balls were even bigger. He smelled different. He even tasted different. It was almost like he was a different man. You might even say, a much sexier man."

"Oh wow. That seems kind of hot. I mean, we are talking about Max here, but girl, that sounds fantastic!"

She wasn't quite getting the picture.

"So, how was the actual sex? Did Max enjoy his fantasy?"

Stalling, I sipped my coffee before answering. "Well, the sex was off the charts. I haven't had an orgasm like that in ... well, ever, I think."

Ellie slapped her hand on the counter, grinning like she'd just won the lottery. "Yes! I'm so happy for you guys!"

I laughed at her enthusiasm, but then quickly sobered. "Ahh. There's a catch, though. I don't even know how to say this." I paused for a moment, regrouping before I continued. "So, last night put something into perspective for me. You know that Max's and my sex life hasn't been that great lately. Well, it's never been that amazing."

"Oh, honey—"

"We haven't been jiving in the sex department for a while now. And I'm not putting that all on Max. We're lucky if we do it once a week lately, with work and our different schedules. And when we do have sex, it hasn't been that good."

"You're just in a rut. It happens to all couples."

I waved off her sympathy and continued, "He doesn't satisfy me. I never orgasm. I thought there was something wrong with me. It just seems to take so damn long for me. And it only takes Max like five minutes."

She put down her mug. "Men can be selfish bastards."

"It's not Max's fault, though. I've been pretty much faking orgasms for years now." As I spoke it out loud, it all seemed so pathetic.

"You need to talk to him, Talia. Tell him what you like."

"I know."

Ellie's eyebrows wrinkled. "But last night was good? You said it was off the charts. So things are good between you two, right?"

"Wrong."

"Huh? You're losing me here."

I took a deep breath. "I didn't have sex with Max last night."

"What? I don't get it."

I rubbed my throbbing temples for a moment. "Last night at the bar, after the fight, Max came here and slept in my bed. And I went to his apartment and conducted Operation Limp Dick. By mistake, I surprise sixty-nined some sexy Adonis-like guy that was sleeping in Max's bed."

The look on her face was priceless. If this wasn't my own life sliding down the shitter right now, I might have laughed.

"Only this guy didn't have a limp dick. He had a big dick. And I had the filthiest, nastiest, best sex of my life."

Her mouth was hanging open in shock. "Oh, my God! Talia! How could you not know?"

I couldn't even look her in the eyes. "I don't know. I was drunk? It was dark? I don't know. I mean, he seemed different."

"My God, what did you do with this ... Adonis?"

I blanched at the memory. "Well, O.L.D. obviously. It was pretty intense. I kind of remember sitting on his face like he was a saddle and I was a cowgirl. And I rode him hard. Like at full gallop."

She gasped at my confession. "No!"

I felt my cheeks grow warm at the memory. "Yes."

"And this guy was really hot?"

Another memory sparked in my mind. Me, hiding my nakedness behind a pillow while checking out this guy. He was big, powerful. Insanely gorgeous.

"Very hot," I confirmed.

"And he gave you orgasms?" Ellie's mouth was still hanging open.

"Multiple."

"My God!" she exclaimed.

"I know."

She took a sip of her coffee. I could see the gears in her brain turning. Good thing one of us was thinking because I couldn't.

"What did he say to you? You know, after …"

"Nothing." I thought back to how I'd run out of Max's apartment. "I don't even know who he is or what he was doing there. When I realized it wasn't Max, I just got dressed and took off as fast as I could."

"Holy Shit! I can't believe it!" Suddenly, her face fell. "Does Max know?"

I threw up my hands. "I have no idea. I haven't seen him yet; I woke up on the couch and he was gone. He left me a note. But he's probably back at his apartment by now. This guy might be telling Max all the juicy details right this very minute."

"Oh, shit." Her soft utterance didn't cheer me up any.

Agitated, I started pacing the kitchen. "What am I going to do?"

"Maybe this guy won't say anything?" she offered cautiously.

I stopped. "Well, I can't keep it a secret from Max."

"You think you should tell him?"

An agonized look crossed my face. Lying wasn't something that came easily to me, especially about something so big.

Ellie looked at me sympathetically. "It's not like you cheated on him on purpose. It was a mistake! An accident. It wasn't your fault. And telling him will open up a whole can of worms."

I grimaced. "I know. What if Max wants details? Oh God, I could never let him know what we did. Or how amazing it was."

"Who was this guy? Was he a friend of Max's?"

I pinched the bridge of my nose. "I don't know. I think he mentioned Max's name, but I can't remember. We were both naked. We had just done ... those things."

"Maybe he'll keep quiet. Not tell Max."

A strange sound escaped my throat. "Right. He went to sleep in Max's bed and woke up to a strange girl sucking his dick and jamming her pussy in his face and he doesn't even mention it?"

Ellie shrugged. "You never know ..."

"What am I going to do, Ellie? I've got to meet Max for lunch in a couple of hours. What am I going to say?"

"You're going to walk in there with your head held high. You're not to blame for this. If Max found out, you'll have to explain it to him logically. Take all the emotion out of it and explain what happened. Clinically."

She saw the look of doubt cross my face. "Hopefully, this guy didn't go into any details, because that'd be brutal. If you need to tell him about the surprise you planned, O.L.D., I'll back you up on everything, but if he knows nothing, I think you should let sleeping dogs lie."

My head was back to throbbing again. "I don't know ..."

"Go take a nice, long, hot shower. You'll feel better."

♪♫♪♩♩

I took my time getting ready for Max's birthday lunch. My headache was better, but my gut was still churning. I was constantly checking my phone to see if a text would come from Max. Nothing came.

Still wrapped in my pink silk robe, I sat down at my vanity to do my makeup. I had four major styles of makeup that I'd perfected for myself: everyday natural, my corporate look for work, a shimmering party look, and a sex-bomb look I pulled out for special occasions.

My aunt, who was very stylish, had given me my first makeup kit when I turned 14 years old. I had no idea how to use anything. I was an only child and my mother wasn't really into makeup or fashion. I turned to the internet and relentlessly copied the how-to videos until I had perfected the art.

In less than 15 minutes, my makeup was complete. I'd chosen my everyday natural look but had embellished it somewhat for added confidence.

Next, I turned to my hair. In the same way that I learned how to do makeup, I learned how to style my hair. Using internet tutorials, I learned how to create dozens of distinct looks with braids, up-dos, curls, or countless combinations. My hair went about halfway down my back and was rather thick; it was perfect for a variety of styles. Today, I thought I'd wear my hair down, but create beachy waves with a curling iron.

With hair and makeup complete, I headed to my closet to pick out an outfit. I dismissed the right side of my closet, mostly my work clothes. Instead, I focused on my casual outfits. I chose a favorite pair of off-white linen capri pants with wide legs and little pom-poms hanging off the hems. Next, I picked out a fuchsia-colored cropped top that tied in front and showed off a sliver of skin.

When I finished dressing, I slipped on some heels and funky jewelry to spice up the outfit and then stood in front of the mirror. As I studied my reflection, I realized only then what illusion I had created. Innocence. I looked like the proverbial girl next door. Innocent and pure. I smiled wryly at myself. If there was one thing I was an expert at; it was dressing for the part. Ellie called me a chameleon because I was always changing my look for the occasion. It was something I did well and enjoyed doing.

I glanced at my phone and realized it was time to head out. I grabbed the large gift bag hidden in the corner of my room that contained Max's birthday present and headed toward the kitchen.

Ellie was still in her pajamas. She eyed me up and down. "You look fantastic. As usual."

I took a deep breath. "That's good. Because I feel like I'm heading to my execution or something."

"You know, Talia, if he doesn't appreciate you, then screw him. You're the most gorgeous, sweetest girl I know. He doesn't deserve you. Especially if he can't even make you orgasm."

I flinched. Maybe I'd blurted out too much information to Ellie in my post-mortem observations of the messed-up situation. Max and I had been together for three years. I wanted to marry him. Right? Spend the rest of my life with him. At least, I thought I did.

All the arguments I felt I should make on Max's behalf were stuck in my throat. "Well, wish me luck."

She smirked. "Good luck, Talia. You've got this."

Chapter 6

Ryder

WHERE THE HELL WAS Max? I'd texted him hours ago, and he said he'd be home soon. Normally, I'd have been long gone by now, but I was sitting around his apartment, practically climbing the walls. I had to talk to him and find out about Angel. I couldn't shake her from my thoughts. I needed to know the lay of the land. Were they dating? Was she off-limits? Did that girl who invaded my very being belong to Max? I couldn't even face the possibility.

I'd showered, scrounged for food, and ate some stale crackers for breakfast. Then, waited some more. All the while, I couldn't stop thinking about her. How she had absolutely feasted on my cock. How she tasted. How she let loose like a wanton sex maniac, but then wanted to retreat like an angelic virgin when I made her come hard.

My band had been on tour for the last nine months. Even though we were just the opening act for the big ticket, Cold Fusion, my bandmates and I quickly got used to girls throwing themselves at us. We had our pick of hot girls every night.

Some of those lays were good; some were pretty mediocre. Most nights, the sex, after hours of partying, wasn't very memorable. It was never hard to walk away when we had to leave for the next city on the tour. I barely remembered any of their faces and never remembered their names, even if they'd told me them to begin with. I never thought about them afterward. But this girl — my angel — her face, her body, her taste, all of it was seared into my memory.

My tortured thoughts finally ended when Max came in the door.

Max threw his gym bag on the floor. "Hey, man. You still here? I thought you had to head to your parents?"

"I do. I just don't want to." I shrugged noncommittally, hoping he wouldn't probe any deeper into that. "You need to go shopping. You don't have any food in this place."

Max grinned. "Sorry, I don't eat here that often. I've got to jump in the shower. I'm heading out to lunch." He paused for a moment and then added, "You want to come? I'm just getting some lunch with my girlfriend at this Italian place down the road."

Normally I would have noped out of there so fast. "Yeah, that'd be great. Unless she'd mind?"

Max waved away my fake concerns as he headed to his bedroom. "Nah, Tal wouldn't care."

I sat down on the couch to wait for Max. Tal? It seemed like a weird name. Was that the name of my angel? I'd flinched when he called her his girlfriend. What the fuck was I doing? Going to lunch with Max and his girlfriend — the girl whose pussy I'd just tongued? I should just leave. Forget about her.

But, I couldn't.

♫♫♪♩♩

I was fucking nervous. I was sitting in a booth across from Max in the slightly upscale-from-a-pizza-joint Italian restaurant. My back was to the door, so I couldn't see anyone coming in. Why had I come? I kept trying to tell myself that I just wanted to quench my curiosity about this girl.

Max and I were making small talk about high school. We were both on the lacrosse team together, so we were friends, but never great friends. Last minute, I'd needed a place to crash near my parent's house, and Max was one of the few people I loosely kept in touch with that still lived near our hometown in central Ohio.

I finally screwed up the courage to ask him about his girlfriend. "So, what's the story with your girlfriend?"

"Tal?" He asked as if he had other girlfriends to choose from. "Yeah, we've been together for a while now. Three years already."

"Jesus!" It slipped out, but luckily, he misinterpreted my meaning.

"Yeah, I know. I was going to propose this past Christmas. I got the ring and everything." He quickly glanced up at me. "Don't you dare mention that, by the way."

I raised my eyebrows. "I won't."

He nodded. "But I chickened out in the end."

"Why?" I probed.

He sat back in the booth. "Cold feet about marriage, I guess. Tal's great and all. She's a totally hot babe. She's nice, smart, funny. I just don't know if I can imagine myself with one person for the rest of my life. Like, I'd never be able to fuck another girl again. It seems so wrong."

"Huh," I replied vaguely.

"And Tal, like I said, she's great and all, but she's a bit boring in the sack, if you know what I mean."

Tal was boring in bed? Maybe I had the wrong girl. Maybe my angel wasn't Max's girlfriend after all; maybe she was just some booty call he kept on the side. Was Max cheating on his girlfriend with Angel?

Whether Angel was his girlfriend or not, his words had opened up the hint of a possibility to me. Angel could be mine.

I wasn't a hundred percent proud of what I said next. But, if my angel really was his girlfriend, Tal, and that's the way he felt about her, I didn't feel too bad about fucking with the unspoken bro code. I'd seen a chink in the armor and couldn't stop myself from going in. "That's rough, man. Maybe you should dump her?"

Max had a pained expression on his face. "Fuck. I've been thinking about that lately, man. But she's like the perfect fucking girl. Except for that."

I dug into the wound a bit. "Yeah, but that is everything."

He shifted around uncomfortably in the booth, looking miserable. "Look, forget I said anything, okay?"

"You got it."

Max took a swig of his beer and then changed the conversation. "You got a girlfriend?"

I shook my head. "No time for girlfriends on tour."

"On tour with Cold Fusion." Max grinned. "I almost forgot that you're a fucking rock star. You must be getting laid by a different chick every night."

"Pretty much."

Max looked envious. "You lucky bastard. Tell me, what's the craziest-"

He stopped speaking and raised his hand in a wave. He must have spotted his girlfriend coming in.

My gut clenched with anticipation.

"Hey, she's coming. Don't mention anything ..."

I grunted. "I'm not a dumb ass."

I watched Max's eyes as he followed her approach to our booth. I felt her eyes land on me. When I turned to look at her, I realized I was holding my breath.

It was her. Angel.

After last night, I had expected to see someone edgier. A total smoke show with attitude. Instead, here was this soft, gorgeous sex kitten. The little hellcat who'd left scratch marks on my skin was this cute little sex kitten.

She was definitely surprised to see me, completely speechless and wide-eyed even as Max was introducing us.

"Babe, this is my friend, Ryder, from high school. And this is my girlfriend, Natalia."

I raised my eyebrows slightly, amused at her stunned expression. "Hey, Natalia, nice to meet you."

I liked the way her name rolled off my tongue. Natalia. So, that explained her weird name.

She was nervous as fuck. Her eyes kept flicking between Max and me, but she still hadn't said anything. It was getting awkward when she stood frozen for several moments and didn't even attempt to sit down.

Max began babbling, explaining why I joined them for lunch, but I wasn't paying attention. My focus was on Natalia and the energy ping-ponging crazily between us. Nothing could cover up the sparks that were shooting through the air. My body was humming in her presence, like 1,000 volts of electricity were buzzing through it. My dick was twitching with the memory of her lips covering it. The reaction was real, and I could tell she felt it too.

I knew Max was mistaking the weird energy in the air, thinking that it was anger she felt because he'd asked me to join them. He had no idea of what had gone on between us only hours before.

I saw a blush washing over Natalia's face and I could imagine precisely what she was thinking about. In all its x-rated glory. I smiled lazily, letting her know I knew exactly which naughty thoughts were in her mind.

Tapping the bench next to him, Max had to coax her to sit down. "Come on, Tal. Have a seat."

Finally, she sat next to Max, placing a large birthday gift bag next to her on the padded booth seat.

She took a deep breath, visibly trying to regain her composure. "So, you're a friend of Max's?"

Max relaxed next to her, but I focused all my attention on Natalia. Max was right. She was fucking perfect. "Yeah. We went to high school together."

Her eyes sparked as she smiled pointedly. "How nice that he invited you to his birthday lunch."

I almost chuckled. I'd inadvertently wormed my way in on Max's birthday lunch. I felt bad for a second. No, I didn't.

Max leaned forward, suddenly nervous again. "Hey, Tal. What's in the bag?"

Just then, the waitress appeared to take our order. It gave me time to study Natalia. She was model-runway gorgeous, but she had a wholesome quality to her. She was ethereal, like an angel, but I'd already seen a flash of something else in her eyes. A feisty spark. If she had a halo, then she also had horns, too.

When she finished ordering and Max began his order, she felt my gaze on her. Our eyes locked and my stomach clenched. I felt that pull between us. It was so strong.

Desire.

Need.

Pure lust.

I sighed when she looked away. I knew I had to get myself under control. If Max saw me eye fucking his girl, he'd start to wonder.

After I gave my order and the waitress left, I casually sat back in the booth and asked, "So, Natalia, tell me about yourself."

She squirmed a bit. "Talia. It's Talia."

"Okay, Talia." I couldn't help but focus on her luscious lips. They were so pink and shiny with gloss.

She paused to gather her thoughts, her tongue poking out slightly as she bit at her lip. "Well, I grew up in Ohio, too. Not too far from here. I work at a company called Cavendish International. I've been there for five years now …"

She trailed off. Maybe she realized I was looking at her tits. The tie knot made her shirt sculpt nicely to her breasts. The shirt was unbuttoned just enough to glimpse a peek of her luscious cleavage. Damn if that didn't make me hard. It was my turn to shift uncomfortably in my seat.

"What do you do at Cavendish International?" I was looking back into her eyes. Eyes that were flashing angrily at me.

"I'm an administrative assistant." Her answer was clipped.

I nodded.

"To the Vice President of Sales. It's a demanding job." She practically spat it at me.

"Nice." I wasn't sure why she was so touchy about it.

My fingers tapped aimlessly against the table. I was always tapping out a tune; I barely noticed it, but Talia's gaze locked in on it. I watched as a deep blush of color stole over her face.

What was my dirty girl thinking about now? I couldn't help the smile that spread across my face. God, I wanted her so bad.

Her breath fluttered, and then she looked away. "Do you live here in Springfield?"

"No, I live in L.A. I'm here visiting my mother. Max was kind enough to let me crash at his place last night." I flashed another mischievous smile at her.

Max looked up at the sound of his name. I realized then that he'd been texting on his phone, unaware of the sexual tension all around us.

Talia blushed again. Desire flitted across her face as she thought about last night. She was an open book, so easy to read. Fuuuuck. My groin pulsed with need.

"How nice," she mumbled and then reached for her water glass.

Max put down his phone and then joined our conversation. He began telling Talia stories about our high school days. Soon our food came. I was content to let Max do most of the talking while we ate.

I kept my eyes on Talia the whole time. Absorbing her. Watching her every move. Reveling in how much she noticed me and pretended not to. She paid very little attention to Max. If I didn't know better, I'd think their relationship was completely platonic. Maybe they didn't do PDA, but besides the brief peck on the cheek when she first slid into the booth, they hadn't even touched each other. If she were my girl, I wouldn't be able to keep my hands off her.

After we'd ordered dessert, Max pointed to the gift bag at Talia's side. "Is that for me?"

She looked uncomfortable. "Yes, but why don't you open it up later?" She turned her head slightly and muttered under her breath, "I should have left it in my car."

Clearly, she didn't want Max to open it in front of me, but he seemed oblivious. "Oh, come on, Talia. You can't bring a gift in here and expect me to wait."

What kind of gift had she gotten him? It wasn't like it was some sexy lingerie; the bag was freaking huge. If I were a gentleman, I'd say my goodbyes and not intrude on the rest of the birthday lunch. Too bad. I wanted to know what was in the damn bag. What was she so reluctant for me to see?

Silence stretched on. Either she'd have to concede and let Max open his gift or make a big stink over it.

Max sounded impatient and a little whiny, "Come on, Tal!"

"Fine." She shot me a dirty look and then passed the gift bag over to Max.

He removed a layer of dark blue tissue paper and then worked a large box out of the bag, holding it up. He seemed a bit underwhelmed, but he faked some enthusiasm pretty good. I had to give him that. "Oh wow. It's a coffee maker. Thanks, babe. I could use one."

She pulled a smaller box out of the gift bag. "And a variety pack of coffee pods to go with it."

Holy shit. Something about the whole thing struck me as so damn funny. I could barely hold back a burst of laughter.

Max glanced my way. *You see what I mean?* "Nice. That's awesome." He gave her a demure peck on the cheek.

Angel suddenly looked upset. "I have to use the ladies' room. Excuse me."

A few beats passed awkwardly as Max and I sat in the booth. Finally, I broke the silence. "She seems nice."

"She is." He nodded. "The coffee maker is nice. I could really use it in my apartment."

I stretched out my legs. "She's cute. Kind of girl-next-door."

"Yeah," he agreed.

"Too bad she's a dud in the bedroom."

He grimaced but kept his mouth shut this time. Didn't matter; I'd landed the blow. Sometimes I was the biggest asshole.

After the mind-blowing night I'd had with his girlfriend, I couldn't believe he actually thought she was cold and boring in bed, but his silence spoke for itself. What the hell was wrong with this guy?

Max got distracted by a new text that came on his phone. I used the opportunity to tell him I was hitting the bathroom. Really, I wanted to talk to Talia. Alone. This would be my only chance.

Chapter 7

Talia

Luckily, no one was in the bathroom, so I didn't have to pretend my world wasn't a spectacular mess. I stood in front of the mirror and checked my makeup. Everything was fine. I looked fine, but I felt awful. If the bathroom had windows, I'd consider crawling out and escaping this impossible situation.

Seeing him here had taken my breath away. Ryder. He looked even hotter than my drunken mind recalled. Sitting across from me with that all-knowing smile. Stripping me bare. Cocky as hell. Making me remember. Sex, sex, sex.

Like a dork, I was tongue-tied around him. The tension between us was inescapable. And the way he looked at me. Like he was going to devour me. My stomach was coiled in knots; I just had to escape to the bathroom and get some distance.

He didn't tell Max.

Last night, I'd only seen Ryder while the light was on for maybe a minute tops. It wasn't a big mystery why, but I hadn't focused on his face so much in that minute. My eyes had zeroed straight in on his naked body. He was a perfect male specimen, underwear-model worthy. Of course, I had seen his cock. And while I had confessed to Ellie that I couldn't picture Max's cock that well, somehow I could picture Ryder's cock in full-blown high definition. It was impressive.

Now I knew the face that went with the cock. He was squirm-in-your-seat gorgeous. The only pretty thing about him was his eyes. They were a darker shade of blue, like sapphires, with a fringe of thick eyelashes surrounding them. The rest of his features were hard, chiseled, and masculine. His hair was dark, almost black, cut meticulously but always appearing rumpled in a stylish way. He hadn't shaved this morning; the rough stubble was swoon-worthy; the type that always made a sexy guy look even sexier.

He looked like he'd just rolled out of bed, ran a hand through his hair, and tossed on some jeans and a T-shirt. Effortless, but deadly gorgeous.

That was the guy I'd had a romp in the sack with. Impossibly sexy. Maddeningly smug.

Giving me orgasm after orgasm.

Dangerous.

At the table, he had watched me with amusement. Judging. Reducing Max's and my relationship to a big joke — practically laughing out loud as I gave my boyfriend a coffee maker for his birthday. Maybe I should remind him that even if the coffee maker was lame, the O.L.D. sex had been strictly meant for Max?

Internally, I was at war. I couldn't figure out if I was mad at Ryder or just humiliated by the whole mix-up. Who was I kidding? I was totally lusting after that perfectly sculpted god and furious at myself for it.

He was a complete stranger, but we had a connection. Chemistry. Hell, an all-consuming fire. I couldn't deny it.

How did Max not notice? Ryder had been eye-fucking me the whole time, and my traitorous body had been responding. We practically had sex right there under his nose.

Sitting across from him, I'd felt myself getting buffeted by wave after wave of pure sexual energy coming off of him. It was so strong. So magnetic. The aftermath of each wave left me struggling in the undertow, feebly trying to keep from being pulled under.

He was too hot. He'd burn me up.

Ryder was the kind of guy that took what he wanted from women and then tossed them aside. No good could come of giving my heart, or even my body, for that matter, to that kind of man. He oozed a no-commitment attitude from his pores. No strings; just delicious, wild, crazy sex. Once-in-a-lifetime sex. And my one time had already come and gone.

I took a few deep breaths; I needed to head back to the table before they started wondering what had happened to me. I'd play it cool. If Ryder was going to keep his mouth shut, then so would I. What happened was a horrible mistake. It was best to forget anything ever happened between us.

I stepped out of the ladies' room and ran nose-first into a solid male chest. I didn't even have to look up to know it was Ryder. He put his hands on my shoulders to steady me and my mutinous body reacted to the sparks that zapped all through me.

Without meaning to, I breathed in a lungful of his delicious scent. It was something unique to him I recognized from our night of passion, something masculine and mouthwatering, a spicy combination of leather, sandalwood, and ... orange, maybe?

The pull between us was irresistible. There was no fighting this riptide.

I was leaning closer to him, sniffing him, for goodness' sake, only one step away from crawling right up his body. Lord help me.

I shook out of my daze, cursed my traitorous body, and stepped back abruptly. "Don't touch me," I said a little too harshly.

He leaned casually against the doorjamb, blocking my way past the narrow hallway. "I wanted to talk to you. Alone."

He didn't have to touch me; his focused gaze alone was too intense. I could barely meet his eyes. My heart was pounding. I swallowed down my nerves and used my most haughty tone. "That's not a good idea."

His jaw clenched. "We need to talk about what happened."

"Nothing happened!" My denial was ludicrous. I knew it. He knew it.

He raised an eyebrow in disbelief.

"You didn't tell him?" I had to know.

"No."

My hands were twisting in knots. "Then why did you come here? To his birthday lunch?"

He shrugged indifferently. "He asked me to lunch. I didn't know it was his birthday. Not until you showed up with the coffee maker. And pods." A sly smile stole over his face.

Bastard was mocking me again.

"It's an inside joke." Why did I feel the need to justify it?

"Oh yeah? What's the joke?" He was daring me.

"That he's a morning person." Darn, why couldn't I keep my mouth shut? I sounded ridiculous. "And that he doesn't have a coffee maker."

This time, the smile was genuine. In fact, he couldn't hold back a growly laugh. "Yeah, that is a funny joke." His sarcasm was not lost on me.

He was laughing at my expense, and yet I couldn't stop the electric pulse that vibrated through me. Straight to my core. Exploding in my nether regions. His smile melted my panties.

And that made me even angrier. I spluttered, "You've got a lot of nerve."

"Why are you mad at me?" his eyes narrowed.

How could I explain it to him if I didn't even know myself? Because I was insanely attracted to him when I shouldn't be? Because he gave me orgasms when my boyfriend couldn't? It didn't even make any sense.

"Why didn't you stop me? You let it go on—"

He took a step towards me. I could feel the heat coming off him. "Stop you? I was sleeping. By the time I was fully awake, things had progressed quite a bit."

"Maybe at first, but ..." I trailed off weakly.

He had a hard glint in his eyes. He was so close to me that I had to tilt my head up to see him. "And you didn't happen to notice that it wasn't your boyfriend's cock you were going to absolute town on? Your boyfriend of three years?"

I cringed. He was right, of course. But as my mother had always told me, I was as stubborn as a mule. Sometimes, to my detriment, it was near impossible for me to back down or not get in the last word. "I may have been slightly inebriated, but what's your excuse? You should have stopped me. Right away."

"Unbelievable!" Agitated, he combed his hand through his hair. "If I recall, it was my mouth that was raped by your pussy."

I inhaled a sharp breath. Speechless.

He reinforced his point quietly, "You didn't exactly get my consent before doing all that, Talia."

My stomach twisted. All the fight left me, because what he said was technically true. "Oh, my God!"

The anger on his face was quickly replaced with concern. "Hey, don't freak out. I didn't mean that. Not really. I could have tossed you off in a second flat if I didn't want it."

I had been selfishly focusing on myself; I hadn't thought about what I'd done from Ryder's point of view. "I'm so sorry," I whispered.

Gently, he captured my chin with his hand and tipped my head to meet his gaze. "It's okay. Really. There was no evil intent behind it. Fuck, Angel, don't look so devastated." His eyes pleaded with me to believe him. "I loved every second of it. You can do that to me any day, any night. Whenever you want. I give you permission from here on out till forever. And retroactively, too. I'm yours."

My eyes narrowed with suspicion. "You just accused me of rape and now you're begging for more?"

He leaned closer and I couldn't help but stare at his lips. Was he going to kiss me? Yes, please. "What are we going to do, Talia?"

I could barely breathe. "About what?"

"Us."

I put my hands up to ward him off. He was so close. Encroaching. Invading my thoughts, crowding out all sanity. My hands ended up resting on his chest, feeling the solid wall of muscle under his T-shirt.

I blinked. "There's no us."

"There's nothing but us."

I was being pulled into him again. We were touching full length now. "But, Max ..."

"Dump him."

My brows wrinkled in disbelief. "I'm supposed to dump Max and become your girlfriend? Just like that? I don't even know you."

The cocky smile was back. He gave me a wink. "Who said I was looking for a girlfriend?"

Of all the nerve! He was messing with me again.

"See you around, Angel." He turned and was gone, leaving me staring after him, open-mouthed.

Chapter 8

Ryder

I COULDN'T DELAY GOING to my mom's any longer. I hopped into the black Nissan Maxima I'd rented and made my way through the heavy main street traffic. It took me at least ten minutes to decide that all the preset radio stations in the car were total shit and then another ten minutes to settle on a station that played halfway decent music. By then, I was on the highway heading west, less than 30 minutes from my mom's place.

It gave me plenty of time to think. Too much time. I'd been on the road, almost continuously, with my band, Ghost Parker, for nine months. We went from venue to venue: setting up, doing sound checks, performing for about 45 minutes, and then partying until the next show. It was simple.

No family drama. Plenty of girls available at the crook of a finger. No strings. No bullshit.

Nothing to worry about. I didn't even have to worry about food. In the early days of the band, our 'tours' were much different. It wasn't uncommon that we'd end up skipping a meal or catching a few bites at some disgusting hole-in-the-wall restaurant if we were lucky. We never had enough food. There were plenty of drugs, lots of booze, and willing women, but never enough food.

This tour had been so different. Opening for Cold Fusion, a hugely popular band, had given us a glimpse of the good life. They had people worrying about that kind of shit for them, so with us riding their coattails, food got taken care of and the schedule never got screwed up. Our two bands ended up getting along well, which didn't always happen. It opened tons of doors for us. Not only were we able to coast off their management team with tour logistics, but with access to their enormous fan base, a whole new audience had discovered us. People who had never heard of us were now diehard fans of our band. We were more popular than we'd ever been.

Coming off this insanely successful tour, we knew that getting our shit together and producing our sophomore album was so important. It was crucial to capitalize on our recent success; this could be the literal make-or-break point for Ghost Parker. The band had scattered for a few weeks' break after the tour, but we'd be back together writing and composing soon. We all knew we had to focus like crazy and hit this next album out of the park.

And I couldn't wait to get back to the million-dollar-plus piece of crap home I'd bought right before our tour started. I smiled, thinking about it. My realtor told me I'd only had a few hours to decide before I made my offer or it'd get snatched up. Properties right on the beach didn't last long at all. This one was a 'teardown' as she called it. The owner, an old hippie dude, accepted my bid, twenty thousand less than the asking price, right away. Suddenly, I was a homeowner.

Before I left on tour, I'd gotten a contractor in there to inspect it, and fortunately, he said we'd be able to fix it up instead of demolishing it and rebuilding.

So while I toured for 9 months, he'd been re-doing just about everything. I made major decisions over text, based on photos that he'd send me. We had two breaks during the tour. The first time that I went back was in March. Most structural issues had been dealt with: the roof, shoring up the deck, an important beam, fixing a plumbing issue. It had been slightly disappointing to see how decrepit it still looked after the massive amount of money that I'd already sunk into it. The last time I went back, it looked much better. The upper deck had been expanded, walls had been knocked down inside to open up the floor plan, and the kitchen had just started getting gutted. I couldn't wait to see it now, three months later.

I just had to spend a couple of days with my mom and then I could get back to my life–my new home, the guys in the band, and making some music that'd make us filthy rich.

So why did my mind keep straying back, over and over, to a certain little hellcat? Talia. I wanted to see her again. I definitely wanted to fuck her again. Multiple times. All night long, this time. Leisurely. Thoroughly.

Frowning, I shifted in my seat. I was heading home in a few days; I'd never see this girl again. So what if I didn't get another chance to fuck her? There would be plenty of girls in California. Besides, this girl was already taken. That was a line I didn't cross. Anymore.

Still, the thought bothered me. I just couldn't pinpoint why.

I didn't do relationships. I had lots of sex — fast, hard, and occasionally amazing sex. It was easy; I didn't have to work too hard, and that's the way I liked it.

I'd never had a proper girlfriend. Sharon, in college, and Kim, right around when Ghost Parker released our first album, were the closest things to actual relationships I'd ever had.

The memories of both girls left a bad taste in my mouth. I'd made the same mistake twice before I'd learned my lesson.

In both instances, things followed a similar disastrous route. It started out slowly, like stupidly letting them stay over after sex, instead of politely kicking them out as I usually did. Gradually, they demanded more and more. Soon, they were wearing my T-shirts. Getting comfortable around my stuff. Leaving their shit in my space. Until, with little warning, they expected everything, usually some form of commitment.

Monogamy.

I'd warned them over and over that I didn't want a girlfriend, and they'd both pretended to understand.

In the end, they didn't.

The breakups had been brutal. The first girl went harder; I was too softhearted. Trying hard not to be a total dick, I let the breakup go on and on. It sucked. I cut off Kim cold; telling myself it was easier for both of us that way. She went full psycho and stalked me for over a year. I still worried about running into her.

I'd learned the hard way to avoid any personal attachments, no matter how small. In the end, it was easier to cut off any of that potential shit before it ever happened. That's why I hardly ever banged the same chick twice; that's why touring was so great. The girls came and went. There were no expectations. Easy.

Forgetting about Talia should be second nature to me. So, why couldn't I? These strange thoughts kept me company the entire drive home until I was pulling into my mom's run-down garden apartment community.

I spotted her husband Stan's car in the assigned parking space but didn't see my mom's car. God, I hoped she was home. I didn't want to spend time bullshitting with Stan. I circled around, but all the visitor spots in front of their cluster of units were filled. I ended up parking two lots away from their apartment and took my time walking to their door. I took a deep breath, mentally preparing myself.

She answered the door moments after my knock.

"Hey, Mom."

She let me give her a hug and a peck on the cheek before she waved me inside. She looked older than the last time I'd seen her, older than her 62 years. Her skin was more wrinkled, her face duller, and she'd given up any pretense of dying her hair. It was now entirely gray, a dark, unflattering steel-colored gray.

"Ryder, honey, I thought you were coming last night?" Mom led me into the kitchen.

"Sorry. Just finishing up with stuff. I should have called."

I sat down at the old kitchen table. It was the same table I ate at as a kid — it must be at least thirty years old.

Mom hovered around in the kitchen. "Are you hungry? I'm making spaghetti tonight and your favorite homemade meatballs."

"Nah. I had lunch. Dinner sounds great, though. Thanks."

I heard the TV playing a sports program in the den. Stan was probably in there watching, but I had no desire to see him and he certainly hadn't come out to greet me. I remained at the table while my mom fixed us both a coffee and then joined me.

We spoke for about an hour. She asked me about the tour, and I gave her the rated PG version of all our antics. She didn't ask at all about Cold Fusion, one of the biggest bands in the world right now, but she wanted to know more about my band. In particular, she was interested in Johnny Parker, our frontman. I teased her about having a crush on him and I finally saw her smile for the first time since I'd arrived, but then she shushed me.

"Don't give Stan any dumb notions."

A sour feeling settled in my stomach. I couldn't stand Stan, but my mother loved him. Why she adored him so much, God only knew.

I changed the subject, bringing up pictures on my phone of my new house. Admittedly, it didn't look like much, especially the earlier pictures of when it was a filthy mess. Until my house was fixed up, the location was the only thing going for it.

"When I get all the work finished, you should come out and visit, Mom."

"Sure, that'd be great."

I knew she'd never come. I swallowed my hurt and asked her about her job at the bookstore and what she'd been up to the past year. We chatted about her life, which seemed terribly empty to me until she brought up the subject of my brother. I knew it was going to come up eventually.

"You should stop in and see Brock before you go back to California."

Brock and I weren't on good terms. "How's he doing?"

Sadness flitted across her face; then she visibly perked up. "Good. And little Joey is so darn cute. Jenny tells me he's rolling over now. He's just so precious. You've got to meet him, Ryder."

My fingers tapped on the table. "I don't know, Mom. I'm not sure Brock wants to see me."

She didn't hesitate. "Of course he does! He's your brother. And Joey is your nephew. You've never even met him yet!"

She let that soak in for a few moments.

"It's time, Ryder."

I tried to keep my expression neutral. "I'll think about it."

She got up from the table, taking our empty mugs with her. "I already told Jenny that you'd be coming over for dinner Tuesday night. So it's all settled. She's very excited for you to meet Joey."

Jesus. I was hoping to be gone by Tuesday, but I knew I wasn't getting out of this — not without Mom's disappointment weighing me down.

"Why don't you come with me?" I said. Mom would help keep things less awkward.

Her eyes shifted away from me. "I can't. I've got to do something for Stan."

"Can't you do whatever it is some other time?" I asked.

"No, sorry."

What the fuck? Stan didn't want her visiting Brock now?

"Don't you want to see your grandson?"

Hurt flashed in her eyes. "Of course!" She looked miserable.

"Are you still going over there every week?" One of my mom's joys was to see the baby. That's all she talked about when I'd called her from the tour.

There was that strange look again. Evasive.

"I'm not going over there so much anymore. But Jenny's been video-calling me several times a week, so I can keep up with Joey. It's so wonderful the technology we have now."

My eyes narrowed. "Why aren't you visiting anymore?"

She sighed softly. "I don't have a car anymore."

"What?" My response was forceful, but I tamped down the anger I felt bubbling up inside.

"Yeah. We sold it. We don't need two cars. Stan has his and I can borrow it when I need to go shopping-"

"But not to go to Brock's house?" I snapped.

She turned her back to me to rinse out the coffee mugs. "He needs his car. There just hasn't been any convenient time to visit when he could be without it for so long."

I let out an angry breath. "I can't believe you got rid of your car. How do you get to work? How can you stand it being trapped here all the time?"

She turned around and glared at me. "Stan drops me off. And I'm not trapped. We're just being more economical. That's all."

Fucking Stan. I couldn't stand it. I stood up. I was going to give that lump of shit a piece of my mind.

My mother's shoulders slumped. "Please, Ryder. Don't."

Fuck.

I hated to see her like this, but she never listened to me. I had no idea what the hell she saw in Stan, but I knew that she'd never leave him. I'd drag her out of here so damn fast if I thought he was physically harming her. He wasn't, so I was stuck watching their joke of a relationship from the sidelines.

I knew my mom clung to Stan because she feared being alone. My father devastated her when he walked out on us. She'd been absolutely crushed. Brock's joining the military and then me leaving for college a few years later had been more blows to her. Then, without warning, one day I found out she was married to Stan. She claimed she needed him — would die if he left her. There was some weird dynamic at play, a dependence that I just didn't understand.

But, I understood Stan. He was a lazy fucking con artist. Leeching off my mom. Using her weakness to scam her money. And in the two quick years after he went through all of her money, he'd turned to me. My fucking money.

Stan was sitting in a brown La-Z-Boy recliner, feet popped up, watching TV. He didn't get up when I walked in. He didn't even turn his head, barely acknowledging me.

"Hey, boy."

I hated when he fucking called me 'boy'.

"Stan." I stared down at him.

He took a sip of beer. "How's that rock band of yours doing? Still raking in the big bucks?"

I ignored his question. "What happened to Mom's car?"

He shrugged. "Just consolidating. Being responsible with the bills and all. Not all of us are swimming in dough."

I looked him over. He had a bald spot on the top of his head. The remaining hair he had was greasy looking. His once-white T-shirt was now a dingy gray color with several nasty stains, probably ketchup, and a few holes torn in it. He wore loose navy pants and completed the outfit with the ugliest, most beat-up loafers I'd ever seen.

"Now Mom can't go visit Brock and the baby anymore. How could you take that away from her?"

He finally looked at me. "She can go. Whenever she wants. In fact, I was just thinking about taking her over there next week. Yeah. I think I'll do that."

Sure he would. I wanted to pound my fists into his ugly face. God, I hated him.

He went back to watching his program. "Is dinner almost ready?"

"I don't know." Disgusted, I turned to leave, but he stopped me.

"Before you go, I need to talk to you about something."

Here we fucking go.

I stopped and waited.

"Your mom's been spending a bit too much money this month."

Yeah, right. "On what?"

"You know ... odds and ends. Women's stuff."

Bullshit. I held my tongue. I'd already learned that arguing at this point in the money grab was useless.

"The rent's late again and the landlord's been making a big fuss this time. I'm going to need some help or we might get evicted."

He didn't even have the grace to look embarrassed.

"Sorry, Stan. I don't have any money. I've got my own bills to pay."

I hadn't spent more than a few days in my new house and I already had a second mortgage on it. I'd needed it to cover for the last hunk of cash I'd handed over to Stan and the renovations on my house were sucking up more money than I'd initially thought.

"You better find some more, rock star. If we get evicted, I can't guarantee I can take your momma with me."

I glanced toward the kitchen. If my mother heard this, she'd be devastated. I tried to keep my voice down as I spat with derision. "My mother can come live with me."

"In California?" he snorted. "She don't want to live with you. She wants to live with me. Work it out, boy. She'd be in rough shape if it came to that."

I strode out of the den before I throttled him. I had to think. Were they really late on the rent? Who knew? I couldn't trust him. I didn't know what he spent the last ten grand I'd handed over to him on. Mom worked at the bookstore; I knew she didn't pull in much money. Stan supposedly worked, but I didn't know what he did and never saw him actually go to work when I was here. I thought that maybe he just sat on his fat ass all day and extorted money from people.

I headed into the kitchen. "Mom, I'm going to get my bags out of my car."

She was stirring some spaghetti sauce. "Okay. Dinner will be ready in about 15 minutes."

"Hey, I was thinking. How about we go out to brunch tomorrow? Then maybe we can go shopping or to the movies. Something fun. Spend the day together."

Her face lit up. "Okay. I'll ask Stan."

Fuck no. "Just the two of us, Mom."

Her lips tightened. She paused for a full beat. "Okay."

Thank God.

"Great."

I headed out to my car, wondering how I'd survive another few days in this house. It looked like I was stuck going to dinner at Brock's house Tuesday night, but I didn't want to spend a second longer than necessary in Ohio.

When I got to my car, I slipped inside and pulled out my phone. Ten minutes later, I purchased a one-way ticket out of Dayton International heading to LAX for Wednesday morning. It couldn't come soon enough.

There was one more thing I needed to do before I headed back inside. I had to see Talia again. I sat back and thought about how I could make that happen. A few minutes later, I began texting Max.

Me: I've got this meeting in town Monday night. Since I'm there, I thought it'd be nice to meet up with some of our old HS friends. Southside Bar on 5th St. 8 p.m. See if James and Becker can come. And others.

I'd never typed so much in one text. I waited a few minutes, hoping Max would respond quickly. Luckily, he did.

Max: Okay, sounds great.

Perfect. Then I added the important part. The part that pulled at his male ego.

Me: Make sure you bring some hot chicks.

He replied a few seconds later:

Max: Definitely.

I was sure that since he'd been dating Talia for three years, he didn't hang around any other hot chicks. He'd round up Talia and use her girlfriends just to look cool, which was exactly what I wanted.

I shook my head and then smiled at my stupidity. What the hell was I doing?

I just wanted to see her. One more time.

Chapter 9

Talia

It was Saturday night. Max was passed out on my couch, his head tipped back, softly snoring. He'd missed the last thirty minutes or so of the movie; I didn't wake him because I could tell he wasn't into it.

I checked my phone. It was just past midnight, and I was nowhere near tired. Ellie wouldn't be home for hours. Max hadn't wanted to go out again tonight, even though by this time last night, he'd already left the bar and was nearly sleeping. At about the same time, I'd been getting ready to head out to conduct O.L.D. on his friend, Ryder.

Ryder.

The guy was an arrogant ass, but I couldn't deny that physically, he was perfection. And sexually …

I couldn't think about it. It wasn't right.

But those orgasms!

Stop thinking about him.

Max had gotten a text earlier. Without him knowing, I'd read the first text as it came in. It was from Ryder. He wanted to go out on Monday night. Stealthily, I tried to see the rest of the messages, but I couldn't without being too obvious.

Then Max casually asked if me and Ellie and some of our friends wanted to meet up with him and some of his buddies who were going to hang out.

God, I wanted to. Not because I was hot for Ryder or anything, but because I wanted Ellie to see this stud who I'd O.L.D'd.

Who was I kidding? The thought of being in the same room with Ryder again made my insides clench. There may have been some tingling going on, too.

But I didn't want to seem too eager. "Monday night?"

Max agreed. "I know. Monday! I don't want to go out on a Monday, but it's the only time everyone can get together."

He hadn't even asked anyone yet. He was making excuses for Ryder. Apparently, Ryder only had to snap his fingers, and Max jumped to attention. He'd go out on a Monday night for Ryder, no problem, but wouldn't go out on a Saturday night for me. I'd swallowed down my annoyance and agreed to go.

I nudged Max on the shoulder and again harder when he didn't wake up at first. He finally popped open his eyes. "What'd I miss?"

"The last half of the movie."

He grunted and rubbed his weary face. "I'm beat. Are you ready for bed?"

"Yeah. Let's go."

While I was brushing my teeth and washing my face, I thought about Max. I still owed him his birthday surprise, but the thought of doing O.L.D. on Max after what occurred the night before with

Ryder was out of the question. The comparisons in my head would be devastating. And Max wouldn't miss what he didn't know about. So, O.L.D. was out.

No, tonight would be about Max and me. We'd have normal sex. Loving sex. Like two mature adults. My thoughts would focus on Max and how good he made me feel.

I finished up and then put on the sexy black lingerie I'd smuggled into the bathroom. Just to make sure tonight was successful, I spent five minutes getting myself ready; it was technically masturbating, but I preferred to call it self-foreplay. That way, hopefully, my orgasm wouldn't fall so far behind Max's. Because I was going to orgasm tonight.

I revved myself up pretty good and then headed back to the bedroom. Max was already in bed.

Passed out.

Snoring.

I left the small bedside lamp on and then climbed into bed next to Max. Nudged him a few times.

There was no response.

Just great.

I pulled the covers off him and studied him for a few minutes. He was a good-looking guy who kept in good shape. As usual, he was in a T-shirt and boxers. Maybe if I played with him a little, he'd wake up. And satisfy me.

Slipping my hand into his boxers, I found his cock. He was small. Squishy. And limp.

Disgusted with myself, I removed my hand from his boxers. Dammit. When had Max stopped turning me on sexually? When did all the romantic feelings disappear? When did I fall out of love with him?

I gasped.

Had I ever been in love with him in the first place? Sure, I loved the idea of him. I loved our relationship. I loved not being alone.

But I didn't love Max. Not anymore.

Stunned by my inner revelations, I sat on the bed, watching him sleep. I'd had some niggling doubts about our relationship for months now, but I'd never allowed my thoughts to take the course they had now.

Deep in my heart, I knew it was undeniable that I needed to break things off with Max. We weren't meant to be. We weren't soul mates.

Would he be heartbroken? God, would he be relieved? Did he still love me? I wasn't even certain.

I was certain that I didn't love Max, and I knew now that I had to dump him.

It had absolutely nothing to do with a certain Adonis-like orgasm-giving god, even though I kept hearing his words over and over in my head. *Dump him.* No, this was all about Max and me — our relationship. This had nothing to do with Ryder, but it took experiencing Ryder for me to finally admit it to myself.

Chapter 10

Ryder

I WAS EARLY. I told Max I had a meeting in town, but that was a lie. I just needed to see Talia again, and I couldn't spend another minute at my mom's place. She'd been at work all day while Stan sat on his fat ass watching TV. I still wasn't sure what I was going to do about his most recent threat. I couldn't keep giving him money; it'd never end — even after I bankrupted myself. But if Stan left her, she'd spiral into depression again. Christ, I couldn't think of any way out of this.

I sat at the bar nursing my beer. Some regulars took up most of the bar stools and a few tables too, but the place was fairly empty. It was a Monday night, after all. What the hell was I thinking? Even if Talia showed up, what was I going to do? She was with Max. Off limits. And I was leaving in two days. This was one of my dumber ideas.

Ten minutes later, a few of my old high school friends started trickling in. By 8:30, there was a decent group of us hanging around the bar. We spent time catching up, but my status as a 'rock star' kept getting brought up. Once one of my friends mentioned Ghost Parker, the girls settled around me like glue and the questions never stopped. I was subtly trying to keep a few of the more forward women at bay. None of these women interested me. I focused all of my attention on the door, waiting for Talia to show up.

A pretty redhead's hand landed on my biceps. "So, you toured with Cold Fusion? What were they like?"

I was still watching the door when I answered. "They're all pretty down to earth. Fun guys."

Another girl, who was introduced to me as Becker's girlfriend, leaned her chest into my arm. "What about Ghost? Does he have a girlfriend?"

Ghost was Johnny Parker, our lead singer. I shifted away from the girl's tits. "Not that I know of."

Where the fuck was Talia? I didn't want to stand in this swarm of handsy women mixed with a few high school acquaintances getting grilled about my band. On tour, I'd pick out one (or two) of them and enjoy a night of casual sex, but I'd done that almost every night for the last nine months. Tonight, I had zero interest.

Plus, on tour, I'd be hanging out with my bandmates, who were like brothers to me. They were guys that I enjoyed being around. Ghost was more elusive, but Knox, who we called Scotty because he was from Scotland, and Sidney, who we called Vicious, were two of my best friends. I was also pretty tight with Sebastian, 'Bash', who was our drummer. We were a tight-knit group that knew how to party hard and have a good time. They also got more than their fair share of attention from the ladies, so this situation I was in now would have been more tolerable if they'd been here. At least it would have thinned out the herd pawing at me a bit.

The redhead was really pressing into me now and giggling about something she said. I was about to put some distance between us when I became distracted by Angel walking in the door. Finally. She was with Max and another girl, but I couldn't take my eyes off her. She scanned the bar and then our eyes met. My cock throbbed a beat in response. I wanted this girl. So fucking badly.

Gone was the girl-next-door look from the birthday lunch; this was a much sexier look. She wore a curvy pink off-the-shoulder top with a flared-out bottom, black skinny jeans, and strappy heels. Her hair was swept back with two braids on each side of her head that met in the back in a high ponytail. Her makeup was dark and dramatic. She was a total knockout.

Talia's eyes drifted to the redheaded girl who was practically molesting me, and she frowned in disapproval. I disengaged from the redhead, watching Talia the entire time. She was whispering something to her friend, and the way her friend was shooting looks my way made me think whatever she said was about me. A few minutes later, Max made his way towards the bar. That's when I made my move.

Talia's friend watched me approach, but Talia kept her eyes averted, pretending not to notice me. I'd ordinarily say her friend was gorgeous. She had long shiny dark hair, a pretty face, and a great figure with an amazing rack, but she couldn't hold a candle to my Angel. No one could.

"Hey, Talia."

She calmly turned my way. "Ryder. Fancy seeing you here."

I took a sip of my beer, letting my eyes wander all over her body and soak her in.

Talia crossed her arms over her chest. "This is my roommate and my very best friend, Ellie."

I smiled politely at Ellie. "Nice to meet you, Ellie."

"Nice to meet you, too."

I switched my attention back to Talia, but I could feel Ellie's eyes accessing me.

"So, can I get you ladies something to drink?"

Ellie started to speak, "Sure—"

But Talia cut her off. "Max went to get us some. We're good."

"Okay."

An awkward silence developed. I couldn't think of anything to say. I barely knew this girl.

"So, how did the rest of Max's birthday go?"

Talia glanced over at Ellie and the fuck if I knew what that silent communication meant.

"It was fine."

We stared at each other for another interval that felt too long when Ellie tapped Talia on the shoulder. "I think I see someone I know. I'll be back in a few minutes."

Talia looked uncomfortable when Ellie left us like she might bolt at any moment.

I stepped in closer, hoping to halt her retreat, and caught the scent of her perfume. Or maybe it was her shampoo. I remembered it from the night she climbed into bed with me — vanilla with a hint of something floral.

"Did the coffee maker work?"

She blinked a few times, and then a telltale red blush crept into her cheeks. With her hair pulled back, I could even see her ears turning red. She looked adorable.

"We didn't get around to testing the coffee maker yet."

My lips twitched. "That's too bad."

She looked past me and I could see her tense with frustration. I followed her gaze. Max was standing in a group of friends, a beer in his hand.

"Looks like he got side-tracked. Let me get you something."

She hesitated for a moment and then smiled tentatively. "Okay. Thanks."

"What's your poison?"

"Alabama Slammer."

I hadn't heard that one in a while. "Drink or shot?"

She smiled slyly and my insides knotted. "How about both?"

Nodding, I asked, "And for your friend, Ellie?"

"Light beer."

I headed to the bar, ignoring the girl who tried to get my attention on the way. Earlier, I had tipped the bartender well, maybe that's why he bypassed a few people and headed straight for me when he saw me waiting.

I ordered the drinks and then waited, stealing a glimpse back at Talia to make sure she didn't escape. One of my high school buddies approached her, but within minutes, he left. Thank fuck. Despite having no right to, I was feeling possessive. Max, the dumbass, was still talking to friends. I couldn't fathom how he could be so inattentive to her.

After I paid, I carefully gathered up the five drinks, two beer bottles and a shot in one hand, and a shot and a drink in the other, and made my way back to Talia.

She laughed when she saw my handful. "What's all this?"

"A drink and shot — both Alabama Slammers." I handed her the drinks. Then I placed the beers on the table near us. "A beer for me and Ellie." I was left holding the last shot. "And a shot for me. You can't do a shot alone."

She was looking at me differently, almost as if her eyes were sparkling. She tapped her shot glass to mine, said 'cheers', and then threw it back.

I followed her lead and then placed my empty glass down on the table. "Fruity. That's a girly shot."

She smacked my arm playfully. Angel was finally loosening up a bit. "Let's play some darts."

She sipped daintily at her drink. "I don't know how to play darts."

"You literally throw the dart at the board. It's not complicated. C'mon." I grabbed the beers and then took her hand. A shockwave of energy surged through our connected hands, creating a needy pull of lust in my dick as I led her toward the empty corner of the bar where the dartboard was mounted. It surprised me when she didn't tug her hand from mine. Progress.

I left her standing behind a line of tape on the floor while I pulled the darts from the dartboard. I returned to her side and handed over the three red colored darts. "Do you want to go first?"

She took a big sip of her drink. "No. You go."

I stood behind the blue taped mark, lined up my shot, and then let the dart fly. It didn't hit the bullseye, but it wasn't too far off. Not bad.

Talia stepped up to the line. She brought the dart up level to her eye, squinted one eye shut, and pouted her shiny red lips. Watching her set my body on fire. I couldn't see those pouty lips without remembering where they'd been a few nights before. Sucking my cock. This time, I couldn't prevent my cock from responding. Within seconds, I was sporting a full, throbbing erection. This monster was probably visible, even hidden beneath my jeans. I'd have to keep it under wraps. I didn't want to scare Talia away.

After she twitched her arm back and forth a few times without releasing the dart, I tapped my foot. "Are you ever going to throw it?"

She screwed up her face in concentration and then suddenly let the dart fly. It flew all right. At least ten feet off course with a crazy lop-sided arc that finally smacked against a glass shadowbox holding sports memorabilia before it clunked to the floor. We were damn lucky that no one was back in this corner of the bar.

"Holy Shit! You're a menace to bar patrons everywhere."

Her hand flew to her mouth. "I told you I never did it before."

"Jesus. That's the worst throw I've ever seen," I snickered.

She sniffed. "You don't have to be so rude about it."

"I'm sorry. You just shocked me. Okay, let's try it again. This time don't side-arm the dart. Use a nice smooth motion, like this..." I demonstrated a nice straight throwing motion.

"I don't think I want to do it again."

"C'mon. Just try. It can't be as bad as the first throw."

She glared at me. "Ha ha."

"C'mon. I'll help you." I slipped behind her and softly grabbed her shoulders. "Put your right foot ahead of your left. Right behind the line. Keep your weight on your front foot."

My hand slid down to her right hand and brought it up. I moved her fingers, fixing her grip on the dart. By this time, her body was tucked perfectly in front of mine like we were molded to fit together. All the while, I breathed in her intoxicating scent and hoped that my cock wouldn't bust through my pants and poke her in the ass.

My mouth whispered near her ear, "You're tiny."

"What?" she half-turned in my arms to look at me. "I am not tiny; I'm five foot eight. That's without heels on. That's not tiny. Maybe you're just big."

"Hmmm. Maybe." I smiled.

She rolled her eyes. "Let's get on with it. Just show me what to do."

Holding her wrist in my hand, I demonstrated the arm motion she should make. God, what I really wanted to do was bend her over and fuck her senseless.

Reluctantly, I stepped out of her way so she could try another throw. "Hold on, let me make sure the coast is clear first."

An eyebrow rose. "Funny."

This time, the dart flew in the general direction of the dartboard but lost momentum and dived to the ground several feet before its destination.

"Better. Try again, but this time put a little more power into it."

She pursed her lips in concentration and then took another shot. This time, the dart landed about two feet left of the dartboard but stuck into the wall. Excitedly, she jumped up and down. "Look at that!"

I couldn't take my eyes off her bouncing tits. "See, you're getting better every time. You're a natural."

That's when Max decided to show up. He glanced my way, looking puzzled. "Hey, Ryder."

"Hey." I nodded.

Talia's face was bright red. "Ryder was showing me how to play darts."

"I see that." Max put his arms around Talia, marking his territory. "Tal, I'd like you to come meet some of my friends."

Without a backward glance, Max pulled her away from me, and they both walked away toward the bar. Fuck. I was cockblocked by her damn boyfriend. I chugged the rest of my beer and then stalked after them.

I set up at a high-top table where I could keep my eye on Talia. Within seconds, a few girls came over to flirt with me, but I blew them off. I was trying to figure out how to get Talia back when another girl joined our table. It was Ellie.

"Hey, Ellie. I got this beer for you." I held up the lite beer I'd been toting around. "It's probably warm by now."

She took a sip. "Thanks. It's still okay."

"So how long have you known Talia?"

"We've been roommates for four years now, but I've known her for about six years." She began picking at the label on her bottle.

"So, you know her pretty well, huh?" I glanced across the room and caught Talia's eye before she quickly looked away.

"Yes, we're very close. We share everything with each other."

"Everything?"

"Yes," she confirmed. "She told me all about O.L.D."

My eyebrows furrowed with confusion. "Old? What's that?"

Her eyes widened. "Oh! No, erhm, I mean, the other night. She told me what happened."

I grunted in reply.

"She's looking over here right now. She's giving me the eye."

I glanced over and saw Talia looking our way. Her lips were compressed in a thin line. She wasn't happy.

"The eye?"

Ellie shrugged. "The stink eye. She's not happy we're talking. I'd say she's jealous."

I leveled Ellie with my sexiest smile. The one guaranteed to melt the panties off the frostiest lady. I draped my arm around her shoulders and leaned in to whisper in her ear. "Angel's jealous? That's something I can work with."

"Oh, Lord!" she moaned. "You're good. Talia's in big trouble."

"I hope so. What's up with her boyfriend?"

Our heads were still bent together in mischief. Ellie sighed. "Max? He's an old habit. Don't ever tell her I said that."

"Good to know."

Ellie began running her fingers along my arm. Hopefully, she was aiming this flirtation at Talia and not at me.

"Why do you call her Angel? She's a sweet girl and all, but she's not that innocent."

I must have gotten a dreamy look in my eyes. "That night, I thought I was getting a blowjob from an angel — like in heaven. I thought I might have died and gone to heaven. And she tasted like—"

She pushed away from me. "Stop. I don't want to hear anymore. The two of you … I can't even."

Chapter 11

Talia

WHAT ON HEAVEN, EARTH, and even purgatory was Ellie doing with Ryder? I was going to kick her traitorous little butt. She was pushing her cleavage so far into his face; he was practically motorboating her.

Max nudged me. "D'ya think, Talia?"

"Sure." I wasn't paying attention to anything Max was saying. I could be agreeing to something disgusting — that roach larvae tasted delicious — for all I knew.

Ever since Max had caught Ryder and me playing darts, he'd kept his hands on me. He had me pulled close to his side, his arm in a vise grip around my waist. I casually tried to break free a few times, but he wasn't having it. Since we'd first arrived at the bar, he'd forgotten all about me until he'd seen me with Ryder. Suddenly, he went all 'territorial' and it made me feel ... well, nothing. It had only cemented the decision that had been running through my head to break up with him.

Nothing highlighted my lack of sexual chemistry with Max more than the zings of heady exhilaration I'd felt around Ryder. I could barely function around that man. He had me all twisted up in knots of desire. And if Ellie didn't step away from him, she was going to feel my wrath later.

Almost as if she could read my mind, she stood up. Ellie headed to the bar, but only moments later, two new girls joined Ryder. My molars ground together. That man was never alone. Women flocked to him like bees to honey.

I stood next to Max and his friends for another thirty minutes of total boredom, trying covertly to watch Ryder at the same time. The man was the sweetest eye candy. I was just fantasizing about taking a lick of that candy when Ellie came rushing over.

She began pulling me away from Max. "Talia, I have to talk to you. It's urgent."

Max didn't want to let me go. He pointedly checked his watch. "Talia, it's getting late. I want to head out soon."

Ellie turned to Max. "Just give me a minute. I have to talk to her."

I wiggled out of Max's grasp. As if I needed permission to talk to my friend! "I'll be right back."

Ellie dragged me over to an empty table at the back of the bar where no one was hanging out.

"What's going on?"

She took a deep breath. "You won't believe this!"

I was focused on Ryder, talking to some more girls, but now she had my attention because her excitement was palpable.

"What?"

Her eyes about popped out of her head. "I was talking to Janine at the bar. That's Becker's girlfriend. She went to high school with Max. And Ryder."

My eyes drifted back to Ryder. "So?"

Ellie grabbed my shoulders to focus me. "So, she told me that Ryder is Ryder Mathis."

"And?" Just spit it out already.

"Ryder Mathis is a guitarist for Ghost Parker!"

My brows wrinkled. "Who?"

"Ghost Parker. The band. Haven't you ever heard of them?"

"No."

She gave my shoulders a little squeeze. "They have a few big singles. You'd recognize them if you heard them on the radio. They just got done touring. They opened for Cold Fusion."

Whoa. Of course, I'd heard of Cold Fusion. "So, you're telling me that he's in a rock band?"

"Yes! And not just a dinky garage band. An up-and-coming major rock band."

I stood staring at her stupidly.

"Talia, you conducted Operation Limp Dick on a friggin' rock star!"

I was struck speechless, but Ellie didn't seem to notice. She was fiddling with her phone. She jammed the screen in front of my face.

"Do you recognize this?" It was a close-up picture of a giant dick, complete with a nice mushroom head and a veiny shaft.

"Wh ... what?"

She swiped on the screen to another dick pic. "It's Ryder's cock. There are pictures of it all over the internet!"

She flipped to a picture of a dick popping out of a pair of ripped jeans. It could have been anybody's dick. "That dick doesn't even look like the first one."

Ellie frowned. "How would you know? We both know that you don't have a good track record with identifying dicks. You couldn't even remember what Max's looked like."

That was just insulting. "I can tell you straight up that this picture is not Ryder's dick. I don't care what the internet says."

"Don't get testy. Okay. Maybe these aren't all legit. But there are so many, some are bound to be real. We'll have to study them later."

I flopped down in the chair. "Ugh. Why does he have dick pics all over the internet? It's just ... gross."

Ellie fiddled with her phone. "Wait till you see all the pictures with girls. God, there are millions. These fan sites have a lot of dirt on him."

Squinting, I closed one eye, not really wanting to see as she scrolled through some more pictures. There were tons of selfies with him and random girls, pictures of him signing girls' breasts, shots of him partying...

My stomach sank. "He's like a walking, talking STD."

Ellie grinned. "He's a total man whore, but I think he likes you."

I pointed to the group of photos. "Oh, my God. It's just too much," I whispered.

"You're not going to walk away from him, are you?" She turned her worried eyes on me. "He's like ... sex on a stick. Irresistible. Talia, you said it, the man's an Adonis. And he gave you orgasms!" Obnoxiously, she squealed the last word.

I shook my head. "He doesn't care about me; he just wants to get laid." I glanced over at him, holding court over a group of fawning women. "And it looks like he's got plenty of choices tonight."

"I shouldn't have shown you all this." Ellie shook her head regretfully. "I was just so ... shocked."

I stood up. "I'm glad you did. Thank God I didn't do anything stupid. I'm going home. You coming with?"

"Hell, no. As long as Ryder stays, I might still have a shot at him. You wouldn't mind, would you?"

"Why would I mind?" I felt a stab of regret run through me. "But, yuck! I can't believe you'd want to hook up with him after seeing all that."

She hung out her tongue and pretended to pant. "Look how sexy he is. You're crazy to pass this up." She held up her phone, flashing me the picture of the giant, meaty cock.

"You're ridiculous!" I left in search of Max. I had to get out of there.

Ten minutes later, Max and I were in his car, heading home. Max was going on about some work meeting he had in the morning while I wallowed. Damn, I didn't want Ellie and Ryder to hook up. I didn't want Ryder to hook up with anyone. Why did he have to be a slutty rock star?

"How come you didn't tell me Ryder was in some famous rock band?"

Max glanced my way. "I don't know. I just forgot, I guess. It's not that big of a band, anyway. He was in a band in high school, too. They kind of sucked."

Silence stretched in the car when I didn't answer. Finally, Max asked, "Who told you? Did Ryder?"

Had Max been trying to keep it from me? "Janine was telling everybody. Ghost Parker — I never heard of them before."

"I guess it's pretty cool that I know him. But, honestly, he seems like a prick now." Max's fingers were tapping on the steering wheel.

I swiveled to face him. "What do you mean? He seemed okay to me."

"Well, he acts like God's gift to women. I guess after having all those groupies throwing themselves at you. He told me he fu ... I mean, had sex with a different chick every night on tour."

I bit my lip. "Sounds like every man's fantasy."

"Well, kind of. Until you meet the right girl." He directed his smile at me, but his eyes slid away from me pretty quickly. He didn't sound very convincing.

I knew I was still going to break up with Max. My eyes had been opened about us. We weren't meant to be. And now, Max had confirmed that Ryder — the man I'd been fantasizing about nonstop for days — was an utter asshole. The insanely beautiful man who caused a riot of butterflies to explode in my stomach, my skin to sizzle with electricity, and my lady parts to throb like crazy was a vacuous, over-sexed and supremely arrogant rock star with an entire website dedicated to his cock. It was too pitiful to bear.

I rested my head up against the car window and fought back tears of bitterness until we got to my apartment. "I know you have that big meeting in the morning, so you don't need to come up with me. I'll talk to you tomorrow."

Max pulled me in for a kiss. A dull, lifeless kiss. "Thanks, Tal. Goodnight."

Chapter 12

Talia

It was the middle of the night when something woke me up. There's no way Ellie was just getting in now, was there? It was a work night. Unless she wasn't alone. My God, what if she brought Ryder back to our apartment to hook up? I would completely die. And after I died, I'd come back from the dead to kill her. I listened closely but didn't hear any noise from the apartment outside my bedroom.

I settled back into my pillow and almost fell back asleep when I heard it again. It was the text notification on my phone. Who could be texting me this late?

I picked it up and opened the text from an unknown number.

Unk: Hey Angel

My heart started beating faster.

> **ME:** Ryder? How did you get my number?
> **UNK:** Ellie gave it to me.
> **ME:** She is so dead.
> **UNK:** Don't be mad at her. I'm very persuasive.
> **ME:** I'm sure you are. Still …
> **UNK:** I want to see you again.

I couldn't help it; I was grinning like a fool.

> **ME:** You mean — you want to shag me again?
> **UNK:** Shag??
> **ME:** Yeah, you know, SEX.
> **UNK:** I won't shag you if you still have a boyfriend.

I rolled my eyes and watched the three dots cycling, waiting for the next text to come in.

> **UNK:** I told you to dump him.
> **UNK:** Yeah, I do want to shag you again though
> **ME:** So you have morals? LOL. You only shag available women?
> **UNK:** What's so funny about that?

I sat up in bed and leaned back against the headboard as I typed my reply.

> **Me:** You really thought I'd dump my boyfriend just because you told me to? You're delusional.

I waited a full minute. There was no reply. Did I hurt his feelings?

> **Me:** Ugh, it's almost one o'clock in the morning. Don't you have better rock star things to be doing right now?
> **Unk:** Right now I'm thinking about us, Angel. I have a very vivid imagination. Would you like me to share?
> **Me:** Huh, there go your morals. I told you there's no 'us'. We're never going to shag!

Ugh! Why did I keep saying 'shag'? I sounded like a pervy Austin Powers.

> **Unk:** You sound like my friend Scotty.
> **Me:** He doesn't want to shag with you?
> **Unk:** God, I hope not. I don't fuck guys.

I pursed my lips. Saying 'fuck' sounded so vulgar.

> **Me:** Don't say that word. I like shagging.
> **Unk:** Now we're getting somewhere! I like it too.
> **Me:** That's not what I meant.
> **Unk:** I like talking sexy with you. <tongue

hanging out emoji>

A rock star was sending me emojis? Why did that make me smile?

> **Me:** I don't do sexting.
> **Unk:** I admit this took a turn I didn't expect, but I'll run with it.
> **Unk:** What are you wearing right now?
> **Me:** White granny panties with period stains on them.

I cackled out loud while I waited for his reply.

> **Unk:** Jesus, you're not that good at this.
> **Me:** Sorry. (Not).
> **Unk:** Don't worry, Angel, I'll teach you.

I saw he was still typing, so I waited a minute until the next text came in.

> **Unk:** Remember that first throw you made at darts? It was a total disaster. Nowhere near the target. With a little coaching from me, you were (almost) hitting the board after a few tries. I'll coach you with the sexting.
> **Me:** Bite me.
> **Unk:** Hmmm, getting better already.
> **Unk:** Are you touching yourself, Angel?

I had to admit that I was getting turned on. An agonizing ache settled between my legs. I'd never sexted with Max before. Every text between us had been strictly utilitarian. It was symbolic of our relationship. Yeah, I wanted to touch myself, because I wanted what we had the other night. Mind-blowing sex.

I gasped as I realized I was taking too long to reply. I quickly typed my answer.

> **Me:** No.

Still, I couldn't stop myself. My hand slid inside my underwear. If only these were Ryder's fingers ...

> **Unk:** I think you are.

I felt like I'd gotten caught with my hand in the cookie jar. My face burned red with embarrassment.

> **Me:** I'm going to sleep now. Goodnight.
> **Unk:** I want to see you tomorrow.
> **Me:** Aren't you going back to L.A. soon?

I held my breath during the long pause before his answer.

> **Unk:** Yeah. On Wednesday.
> **Me:** So, what's the point of this?
> **Unk:** The point is I want to see you again.
> **Me:** This is stupid, Ryder.

Unk: Don't turn me down.
Me: I have work tomorrow.
Unk: After work.
Me: Max won't want to go out again.
Unk: I DON'T WANT TO SEE FUCKING MAX
Me: Jeez, don't yell
Unk: Then say yes
Me: FINE! Will you let me go to sleep now?
Unk: <grinning emoji> What's your work address? I'll pick you up at 5.

Was I really doing this? I hadn't stopped grinning the whole time. Yeah, I might actually be doing this.

Me: 1000 Cavendish Dr. in Fairborn. Where are we going?
Unk: To my brother's house for dinner.
Me: This sounds like a date, Ryder.
Unk: It's not a date. You have a boyfriend. Remember?
Me: Ugh. Fine. I'll see you at 5.
Unk: Sweet dreams, Talia.

I quickly scanned through the emojis for something appropriate. I chose the sleepy face with the zzz's, but when I pressed send, I realized I hit the wrong emoji — the one next to it.

Me: <weird derpy face emoji>

Oh no! An internal battle took place as I tried to decide if I should send a new text. What would I say? 'Oops, wrong emoji?' It seemed so dumb.

When I didn't hear from him, I decided to let it go. I should put down my phone before I humiliated myself more. But despite being so tired, I read through all our messages again. And again.

I was going to see Ryder tomorrow. It was the dumbest, stupidest thing I'd agreed to in a long time. Perhaps ever.

Then how come I was still grinning ear to ear?

Chapter 13

Ryder

It wasn't quite 5 p.m. yet when I followed the arrow on the lane painted with the word 'visitor' and drove up to the security hut. I rolled down my window and waited.

The bored-looking security guy leaned out his window and peered into my car. "Can I help you?"

"I'm here to pick up a friend."

He peered down his glasses at me. "Name?"

"Talia …" Fuck, what was her last name? "Uh, Natalia something. I don't know her last name."

He flashed me an impatient look. "Real great friend, huh?"

My jaw tensed. "Can you just look her up by the first name? How many Natalias could work here?"

"Sorry, can't do that."

I sighed. "Okay. Hold on a second." I grabbed my phone and began texting Talia.

> **Me:** What's your last name?
> **Talia:** Bennett.
> **Talia:** Are you here?

I spoke to the security guy, "Bennett. Natalia Bennett."
"One moment." His head disappeared back into the hut.

> **Me:** Trying to get past security.
> **Talia:** OK, I'll be down in 5.

The security guard took some information, handed me a temporary parking pass, and then said with a robotic tone, "Follow the signs to the visitor's parking. Stop by the reception desk if you need to go inside. Have a nice day."

The red and white striped gate arm lifted, and I drove through. I parked in an empty visitor's slot near the front door, turned off the engine, and then waited. I flipped my sunglasses up on top of my head and then sat back and watched the people exiting the building. I was eager to see Talia.

I'd been bitterly disappointed last night when she left Southside Bar without even talking to me again. I'd left shortly after she did, but not before I'd gotten her phone number from her roommate. And in case she didn't answer my text, I'd gotten Ellie's number too, as a backup plan to get to Talia. I was a pretty persistent asshole.

My eyes locked onto her as soon as she exited the building, but I didn't even know it was Talia at first. My eyes naturally honed in on hot women. This woman was smoking hot in a 'throw me down and fuck me on the conference room table during a board meeting' kind of way. A second later, I realized it was Talia.

She looked different, yet again. She was wearing a black skirt and matching suit jacket, black pumps, and her hair was pulled back in a large, loose bun. From afar, she looked like the CEO of the company. Despite showing hardly any skin, I noticed at least two guys checking her out as she walked by. She definitely turned heads.

I hopped out of the car and met her at the passenger's side door. She eyed me up and down as she neared, making that thrum of awareness jump-start my body.

"Hi, Ryder." She held out a bottle of wine in a gift bag. "Hold this for me."

My lips twitched. It was bossy Angel again. "Hello, Ms. Bennett." I took the wine and then she shoved her purse into my hands. By purse, I mean — a giant, black leather bag that could easily hold the contents of my duffel bag plus a few ten-pound weights to spare. It was heavy. "What are you carrying around in here? Bricks?"

"I'll never tell." She gave me a sassy look and then began peeling off her suit jacket. Underneath, she wore a white blouse that had a very feminine fit with sleeves to her elbows. She began unbuttoning her blouse, first the top button and then the next.

My cock stirred as I watched, mesmerized. "You sure know how to greet a man, Talia."

Her fingers undid a third button. She looked up into my eyes, laughing, and then she took back her purse. "I hope your brother likes red wine."

I opened the car door for her and she slid in. "I'm not sure, but Jenny probably does."

Her skirt reached modestly to her knees, but I spied a lovely piece of mouth-watering skin before she adjusted the slit that had exposed high up her creamy thigh. I closed the door and then walked around the back of the car, giving my cock time to settle down.

When I got behind the wheel, I stopped to watch her for a minute. She'd already kicked off her heels and was digging out a new pair from her bag. She slipped on, and then buckled, a pair of black heels with straps that zig-zagged across her foot with one thicker strap that circled above her ankle.

Then she dug into her monster-sized purse and pulled out a metal belt, which had large silver disks that were connected by a thick chain. She fastened it across the high waist of her black skirt, letting it drape a bit.

She glanced up at me. "Are we going?"

I shook myself into action. "Sure. I'm just amazed at what's going on over there." I started the car.

"I just need to make a few adjustments." She wrinkled her nose. "I can't go to dinner in a business suit."

She'd looked perfectly fine to me before, but I was already digging the transformation. I began backing out of the parking lot while she started touching up her makeup. I slid my sunglasses back over my eyes; that way I could watch her slyly as I drove.

"Try not to hit any bumps." She began adding more eyeliner to her eyes — giving them that cat-eye look. I was silent, not wanting to disturb her.

Next came mascara. "So, who's Jenny?"

"Jenny's my brother's wife."

She held the mascara wand in the air for a moment and glanced my way. "What's she like? Is she nice?"

"Nice? I guess. I don't know her too well."

She went back to attacking her eyelashes. "How long have they been married?"

I thought back to their wedding. My brother and I hadn't seen each other for years before the wedding. I only went because my mom had begged me. My dad had shown up with a new woman he'd been dating, pissing off my brother and devastating my mom. It had been a complete shitshow of a wedding from my point of view, which I'd witnessed from afar on the sidelines.

"Around four years, I think."

She was screwing the cap back on the mascara. She looked over at me speculatively, but my eyes were peeled to the road now. "Four years and you don't really know her?"

I tapped the steering wheel nervously. "She's kind of quiet. Hard to get to know."

"Oh, great!" Talia huffed. "Well, she must not be too bad. It was certainly nice of her to invite me along with you."

I was silent as Talia watched me like a hawk.

"Ryder?" Her voice sounded urgent.

"Yeah?" I couldn't look at her.

She turned in her seat, facing me. "They DO know I'm coming, right? They invited me?"

I winced. "Not exactly."

"What?" she hissed.

I glanced her way. "They didn't invite me either. Not really. My mom set it up. I'm not really on great terms with my brother."

"Terrific! They don't even know I'm coming?" The pitch of her voice grew steadily higher. "So you're just going to show up with me in tow? That was your plan? And who are you going to tell them I am? Your good pal? Your oral sex buddy? Because, don't you dare tell them I'm your girlfriend!"

I swept a hand through my hair. She was getting mad and all I could focus on was her saying oral sex. "I won't call you my girlfriend, don't worry. Look, I know this is awkward, but I didn't want to disappoint my mom. I'm leaving for L.A. tomorrow, and I really wanted to see you again. This sort of ... killed two birds with one stone."

Her mouth dropped open. "Are you serious?"

I began to sweat. "Hey, I didn't mean it like that. I really wanted to see you, but I promised my mom I'd see little Joey, too."

Her brows knitted in confusion. "Little Joey? Is that your brother?"

Oh fuck. "No, that's my nephew. I haven't met him yet."

Her sexy cat eyes bugged out of her head. "Are you kidding? Tell me you're kidding! You're going to meet your nephew for the first time? Why the hell did you ask me to come, Ryder?"

"I told you why. I wanted to see you." She turned away from me and sat back in her seat in a huff. Before I could stop myself, I asked, "Why did you agree to come?"

Her voice was barely above a whisper. "I don't know. I must be nuts."

She sat silently steaming for a few minutes before she chuckled. "You didn't even know my last name. You're ridiculous."

I know. I nodded my head in agreement and then watched out of the corner of my eye as she resumed her transformation. She applied some lipstick and then made a pouty face in the mirror, put some long, dangling earrings on, and then pulled the pins out of her bun and lowered her hair. God, she was beautiful.

She was finger-combing through her hair when she suddenly turned to me, looking flustered. "Do you have a gift for your nephew?"

I hesitated. "No ... I'm sure they're not expecting one."

"Ryder!" She pressed her lips together in a thin line. "How old is he?"

Fuck. She was going to think I was the biggest asshole. "I don't know. He was born in the spring ... I think."

She covered her face with her hands. "Ugh. You don't even know your nephew's birthday. You're just meeting him and you don't have a gift. And you're showing up with some random floozy."

"You're not a random floozy. You're my oral-sex buddy. Plus, we've got the wine." I shrugged like it was all going to be okay.

She peeked at me from behind her fingers. "I'm not sure little Joey will appreciate the wine." She grabbed her cell phone and began madly typing something into it. "We've got to stop for a gift. You can't show up empty-handed. My God! You're such an idiot."

I chuckled.

A few minutes later, she announced that she'd found a store that was only a few minutes out of our way. While she gave me directions toward the store from her phone, she began messing with her hair. She repositioned where her part was, and then her fingers began flying through her hair, braiding it. I could barely keep my eyes on the road; I was fascinated by what she was doing. When she got to the end of the section of hair, she began pinning it in place with the pins she'd taken out of her bun.

Most of her hair was hanging straight down, but she'd braided a large chunk of it that somehow wrapped over the top of her head like a headband. It was a headband made of a shiny golden braid of hair or a halo for an angel. Either way, it was stunning.

"How do you do that?"

She checked her hair in the visor mirror and then shut it. "Lots of practice. We get off at the next exit."

Five minutes later, I parked in front of the giant warehouse of a store. I jogged across to the passenger side of the car, but Talia was already getting out. It was the first time I could see her complete transformation. Fifteen minutes ago, she looked like the professional, but highly fuckable, CEO I wanted to shag, I mean fuck, in the boardroom

— and now she looked completely different. Now, she looked like a sexy siren calling me to my destruction.

I knew I was moving too close to her. She shut the car door, and I stepped toward her, not away. She was backed against the car and yet I felt myself moving closer. Our bodies were only inches away, but not touching.

"You look amazing." My voice was rough and growly. My pants were tight as fuck.

"Thanks." It was a breathy whisper.

I couldn't back away from her. I should. Right now. But, my body wouldn't listen. I lifted a finger to trace down the side of her face. Her eyes locked onto mine. My gaze flicked to her lips. I wanted to kiss her. I needed to.

"Ryder ..." She was breathing heavier. "We need to get a gift. Let's go."

Fuuuck. It was torture keeping my hands off of her. Why did I do this to myself? I took a step back and heard her sigh — of what? Relief or regret?

We walked through the parking lot, through the first and then the second set of automatic sliding doors. I stopped dead in my tracks.

The sight before me was alien. Elevator music assaulted my ears while the bright fluorescent lighting lit up a giant megalopolis of everything baby. Miniature human clothing surrounded us, but beyond that were aisles and aisles, and different grouped-off sections of baby stuff for as far as the eye could see.

"What the fuck!"

Talia turned to me. She looked concerned. "What's the matter?"

"What is this?" I was still taking it all in.

She put her hand on her hip and rolled her eyes. "It's a baby store, Ryder. Have you never been in one before?"

"No." I swallowed. "I think my balls are shriveling up."

Her eyes narrowed. "Oh, for Pete's sake! C'mon. Let's find a gift for Joey."

When I didn't move, she took my hand and started leading me onward into the jungle of baby clothing.

"How much shit could a baby need? This is nuts." I was still looking around. She ignored me, so I continued, "How does this place even stay in business? Look how freaking huge it is!"

She was holding up some tiny blue pants. "Babies are born every day. And they need a lot of stuff, but I bet Jenny already has most of this stuff. That's why you should get him a cute baby outfit."

I couldn't keep up with her. She was flitting from rack to rack, picking out tiny baby clothing and gushing over every little thing. "Look at these cute onesies!" It gave me time to look at her without her noticing.

She held up a pair of blue swim trunks. "Oh, my God! Look at these. So cute! And this little rash guard."

She pulled a tiny blue shirt off the rack. It had a grinning cartoon shark with exaggerated teeth on it with the word 'GOTCHA' printed under it.

"It's kind of cute, I guess, but do babies really swim?" I asked.

"Of course, they swim! Why would they make bathing suits if they didn't?" She held up some shoes and squealed, "Look at these. Tiny little sandals! And a matching sun hat! Adorable."

I couldn't help but laugh at her. "Talia, they are cute, but Brock doesn't have a pool. And it's the end of summer. In Ohio. I'm not sure a bathing suit is the most practical gift."

Her bottom lip stuck out in a pout for a moment. "You're right. But they're so darn cute. Hmmm. How about some fall clothing? Let's see …"

She moved away from the swim stuff and headed to a different rack of clothing. "When was he born again?"

I frowned. "While I was on tour. I can't remember exactly. The days all sort of blur together. April, I think? Or May?"

She was looking at the tag on a miniature jeans jacket. "Is he a big baby or a little baby? What size would he be?"

I tried to think if my mother had ever mentioned it, but I had never listened carefully when she talked about Joey. Now, I kind of regretted that. "I'm not really sure."

She hung up the jacket and sighed. "We shouldn't get clothes then, since you're not sure. How about some toys instead?"

I liked how she said 'we' like we were in this together. I flashed her a genuine smile. "Good idea. Lead the way." I held out my hand for her to take.

She stopped and stared at me for a long moment. Hungrily. It felt like all the blood in my body pooled in my cock. I wasn't sure why she was suddenly looking at me like that, but fuck, I think the air was rippling around us. I shifted uncomfortably. I was going to have the biggest case of blue balls before this night was through.

Talia blinked and then grabbed my hand. "Let's go."

She led me through aisles of baby toys, all the while giving me a running commentary on the pros and cons of each one. We got to the end aisle in the back corner of the store. Next to us was an open space with at least 20 cribs set up with different colored frilly bedding and playful mobiles attached to them.

Talia was extolling the virtues of some baby contraption. It was called an activity center, and it apparently had enough lights, bells, and whistles to keep a baby active for years. When the baby got older, according to the box, you could fold it up like some plastic origami Transformer and turn it into a walker. I was sold.

Her head was currently buried in a large floor bin filled with stuffed animals. Her deep dive was giving me an unforgettable view of her ass, and I was taking advantage. She came up laughing and holding a stuffed monkey. "Got it!"

My breath caught in my throat. She was just so damn beautiful and radiant, bouncing around, looking so happy. I wanted to pull her down behind those cribs and fuck her senseless.

I couldn't help it. I pulled out my phone and sent a text to her:

Me: I want you.

I watched as she transferred the stuffed monkey from her hand to clutch it under her arm and then dug into her behemoth-sized purse to find her cell. I knew exactly when she read my message. She shot a look at me with those blue eyes and chewed on her lip.

Fuck.

The energy zapped through me. The fierce tightening in my groin. The nervous butterflies. I was combusting. Burning up from the inside.

We stood like that, frozen to the spot, for way too long. Finally, I nudged myself forward. I went over to the aisle with the activity center/walker toy and hefted it up into my arms. By the time I reached Talia's side, she was moving again.

She followed me to the checkout and waited without speaking until I had paid for the toy and the monkey. I couldn't look at her anymore. If I did, I was sure I'd drag her off somewhere like a caveman.

Her hand brushed my arm before I exited. "Hey, there's a wrapping station over there. Let's go wrap this up."

I nodded, and we headed over to the table with the wrapping supplies. She began making quick work of wrapping the bulky box in baby blue wrapping paper.

She was shooting me shy glances while she worked. "So, I guess your balls are breathing again?"

God, if she could only feel my balls right now. Shit, that thought sent a fresh twinge of pleasure to my cock.

"You seem to think about my balls a lot."

Just then, a sweet grandmotherly lady shuffled by and pierced me with a nasty look. Talia's clear laughter rang out.

After she finished wrapping the gift, we left the store and headed to my car. I placed the box in the trunk and then got into the car. Talia looked ... happy and carefree, more relaxed than when I picked her up.

She flipped the radio on while I started the car and backed out.

"Do you like classic rock?" I asked. An obscure Pink Floyd song was playing.

"Yeah, sure."

Talia was silent as I navigated out of the busy parking lot. The song ended and then switched to Stevie Nicks' *Edge of Seventeen*. Her foot started tapping to the strong opening beat. She liked this song; she was really getting into it.

When Stevie started singing, Talia was singing right along, fairly off-key. Belting it out with no care in the world. And holy shit! What the fuck was she saying?

"Just like a one-winged dove ..."

No, I must have just misheard her.

Even louder this time- "Just like a one-winged dove ..."

My head swiveled toward her, and my jaw slackened. "What the fuck, Talia?"

She stopped singing and looked at me confused. "What?"

"Those aren't the words!"

"What?" Her eyes narrowed. "Yes, they are!"

A quick burst of laughter escaped my lips. "No, they aren't. What the fuck is a one-winged dove? Have you ever seen a one-winged bird? Ever?"

Her lips twisted thoughtfully. "It's an injured bird, obviously. It's a metaphor for loss and pain. Not being able to fly. The lyrics are beautiful."

Holy shit! This girl. I held back more laughter. "Whatever you say."

I almost felt bad for speaking up because she totally stopped singing. She was busy punching something into her phone.

The song was almost over when I heard her strangled cry. "No! What? It can't be!"

"What's wrong?"

She slapped her phone down on her leg. "It's white-winged dove! That's even the subtitle of the song. Dammit, you were right. What the heck? White-winged dove? It doesn't even sound like she's saying that. God, it should be a one-winged dove. That sounds so much cooler."

My shoulders were shaking as I tried to hold back my laughter. "You're a pretty terrible singer."

"Oh, excuse me, Mr. Rock Star." She slouched down in her seat and mumbled, "I should have known better than to sing around you. I forgot who you were for one brief moment."

God, she was so cute that I couldn't help but tease her some more. "That's the third thing I found that you're awful at."

She sat up, her eyes flashing indignantly. "What? What else am I awful at?"

"Darts."

"Oh, that's true." She shrugged nonchalantly. "What else?"

"Sexting."

A haughty eyebrow lifted. "I'm probably pretty good at sexting. I wasn't even trying, so you can't judge me by last night. I bet I'm an amazing sexter!"

I turned my head to her. "We shall see."

Too bad I had to drive. Watching the blush creep over her face was too adorable.

A Van Halen song came on next, and her foot started tapping. I was braced for what was going to come out of her mouth, but then she saw me watching and waiting. She leaned over and switched off the radio.

I chuckled. "What's your favorite song, Angel?"

She fidgeted next to me. "Um, just so you know, this morning Ellie told me why you call me that."

"Okay. It wasn't a secret."

"So, are you going to keep calling me that?"

"Absolutely, Angel." I gave her a wink.

She sucked in a breath. "Then I'm going to give you a nickname."

"Okay. Let's hear it."

She was silent for a couple of minutes. "Gah, I can't think of one that's right. I would say Devil to go with the Angel theme, but that's lame. It could be OSB, but nah, that doesn't roll off the tongue nicely. O.L.D. buddy? Nope. I guess it'll have to be Mr. Rock Star."

I huffed. "That's not very original. What does OSB and the other one mean? Old buddy?" I'd heard that strange phrase before — with 'old' spelled out. Ellie had said it last night at the bar, but I couldn't remember the context.

"Well, OSB is oral sex buddy, of course, but I probably don't want to keep reminding you of that."

She was right. My dick was coming to life again. "What about O.L.D.? What does that mean?"

"That's super top-secret. Don't you worry about it, Mr. Rock Star."

I was going to find out. If she didn't tell me, I knew I could get Ellie to crack. Getting her number was genius.

"So, you didn't tell me, what's your favorite song?"

I could tell that she thought of one right away, but she started nervously fidgeting in her seat.

"I don't really have one."

"Yes, you do. Tell me."

"No, I don't." She was blushing. "I like a lot of different music."

I was tapping on the steering wheel. "It must be really embarrassing the way you're blushing. Is it the Jonas Brothers or something?"

"What? No!" She denied it vehemently. "And I like them, by the way."

"Hmmm." I rubbed my jaw. "Taylor Swift?" I loved teasing her.

"What's wrong with Taylor Swift?"

I laughed at her hurt expression. "C'mon. Just tell me. Is it a Ghost Parker song?"

She got quiet. "You know, I'm not really big into the music scene. I'd never heard of Ghost Parker until Ellie told me last night. She told me I'd definitely recognize some of your songs though. I just haven't had a chance to look them up yet."

I exited the highway. We were about 20 minutes from Brock's house. "Yeah, we're just starting to get some radio play now after this tour."

"That's exciting for you guys. How did you become Mr. Rock Star anyway?"

I relaxed in my seat. Of all the questions I was bombarded with about Ghost Parker almost daily, I'd never been asked how I personally had started out in music.

"My dad got me started, actually. Right before he walked out on my mother, he bought me my first acoustic guitar and got me lessons. I practiced like crazy, always hoping that if I were good enough, maybe he'd notice me again. Maybe he'd come back."

"Oh, Ryder." Her voice was soft. "How old were you?"

"Nine."

"Your parents divorced?" She asked.

"Yep. He crushed my mom. She was never the same. And then he married a lady with 3 kids about a year later. They were all really young, so when me and Brock went over there every other weekend, it was miserable. Dad and Suzie were too busy taking care of the little kids. It was boring, and I hated going. Hated leaving my mom 'cause I could see her holding back tears every time we left."

Her hand rested on my leg. She meant it as a soothing gesture, but damn, it just gave me dirty thoughts.

"How old is Brock?"

"He's 6 years older than me. He started refusing to go to Dad and Suzie's house after a while. Then Dad ended up divorcing Suzie. She was pretty nice to me but after the divorce, I saw none of them ever again. Dad lived alone in an apartment for a few years after that, but I was a rebellious teen by then. I wasn't interested in much of a relationship with him. He's now remarried again. He's got another ready-made family, so I still don't see him much."

I touched her hand gently and then laced my fingers through hers when she didn't pull away.

"And your mom? Is she remarried?"

"Yeah. About three years ago. She was so lonely after Dad left. Then Brock joined the Marines without telling her ahead of time and then right after I went to college. Everybody kept leaving her. She was just so broken all the time. I couldn't stand it. Then three years ago, I came home to visit and found out that she got married." My jaw clenched.

"That's a good thing, right? If she was so lonely?"

I squeezed her hand. "Except Stan, her husband, is a complete asshole. They were only married a year before they sold our house, the house I grew up in, and moved into a shitty apartment. Then he drained her savings account. I had to buy her a cell phone and put her on my plan last year when I found out he wouldn't even pay for that. A fucking phone! When I came home this time, I found out that he sold her car. He's just draining her dry."

"But if they love each other ..."

"I don't know what she feels for him, Angel. It's something I don't understand. But, he doesn't love her; he's just using her. Stan saw her weakness and exploited it. He's already making weird threats about leaving her. As soon as he runs out of her money, he'll be gone. And I don't know if she can survive a man leaving her again."

"What does your brother think about this?"

"We haven't ever talked about it, but I might mention it tonight. I'm at my wit's end with that fucker, Stan."

The car fell silent.

Absently, I stroked her hand with my thumb. "Thanks for listening to all this."

"No problem. I wish I could help." She sounded a little sad.

"You have helped. Just by listening."

I wanted to replace the somber mood in the car, so I spent the next ten minutes telling her about the house I bought in the northern part of Huntington Beach. I had her laughing when I was describing the horrible condition it was in when I bought it. She seemed interested to hear about the renovations, so I dug out my phone and showed her some pictures.

After we went through all the house pictures, she suddenly seemed uncomfortable. "What's the matter?"

I had lost her hand when she was looking at the pictures on my phone, and I missed it.

"I was just reminded of some pictures Ellie was showing me on her phone last night."

I glanced at her. "Last night? At the bar? Right before you took off?"

She looked up. "Yeah. How did you know?"

I shrugged. "I was watching you." Was that too stalkerish to admit? "Oh."

She seemed like she wanted to drop the subject, but it was clearly something that was bothering her. "What were the pictures of?"

"You," she answered quietly.

"Me?" I frowned. "How did Ellie have ... Oh!" I scowled. "Shit from the internet."

Her voice was small. "Yeah."

Fuck me. "Pictures of what, exactly?"

"Oh, I don't know, Ryder. Pictures of you with half-naked girls hanging all over you. Partying it up. One of you with your face buried between a giant pair of tits." I flinched, but she wasn't finished yet. "About a million pictures of your dick in all its glory."

We were just pulling up the driveway of my brother's suburban house. This was definitely not the time for this conversation, but I knew I couldn't put it off. This was really upsetting to her.

I turned off the engine and then turned in my seat to face her. "Those pictures are bullshit, Talia. Just a lot of crazy, fun, partying stuff that happens on tour. It doesn't mean anything. I don't even know those people in the pictures. It's just a bunch of fans having fun."

She about melted me with her tortured blue eyes. "And the dick pics? What about them, Ryder? You're a ... a total man whore!"

My lips twitched. "You and Ellie were studying my dick pics last night?"

She wasn't amused. "Yeah, I guess we were. Why would you plaster your dick all over the internet?"

I took a deep breath. "Well, first off, I doubt all those pictures on the internet are of my dick, but I haven't studied them like you have. Of course, that doesn't mean that a few of them aren't my dick — I don't know. I'm not proud of this, but, it's happened before, during some drunken partying on tour — that some, uh, let's call them enthusiastic fans, have taken some pictures without my knowledge and they got posted on social media."

Talia frowned, but I shrugged it off and continued.

"Bands, like Cold Fusion, have teams of people cleaning the internet for them. Our manager keeps the terrible stuff off the internet, but clearing the supposed dick pics of all five of us would be a full-time job — more just keep popping back up. And fan sites, even unofficial ones, are beneficial for the band at this point in our career. We leave all that shit to our manager; I stay off social media. It's much easier that way."

"It's all just so crazy," Talia mumbled.

I grabbed her hand and stroked my thumb against her palm. "No one has ever actually cared about me enough to actually give a fuck about me having dick pics on the internet. That is, not until you."

She looked up at me with those big blue eyes. "I do care about you."

"Thank you." I gave her hand a squeeze. "We better get inside. I'm sure they saw us pull up; they're probably wondering what we're doing out here."

We got out of the car and I had a full texting conversation with Ellie while we were gathering up the stuff we needed to bring inside.

> **ME:** What's Talia's favorite song?
> **ELLIE:** Aren't you with her? Why don't you ask

her?
ME: I did. She won't tell me.

I opened the trunk and removed the baby gift.

ELLIE: It's Rebel Yell by Billy Idol.

Huh. That wasn't what I was expecting, at all. Why was she so embarrassed to tell me that?

ELLIE: But don't tell her I told you.
ME: Thanks.

I was cradling the baby gift package in my arms like a guitar. I thought of the opening notes of *Rebel Yell*. My fingers plucked at imaginary strings as I went through the chord progressions in my head. Then, a bass riff in B — I could hear it all clearly.

I was itching to pick up a real guitar and mess around with it. There was even a pretty awesome guitar solo in that song. Yeah, I could learn that song easily. It would be fun to play, but why was it her favorite?

It was harder for me to remember the lyrics than the guitar work. I had to concentrate, humming the melody in my head until I could remember the chorus.

In the midnight hour, she cried more, more, more.

I was standing on the porch with a stupid grin on my face. Oh, Angel, you naughty girl.

Chapter 14

Talia

I HAD A MUCH-NEEDED few minutes to think after our conversation in the car because Ryder was busy texting on his phone. I hadn't wanted to confront him with all the fan photos and dick pics that I saw on the internet, but it slipped out. It obviously bothered me more than I realized, which was odd because I didn't have any reason to care so much. We barely knew each other.

Yet, the more I got to know him, the more I liked what I saw. He'd opened up to me about his life: his new house, his band, his parent's divorce, his worry about his mother — all about his personal life, while keeping me laughing the whole time. He'd tease me mercilessly one moment and then lay on the smoldering heat the next. I wanted to be near him. I actually liked him. And above all, I lusted after him like crazy.

But he was leaving.

He'd even told me he was 'killing two birds with one stone'. This dinner was an obligation he couldn't skip, and he wanted to see me again. When I translated that into rock star speak, it meant he wanted to have sex with me before he left town. And that might be a problem because I was developing an interest in him beyond that of a one-night stand.

The sexual chemistry between us was undeniable. I think that's why I'd agreed to this ridiculous dinner 'non-date' in the first place. Maybe I thought I could take a taste of that forbidden fruit once again, but now realization was hitting me hard. It wasn't just lust. I enjoyed being with him; I liked the way he made me feel, how he made me laugh, and how he drove me crazy.

I wanted more from him. A connection. A relationship of some sort.

His explanation about the dick pics made me acknowledge to myself that I had absolutely no claim on him. Of course I didn't, we'd just met. And Ryder had stated several times he didn't want a girlfriend. He'd be gone from my life tomorrow — back to his rock star life, which a random girl from Ohio certainly didn't fit into.

I wasn't deluding myself; I knew what his goal was. All signs pointed to him trying to have sex with me tonight. I had known that when I'd let him talk me into accepting this invitation. Hell, it had excited me.

So, did I have the willpower to resist him when he inevitably tried to make his move? Could I dismiss the once-in-a-lifetime chance of molten hot sex with a rock star? When Ryder was gone, would I remember our night of passion with exhilaration or with guilt and deep regret? And I couldn't forget that Max was still in the picture, no matter how strong my intentions to break up with him in the future were. For now, Max and I were still technically dating.

I clutched the gift bag of wine and stood on the porch waiting with

Ryder after he rang the doorbell. This dinner could be an unmitigated disaster. He hadn't told them I was coming and apparently; he wasn't on good terms with them either. It was so absurd that I'd let him rope me into coming with him. If I was with anyone but Ryder, I'd probably consider this the worst date I'd ever been on in my life, and yet, so far, it had been the exact opposite. I'd been having so much fun.

I held my breath as the door opened. There was no doubt the man who stood before us was Ryder's brother, Brock. The few differences that stood out — lighter color hair, a few extra pounds, and a slightly older face — could not disguise the fact that they were brothers.

I shifted on my feet awkwardly as he stood at the door staring at us, not saying a word. A few seconds later, his wife, carrying little Joey, joined him.

Jenny's eyes landed on me, wide with surprise, but she recovered quickly. "Well, Brock, are you going to let them in?"

Brock moved aside and motioned for us to enter. We stepped into their house, and then Ryder began introductions. "Jenny, Brock, this is my ..." he paused for a moment and glanced my way, "friend Talia. She's already yelled at me for not asking you if it was okay that I bring her." He flashed Jenny a disarming smile. "Sorry, Jenny. I can be a rude bastard sometimes."

She waved away his concerns. "It's no trouble at all. I'm glad you came, Talia. And here is your nephew! He's been waiting to meet you. Joseph Leslie." She lifted Joey's hand and made him wave at us.

Ryder cocked an eyebrow. "His middle name is Leslie?"

Jenny laughed. "Yeah. He's named after my grandfather. Your mother and Stan hate it, though. Said it was too girly."

"Mom has had nothing but praise for Little Joey. It's probably just that douche, Stan, that hates it," Ryder replied.

Brock grunted but said nothing.

Jenny began leading us into the family room. "Is that a gift for Joey? How nice! Why don't you put it near the couch? I just need to go check on dinner."

Ryder shot me a pleading look when I said, "I'll come help you." I escaped the chilly atmosphere between Ryder and his brother and fled to the kitchen with Jenny. "I hope you like red wine?"

"Oh, that's fine. Thank you. It was nice of you to bring it and the baby gift." She took the bag from my outstretched hands.

"Can I help with anything?"

"Do you mind holding the baby?" she asked.

"Not at all. It's been a while since I was around someone this little. How old is he?" I held out my arms to take Joey from her.

"He was born March 28, so he's about five months old now."

I made a mental note to put Joey's birthdate into Ryder's calendar for him. Joey stared at me as I balanced him on my hip, but didn't fuss at the transfer.

Jenny began stirring something in a pot on the stovetop. "We're just having spaghetti and meatballs. Nothing fancy, I'm afraid. Grace told me it's Ryder's favorite meal."

"Spaghetti and meatballs are fine. I hope I'm not intruding ..."

"No, not at all." She shot me a glance. "I wish Ryder had told me, though. I would have made more of an effort to wear something besides these nasty maternity jeans and a hoodie. You must think I'm a slob. I just haven't been able to fit into my regular clothes yet."

Jenny looked comfortable. She was a petite girl, probably six inches shorter than me right now since I was currently in heels. She had a pretty face with just a touch of makeup and her blonde hair was cinched up into a high ponytail.

I was feeling decidedly out of place. "You look great. Ryder picked me up from work. I feel a bit overdressed."

"God, you look gorgeous." She waved her hand. "I hope Joey doesn't spit up on you."

I laughed and removed a fistful of my hair from Joey's tiny hand.

Jenny opened a cabinet and pulled out two wine glasses. "So, are you a model or something? An actress?"

"No." I shook my head. "I'm an administrative assistant — AKA a secretary. I work at Cavendish International in Fairborn."

She looked stunned. "Really? I just thought ... I mean, Ryder ..." Her voice trailed off.

"I know. He's a rock star." I sighed. "What's he doing with me?"

"Look at you! Of course, he's with you. You're beautiful."

She began filling our glasses with the wine that I brought.

"I'm sorry, Talia. I didn't mean that at all. I was already nervous about Ryder coming over here. And then you showed up and you're so — just so put together." Her words began spilling out faster and faster. "And look at me. I look dumpy and I'm huge — I still haven't lost the baby weight. And I'm serving spaghetti. And the house is a mess if you actually look closely. And I'm going to have to pump and dump later, but I'm drinking this wine, dammit."

My eyes popped open wide at her rant. I tried, but couldn't suppress the little giggle that escaped when she finished.

Suddenly, we were both laughing. When we finally settled down, Jenny said, "We'd better go check on the boys."

She grabbed a beer from the refrigerator and then motioned for me to follow her. The room was silent when we entered. They were watching TV, ignoring each other.

Jenny handed the beer to Ryder and then sat on the ground near the baby gift. "Joey, come help me open up your gift."

I brought Joey over to her. Jenny began tearing at the wrapping paper and then handing large pieces of it to Joey. Evidently, he enjoyed mashing up the paper.

"Oh, wow. An activity center. Joey's going to love this! Thanks, Ryder."

Ryder glanced at me before replying, "You're welcome. Hope he has fun with it. He's not walking yet, is he? It turns into a baby walker."

Jenny snorted. "No, not yet. This will be perfect. Why don't you and Brock assemble it while Talia and I finish up dinner?"

Ryder begged with his eyes for me to stay, but Jenny rounded the coffee table and plunked Joey down on his lap.

Once back in the kitchen, Jenny refilled our wine glasses. "He doesn't know too much about babies, I take it."

"No, I don't think so."

"Well, he and Brock might kill each other trying to assemble that baby contraption, but at least they'll be forced to talk to each other."

I wanted to ask her why the two were estranged but didn't feel it was my business. If Ryder hadn't felt comfortable telling me, I shouldn't be trying to pry it out of his sister-in-law.

For the next forty-five minutes, Jenny and I drank wine and had a great time talking with each other. She was really down-to-earth and friendly. We ended up talking about everything from the details of Joey's birth to the insane conversations I constantly had with a gay coworker of mine who was in love with my married boss. I found out that Jenny was a third-grade teacher and couldn't wait to get back to her classroom at the start of the school year, yet she was dreading leaving Joey and putting him in daycare.

We had talked about hairstyles and before I knew it, I was braiding her hair in a half-fishtail braid and promising to send her the video tutorial link so that she could learn to do it herself.

She was so easy to talk to; I felt we were becoming fast friends. I had no clue why Ryder said she was hard to get to know. Somehow, I even offered to babysit little Joey when she told me how long it had been since she'd last had a night out.

After we finished our third glass of wine, Jenny stood up. "I've got to get the pasta started. Can you ask Ryder to bring Joey in here and put him in his highchair? He needs to eat his dinner. Maybe Ryder can help feed him for me?"

"Sure."

In the family room, I stopped to survey the scene. Ryder sat on the ground with Joey in his lap and was playing peek-a-boo with him. It was adorable. Watching them sent a gooey twang to my ovaries that I fought to ignore. Brock had the activity center assembled and was applying stickers to it while Ryder critiqued from the sidelines.

"Jenny wants you to bring Joey in for his dinner, Ryder."

I returned to the kitchen. Jenny was placing pasta in a pot of boiling water. "Everything okay in there?"

I nodded. "The activity center is assembled. They're just fighting over the sticker placements now."

Ryder came in with Joey and I helped him get the baby strapped into the highchair while Jenny started stacking plates and utensils on the island. "Talia, can you set the dining room table?"

"Sure." I began my task.

Then Jenny handed a bib to Ryder. "Would you feed Joey for me while I finish dinner?"

I watched out of the corner of my eye as Ryder struggled to get the bib on Joey. Then Jenny handed him two plastic baby bowls, each with a baby spoon in them before she went back to cooking.

Ryder sat down in a chair next to Joey's highchair. "All right, little man, time for dinner."

He took a spoonful of some orange puree and put it into Joey's mouth. Ryder frowned when the food oozed back out and dribbled down Joey's chin. He glanced over at Jenny, who wasn't paying attention, and then repeated the same thing. More food slid down Joey's chin.

"He doesn't like it."

I could hear Jenny's answer. "He likes it. You've got to scoop up what he pushes out of his mouth and put it right back in. Multiple times."

"What? That's gross."

I giggled at the disgust I heard in Ryder's voice. After arranging the plates and silverware, I watched Ryder feed his nephew from the threshold of the dining room.

Suddenly, after another scoop of food, Joey's hand swept across the tray and launched one of the food bowls into the air. Liquid food landed on Ryder's pants while the bowl clunked to the floor, splattering food everywhere. Ryder used his finger to scoop the glob of food off his pants and then popped it into his mouth.

He immediately screwed up his face and gagged. "Oh God, what is that? It tastes horrible."

"It's squash." Jenny came rushing over and swatted him on the arm. "Cut it out! Don't let him see you making faces." She scooped up the other bowl and grabbed the tiny spoon. "Ryder, eat a scoop of this and pretend you like it. You better pretend you like it a lot!"

Ryder looked confused. "What?"

"Just eat it and gush about how good it is." Jenny jammed the spoon in his mouth. "Yummy. It's so yummy, right, Ryder?"

Ryder clamped his mouth shut, holding in the food, but refusing to swallow at first. It looked like his eyes were watering, but like a champ, he started talking in a sing-song voice, "Yes, it's very yummy. Sooo good." He maintained his exaggerated cheerful voice, but the sentiment quickly changed. "What is this? It tastes like crap. I'm about to start dry heaving. Quick, get me some water!"

Jenny was watching Joey carefully. "Suck it up, Ryder. And be careful what you say, or I'll give you more. Now feed him the rest of this chicken puree while I clean up the floor."

Ryder noticed me laughing from the doorway and joked, "You think this is funny, Angel?"

I walked into the kitchen and got a washcloth from Jenny to clean off the gobs of food on Joey's face and hands. "Ryder, the goal is to get him to eat it, not wear it."

Ryder shoveled in another scoop. "It's not so easy when his mouth keeps leaking."

Ten minutes later, we finished feeding Joey. Brock had helped serve dinner, and we were all eating in the dining room, with Joey strapped into a bouncy seat.

Dinner was a more subdued affair. Brock and Ryder in the same room seemed to strain the flow of conversation. Jenny tried to ease the situation by asking Ryder a lot about his band, but Brock remained fairly silent. After about ten minutes of eating, Joey got fussy. Brock took him out of his seat and held him on his lap.

"He's getting tired. I'm going to give him his bath." Brock got up and headed upstairs with Joey.

Jenny watched them leave. "Brock and I are used to eating quick dinners but don't rush. Relax and enjoy dinner. Joey loves his bath; he'll be in there for a bit."

I sipped my wine. "He's such a wonderful baby, Jenny. That was the first time I saw him fuss at all. He hasn't made a peep all night."

She smiled. "He really is, but wait until Brock takes him out of the tub. You'll hear him then. In fact, I'm going to go warm up a bottle for him. Once he's out and in his pajamas, it's a bottle and bed for him."

Jenny left us at the table, but we were both finished eating, anyway.

Ryder leaned back in his chair. "I think I've had enough spaghetti and meatballs to last a lifetime these past few days. My mom thinks it's my favorite meal, I guess. Maybe, when I was ten years old, it was, but now ..."

"It was delicious, and it was nice of Jenny to cook for us." I felt like I was defending my new friend.

Ryder grinned. "I know it was. Maybe we should help clean up?"

I nodded my agreement. We began stacking dishes and bringing them into the kitchen. Jenny protested our help, but we ignored her. It didn't take long for us to clean off the table and load the dishwasher. Ryder was cleaning the saucepan when we heard Joey screaming bloody murder upstairs.

"He hates getting pulled out of the bath." Jenny shook her head. "They'll be down any minute. I better make sure his bottle is ready."

A few minutes later, Jenny was handing the bottle off to Ryder. "Can you feed him when they get down? Talia, make sure he's doing it right, so Joey doesn't suck down any air. He doesn't need to be burped anymore — he'll fall asleep while he's eating. Just hold him and hang out until I come back down. Is that okay, or do you have to go?"

Ryder answered for us. "No, we can hang out for a while."

Jenny rushed off upstairs and we finished cleaning up what we could in the kitchen. Brock came down with Joey and I helped set them up on the couch in the family room. I showed Ryder how to position the bottle correctly and then watched as he fed his nephew.

Brock had disappeared, so it was just Ryder and me. I was having a vibrating ovary moment again. Maybe it was just vestigial remnants of some primitive mating instinct, but seeing Ryder with a baby was completely turning me on. Joey's fuzzy blonde head nuzzled cozily into Ryder's side and he looked blissful as he sucked on the bottle with eyes half closed. The sight was making me think about all kinds of things I had no business thinking — crazy, long-term things with a certain rock star.

Ryder looked up at me. "I'm glad I got to meet little Joey. He's a cute little bugger."

I agreed. "He's really taken to you. You two speak the same language, I think."

He arched an eyebrow in answer and then looked around the empty room. "What happened to Jenny? Did I scare her off with those stupid stories about the tour?"

"No. She just had to do something. Don't worry, it had nothing to do with you."

Ryder looked confused. "You obviously know what it was. What am I missing?"

"I, er—" I looked around awkwardly. "I believe she had to pump."

"Pump?"

I put my hands on my hips. "Yes. You know, pump. Milk."

His face fell. "Oh, jeez. You didn't have to tell me that!"

"You asked!" I rolled my eyes. "Real mature, Ryder."

Ryder shook his head. "I didn't need to know my sister-in-law is pumping milk right now." He chuckled. "Yeah, you're right. I suppose I am immature."

His gaze dropped to my chest. I crossed my arms over my breasts and warned, "Ryder ..."

"Sorry." He averted his eyes and looked down at Joey. "I can't stop thinking about your tits now. It's not my fault."

I decided we needed a change of subject. "Did you get a chance to talk with your brother?"

"We didn't do much talking, but I asked him about my mother and Stan. I think we're on the same page with that, so that's good. Hopefully, we can figure something out."

"Good. It looks like Joey's falling asleep. I'm going to go find Brock." I needed a little distance. The Ryder / Joey combination was too lethal.

Brock was drinking a beer on the back deck. I hesitated before joining him because we had barely spoken all evening. I took a deep breath and then stepped outside.

"Joey is almost asleep."

Brock turned to face me for a drawn-out second and then gestured to the empty chair next to him. I took the seat and then grappled for something to say. "It's so nice out here. Quiet, too."

We fell into silence for a few minutes. I was thinking about getting up and leaving when Brock finally broke the uneasy silence.

"So how long have you been dating Ryder?"

"We're not really dating. We only met recently."

Brock squinted and nodded like what I said wasn't unexpected. A few minutes later, he said, "Yeah, Ryder doesn't 'date' women. You seem like a nice girl. Not his usual type. Just be careful with him."

My eyes flew to his face. "What do you mean?"

Shifting in his seat, he took a long sip of beer. "He's a cheater. He has a habit of taking what's not his."

His words floored me. This was Ryder's brother, warning me away from him. Did Ryder mention to him that I had a boyfriend? Why would he? They weren't close at all. Was he talking about something else?

Before I could formulate a response, Brock spoke again. "He likes to wreck things that are good. He doesn't care about anyone but himself. I'd hate to see you get hurt."

I don't know how long I sat there stunned. Brock got up and went into the house, but I stayed to gather my chaotic thoughts. Only minutes before, I was considering throwing my self-respect out the window to have sex with Ryder before he left town. I was thinking that even one night with him was better than none. I'd had the justifications for essentially cheating on Max all worked out in my head.

Then Brock confirmed my worst fears, and it felt like a kick to the gut. I couldn't move. I couldn't think. Brock's revelation felt ... devastating.

At some point, Ryder came outside to collect me. We said our goodbyes to Jenny and Brock. I had already exchanged phone numbers with Jenny earlier; she seemed like she could be a great friend, but now I knew I'd probably never contact her. I'd avoid her messages too, all because of Ryder. He'd already managed to mess with my head.

Ryder was pretty talkative when we got into the car. "That didn't go too bad. Brock was a moody asshole, as usual, but Jenny was cool. And Little Joey was awesome. How do you know so much about babies, anyway?"

I was staring out the side window. My tone was flat. "Babysitting."

Ryder was backing out of the driveway. "It's still pretty early. Do you want to go out somewhere?"

I didn't even look at him. "I've got work tomorrow. I just want to go home."

"Okay. Is your roommate there? Maybe we can all hang out?" His fingers were nervously tapping on the steering wheel.

I looked over at him. "Don't you have a flight to catch tomorrow?" It came out sounding about as bitchy as I felt.

His jaw ticked. "Yeah, but I thought we could spend some time together before I left."

"Spend some time together? Or do you mean fuck? Or were you looking for a threesome: me, you, and Ellie?" For some inexplicable reason, I added jazz hands to that.

He looked shocked at my outburst. "What the hell, Talia? Did I do something wrong? What's going on? I was talking about hanging out. Not sex."

Wow. He looked so sincere. I almost believed him. "Let's just drop this whole stupid charade. You're leaving tomorrow and I have a boyfriend. This is the end of whatever you were hoping to accomplish."

He was quiet while the car ate up miles on the road. Finally, he spoke again. "I thought we were having a good time together tonight? I know I was. What happened? Was it seeing my family? The baby? Was it too much?"

"Your family's not the problem, Ryder."

He was squeezing the death out of the steering wheel — white-knuckling it. "So, it's me. Is it about the dick pics?"

I threw up my hands angrily. "Yeah, the pictures are part of it, but it's the entire package. The whole slutty rock star thing. The 'fuck a new girl every night' thing. I won't let you use me like that."

The muscles in his jaw were working overtime. "You think that's what I want to do with you? You really think that little of me, don't you?"

"So, what were we doing tonight?"

He glanced my way. "We were having fun — getting to know each other. Tonight's not the end. I want to see you again after tonight."

My hands clenched into fists. "I have a boyfriend, remember?"

He couldn't keep the look of disdain off his face. "If you care about him so much, why did you come out with me?"

It was a damn good question; one that I evaded because I couldn't answer without giving my foolish self away. "So, you want me to cheat on him?"

He gritted his teeth and practically forced the words between them. "No, I want you to dump him. Like I told you already." He ran his hand through his hair and blew out a breath. "Then I want you to come out to L.A. and visit me. I want you to be with me. Only me."

His words had me gulping for oxygen. It was like I'd forgotten how to breathe. Every cell in my body wanted me to give in to Ryder. Believe his words. Listen to his lies. Experience one night with him. Hot, sinful sex that I knew only he could give to me. I wanted it.

Instead, I heard words fly out of my mouth — words that parroted what Brock had told me earlier. "You want me to wreck my relationship? For a lousy fling with you?"

It was quiet in the car for a really long time after that. When we got closer to my apartment, Ryder finally spoke. His voice was steady and calm. "Talia, did I read the signs wrong? I thought you were interested in me? I felt something between us. A connection. Chemistry ..."

"You felt my lips around your cock. That's all it was." I immediately regretted what I said when Ryder flashed me a hurt look. I was lashing out like a toddler because I wanted Ryder to want me as more than just a hookup. I didn't want to be a notch on his rock star belt, but commitment wasn't written in his DNA. And that really upset me.

"Don't say that. Don't pretend there's nothing there, Angel. If I said something wrong back there, I'm sorry."

I remained quiet. A few minutes later, we pulled up in front of my apartment building. I quickly popped open the door. I wanted to get out of there before I did something really stupid, like cry.

"Angel ..."

I slipped out the door and then turned to him. "Goodnight, Ryder. Good luck with Ghost Parker and have a good flight out tomorrow."

I saw his jaw clench. "I want to see you again."

My hands were shaking. "That's not a good idea."

"Talia ..."

"Goodbye, Mr. Rock Star." I shut the car door and then walked away without looking back.

Chapter 15

Ryder

I FORCED AN EYELID open and looked around. A coffee table — littered with empty beer and liquor bottles, a discarded red bra dangling off the edge, and a dirty-looking bong — rested about a foot from my head. I rubbed a hand over my face and slowly sat up.

This was the second time in the past week that I'd crashed overnight at Sid and Bash's place. I looked around for my T-shirt and found it sticking out from under the couch. I'd passed out wearing my jeans, which was as uncomfortable as fuck. I slid my T-shirt on and stood, idly wondering where my shoes were. I wasn't sure if it was safe to walk around this apartment barefoot.

I loaded up my arms with empty bottles and then headed for the kitchen. After disposing of the bottles in the recycling bin, I began making myself a cup of coffee. I pulled a water bottle out of the refrigerator and downed it while I waited for the coffee to brew. My head wasn't aching too badly, considering how much I had drunk the night before.

I winced at some of the memories as they flashed through my head. Every night was a party night at Sid and Bash's place, but last night had been pretty wild. The girl-to-guy ratio had been about 5:1, so the party had been almost orgy-like at one point.

Last night, I had only one goal: to get laid. It was something that had eluded me in the week I'd been back home. I'd had plenty of opportunities, but couldn't seal the deal. At first, I told myself it was just because I was being too picky. After a full week, I was wondering what the hell was going on. It definitely had something to do with Talia, but I was desperate to overcome whatever the fuck it was.

None of the women I met, no matter how hot, made me feel the way Talia did. There was no crazy pull. No spark of excitement. No all-consuming need to be with them. So I tried to use alcohol to dull the emptiness I felt around these other women.

I'd gotten pretty trashed at the party and chose a petite brown-eyed girl with long, dark hair to drown my sorrows in. She was almost the opposite of Talia looks-wise, which suited me just fine. I'd stuck my tongue down her throat. And felt nothing. She'd rubbed her killer body up against me all night. I felt nothing. She'd slid her hand down my pants and grabbed my junk. No fucking reaction. I had no desire to fuck her. Disgusted with myself, I sent her on her way. I tried with two other girls that I remember before I gave up entirely.

I was adding some suspect milk to my coffee when Sid stumbled out of his room sporting some outrageous bedhead and wearing nothing but a pair of boxers.

He wandered into the kitchen. "Stroke, you sleep on the couch by yourself again last night?"

The guys in the band called me Stroke, a nickname I purposefully hadn't mentioned to Talia when we were talking about nicknames. Ostensibly, the name came from my guitar-playing skills, but the guys would swear it had a more sexual meaning just to mess with me.

"Morning, Vicious. Had to crash here. I couldn't drive home last night. What are you doing up so early?"

It was only 10 a.m., about two hours before anyone would normally begin to stir around this place.

Vicious groaned. "Yeah, fuck. This chick is snoring her ass off in there. Like a lumberjack. I tried poking her awake and rolling her the fuck over so she'd shut up, but fuck. It's driving me crazy."

I nodded sympathetically. "Well, the couch is free now."

"I want to sleep in my own fucking bed. Without the snoring chick. If I pinch her nose closed, you think she'd shut up? Or is that a bad idea? I don't want her to die, just shut up."

I shrugged. "How about using some earplugs?"

Vicious snarled, baring his teeth. "Fuck. I'd go curl up with Bash and whoever he's got in there, maybe get some nice morning action, but I know he had at least two girls with him when I retired with the lumberjack. Lucky bastard. Probably not enough room in the bed for me."

It wouldn't be the first time those two guys took part in a threesome or moresome together. They still argued about the last time it happened when some mysterious mishap had occurred, but neither of them would tell. It had freaked them both out, though, so the rest of the band teased them mercilessly about it.

I raised an eyebrow. "You wouldn't want IT to happen again, though, would you?"

"Don't fuck with me, Stroke. It's too damn early. So what's your fucking deal? How come you keep striking out with the ladies? It's not like you, man. It's kind of pathetic."

I took a sip of coffee to avoid his gaze. "I'm not striking out. Just being a little more discriminating."

Vicious snorted. "Discriminating? Hell, you haven't gotten pussy since you've been back. I know; I've seen your sorry ass every night. What gives?"

What gives was a certain Angel that I couldn't shake from my mind — something that I was sure Vicious would never understand.

Especially when she'd rejected me after she'd worked her way right under my skin. Deep under. She'd left me reeling, nursing the hurt and disappointment. Those were feelings I'd never experienced so acutely, and I had no idea what to do with them.

I shook my head to clear it from Talia memories and muttered, "I just can't have sex right now."

Surprisingly, Vicious nodded in understanding. "Fuck, it's that bad?"

My lips twisted into a frown. "Yeah. It's bad."

Even though Talia left me wrecked that last night in Ohio, and wounded me in a way I didn't think a girl ever could, I couldn't stop thinking about her. What the fuck was wrong with me?

Vicious looked sympathetic to my girl troubles. "Sorry that you're going through this, man." He patted my arm awkwardly.

"Thanks." At least I still had my band. They were a bunch of juvenile assholes, but they were like brothers to me.

"Is it ..." he swallowed, "permanent?"

"Jesus Christ, what? I hope not!" I was getting agitated. "What if sex is never the same? What if it's ruined forever? Is that even a thing? God, this is so fucked up!"

Vicious rubbed the back of his neck. "So, which one is it?"

"Which what?"

He was avoiding my eyes. "Which one? Is it the herp?"

"The herp?" I repeated dumbly.

"Yeah, what you got? The Herp? The Clap? Crotch Crickets? Fuck, not HIV?"

My mouth fell open. "I'm not talking about an STD, you dumb shit. I'm talking about a girl. I can't have sex with anyone because of this girl. She's in my head. Wrapped around my brain."

Vicious looked confused. "Unless she's wrapped around your dick, of course you can have sex with anyone. You're not even making sense."

I was pacing the floor, tense as fuck. "Well, I really liked her, but she rejected me. She doesn't want to get to know me — or even give me a chance. I can't even think about any other girls. She's ruined them."

"You're not having sex because of some girl who rejected you? Fuck, man. You're twisted." He looked like he'd just tasted something sour. "Have you even tried winning her back?"

I stopped pacing. "She made it pretty clear. She's got a fucking boyfriend, too."

He shrugged. "So, you might have to work for it a bit, Stroke. Did you ever have to do that before? Work for the pussy?"

"No." I shook my head. "Not really. Never wanted to bother."

"Who is this girl?"

"A girl from back home — in Ohio."

He pulled on his lip. "Have you talked to her since you've been back?"

I looked at him hopefully. "We've exchanged some pictures."

"Well, fuck. That's a good sign. Let me see them."

Vicious followed me into the living room, where I found my phone on the coffee table. I pulled up our text messages. On a whim, a few days after I got to California, I sent a photo of my new kitchen remodel to her. I told myself that maybe she'd be interested in the renovation, but really, I just wanted any contact with her. I practically had a coronary, hoping she'd answer my text. A few hours later, she did. She sent a picture of what I presumed was her kitchen cabinet door hanging precariously from a broken hinge.

The next day, I sent her a picture of a palm tree I took from a cool angle. She replied with a photo of a sad-looking pine tree. Each day after that, I sent her one photo, and she replied with her own. Receiving her answering photo became the highlight of my day. The snapshot of the sun setting over the ocean from my deck was met with what looked like the sun rising over a dingy parking lot. Yesterday, I snapped a shot of my guitar propped up on an Adirondack chair on my deck with a bottle of beer resting on the armrest. I laughed when I received a photo of a beat-up lawn chair sitting on a patch of dirty concrete with a crushed can of Budweiser sitting on it.

Vicious scrolled through the photos and scowled. "I thought I was going to see a nudie of this chick. Instead, I'm seeing a rusty lawn chair. Fuuuck."

"It's a good sign that she's answering my texts, right?"

Vicious handed me my phone. "Fuck, I'm going back to bed. Just send her a dick pic already."

I frowned. "She's seen my dick pics already, and she doesn't like them."

Vicious was already walking away, but he stopped and turned back to me as he shook his head sadly. "Holy fuck, Ryder. You're in big trouble with this chick."

"I know."

Chapter 16

Talia

I RAN INTO MY apartment shouting, "Ellie! Ellie! Get over here!"

Thank God she was home before me! I headed toward the kitchen, dropping my purse and ditching my heels along the way.

Ellie was in the kitchen chopping up a bell pepper. "Did you get another picture from Ryder?" For some reason, she didn't seem to share my enthusiasm.

"Oh, God! I couldn't stop looking at it on my drive home from work. I almost took out a garbage can that rolled into the road." I was still panting from running up the stairs.

Ellie lifted an eyebrow. "Let me guess, is it a seashell on the beach? A dolphin jumping through the waves?"

"Look!" I squealed and then held up the phone so she could see the newest picture Ryder had sent me.

This time it was a selfie and Ryder looked absolutely mouth-watering. He was on a beach with some blonde beach-bum type guy who was carrying a surfboard. It looked like they were walking toward the surf, but they both glanced at the camera and smiled. They were shirtless, but because Ryder was closer to the camera, only his bare shoulders and an arm were visible. It was a carefree candid shot, not a staged selfie like the ones I occasionally posted on social media.

Ellie put down the knife and grabbed my phone for a closer look. "Holy shit, Tal. That looks like Tommy from Cold Fusion! Look at that body! Oh my God, look at those tattoos!"

I pulled the phone back towards me. "Is it? I didn't even notice that guy. Let me see."

I wasn't an expert on Cold Fusion, but it looked like it could be the drummer. "He is kind of hot, but look at Ryder! That smile! It just slays me. I wish I could see more ..."

I slid my finger along the phone, hoping to scroll down the picture and see more of Ryder's body.

Ellie laughed. "You're not going to magically reveal more of him, Tal. But damn, just seeing that arm, you can tell he's super ... fit. Enlarge it a bit. I want to see some of Tommy's tattoos better."

"You really think that's Tommy?" I couldn't pull my eyes away from Ryder's smiling face.

Ellie came around the island to see the picture, since I was no longer sharing my phone. "We could find some online pictures of Tommy and compare the tats. Then we'd know for sure."

"Oh, God!" I groaned. "You know what this means? I have to send a responding selfie. And you have to be in it."

Ellie backed up like she'd been burned. "I don't want to be in it. Oh, hell!" She frowned as acceptance settled in. "This is going to take hours, isn't it?"

She knew me well. "Where are we going to take it? Oh, we have to look amazing. I can help with your hair. We'll do our hair and makeup fancy, but you can't look better than me."

She squinted at me. "Wait, don't you send him kind of the opposite pictures? So, really, we should dress in sweatpants and look terrible."

"No way." I shook my head. "I can't do that."

She had a stubborn glint in her eye that I knew all too well. "Forget makeup. We'll wear mud masks and put our hair up in messy buns. It'll be funny."

"No!! My God!" I screeched.

She grabbed my arm. "C'mon. You've got to do it!"

"Like hell I do."

She wouldn't give up. "It'll be funny. He'll laugh and think you're a totally cool chick."

I made a face. "Or he'll think I'm a total nut job."

"He'll love it. And then later, you can send him a really pretty one of you. Or, better yet, a sexy one. Maybe a lingerie shot?" She raised an eyebrow suggestively.

I sucked in a breath. "No. Then he'll read more into it."

She went back to slicing up her peppers. "What do you mean?"

My heart was suddenly pounding. "He'll think I like him. That I'm coming on to him."

She huffed her impatience. "You do like him! You'd jump his bones in a minute if you could undo all that bullshit you laid on him in the car."

I was nervously wringing my hands. "But he still thinks I'm with Max."

"Don't you think it's time you told him? Tell him tonight."

Her calm and reasonable words had my heart galloping like a racehorse. I'd broken up with Max the day after I'd said goodbye to Ryder. Even if I'd never heard from Ryder again as I'd expected, I knew it was the right thing to do.

The breakup itself hadn't been easy. Max hadn't let me off the hook without a long, drawn-out, and messy rehash of our relationship. For the amount of staleness in our relationship that I knew we both felt, Max put up quite the resistance to the end of us. He even confided that he'd purchased an engagement ring, but I only felt relief that he hadn't gotten around to proposing yet.

That I'd spent the last week mourning the loss of Ryder and not even thinking about Max reinforced my decision. Ryder was the man I really wanted to be with. Ryder. A freaking rock star.

"I love you, Talia, but you're making me crazy with this Ryder stuff."

I looked up at her.

"I just don't get you. You like him. A lot. I've had to deal with you this whole week. The hours of conversation with you worrying that you made a big mistake. He's shown you he cares. You blew him off big time and he's still contacting you. It wasn't just about sex, or whatever your dumb hang-up was about. He's still freaking texting you! From California!"

"It's not so straightforward, El. You know that."

"God, Tal. You're the one making it complicated." She began chopping more aggressively. "Max is out of the picture. So what's your excuse to sabotage your life now?"

I didn't answer.

"You know that you're allowed to have fun, right? You're allowed to enjoy life. Even to enjoy sex!"

My face felt like it was on fire. Did Ellie believe I was that lame? Was I?

"Oh my God, Talia, fucking go for it!" She pointed the knife at me, punctuating her words with it. "Or. I. Will. Kick. Your. Ass."

I ended up putting myself in Ellie's hands because I hadn't done a bang-up job with Ryder in the first place.

We fooled around, not for hours, but for maybe forty-five minutes, and took a crazy selfie of the two of us. We sat together on the couch with our faces slathered in brown clay and our hair wrapped in towel turbans. Ellie convinced me to put on a padded push-up bra to create maximum cleavage under my artfully draped pink silk robe, and we spent the most time taking millions of shots to find the one with the perfect hint of luscious cleavage.

Then it took much longer, another two hours, to capture the perfect lingerie shot. First, I had to redo my hair and makeup after our facials messed it all up. Then, thousands of poses were struck, lamps were moved to create the perfect lighting, five different panties and two pairs of stilettos were tried to find the perfect combination and finally, one lingerie "selfie" that I didn't actually take myself because it would ruin the perfect angle I needed, was painstakingly chosen out of hundreds of shots.

I chose one that cut off my face above my shiny red lips because sending anything too identifying was too scary. I wasn't kidding when I'd told Ryder I'd never sexted with anyone before.

I stared at both pictures, the mud mask and the lingerie selfie, almost equally dreading sending either. "Does my stomach look weird?"

Ellie repeated her reassurances for the fifth time. "You look amazing. Your legs look super long — like a model's. Your tits look huge in that push-up bra and your stomach looks pretty darn flat."

"I'm terrified to send this." I slipped my robe back on.

"I know. Send the funny one. Let's see what he says. He's probably been waiting for your reply."

I chewed on my thumbnail as I stared at the lingerie photo. "There's usually a gap before I send him a picture back, so I really have more time."

"Talia … send it now."

I blamed it on the two glasses of wine I had when I was trying to loosen up for the photo shoot, but I picked up the phone, selected the mud mask picture, and sent it to Ryder.

Ellie stood up. "Now, we wait. Let's put on some music and finish cleaning up dinner. And I will hold your phone and let you know when you get a reply."

I handed over my phone. "Can we listen to Ghost Parker?"

Ellie rolled her eyes. "Again? Okay. You're becoming quite the little groupie."

I glanced at my phone in her hand. "He's probably not going to say anything. We don't comment on the pictures. That's the … thing we're doing."

"Okay." Ellie slid my phone into her pocket. "That's fine. We stick to the plan. Wait an hour and then send the sexy picture."

"You won't send it while I'm not looking, will you?"

She smiled. "Promise I won't. But in exactly 60 minutes, I'm going to force your finger to hit send if you don't do it."

"Ugh." I bit my lip nervously. "Let me get out of this lingerie and into sweatpants so I can help you clean up."

Sixty minutes later, our dinner was cleaned up and Ellie and I were sipping another glass of wine at the kitchen table. No new text from Ryder had come in. Just as I thought, he was sticking to our 'thing'. The problem was that I didn't know what he thought about any of the pictures I sent him. Did he think they were funny? Or just plain stupid?

"Time's up, Tal. You gotta send it now."

I felt like I was going to puke. "I've been thinking; it's only about 7 p.m. in California right now. It's too early. I don't want to send him a sexy picture while he's eating. It seems gross."

"Oh, my God!" She slapped my phone onto the table. "Send it."

"Ellie, let's be reasonable. This is the dumbest idea we've ever had. It's going to look so damn desperate and slutty if I send that picture to him. I'd rather sleep on it tonight and revisit this again tomorrow when my head's clear. You've been plying me with wine all night—"

Ellie picked up my phone and ran into the bathroom with it. I chased after her, banging on the locked door, screaming the entire time. "Ellie, don't you dare."

I begged and I pleaded. Moments later, the door opened. She walked out and handed me my phone. "You'll thank me later."

I looked down at my phone with absolute dread. She'd sent the picture with a message. It said, 'I miss you.'

No! Please, no!

The deed was done.

I was going to be sick. Or pass out.

I stumbled back to the kitchen table. Ellie followed, "Hey. Are you okay?"

My stomach was churning. My body was trembling.

My eyes were fixed on my phone.

I was sweating.

Dreading.

Waiting for those three dots to appear, indicating an incoming response.

Agony.

The phone rang, and I shrieked. Ellie laid a hand on my shoulder to calm me.

"It's Ryder! Oh my God! What should I do?" I was borderline hysterical.

"Take a deep breath and answer it."

I was freaking out. "But it's a video call! My God, he'll be able to see me! Help me, Jesus."

Ellie picked up my phone and held it out to me as it kept urgently sounding my ringtone. "You look fine. You just redid your hair and makeup for your sexy photo shoot, so you look amazing, Tal. C'mon, this is exactly what you wanted to happen. This is good! You've got this!"

I took the phone from Ellie, and with a shaky hand, swiped to answer. "Hey."

"Angel, you know what you're doing to me, right?"

Chapter 17

Ryder

After I left Sid and Bash's place, I headed to Rincon Point to meet Tommy for another kiteboarding lesson. He'd already spent two days teaching me how to maneuver the kite on land; so when he said I was ready to hit the water today, I was excited. I was a decent snowboarder, so I thought this sport would be pretty easy to pick up.

Handling both the kite and the board while fighting deep swells and constantly changing winds proved to be trickier than I thought. I just started learning how to water start solo and ride downwind, but riding upwind was going to take more practice. Meanwhile, Tommy was doing jumps and tricks all around me. Still, it was really fucking fun and I couldn't wait to get better.

When we got back to Tommy's Jeep and loaded our equipment, I checked my phone for new messages. There were a few, but not the one I was looking for. Talia hadn't responded to my picture yet. I'd snapped a photo of Tommy and me on the beach before we headed out. It was the first time I'd included myself in the picture I sent her, so I wondered if Talia would answer in kind, like she'd been doing with the others.

Tommy invited me back to his house for dinner and I accepted. I still hadn't gone grocery shopping, and I was getting tired of eating takeout. He had an enormous house on the beach with private access to the ocean. It was decked out with every convenience and professionally decorated. It was close to how I imagined my dream home and made my newly renovated beach house look like a rundown shack.

Dinner was a chicken dish that was delicious. I found out that they had a personal chef that came in twice a week to prepare a bunch of meals for them to heat up. I'd met Tommy's wife, Livvy, while we were touring, but her reputation as a crazy chick had long preceded her. Tommy took a couple of months off the tour when she gave birth to their second kid. The baby girl was four months old now and their son had just turned three. We spent a bit of time playing with them. Luckily, visiting my brother last week made me feel a lot more comfortable around babies.

I couldn't help but be awed by my friend's life. He had it all. He loved what he was doing, made tons of money, and had an amazing home and a great family that he clearly loved. It was pretty inspiring; something I could only hope for someday.

When we finished dinner, I checked my phone again for messages and was excited to see I'd gotten a new photo from Talia nearly 30 minutes ago. I couldn't keep the dumb grin off my face when I saw what she sent me. She and Ellie had some kind of shit smeared all over their faces, like they'd just come from the spa.

"What the hell is that?" Tommy was looking over my shoulder.

I laughed. "That's the girl from Ohio I was telling you about. The one who's driving me crazy."

"The crazy ones are the best ones. Right, Liv?"

Livvy came back into the room from the kitchen and walked over to my side to see what we were looking at. "Who's that?"

Tommy answered, "That's his girlfriend."

"She's not my girlfriend … yet."

Livvy studied the picture. "Which one?"

"The one with the brown shit on her face." Tommy shrugged. "It doesn't matter. You can't see either of them."

I pointed to Talia and smiled. "This one's Talia. The other one is her roommate, Ellie."

Livvy squeezed my arm. "Well, any girl who has the balls to send you a picture like that is good in my book. When do we get to meet her?"

"She lives in Ohio, so that's a problem."

"Well, get her out here, Ryder. Show her around California. You've got to lure her away from Ohio. Shouldn't be too hard. I'd love to help you out." Livvy picked up another stack of dishes and headed back to the kitchen.

Tommy fixed a warning glare at me. "You do not want Crazy helping with anything or rubbing off on your girlfriend in any way. Trust me. You might think you're prepared, but you have no idea how much crazy my wife can unleash."

I'd heard a few stories, but the Livvy I met seemed so sweet and innocent. In fact, it'd impressed me when I saw how down-to-earth she was, considering she was the wife of a world-famous rock star. Tommy had to be exaggerating.

Tommy and I hung out on his amazing deck for a bit after dinner. Just when I was thinking it was probably time to head out, I got a new text from Talia. I was mid-sentence when I saw the picture, but I just stopped talking. I don't even know why, but I stood up. Holy hell.

"Everything okay?" I barely registered Tommy's question.

A monster boner was growing inside my pants. Holy fuck. She did not just send me this photo. My body was actually shaking in reaction. I wanted to crawl on top of her, get inside her, and fuck her senseless, but she was thousands of miles away. I stood glued to the spot, staring at Talia, looking sexy as fuck. What did it mean?

"You okay, man?" Tommy was standing up.

"Yeah." My voice sounded strange. "I've got to use the bathroom."

I bolted from the room. The call I didn't even realize I was making was just going through as I shut and locked the bathroom door.

Talia's face popped up on the screen when she answered. "Hey."

"Angel, you know what you're doing to me, right?"

She smiled a bit mischievously. "What am I doing?"

Talking to her had my heart racing. "You really miss me?" I inwardly cringed at the desperate-sounding question.

She paused for a second, but then nodded.

God, I still had a chance with this girl. "The other night ... I didn't want to leave like that. You said—"

"I know. I'm sorry. I totally freaked out."

"Why? I thought everything was good?"

"Your brother said something ..."

Fucking Brock. He'd barely spoken the entire night, but obviously, he'd gone out of his way to say something shitty about me. "What the fuck did Brock say to you?"

She frowned. "I don't want to ... Let's just forget about it."

I knew the gist of what he probably said. It was the last thing I wanted to talk about right now after she'd just sent me that scorching hot picture, but I knew I had to explain. "Please, Talia. Tell me what he said."

She sighed and then stood up and started walking around. Finally, she plunked down on what looked like her bed. I was hoping to get a glimpse of that sexy underwear she was wearing, but she kept the phone focused on her face.

"He said I should be careful because you were a big cheater. That you liked to wreck relationships and take what wasn't yours."

The fucking prick. I was pissed, but kept my voice neutral. "Okay. I can see why you freaked out."

"Why did he say all that, Ryder? Obviously, something happened between you two."

"Yeah, something happened. I wish I were there with you right now, Angel. This sucks telling you over the phone." I ran a hand through my hair. "So, I had sex with Brock's girlfriend — actually, she was his fiancée at the time—"

She sucked in some air. "Jenny?"

"No!" I flinched. "This was years ago. When I was 17. God, it was the stupidest thing I've ever done. He's never forgiven me."

"You were 17? Isn't Brock a lot older than you?"

"He's six years older. Diane, his girlfriend, just started flirting with me a lot. She was older, so it really stroked my ego. I don't know, eventually, I gave in to it. I was really immature and stupid. And she was the most gorgeous, sophisticated woman who'd ever paid attention to me."

Talia wrinkled her nose. "That's gross, going after your fiancé's much younger brother. You weren't even an adult yet."

This conversation was acting like a wet blanket to my libido, but I had to finish it. "Yeah, she was a piece of work, but I knew exactly what I was doing. I knew it was wrong. I knew it and I did it, anyway."

"And Brock found out?"

Sighing, I leaned up against the bathroom door. "I told him what I did a couple of months before the wedding. I don't know; maybe I shouldn't have. He's hated my guts ever since that day. I just thought that he should know before they got married. I don't think I was the only one she cheated with."

She was chewing on her lip. "He's been mad at you this whole time? It's been what, 10 years?"

"Yeah, that was the end of any relationship that we had. I never meant to hurt him. And, I've apologized — a bunch of times. But, I betrayed my brother. I get it. I hoped it would get better. He has Jenny now and Joey, but I guess he still hasn't forgiven me."

She was quiet for a few moments before she stated, "he probably dodged a bullet with that girl."

I'd been thinking the same thing for ten years, but never said it out loud, because it still didn't make what I did right.

"Angel, I want you to know that I learned my lesson. What Brock said, that I liked to take what isn't mine — that I'm a cheater — it isn't fucking true. I've never done that again. That's why I told you to dump Max. There can't be anything between us if you're still with him."

"I thought you said you didn't want a girlfriend?"

Girlfriends made things so complicated. The thought caused a flutter of nerves in my belly and made me shift my stance as a rush of excess energy flooded my system.

"I don't." I squeezed the phone tight in my hand. "But I'd make an exception ... for you."

Her eyes widened with surprise. "Okaaay."

It's not like I'd been keeping my feelings to myself; she knew where I stood. And, shit, she'd sent me that sexy picture; that must mean something. That she was talking to me right now wearing that and I couldn't even get a glimpse was killing me. "I liked the picture you sent me. A lot."

Even over the phone, I could see the blush tinting her cheeks.

I raised my eyebrows suggestively. "Just give me a little peek."

She squirmed against her pillow. "Ryder, I'm not—"

"Just real quick. That way I can go to sleep tonight with a smile on my face."

She rolled her eyes. "You can just look at the picture."

"Just one peek ..."

"Ryder—" A quick giggle escaped her lips.

"Real quick ..."

She moved the phone camera so I could see her body.

I squinted at the image. "Shit. That doesn't look like the picture."

"I changed into sweatpants and a hoodie after I sent it."

I swiped a hand through my hair. "Ah, well, it's probably better. I'm locked in the bathroom at my friend's house. They're probably wondering what I've been doing in here for so long."

"You should get back to your friends." She added softly, "I'm glad you told me about Brock. Can we talk again?"

I wasn't about to leave it so open-ended. "I'll call you tomorrow night."

"Okay." She sighed. "I'll be waiting."

I wanted to say more, prolong the call, but I didn't. "Goodnight, Angel."

"Goodnight, Mr. Rock Star."

I was feeling pretty damn good when I went back onto the deck to find Tommy. Livvy followed right behind me with a glass of wine.

She sat down next to Tommy on a sofa, setting down her full wine glass on a wicker table, leaving it perched precariously overhanging the edge. "I love this time of night. The kids are sleeping and I can just relax."

Tommy leaned in to give her a prolonged kiss, but really he was distracting her while he pushed her wineglass to safety.

When he let her come up for air, Livvy laughed and punched him jokingly on his arm. "Do you want another beer, Ryder?"

"No thanks. I should probably get going." I'd been hanging out with Tommy all day; I didn't want to intrude on their time too much.

Tommy stood up to walk me out. "Everything okay?"

"Yeah." A smile crept across my face. "I think everything's gonna be great."

Tommy and I headed back into the house. Suddenly, Livvy rushed over and grabbed my arm. "I'll walk him out."

I almost laughed at the face Tommy made.

Livvy made shooing motions for him to leave. "I just want to give him some love advice. Privately."

Tommy actually grimaced. "Alright, Crazy, just give me a minute."

Livvy reluctantly let go as Tommy pulled me aside and urgently spoke in a low warning voice, "Jesus Christ, don't listen to a damn thing she says. I'm warning you — as a friend."

We parted with a manly bro-hug and then Livvy walked me out to my truck. "So, Ryder, I noticed that you have a nice, big ... truck."

"Uh, yeah."

She looked behind us to make sure Tommy wasn't following. "I need a favor. A secret favor."

"Okay?"

She leaned in conspiratorially. "I'm throwing a party for Tommy's birthday. It's a surprise. You'll get the invitation soon. You better be there. I want all his best friends there."

"Okay, sure. Sounds great."

She grabbed my arm like she just had the best idea. "You should bring your girlfriend. It's going to be so much fun. Lots of music people will be there, some actors, hopefully, everyone from Ghost

Parker and Cold Fusion, of course — Sunglasses already said he'd be there; he can usually bring the ladies. God only knows why—"

"Sunglasses?"

She snorted derisively. "Tyler. Did you hear that he might be filming a reality TV show? One of those music contest shows where he'd be a judge or some nonsense. Can you imagine if that happens? Holy hell. His ego. I can't even right now." She shuddered.

Tyler was the front man for Cold Fusion — Rock God status. He was best friends with Tommy, but I'd noticed he and Livvy had a love-hate relationship. They loved to bust each other's balls.

"So make sure Ohio comes. We'll straighten her out for you."

"I'll try, that's for sure. I ... miss her." The last part kind of slipped out.

"Oh my God, Ryder," she threw her arms around me in a hug, "you're so cute."

"Thanks for dinner, Livvy. And I promise, I won't give away your secret."

I hopped into my truck and started down the sloped drive. Luckily, I glanced in the rearview mirror because Livvy was running down the driveway after me. I stopped the truck and rolled down my window.

She was out of breath when she caught up to me. "Jesus, I got all distracted. I almost forgot to ask you — I bought Tommy a custom surfboard for his birthday. Somehow, I have to get the surfboard from the shop to the restaurant. I've got a tiny car; I turned in the minivan — are you kidding me? I'm not a minivan girl. And I can't take Tommy's Jeep."

I cut in when she had to suck in a huge breath. "You need help with the surfboard? Just tell me when and where, and my truck is available to you."

"Thanks, Ryder. The restaurant can't store it for long, so I'll want to get it there right before the party. I'll text you with the details when I figure it out."

Chapter 18

Talia

Two weeks ago, I sent Ryder that crazy picture of me in skimpy lingerie. Since then, we'd spoken or texted every day. Most of the time, we exchanged quick and flirty text messages. A few times we spoke for hours, leaving me bleary-eyed in the morning when I had to get up for work.

I'd learned a lot about him. I'd gotten a glimpse of the rock star life he led, but more than that, I'd discovered more about the man beyond all that. What I initially thought was a superficial reaction to his appearance was turning much deeper. I was developing genuine feelings for him, feelings that excited and terrified me at the same time.

Bit by bit, I'd shared personal things about myself with him. We talked about my work, my family, my goals, and even my frustrations. I'd doled it out slowly; always afraid that a rock star would find my life totally boring, but Ryder always seemed interested. In all the years I'd dated Max, I'd never remembered sharing even half as much with him.

Things felt right with Ryder. We clicked. There was no doubt that I was completely infatuated with him. He constantly invaded my thoughts and my every dream at night. In my imagination, I relived, in excruciating detail, his hands on my body and his mouth devouring my pussy, over and over. Those thoughts were stuck on repeat. And it was making me crazy.

I wanted to be with Ryder.

In the very biblical sense.

And re-experience those amazing orgasms.

In my little infatuation bubble, I tried to pretend that things were perfect with Ryder. But things weren't perfect. He was thousands of miles away. Three time zones away, in fact. I believed him when he said he wasn't a cheater, but there were millions of single women in California. He had no attachment to me. We weren't a couple. He could, and probably was, having sex with other women. God, I hadn't even told him I'd broken up with Max yet. I hadn't wanted to bring his name into our conversations just yet.

Forget the infatuation bubble, I was in a bubble of delusion. If I could put aside the crushing insecurity of wondering why he'd want to be with me, a secretary from Ohio, I thought of about a million other different obstacles. The number one was other girls, of course — girls that could satisfy him. He was so attractive. He not only exuded sex appeal, but he had that rock star fame and fortune going for him. Girls loved that. And, his online pictures showed he didn't live the lifestyle of a monk.

I was jealous and afraid he'd move on. How long would he trade texts and PG-13 phone calls with me?

The worst thing I could do to feed my insecurity was compulsively stalking his internet dick pics. At first, I'd just wanted to see pictures of him. Then, I wanted to know about the band. I'd quickly become a fan of Ghost Parker. From there, it escalated rapidly. I became enthralled with that world. It fascinated me.

In other words, I turned into an obsessive psycho over Ryder.

In the back of my mind, I knew I was caught in a slow-motion train wreck, but I was helpless to get off and avoid it.

I was so screwed.

It was 8 p.m. when Ryder called, which made it 5 p.m. his time. He never called that early. Sometimes he would text, especially if he wouldn't be home that evening, but he never called before midnight.

"Hey there," I answered, trying not to sound too excited.

"Hey, Angel. I was hoping I'd catch you. I won't be able to talk later, so I thought I'd try now."

For me, Tuesday was a work night. Of course, I was sitting at home waiting to talk to him. I must seem so lame. "Big plans tonight?"

"Yeah, Knox is back from Scotland. He's our lead guitarist. We haven't seen him since the tour, so we're all getting together tonight. We'll do some partying and play some music together. It should be ..." he laughed, "pretty insane."

I knew Knox Stewart was the lead guitarist for Ghost Parker. I also knew that Ryder played rhythm guitar, but sometimes switched with Knox to play lead. And Sid was the bassist. I'd even researched to find out what the differences between them all were. Yeah, I was becoming the type of FAN that added the extra letters ATIC to the end. I'd keep that to myself, though.

"That sounds cool."

"It should be. What have you been up to?"

Nothing that didn't involve stalking you. "The usual. Work. Rinse and repeat. Some of Ellie's friends are going to take us repelling Saturday. I've never been before."

He was quiet for a moment. "Huh. That sounds fun."

I couldn't interpret his comment at all.

He continued, "She has friends who repel?"

"They're some kind of mountain dudes. She assured me they really know what they're doing, so we'll be safe. She has the hots for one of them, so I couldn't say no."

Maybe I was playing up the mountain dude aspect a bit. I'd met them once. They were nice, but kind of dorky in reality. More hippie granola than manly ruggedness — not exactly my type. We'd probably get a two-hour course on harness safety before we even stepped one foot into nature.

I waited for Ryder's response, but he was strangely silent.

"Ryder, are you still there? Did we get disconnected?"

"No. Sorry. It just sounds like a date."

Oh God, he sounded a teeny bit jealous. The flutters started up in my stomach as I secretly smiled. "Well, it is a date for Ellie. I'm just being her wingman. Like any good friend."

"Right."

I took a deep breath. "And now that I've broken up with Max, I've got to date again. I guess."

"Wait!" That got his attention. "Rewind a second. You broke up with Max?"

"Yeah, a while ago. The day after you left, but it had been a long time coming." I tried to sound casual, but my voice was pretty scratchy.

"Shit, why didn't you tell me?"

"I just wanted to make sure I did it for the right reasons."

"And, did you?"

"Yes. Definitely."

"Well, shit, Angel. This changes everything." I could hear the sly smile in his voice. It made my insides clench in reaction.

I heard a male voice in the background calling out. It sounded like they said, "Let's go, Stroke."

"Ah, Talia, I have to go. Listen, I want to ask you something. There's a big party coming up for Tommy Erikson's birthday. He's the drummer for Cold Fusion and he's a good friend of mine. I want you to come with me."

My stomach did a funny little flip, and my heart thundered in my chest. "Where is this party?"

"It's here. Come to L.A. Stay with me. I have a big house. You can stay for as long as you want. I'll show you around." His friends began harassing him in the background again. "Just say yes."

My brain disconnected from my mouth. "Um, okay."

"Okay?" he repeated.

"Okay."

It was so out of character and way too spontaneous for me to throw caution to the wind and accept. But, thank God, I did.

He laughed. "Okay, Angel. We're going to do it. I've really got to go. They're busting my balls. Talk later?"

"Okay. Goodnight Ryder."

And then he hung up. I sat there stunned for about 10 seconds before I jumped up and twirled around the room, screaming like a madwoman. I couldn't wait to tell Ellie.

♫♫♪♪

It was 3 a.m. when my phone woke me up. I had gotten into the habit of sleeping with it under my pillow in case Ryder texted late. Half asleep, I groped around until I finally found it.

> **RYDER:** You awake?
> **ME:** I am now.
> **RYDER:** Sorry.
> **ME:** It's okay.
> **RYDER:** I just checked the time. It's after 3 a.m. there. I'm a jerk.

I sat up in bed, shaking off the sleep pretty quickly.

> **ME:** What are you doing?
> **RYDER:** Party. Lots of drunk and high people.

He was still texting something, so I waited.

> **RYDER:** Sitting here thinking about you.
> **ME:** Are you drunk?
> **ME:** Or high?
> **RYDER:** Maybe a little.

Ryder was drunk texting me. In the middle of a party. Thinking about me.

> **RYDER:** Did you change your mind?
> **ME:** About?
> **RYDER:** Coming to L.A. to see me.
> **ME:** No. Did you want me to?

I winced when I hit send. Why couldn't I just play things cool? Did I sound lame?

> **RYDER:** No. The party is in three weeks.
> **ME:** Okay. I'll see what kind of time I can take off work.
> **RYDER:** Lots of time? Weeks?
> **ME:** You don't want me there for weeks.

Self-doubt was a bitch. I held my breath, waiting to see how he'd respond.

> **RYDER:** What are you wearing right now?
> **ME:** Uh, are we sexting right now?
> **RYDER:** It would be hard to. There are people all around me.
> **RYDER:** When can you come here?

He sounded drunk. The conversation was disjointed. He was in the middle of a party, so, of course, we couldn't do 'sexting'. Whatever the hell that actually was. But I wanted him to think about me right now. Not about the other girls that were at the party, circling around him like sharks. Maybe I could give him something to keep his mind on me.

> **ME:** I'm sliding off my panties right now.

I held my breath.

> **RYDER:** What do they look like?
> **RYDER:** DO NOT tell me granny panties.
> **ME:** They look gone.

Now what did I say? Jeez, I was so bad at this. I typed in a few words and then immediately backspaced them. I typed in a new sentence and stared at it.

> **ME:** It feels so achy between my legs.

Screw it. I hit send.

What if he didn't answer? He was at a party, for goodness' sake. Gah!

I quickly typed out more. In for a dime, in for a dollar ... and all that.

> **ME:** I need to feel you inside me.

Waiting for a response was excruciating. Why did I start this with a rock star, of all people? Why, oh why? I had no damn clue what I was doing.

> **RYDER:** Oh fuck. Are you touching yourself?

Thank you, Jesus, he answered. I took a deep breath. If I just followed his lead, I could do this. Plus, he was drunk. How hard could it be to make a drunk and horny guy think sexy thoughts about you?

Me: Mmmm. Your mouth would be better.
Ryder: Fuck! You're killing me.

See, easy-peasy.

Me: I'm so wet right now.

I took a sip from the glass of water on my nightstand. Hmm, what should I say next? I opened the web browser on my phone and typed in 'great lines for sexting'. Ooh, there were some good ones! I picked out a few potentials and then realized I wasn't getting a response. It had been a few minutes and … nothing.

Oh my God, was that it? That was the worst way to end a sexting session! What did it mean? Did he get distracted? Right in the middle of my lame sexting? How embarrassing!

Should I say anything else? And have it be ignored? No! More minutes passed by. No dots appeared. He wasn't going to text back.

Kill me now. If only there was a 'take back your text' function, I'd use the shit out of that. I slapped my pillow aggressively to plump it, then collapsed against it. How was I going to sleep now? I'd be picking apart my stupidity for the rest of the morning.

What if, right this very second, he was showing everyone at the party my—

My phone rang.

Shit.

It was Ryder.

Double shit.

No, this was good.

Answer it!

Oh God!

"Hey."

His voice sounded gruff. "Angel, you're making me crazy. I want to hear you cum."

"Oh." Oh, my.

"Fuck! You didn't orgasm already, did you?"

"No." Shit. Now what did I do? Was I supposed to masturbate? Right now? Or should I just fake a pornstar orgasm, because I was an unusually quiet masturbator? "Aren't you at a party?"

"I'm locked in the bathroom, so I have some privacy and can hear you better. I've been thinking about all the things I want to do to you. Filthy things. Talia, I want you to think about me when you cum."

I took a shaky breath. "That will be easier if I'm hearing your voice. Will you help me?"

"Fuck yes," he growled. "Are you touching your pussy right now?"

"Uh, no."

I was about to masturbate on the phone for Ryder. Hmm. This was kind of hot. Even the sexy tone of his voice was turning me on.

"Put the phone on speaker and lie back. Then spread your legs real wide for me."

Oh, my God! "Let me just take off my jammies …" I put the phone on speaker as ordered and then began tugging off my pants and underpants.

"Talia?"

"Yeah?" I asked breathlessly.

"You told me you took off your panties already. Were you lying?"

Oh shit. Busted. "That might have been a slight exaggeration."

Did he just chuckle? "And was touching yourself an exaggeration too?"

Oops. "I was just about to get around to it."

He growled. "You've been a bad girl; you need a good spanking. But now, you need to listen to me closely. Do whatever I tell you. Exactly what I say. You understand?"

"Yes."

"What are you wearing right now?"

"Just a T-shirt." I moved the phone closer to rest near my head on the pillow.

"Lose the T-shirt. Are you under the covers?"

I pulled my T-shirt off so that I was completely naked. "Yeah."

"Get on top of the covers. No hiding. And spread those legs wide, Angel."

I scrambled to follow his directions. The way he was ordering me around was so sexy. I could already smell my arousal. I shivered with anticipation.

"Move your fingertips to your inner thigh. Just your right hand."

I was starting to get that achy feeling now.

"Don't move them unless I tell you," he warned.

"Mmmh," was my only answer.

"Slide your other hand over your tits. Circle your nipple with your fingers. Slowly."

My hands were on automatic pilot, doing whatever Ryder told me to do. "Ooh. Feels good."

After a few minutes of his orders entirely focused on my breasts, that achy feeling between my legs was growing much more insistent. "Ryder, I need—"

He interrupted. "Are you still pinching your nipple?"

Damn. "Yes."

"A little bit harder, Angel."

I sucked in a breath when I increased the pressure. It was driving me crazy. What I really needed was a cock between my legs right now.

"Now, the other one."

I moaned in response.

"Would you like to rub your clit?"

"Yeessss!" I hissed.

"Not yet."

"Please, I'm ... throbbing. Your voice is so sexy. I'm really ... ahhh."

"Angel, I want my mouth all over your body. Licking ... and sucking ... and tasting. Everywhere. I'm going to tell you where I'm kissing you, and I want you to trace your fingers there."

"Yes," I forced it out of my lips.

"First, I'm kissing your lips. They have the faint cherry taste of your lip gloss lingering on them. Mmm. I'm licking them. And my tongue is sliding into your mouth."

I imagined Ryder's lips on me, something I'd fantasized about hundreds of times in the past weeks.

"Use your middle finger, Talia. Suck on it. You better be still playing with your tits."

Oh jeez. This was more erotic than my PG imaginings had been. My only response was another moan.

"My tongue is sliding over your bottom lip. Across your jaw. Under your ear, slowly down your neck."

His voice melted over me like honey, while my fingers followed the path of his kiss.

"Wet your finger again, because my tongue is circling your pink nipple now. My teeth are tugging it. I'm kissing the other one now. Tell me, how do they feel?"

"Ungh," I choke out. "They're so tight. They almost hurt. And with every pinch, I feel something down below."

"What do you feel?"

"I feel like ... I need something. Ryder, I need your cock. So bad."

Wow, with my breathy declaration, I sounded like a professional phone sex operator, but it was completely genuine. I was needy as fuck right now.

"Soon," Ryder promised. "My mouth is moving, Talia. Follow me with your fingers. I'm kissing between your breasts. Sliding lower. Across your rib cage. Down to your hip bone. I love the way your silky skin feels under my lips."

"Mmmm. Yeah."

"Wet your finger, Angel. I want to taste you. I'm sliding my tongue through your folds. Spread yourself for me so my tongue can taste everywhere. You taste like heaven, Angel. I remember. I'm circling your clit with my tongue. Then sliding it, dipping it inside so slowly."

For the next few minutes, my fingers mindlessly followed his every word, alternating between massaging, pinching and teasing my swollen clit, plunging into my pussy over and over, and rubbing everywhere in between. I couldn't stifle the moans and whimpers coming from me, even if I wanted to. The sweet crescendo was building.

Ryder's orders were coming at a more clipped pace. "Fuck. You sound so sexy moaning like that. I can picture you fingering yourself and it's hot as fuck, Angel. My dick is fucking seeping over here for you."

"Ryder ..." I begged.

His voice sounded thready. Gritty. "Use more fingers, Angel. That's my cock. It's sinking into your tight, wet pussy. I'm pumping into you. Again and again. Rub your clit with your other hand. That's me fucking you, Angel."

"Oh my God, Ryder. It's happening! I'm gonna come! Don't stop." I was about to topple off the edge of the highest cliff. Shatter to dust.

He let out a long hum. "Keep going, Angel. I wanna hear you cum. Pound that pussy for me."

I was writhing on the bed, hips thrusting upward to meet my hand. My teeth clenched and I let out a warbling moan. A second later, I climaxed. I slowed down my frantic fingers as I rode out the spasms.

I was still panting and making little noises. "Fuck, it felt so good."

I don't think I'd ever touched myself so thoroughly. I was spent, still trying to collect my runaway breathing.

"Ryder, are you still there?"

He took a deep breath. "I'm right here."

I slipped back under my bed sheets. "God, Ryder, you're so good at that. That was ... amazing. I've never ..." I took a quick breath. "I've never done that before."

He was quiet for a few moments. "Just remember this when you go repelling with the lumberjacks."

His jealous grumbling struck me as hysterical. I burst out laughing.

Chapter 19

Ryder

IT WAS A PICTURE-PERFECT California afternoon: blue skies, warm temperatures, and cool ocean breezes. The Pacific Coast Highway stretched out before me, meting out nonstop gorgeous scenery. All the windows were rolled down in my truck and the radio was blasting out tunes.

Tommy's wife, Livvy, sat in the passenger seat, but it was impossible to talk between the wind and the radio. Every time I'd met her before, she'd been a chatterbox, so I was surprised that she wasn't singing along to the music, even when the current Cold Fusion chart-topper came on. I couldn't help but remember how Talia loved to belt out songs with no hint of embarrassment until I teased her. Shit. One-winged dove. A smile curled my lips.

Livvy had insisted on driving to my house because she didn't want me 'driving all over California' to help her. From there, we took my truck to the surf shop to pick up the board she had custom-made for Tommy. I spent some time checking out some boards and talking to the owner there. I'd have to go back. The shit he had in the shop was damn cool. I wouldn't mind my own custom board and I needed my own kiteboarding equipment even though Tommy had offered to give me his old stuff.

Now we were heading to some restaurant on the coast where Tommy's party would be held in two days. Tomorrow night, I'd be heading out to LAX to pick up Talia. She was staying for almost a week, not enough time, but it was all I could coax out of her. To say I couldn't wait to see her was an understatement. Phone sex wasn't good enough. I mean, just her voice alone could get me off, and the quick flashes of her naked body that she'd allow me to see on video calls had me coming in my hand, but I wanted more. Talia and me, separated by nothing — no miles and no clothes. Christ, I'd had an honest-to-God wet dream the other night — something I hadn't experienced since my early teens. I really fucking couldn't wait to see her again.

My GPS indicated we were near the place, so I slowed down and then turned when Livvy pointed at the sign by the road. We followed a curved drive toward a group of buildings. This place looked like a resort that held weddings and stuff. The landscaping alone shouted big bucks. Livvy guided me past a large fountain toward the far end of the complex, where we parked in the large parking lot that was almost completely empty. I guess they didn't have many patrons on a Thursday afternoon.

Livvy returned the oversized sunglasses to her eyes and plopped a navy baseball cap that said 'beach babe' back onto her head. She was wearing cutoff shorts and a T-shirt. I'd never seen her looking so casual before.

We met at the back of the truck and I teased, "Sorry, I forgot my disguise."

Livvy laughed. "I know the guys at the surf shop are cool, but I don't want anyone here snapping my picture and ruining Tommy's surprise somehow. It'd be just my luck."

I pulled the surfboard out of the bed of the truck. "Do you get recognized a lot?"

She snorted. "More than I used to. After Lena and I got busted dirty dancing in a club in Dallas last year, the paparazzi have been more interested. It's so annoying; I can't take Mason to the park anymore without it potentially getting online. It's worse here in California than it was in Dallas. You'll find out soon enough."

I was busy checking out Tommy's surfboard. "Who designed the artwork on the board?"

Her hand swept over the board lovingly. "I worked with an artist to come up with the design. Everything represents something important to Tommy. Some of these," she pointed, "are copies of Tommy's tats. Some represent really cool times we had together." Her fingers briefly caressed an intricate drawing of handcuffs and a whip embedded in a swirling design.

Three sets of footprints were interspersed within the design near the top of the board. A bigger set said 'CRAZY' under them. Two smaller sets were labeled, 'MASON' and 'ROXY'.

She saw me looking at the footprints. "It's so when he's surfing, we're all with him in spirit. And, of course, he might remember how those kids came about. Let's just say that surfing may have been involved."

I made a confused face, and she laughed. Was she talking about sex on a surfboard? Maybe she was a little crazier than I'd given her credit for.

I hefted the board under my arm and we headed toward the building. "Place looks nice."

"The party will be on the terrace out back. Maybe we can peek in and look."

Livvy held the door for me so I could maneuver the surfboard inside. The place looked empty. She checked her watch. "Elliot said he'd be here."

She started moving further through the open lobby and down a small hallway on the right. I followed.

"Elliot?" she called out a few times.

No one was in the small offices located off the hall. She turned around, headed back through the lobby area, and then through some double doors into a banquet room. A pimply-faced kid with earbuds in his ear was rummaging through some boxes at a long table.

Livvy approached him. "Is Elliot here?"

The kid looked up, reluctantly pulling out his earbuds. "No. He had to go to the Palms to get something."

Livvy frowned. "Oh. He said he'd meet me here."

The kid shrugged. "He just left. He won't be back for hours."

"Maybe you can help me?" Livvy pulled off her sunglasses and smiled. "Elliot said I could store this surfboard here until Saturday. I'm hosting a party on the terrace? He said I could keep it in the wine cellar?"

The kid looked bored. Even Livvy's killer smile didn't seem to affect him much. Weird.

He huffed a breath. "Sure, I'll go get the key."

The kid left and Livvy motioned me to follow. "Let's go look at the terrace."

Still carrying the surfboard, I followed her to the back of the banquet room and out through one of the four sets of French doors.

The terrace was pretty awesome. It was a roomy space anchored on each side by two giant outdoor fireplaces. Individual stone fire pits were interspersed with dozens of plush outdoor chairs and small bistro tables throughout the lounge area. Huge planters were overflowing with colorful flowers throughout. The Pacific Ocean stretched out behind the terrace, providing a breathtaking view.

"This is a great place, Livvy."

She agreed. "Yeah. And Tommy's going to be so surprised. His birthday was actually last week. We had a family party for him and got him a few gifts, so this is going to catch him off guard. He has no clue. He thinks we're just going to be meeting Tyler for dinner."

I followed her back into the banquet room and a few minutes later, the kid was back holding out a set of keys. "Just leave the keys in Elliot's office when you're done."

Livvy took the keys from him. "Okay. Where's the wine cellar?"

The kid went back to his boxes. "Downstairs past the bar, you'll see a hallway. There are stairs at the end that lead to the cellar. Just inside the door is a flashlight if you need it."

"Thanks."

I followed Livvy out of the room. "Do you know where we're going?"

"I know where the downstairs bar is, but that's it. I'm sure we can find it. Doesn't seem like that kid is too interested in helping us."

We found it pretty easily. The stairs heading down weren't lit very well, so I cautiously followed behind Livvy. At the door at the bottom, she fit the key in the lock and then jiggled it until it unlocked. She held the door open for me as I carefully angled the surfboard inside. She propped the door open with a wood block that was obviously used as a doorstop, so we had some light until she found a wall switch. The light from the two bare bulbs overhead didn't penetrate the gloominess of the room very well.

"Do you see the flashlight?"

The door opened onto a small landing, then there were two more steps down into the cellar.

Livvy crowded onto the landing with me, looking for the flashlight. "Here it is."

She clicked it on and then swept the beam of light around the musty room. "Some wine cellar."

It was a more utilitarian storage room than a fancy wine cellar. The back wall held racks of dusty wine bottles, but boxes of alcohol and cheap wine scattered about haphazardly crowded most of the room. "Where should I put the board?"

She shined the light across the room on an empty spot of wall where I could prop it up. "I guess over there."

I waded through the cobwebs to the far side of the room and was gently leaning the surfboard against the wall when I heard Livvy let loose a high-pitched squeal. I spun around to see the flashlight beam thrashing wildly through the air, followed by her making a panicked lunge for the door. Instead, she fell to the ground with a thudding sound, while the propped door swung shut.

"Livvy? Are you okay?"

She scrambled to get up and was dusting herself off before I could make my way back over to her.

She swept the flashlight beam all along the floor by her feet. "God, something crawled across my foot. One of those fast bugs with a bajillion legs. Ugh, I hate those."

I bit back a laugh.

"Let's get out of here." She pulled at the door, but it didn't open. "Damn, the door's stuck."

I stepped in front of her and tried to turn the doorknob. It didn't even budge. "Fuck." I pulled hard on the door. "It's locked."

"What?" She grabbed my arm, squeezing hard.

There wasn't even a lock on this side of the door. "Where's the key?"

"I left it hanging in the lock."

I went at the door again, this time more forcefully. "If the key's still in the lock, how the fuck is this door locked? Did you turn the key back after you unlocked it?"

"I don't know. It was kind of hard to open."

While I was ineffectually jiggling the doorknob, Livvy pulled out her cell phone. "Oh my God, Ryder. I've got no service."

I pulled out my phone. Fuck. No service and the battery was fucking low. I moved my phone around the space, holding it near the door, holding it up as high as I could and walking all around the dingy space, but didn't get any signal.

"That kid's going to realize we didn't come back and come looking for us," I was trying to reassure her, but I didn't have all that much confidence in the kid upstairs. He didn't seem to give any fucks at all about us.

I went back to the surprisingly sturdy door and began pounding on it with my fist. In between each wave of bangs, I'd shout out, hoping someone would hear me. I gave up pretty quickly. After maybe two or three minutes of shouting and banging, I realized it was hopeless.

Livvy was just standing there, hugging herself with her arms. She was fucking cold. It wasn't even sixty degrees down here and she was wearing short shorts, a T-shirt, and flip-flops. I had jeans and a T-shirt on, plus shoes. The coldness wouldn't bother me, but she was a chick. She was probably already freezing.

I figured our best chance of someone discovering us was when that Elliot guy returned from wherever he went. The kid said that would be hours from now. Fuck. I didn't want to mention it to Livvy, but I was pretty sure we were screwed. At least for the next several hours.

"Fuck," I muttered for the hundredth time.

Livvy moaned. "I'm so sorry, Ryder. This is all my fault."

I squeezed the back of my neck, trying to relieve some tension. "I'm not mad at you, Livvy. I'm just mad at the situation."

"But I was the one who knocked the door closed. It's just that ... something attacked me."

I grunted in reply. I was still trying to figure out how to get out of there.

"That thing is in here somewhere." She was shining the flashlight all around her feet.

I stepped back and then slammed my foot against the door as hard as I could. The door was fucking solid, and I was fighting against the frame too, because of the direction the door opened. Kicking it open would not work.

"Fuck." My vocabulary had diminished severely in the last few minutes.

Livvy was now inspecting the rest of the room with the flashlight. "You think there are bats in here?"

"No, there are no bats in here," I muttered.

"Rats?" She shivered.

Fuck! Did I say that out loud? "There're no rats."

"Mice?"

There were probably mice. "No, even mice wouldn't hang out in here."

"Bugs?"

I grunted in response.

"Spiders?"

Fuck, yes. There were all kinds of nasty shit in here, but I kept my mouth shut. She was already on the verge of panic.

We both huddled on the landing, not knowing what to do. She was busy sweeping the flashlight's beam around us, keeping guard against creepy crawlies.

"It's freezing in here."

Fuck, I didn't have any extra clothes to give her. I checked my phone again, hoping a bar mysteriously had appeared. No luck.

"I've got to get home before Tommy does. I don't want to ruin the surprise."

There was no way we were getting out of here that quickly. "There's nothing we can do but wait."

"What if nobody realizes we're down here? What if we never get out? Maybe everyone will show up for the party on Saturday and we'll still be down here. Starving to death while they're partying."

I put my arm around her shoulder. "I'm sure they come down to the wine cellar all the time. All their booze is down here. We'll get out."

♫♪♩♩

Four hours later, a strange calmness had set in between us. It didn't seem like anyone was going to come to our rescue anytime soon, but we were halfway to pleasantly plastered to bother worrying too much.

We were on our third bottle of wine. I'd flattened a bunch of cardboard boxes and used them to build us a makeshift 'fort' on the landing. I hadn't gotten Livvy to sit until I'd lined the entire landing with cardboard. Then I lined the sides because she was so damned worried about bugs or whatever attacking.

When she went from merely complaining about the cold to chattering teeth, I'd begun to worry. We sat side by side, my arm around her shoulder and my hand briskly warming up her bare arm on occasion. That was all I felt I could do to keep her warm.

I hoped like hell that hypothermia wasn't an issue, but if we had to stay here overnight, who knew? Her body was physically shaking with cold. She was way underdressed for the room temperature.

When she decided to break into a bottle of wine, I didn't stop her. She rummaged through a bunch of labels and selected a red, probably the house wine, with a twist-off cap. We needed something to ward off the cold and boredom. At least the wine had helped her stop obsessing with spiders and mice.

Two bottles in, I decided Tommy would kill me if I let his wife die of hypothermia in the name of propriety. When Livvy came back to the fort after picking out the third bottle of wine, I patted my legs. "Come sit over here, Liv. You need to warm up."

"On your lap?"

I nodded. "I'll be a perfect gentleman. I promise."

She wavered for a moment and then relented. Gingerly, she parked herself on top of my lap, and then I pulled her back against my chest.

She sighed. "How are you so warm? It's not fair. I think my feet are numb."

I did my best to use my body to warm her up, but damn, it was awkward. I was only human, after all. "Do you want to wear my socks? I should have offered before. I didn't think about it."

"Oh, God. Yes."

I shifted until I could pull off my shoes and socks, and then handed the socks to her before I put my shoes back on. "You're lucky I don't have athlete's foot or anything."

"I don't care!" She slid them over her feet and pulled them up as far as they would go. She moaned, "Oh, this feels so good."

"Jesus, this is ridiculous."

She giggled. "I have a horrible tendency of getting myself into situations like this."

"Is that why they call you Crazy?"

"Yeah, Tyler started that and I guess it stuck. I was kind of star-struck when I found out Tommy was a member of Cold Fusion. I was trying to impress him and I ended up getting into some ... well, crazy situations."

While we polished off the third bottle, Livvy told me all about her crazy exploits when she was dating Tommy. Stories of her epic 'date' fails and the absurd predicaments she got into at a sex club in Dallas had us both laughing. I could see why this woman, beyond the obvious, was perfect for Tommy.

She took a swig from the wine bottle. "We haven't done anything crazy like that since Roxy's been born. I haven't completely lost all the baby weight yet, but I'm tired of waiting. I ordered this corset thing — my boobs are still huge from the pregnancy — and the material is like Spanx. It can suck in all the extra stuff pretty good and it still looks hot as hell."

"Hey, Liv?" I grabbed the wine bottle. "We better not talk about your Spanx corset."

"Oh, right." She squirmed. "I forgot. You're easy to talk to. I'm drunk. So anyway, tell me about your girlfriend. How did you meet?"

I didn't think I'd be able to go into the sexual details of my first encounter with Talia to Livvy, considering she was currently sitting between my legs, but with her nonstop prompting and interrupting with endless questions, she dragged the whole story from me complete with glorious and intimate detail. After hearing all her crazy stories, I laughed when she gasped in shock at some parts. Mostly, she laughed hysterically and slapped my leg, exclaiming 'No way' over and over.

"That's one hell of a first impression she left. She sounds like my kind of girl."

"She's pretty unforgettable." I put the wine bottle aside. I was feeling the alcohol.

"You said she's coming to the party. What are your plans? I mean, with her. She's not a groupie-type girl. She won't put up with a one-and-done."

"That's not what I want either."

"Hmm." She was looking for the wine bottle. "What do you want?"

That's what I'd been wondering since I'd met her. "I'm not the type to have a girlfriend, but she feels like girlfriend material. But what happens when she goes back to Ohio? What do I do? I'm not the long-distance relationship type of guy."

"You've got to get her here. Permanently."

Right. How the hell was I going to do that? "I can't wait to see her again in person. I want to see if we still have that connection — make sure it wasn't all my imagination. Then I'll figure it out."

She suddenly tensed. "Oh, my God. We've got a big fucking problem."

"No kidding."

"I mean, we have a big fucking problem on top of our big fucking problem. And I never say the word 'fuck'. So, it's bad."

"What is it?" What could be worse than being stuck in this dungeon? Since she'd been in my lap, she'd stopped shivering and her skin even felt warmer. I didn't think she was about to freeze to death anymore.

"I have to pee."

Oh shit. Come to think of it ... "Can you hold it?"

She groaned. "For a bit. Maybe an hour, tops. But we're not getting out of here tonight, are we? What time is it?"

I'd been trying to distract her while time passed, but I couldn't forever. "It's after nine."

"Holy shit! My kids. I said I'd be back by five o'clock. Tommy probably came home, and I didn't tell the sitter where I was going. He's probably so worried! The terrace doesn't get used during the week. You saw how empty it was. No one is coming for us, Ryder!"

I tried to be soothing. "Someone will come down here — if a guest orders a fancy wine or that guy, Elliot will come down looking for the key."

"Where am I going to pee? This is horrible!" her voice wavered.

Fuck, she was close to crying. "Well, we have empty wine bottles."

"Oh. My. God. That's crazy!"

Unfortunately, she didn't have a choice. She made me turn my back, even though she was on the other side of the room and behind some boxes. I heard her muttering and cursing.

"How the hell is this going to work? The opening is too small."

A few seconds later, "Damn, this is pretty obscene."

I held back laughter.

She was quiet for nearly a minute. "I'm getting stage fright. You need to sing. Loudly."

Anything to get her to piss already. I started singing a Ghost Parker song that I usually played lead guitar for. I was repeating the chorus for the third time before she started heading back to our fort.

"How'd it go? Success?"

She wouldn't even meet my eyes when she returned. "Let's not talk about this ever again. Ever."

I laughed and grabbed another empty bottle. "My turn."

She shook her head. "Just don't go over to my corner. Pee somewhere else."

"What difference does it make?" I headed off to a different corner.

"I don't want you to see my piss."

In less than a minute, I was finished with my business. Crazy sang 'Yankee Doodle' really loud while I did it. It was funny how I was thinking of her as Crazy now. Shit.

I got back to the fort, and we settled back into the same position.

"This has got to be uncomfortable for you."

It fucking was — in more ways than one. My back and neck were getting stiff. "But you're not freezing anymore. And you're keeping me warm, too."

She sighed and snuggled in. "And you're protecting me from the bats and spiders and stuff."

"Yeah," I replied, but I think she had already passed out by then.

♫♪♩♪♩

Something woke me up. The first thing I realized was that I was physically miserable. Every muscle in my body was sore. Then I remembered why there was a girl lying on top of me. It had nothing to do with sex. It had to do with a dungeon/wine cellar that I was locked inside of with my friend's wife. My head was pounding like a jackhammer. I remembered swigging wine straight from the bottle, and I was no wine drinker.

I opened my eyes slowly. Livvy had turned on her side and was curled up in my arms, her hair spread out against my chest, her legs, and arms wrapped around me like an octopus.

That's when I realized there was a guy standing over us. Peeking into our fort and oh, fuck — taking a picture with his phone.

"What the fuck are you doing?" I growled at him.

I started trying to sit up, half pushing Livvy off of me because the fucker was still taking pictures. Trying to stop him, I reached out to grab his phone, but he pulled away and started running back up the stairs. At least he left the door open.

Livvy was slowly waking up. She looked like I felt. I grabbed my phone to check the time, but the battery was dead.

I untangled myself as gently as I could from Livvy. "Hey, the door is open. We're free. What time is it? My phone's dead."

She groaned. "I think I'm still drunk. I've got to pee so bad." She found her phone and flicked it on. "Oh God, it's after 10 a.m.!"

No one would have been worried about me last night, but I knew Tommy was freaking out about Liv disappearing. "We've got to get out of here. Some dude was just here, and I think he was taking pictures of us."

Her eyes widened with shock. "You're fucking kidding me? Just great! Could this get any worse?"

"Let's just get out of here." I stood up and stretched my legs.

"We can't leave the wine bottles here." She looked panicked.

"What, the piss?"

She nodded. "Yeah. We have to take them."

"Fuck no. We'll pay for the wine and we'll leave a big tip for whoever has to take care of it." Was I standing here arguing about piss bottles with her? Jesus.

"Ryder, if they have pictures, this whole thing could blow up. The last thing I want the press to have is any information about our piss bottles. It would be so humiliating. You know they'd love to add that in. It'd make the story extra juicy. They'd probably auction off the piss bottles or something for more publicity."

I stared at her like she was nuts. "We'll call the manager. We'll get him to take care of it discreetly for us. I'm not carrying around bottles of piss, Liv."

She was stubborn. "Ryder, we've peed together, we've slept together, and we've shared deep, dark secrets. Sorry, but we're besties now. BFF's. And that means you'll grab the piss bottles to protect us both from total humiliation."

I didn't want to spend any more time arguing before that dude upstairs rounded up more trouble for us. "Fine, I'll take the fucking piss bottles. At least they're capped."

I grabbed the bottles and then we hurried up the stairs.

"Ryder, I've got to use the bathroom before we go."

A few employees were gathered near the bar when we came up almost as if they were waiting for us. I tried to keep the piss bottles low and out of sight.

Livvy rushed straight to the restroom. I waited in the shadows for her to finish. The employees were chattering and snickering, and the snatches of conversation that I could hear were not good. A few more employees showed up. Yesterday, this place was a ghost town. Now suddenly, people were crawling out of the woodwork.

I tapped on the ladies' room door. "Liv, hurry."

She must have been in there for five minutes already. I cracked open the door and saw her leaning against the sink. She was on the phone.

I slipped into the restroom. "Livvy, c'mon, we gotta go. A crowd is gathering."

She held up a finger, turned her back, said a few words quietly into the phone, and then hung up.

"What's going on?" She was frowning at her appearance in the mirror. Her hair and makeup were messy. She looked like she'd just had a healthy tumble in the sack. Fucking great.

"Where's your hat and sunglasses?" I asked.

She frowned. "I don't know. They must be in the wine cellar."

"Well, we've got to get the fuck out of here. We don't have time to look for them; people are gathering."

She glanced down at the bottles in my hand and then nodded. "Let's go. We'll walk really fast and ignore everyone. Hopefully, no one takes pictures."

I didn't tell her, but that ship had sailed. I'd seen a few phones held out awkwardly, probably recording video, as I waited outside the restroom. We'd been busted, and I knew this was going to be bad. I wished it could be bad without me holding two bottles of piss, but hey — life was crazy.

We'd gotten about two steps outside the restroom before a pack of people began trailing us. They were definitely recording shit. I didn't know if they knew who we were or just sniffed the scent of scandal. We didn't speak to each other; we just made a beeline for the exit.

About five people followed us into the parking lot. One guy shoved his phone way too close to Livvy's face. I transferred the wine bottle in my right hand to the other, so that I was gripping both in one hand. Please God, don't let me drop this bottle. I used my arm to push back the phones and keep the people away from her.

I heard someone snicker 'Tommy Erikson' and I saw Livvy flinch. I tried to use my body to block Livvy from the cameras, but the fucking piss bottles were really impeding me. Finally, we got to my truck. I unlocked the doors and then helped her in before I went around to the driver's side. I tucked the piss bottles behind my seat, praying they wouldn't leak or break, and then hopped in behind the steering wheel. Within a few seconds, we were roaring away.

"Fuck, that might be bad."

Livvy slumped back in the seat. "I'm just so happy to be out of there. I called Tommy. He had his security guys looking for me last night because the police wouldn't do anything yet. They tracked my car to your house, but they couldn't find us, obviously."

I glanced at her nervously. "So, what did you tell him?"

She sighed. "I told him I was safe, and I'd call him back. I can't give away the birthday party surprise! This'll be tricky." She chewed on her lip.

My mouth fell open. "I think you'd better give it away. I don't want my ass getting kicked by him."

"My head is killing me." She pulled out her phone and made a call. It was answered immediately. "Hey, babe. I'm going to put you on speakerphone. I'm with Ryder."

Tommy's voice came through the phone. "Where are you? Are you okay?"

"I'm with Ryder. We're in his truck." She looked at me. "Where are we heading?"

I shrugged. "I guess I'll take you home?"

Tommy didn't sound too happy. "Where are you? I'm getting in the Jeep now. I'll meet you."

I looked at my GPS. "Pacific Coast Highway heading towards you. I'll meet you at the surf spot in Malibu."

"Tommy, we had a bit of a ... mishap. I can't explain everything to you right now, so you just have to trust me. Plus some, uh, pictures might come out, but they are not what they look like. And, I just want you to know that none of this is Ryder's fault."

"That I can believe," was his dry answer.

I looked over at Livvy like she was crazy. That's all she was going to tell him? "Tell him what happened, Livvy."

Tommy chuckled. "Don't worry, Ryder. I'll get everything out of her. Just focus on bringing her back to me. She scared me to death."

Chapter 20

Talia

If I hadn't been stalking Ryder on the internet, I'd never have seen it. And this stuff had made it to the legit gossip sites, not just the unauthorized Ghost Parker fan sites. It was breaking news in the sleazy world of celebrity gossip.

I was staring at a picture of Ryder sleeping with a girl curled up on his chest. Even sleeping, he looked good. His hair was rumpled and he was rocking some delicious 5 o'clock shadow. He was also rocking a pretty girl with auburn hair on top of him.

Ellie came into the kitchen. "Are you finished packing?"

We'd already spent an hour picking out the sexiest outfits and lingerie for me to pack — figuring out what to wear when you're with a rock star and all that.

When I didn't answer, she came over to the table to see what I was looking at on my laptop. "Holy shit! Is that Ryder?"

I groaned. "Yeah. And according to Buzzed Life, he's with the wife of Tommy Erikson. You know, the famous guy whose birthday party I'm supposed to be going to with Ryder."

"What the absolute hell?" Ellie managed to pinpoint exactly what I was thinking.

I showed her a few videos from the site: Ryder and the girl exiting a ladies' restroom, Ryder shielding the girl from the camera, Ryder holding a bottle of wine and helping her into a truck.

Ellie broke the silence. "I have to say, that girl looks properly fucked. The perfectly tousled hair and messy makeup. Shit, and he's carrying two bottles of wine."

"Yeah," was my quiet answer.

Ellie pursed her lips. "Go back to that first picture."

Reluctantly, I clicked back on the picture of the two of them sleeping.

"Tal, they're not naked. They're both wearing clothes. The same clothes they had on in all those videos. And they look like they're sleeping in a homeless camp. Look at that weird cardboard shit."

She was right. I hadn't noticed anything beyond the two of them before. "What is that? It is odd."

"Before you flip the absolute fuck out, ask for an explanation. Don't cancel the trip based on a knee-jerk reaction." She was staring at me intently.

I snapped the laptop shut. "He told me he wasn't a cheater. Either he's a big fat liar and he's sleeping with his good friend's wife, or there's some insane explanation for this. Either way, I'm going to California. Even if I have to stay in a hotel and vacation by myself for a week."

Ellie released a breath she'd been holding. "Good. This might be entirely innocent despite how bad it looks."

"That's true, " I agreed. Inwardly, I kept repeating the warnings

Brock had told me.

He's a cheater.
He doesn't care about anyone but himself.
He takes what's not his.
He wrecks things that are good.

How well did I really know Ryder? He was a rock star. All the doubt, mistrust and insecurities came flooding back despite my best efforts not to slide into a complete tailspin over those damning videos and pictures.

Ignoring my cautious nature and letting Ellie prod me along, I loaded my suitcase into Ellie's car and we set out for the airport. She kept up a constant stream of chatter the whole way there. She dropped me off curbside with a hug and then went on her way. There was no turning back.

While I was sitting at the gate, waiting to board my flight, I got a call from Ryder. My heartbeat quickened as I picked up the phone and said hello.

"Hey, Angel. Are you at the airport yet?"

"Yeah. I'll be boarding soon."

"Good. Is everything okay?" He sounded a bit concerned. Perhaps, even guilty.

I closed my eyes. "Um, maybe you should tell me?"

"Did you see the pictures?"

"I did."

He blew out a breath. "Fuck. And you're still coming?"

"I'm at the airport, but I could turn around." I tried to keep the tremor out of my voice.

"No! Look, Talia. I can explain everything. Whatever you read, it's all bullshit. I was helping Livvy with Tommy's birthday present and we got locked in a wine cellar. And absolutely nothing happened between us. I would never do that to Tommy. Or you. I promise, Angel. I want to explain it all to you, all of it, but I'd like to do that in person. It's an absolutely ridiculous story, but it's the truth."

For some reason, I believed him. I really did. Maybe I just wanted to. "Okay. You can tell me when I get to California."

I could hear his sigh of relief over the phone. "Thanks, Angel. I'll see you soon. Can't wait."

We hung up and I felt better. I texted Ellie:

> **Me:** I think you were right. There must be a crazy explanation for those pictures. I don't think he's a cheater.

She didn't reply because she was still driving home. The plane began boarding, so I put away my phone.

♫♪♩♪♪

I was leaning against a post waiting for my suitcase in the baggage claim area when I saw him. He was still far away and there were tons of people in between us scurrying about.

Our eyes connected from two baggage carousels away and I felt a zing — a flash of awareness that zigzagged through my body. I swore that my heart stopped beating for a few beats and then violently jump-started, now beating way too fast. Tension bloomed in the pit of my stomach. A curl of desire unfurled, pulsing obtrusively between my legs.

He was so achingly beautiful with his dark messy hair and penetrating blue eyes. I saw heads turn his way, mostly female. He had such a presence about him that I was sure he was often mistaken for a movie star or a model in this city. He was wearing snug jeans with a black leather studded belt and a tight, fitted black T-shirt that showed off his broad shoulders, toned muscles, and the tattoos on his right arm. He looked delicious. And he was holding a single long-stem red rose. Swoon.

Without realizing it, my legs began moving. I took steps towards him; I was invisibly pulled to him. It was as if I had no choice, I was drawn to him like a moth to flame.

He approached, never taking his eyes off me. We met somewhere in the middle. Without heels on, he was much taller; I had to tilt my head up to meet his gaze. Neither of us spoke; I wasn't sure I could get a word out of my mouth if I tried.

We'd stopped in the middle of a crowded stream of busy travelers; the crowd had to part for us, but I didn't care. Ryder gently cradled my face in both his hands and stared into my eyes. He looked hungry.

The world seemed to slow down around us. It gradually disappeared as his thumb caressed my cheek and then very slowly swiped across my bottom lip. My lips parted with a shaky moan.

His eyes zeroed in on them and then his gaze darkened. It grew molten. I drew in a ragged breath as his hand slid around the back of my head, guiding me closer for a kiss. Our lips touched.

Fireworks.

My tongue reached out to taste him and was met in kind. His fingers threaded through my hair as he deepened the kiss. Our tongues tangled together, stroking, exploring until I was weak in the knees. My hands fisted in his shirt; I felt his hard muscles against my fingers as I took everything he could give.

My body was answering his overpowering call. Throbbing. Feeling tight. Swollen. Needy. I was slowly losing all control as my senses were overwhelmed by him. His taste. His smell. His body against mine. He had full command of me and I couldn't get enough. I was drowning as he plundered my mouth, taking and taking. I was about to melt into a puddle at his feet. His arm slipped around my back, pulling me closer, maybe even holding me up, just when I thought my knees might buckle.

His tongue was stroking my mouth so erotically, in and out in perfect rhythm to the needy ache that pulsed between my legs, that if we kept this up, I was sure to embarrass myself. I was already pressing into him and the moans coming out of my mouth bordered on public indecency.

When I felt the hardness under his pants pressed up against my softness, I whimpered.

Unfortunately for me, Ryder had enough sense to put the breaks on our overheated public display. He broke our kiss and rested his forehead against mine for a few moments while I fought to steady myself. He gave me time to shake off the dizziness that his lethal kiss had induced. I'd never felt a kiss like that one. Explosive. And so intensely sexual.

His hands slid down to the sides of my arms. "Angel, I missed you."

I felt so vulnerable with him staring at me with such naked lust. He was looking at my lips like he might kiss me again. I slid my tongue across them feeling suddenly shy. "Ryder," it came out like a breathy whisper. "That was ... wow."

I wanted to smack myself for ruining the moment by saying something so corny, but a slow, cocky smile spread on his handsome face making my insides turn to quivering mush.

"Let's collect your bags so we can get out of here."

♫♫♪♪

I was so nervous. Ryder said that it would take a little over an hour to get to his house from the airport. Even though my entire being was acutely aware of him sitting next to me in his truck, I felt a slight reprieve from the predatory heat in his eyes, because it wasn't like he could do anything right now but drive. There was some safety in that. Back in Ohio, I had used Max as a barrier against the wild and uncontainable physical intensity I felt between us. When we got to his house, there would be nothing left to keep us apart.

It was scary. It was also thrilling beyond words. My body was buzzing with anticipation. Butterflies were rioting in my stomach. My mind was racing a mile a minute. I wasn't sure exactly what Ryder expected. A week of non-stop sex? Could I even do that? I hadn't really ever done anything like that. With Max, even at the beginning of our relationship, we'd had sex on the regular, which meant a couple of nights each week. What if I couldn't keep up with Ryder? What if he was disappointed in how ordinary I was?

Ryder held his hand out for mine. I slipped it into his and then he squeezed it, looking at me. "You're pretty quiet."

"Sorry, I'm just a bit tired." I dug for excuses. "And hungry, too."

His eyes returned to the road. "I made a salad and some chicken and rice that I just have to heat up. I thought you might be too tired to go out tonight?"

"That sounds perfect."

"I don't know about perfect. I'm not much of a cook, but I followed a recipe."

"Okay," was my lame answer.

A few minutes of silence passed before Ryder spoke up again. "So, tomorrow night we're going to Tommy Erikson's party. It's a surprise birthday party. He's the drummer for Cold Fusion," he glanced at me, "you've heard of them?"

I nodded.

"We opened for them on our last tour. I've become pretty good friends with Tommy. He lives in California too, and he's big into surfing and he's been teaching me to kiteboard since we've been back home."

I knew a lot more about both Cold Fusion and Ghost Parker than when I first met Ryder, but I wasn't ready to admit the whole obsessive stalking thing. "Kiteboarding? Is that where a sail is attached to the surfboard?"

"No, that's windsurfing. Kiteboarding is like wakeboarding, except there's no boat; you're holding a power kite that propels you through the water really fast. I'm sure you'll see them at the ocean while you're here."

I snuck a look at his profile. "Hmm. I don't think it's that popular in Ohio."

He grinned. "Probably not." He took a deep breath and then grimaced for a moment like he didn't particularly want to get into the next part. "So, Tommy's wife, Livvy, got him a surfboard for his birthday and she asked me to help her bring it to the place where she's having the party because I had a truck. With some really bad luck, we ended up getting locked in a wine cellar overnight and we didn't get out until this morning. That's what those pictures were on the internet."

I frowned a bit. "You got locked in a wine cellar?"

He spent the next five minutes detailing what happened. It sounded pretty horrible, but I still couldn't help but feel a slight twinge of jealousy toward Livvy. The picture of her sleeping on Ryder's chest, as innocent as it turned out to be, still brought out the green-eyed monster in me.

"I guess Tommy's party is no longer a surprise?"

He raised an eyebrow. "Actually, I think it is. Livvy wasn't going to tell him any details of what happened. She was determined not to ruin the surprise. I'm hoping he doesn't see the crap online before the party tomorrow, but he knows she was with me. He was pretty worried when she didn't come home."

"And he's okay with her not telling him? Do they have an open relationship or something?" I started feeling nervous again. I felt so out of my element in this rock-star world.

"Hell, no. He definitely wouldn't let another man near her. They just trust each other. They have two kids, Roxy and Mason; they're both really cute. Everyone calls Livvy, 'Crazy', because she does crazy stuff that ends up getting her or Tommy into trouble, so he wasn't exactly shocked that something ridiculous happened. You'll see tomorrow night when you meet them."

When I didn't answer, he picked up our intertwined hands and kissed the back of my knuckles. "You okay with everything?"

"Yeah. I believe you about everything. I guess I'm more nervous about fitting in with all your famous friends and stuff. I'm pretty boring."

"Jesus, don't be nervous." He looked genuinely surprised. "My friends are a bunch of animals, for the most part. They'll all be wondering how I got so lucky and I guarantee that they all hit on you. That's why I'm going to stick close by your side. Like glue. I don't trust them."

Laughter bubbled out of my mouth. I relaxed back in my seat. Being with him was so easy. So right. I snuck a glance at him. I had to be really careful. I already wanted more than he could give. I was here to enjoy life, not lose my heart.

As we neared his house, the unmistakable scent of the ocean wafted through the air, a mixture of salt, brine, and seaweed. I could catch glimpses of the ocean between the crowded facades of businesses and houses. We turned off the main street, heading toward the ocean onto a street that ran parallel to the beach beyond. The road was packed with houses, each three stories high, sitting one after another about an arm's span apart from its neighbor.

Ryder pulled into the driveway of house #3522. It looked pretty similar to all the others, except a bit more unkempt.

"Here we are." He leveled his five thousand megawatt smile on me.

I hopped out of the truck to avoid commenting on it. The façade was ugly, with no architectural embellishments, not even many windows broke up the monotony of the shabby-looking structure. I knew this rectangular box was on prime oceanfront real estate in California, so it must have cost an arm and a leg. The same money would have bought a luxurious mansion in Ohio.

Ryder hefted my fifty-pound suitcase out of the truck with ease and then motioned me to follow. He gave me a tour of the place the way only a guy can, giving me only a few seconds to linger in each spot. It was hard to take in so quickly.

The bottom floor was surprisingly small. It was wide open and mostly empty. I only had time to notice that the floors needed serious replacement before Ryder guided me to the stairs. The stairs were ugly. The dirty cream-colored walls needed new paint. The handrail looked really unstable.

The second floor contained an open gathering room and two bedrooms each with its own bathroom. Ryder deposited my suitcase in the first bedroom. "I thought you might like this room better. The bathroom is ... cleaner in this one."

The room was empty except for a twin-sized bed with sketchy-looking bedding on it. I didn't have time to check out the bathroom, because Ryder had grabbed my hand and was pulling me upstairs. I didn't even have time to worry about the implications of Ryder parking my suitcase in the guest room, which was probably a good thing.

The third floor was the showstopper. The back wall was almost all window, showing off the amazing view of the ocean beyond. The space was entirely open, a great room with a raised ceiling, which combined a modern kitchen with a large island, a comfortable living room, and a large dining table tucked off to the side.

I gasped as I spun around to appreciate the space, "Ryder, this is awesome!"

He grinned. "Everything up here is new. I needed a new roof, so my contractor convinced me to raise the ceiling to make everything more open. I didn't want to spend the extra money, but it made such a difference. We also extended the deck. That was a huge bill, but it's my favorite part of the house. Let me show you."

I followed him out through the sliding doors. The deck spanned the entire width of the house and hung out at least twenty feet. From here, the view of the ocean and beach below was virtually unimpeded. An ocean breeze kept the warm, salty air from being stagnant. Ocean waves crashed onto shore creating a hypnotic soundtrack while the setting sun bathed the evening in a romantic glow.

"It's gorgeous."

My eyes swept over the eclectic mix of deck furniture that looked hastily thrown together. A sun umbrella against a wall next to a giant, brand-new grill.

The décor was lacking for such a great space. I could imagine a few seating groups consisting of comfortable chairs and sofas. In my head, I placed a few outdoor rugs, two matching market umbrellas, and a small dining table around the space I imagined. A string of outdoor lights and a few lanterns set randomly about would complete the look.

Ryder had inched up to me as I was daydreaming. "What are you thinking about?"

I felt my cheeks heating up. "I, uh, it's nothing."

He moved closer. His hands rested on my hips and then pulled me against him until my legs were surrounded by his wide stance. "Tell me."

I ripped my eyes from the outline of his well-defined pecs. Being this close to him made my neurons misfire. Finally, I confessed, "I was mentally redecorating the deck."

His finger tapped my nose and he laughed. "You don't like my efforts?

"I do."

His gaze darkened and he pulled my hips even tighter against him. I couldn't keep my eyes off his mouth or my thoughts off the devastating kiss he'd planted on me at the airport. I was hungry for more.

He dipped his head to my lips slowly, giving my stomach plenty of time to turn riotous somersaults. The kiss started slow and sweet, but quickly heated up until I felt every inch of my body responding. I was on fire for him.

I may have moaned at the loss of his lips when he broke away.

He released me and took a step back. "I know you're hungry. I'll go heat up dinner. It shouldn't take too long." I immediately missed the contact with his body.

I followed him into the house. "Can I help with anything?"

"Nope." He began pulling items out of the refrigerator.

I sat at a barstool in front of the island and watched him work for a bit.

"Where do you sleep?" Darn it, was I blushing again?

He lifted an eyebrow, but his face remained neutral. He pointed to a closed door near the top of the staircase. "That's my bedroom. You can go check it out if you want."

I wasn't going to pass up the chance. Curious, I got up and headed to his bedroom. It was large, but fairly empty and stark looking. A large bed with a gray comforter was on the wall next to the sliding door with the ocean views, which must have opened onto the same deck. The only furniture besides the bed was a single nightstand and a tall dresser.

He needed more furniture, new bedding, window treatments, and a few area rugs scattered around the wide plank wood floors. I'd also preferred the walls not to be painted white, even though I could tell they were freshly painted. It seemed that I was a compulsive redecorator.

I crossed the room to the door that led to the bathroom. No expense had been spared in the large space. The beautifully tiled walk-in shower had two shower heads on opposite walls plus a rainfall shower head overhead, bench seating, built-in niches, and what looked like a sound system all enclosed in glass. I swallowed hard because my imagination suddenly started going wild. I took in the rest of the room noting the dual vanities, soaking tub, and heated towel racks. The space was near perfection. A few fluffy bath mats and coordinating towels were all it lacked.

I peeked in the small linen closet and then opened the last door that passed through the bathroom into the huge walk-in closet. It was currently only about a quarter used.

I'd been poking around for far too long, so I hastily made my way back to the kitchen. "Did you pick out all the stuff for the bathroom?

It's amazing."

Two dinner plates filled with chicken, rice, and vegetables sat steaming on the island. Ryder was busy filling two bowls with a salad he'd tossed together. "I did with a lot of coaching from my contractor. He knows what kind of things are good for resale."

My eyes widened. "Are you thinking about flipping this place?"

He shook his head. "No. Not for a while anyway. But, I probably won't stay here forever. Not if the band takes off like I hope it does. You should see the place that Tommy has on the beach. It really puts this place to shame, but I've got a ways to go before I can afford anything like that."

"Your house is really nice, Ryder. You could use a decorator, but the renovations you made are amazing."

"Thanks." Ryder handed me my plate. "I usually eat out on the deck. That okay?"

"Sure."

"What do you want to drink? Wine, beer, water ... Alabama Slammers?"

He remembered my drink. "Red wine would be great."

He pulled a bottle of wine from a built-in wine refrigerator, poured me a glass, and then grabbed a beer for himself.

I followed him out to the deck where we ate dinner watching the sun sink over the Pacific.

Chapter 21

Talia

Even though I was like an adolescent boy with one thing on my mind — sex, sex, and more sex — conversation during dinner flowed smoothly. We spent most of the time discussing things we could do in California while I was visiting. Ryder told me that his band was getting together every morning, starting Monday, to work on new music. He planned to blow off one of those days but hadn't told the band yet, because they were already irritated that he asked them to change practice to mornings this week. It apparently crimped their party lifestyle to get up so early.

I was going to have a few mornings to myself. I could sleep in late, walk the beach or even rent a car and explore. Maybe I'd ask Ryder to take me into L.A. with him one morning and just check out that part of the city while he practiced with the band.

The sun had long set, so darkness spread out beyond the deck.

The constant sound of waves crashing to shore reminded me that the endless ocean stretched out in front of us. Ryder went back inside the house to get us each a fresh drink.

When he came back out, I decided I wasn't going to wait for him to make the first move. Those two kisses we'd shared earlier had stirred me up. Throughout our dinner, in the back of my mind, I kept fast-forwarding to the part where we had sex. Anticipation was sweet, but I was ready for the main course.

When he sat back down in his chair, I stood and seductively prowled over to him. Wordless, he watched me approach, accommodating me when I slid onto his lap, straddling him on the Adirondack chair. His hand slid up my bare calf while our eyes locked on to each other, but he didn't make any other move.

He raised an eyebrow as if to say, 'Your move'. I wanted those lips on me. Those hands. All over me. I peeled off my T-shirt and tossed it aside. Then I waited an eternity for him to look at my breasts. When he finally did, I physically felt the smolder in his eyes. It heated me. Left me breathless.

His fingers traced the skin along the top of my demi-cup bra before pushing down the lacy material until my breasts were exposed and resting on top, pressed high and plump by the gathered fabric. I found the bottom of his T-shirt and tugged it off when he raised his arms obligingly.

There was just enough light from the two light fixtures to study his muscular chest and tattoos. My fingers wandered over the half-sleeve of tattoos on his right arm, a detailed sailing ship surrounded by intricate waves, which inked the granite muscle below. I skimmed over the patterns of the tattoo, which stretched up his arm and artfully connected with the tribal sun and moon tat on his right pec. From his broad shoulders and well-defined chest, I continued to explore lower:

down his slender torso, across the ridges of his hard six-pack, down the funnel of the V that led to the light dusting of hair under his navel that beckoned my hand even lower. He was stunningly beautiful.

I couldn't fully concentrate on my exploration because his fingers had worked my nipples into two taut peaks. They teased, pinched, and pulled until I was moaning for more. He lounged back in the chair, looking delicious as his hands slid slowly down my sides to my hips, firing sparks of desire along the way. With his hands on my hips and his fingers splayed along my back, he eased my torso forward.

I couldn't tell if I was leaning in or being pulled in, but before I knew it, his lips were pressed against my breast. All sense of time evaporated as his tongue swirled over my tight nipple, flicking it back and forth before drawing it into his mouth. His other hand worked the other breast mercilessly.

When his mouth slid to my other breast, I realized I was grinding my pussy against his hardness. I tried to contain myself, but when his teeth started pulling on my other nipple, my head fell back as I gave into the pleasure. The ache between my legs was coiling so tight I thought I might actually orgasm from breast stimulation alone.

My fingers were weaving through his hair, trapping his mouth against my chest. I was surprised to realize that at some point, Ryder had unhooked my bra. When his tongue trailed over my cleavage and headed toward my throat, I took the opportunity to disengage my bra straps so I could fully discard it.

That was when I saw the man from the house next door staring at us from his own deck. I froze.

Ryder began teasing my nipple with his tongue again, and I automatically rocked my hips into him. All while I stared in shock at this man.

Before the renovation, Ryder's deck had been identical to his neighbor's. But now, Ryder's deck extended further toward the ocean, giving the man a front-row seat to our antics. We locked eyes for what seemed like forever before he turned and went back into his house.

Belatedly, I collapsed against Ryder's chest with a high-pitched shriek that escaped my lips. I buried my face against his neck.

We were both breathing raggedly. "Angel?"

"Someone's watching."

He rubbed a soothing hand down my back. "We're three stories up. No one can see us."

"Your neighbor. He saw us."

Ryder turned his head toward the now empty deck. "Fuck. That asshole? I thought he was away."

"He went back inside," I added lamely.

Ryder wrapped his arms around my waist and then stood up with me in his arms. I hooked my legs around his hips and then he walked us through the sliding doors leading into his bedroom. "Let's finish this in here."

He flipped a wall switch, which lit up a lamp on his nightstand; then he walked me over to his bed and tossed me onto it. I'd barely landed on the covers when he crowded over me, trapping me beneath his hard length. He gave me a scorching kiss, reigniting the frenzy of desire I'd felt before the man's gaze had intruded on us.

His tongue tangled with mine as he popped the button on my shorts and pulled down the zipper. I missed the feel of his demanding mouth when he lifted away to slide my shorts down my legs, whisking them off, leaving a skimpy piece of silk covering me. Excitement sparked higher as he took his time, sliding my panties down my legs, making me squirm under his heated gaze.

He climbed on top of me again and kissed a trail across my body — finding the sensitive spot in the crook of my neck, paying attention to each breast before trailing lower, sliding down my side to my hip bone.

He pulled up to look at me once again. "Angel, you don't know how much I want you right now." His voice sounded heavy with need.

Kneeling between my legs, his hand drifted down my leg to my ankle. He circled his fingers around my ankle and then slid it forward, bending my knee until it was pointing straight up. Never breaking contact with my eyes, he repeated the same process with my other leg. Then he put his hands on both my knees and spread them apart.

I was arranged on display for him, but instead of feeling dirty, it felt so incredibly sexy. He deliberately looked between my legs, causing my heart to pound even harder in my chest. Reaching upward, he touched a finger to my mouth, slightly pulling on my bottom lip. It took me a few seconds for my brain to work, but then I wrapped my lips around his finger and sucked.

When I released it, that same finger trailed down my body until it got to the aching, needy center of me. His finger slid over my clit and my hips bucked upward.

I writhed. I needed more.

His finger circled my clit and then worked to my entrance over and over, each time dipping a tiny bit further into me. He sucked his finger, tasting me, before teasing me all over again, each time even more intensely.

"So sweet. I've waited so long to taste you again."

He hadn't even gotten a finger all the way inside of me with his endless torment when I felt the pressure of an orgasm rising. My thighs trembled and my hips bucked against his gentle torture.

"Ryder. Please." My voice was breathy and urgent.

He lowered his mouth to my pussy and worked my clit with his tongue and lips. As soon as he slipped his finger inside me, all the way inside, I shattered around him. I exploded, clamping my thighs around his head, grinding against his mouth, while I rode out the spasms.

He released me for a moment, while I held onto the blissful orgasm as long as I could. When my brain slowly started working again, I squinted open my eyes. Ryder was taking off his pants. I sat up on my elbows to watch.

His cock was just how I'd remembered it. Perfect. Straining. Mouthwatering. Ryder dug through the drawer in his nightstand and pulled out a condom packet. He ripped it open and then rolled it onto his cock in record time.

He parted my thighs. "How do you want it, Angel?"

Shocking myself, I blurted out what I wanted. "Really slow and sensual." I met his eyes.

Ryder licked his lips. "Fuck. You're going to kill me."

He lined up his cock with my entrance and pushed in with a measured pace. He switched between watching where our bodies joined and holding my gaze. By the time he pushed all the way inside of me, we were both panting with lust.

My breath hitched when he finally filled me. It felt heavenly, something I wanted to remember forever. He didn't withdraw, but pulled close to kiss me — one of his toe-curling kisses that sucked away any remaining oxygen in my lungs.

He began sliding in and out of me slowly. "Talia, look at me."

My eyes snapped open; I'd already been dazed and half consumed by his kiss. Our eyes connected as he pumped into me in a controlled rhythm that was turning out to be just as deadly and lethal as his kisses were. His arm muscles strained, while his jaw clenched from holding back as the pleasure built. I wished we could go on forever like this, but on the back of my earlier orgasm and the sheer intimacy I felt while he watched, I knew I was going to come soon.

He licked a finger and then began massaging my clit in a rhythm with his slow-motion thrusts that had me moaning all while his eyes never flickered from my face. Suddenly, this felt too intimate. I should have told him to go hard and fast. This was way too much.

I was fisting the sheets and moaning unintelligible words, fighting the quick, hard rise to orgasm, but I had no control over this.

"I'm going to make you scream, Talia."

More garbled noise burst out of my mouth, louder this time. I couldn't even process words, let alone speak. I think I groaned/shouted, "More."

Ryder did not pick up the pace. He was expertly maintaining this rhythm that was keeping me on the edge of the precipice. I was at that white-hot, insanely intense moment right before orgasm, but it was lasting forever.

"I can do this all night, Angel."

My eyes must have bugged out in my face because he laughed.

"Tell me what you want."

I groaned, low and long. "Please," I panted. "Make me come."

He increased the tempo and pounded into me harder. When he squeezed my swollen clit, that's all it took. I was done. Gushing. Melting. Jerking with spasms. And, yes, I was screaming.

Luckily, he followed pretty closely behind me because I was still screaming out weird stuff — something like 'Oh yeah, give it to me, baby'. At least I didn't call him Big Daddy or something else equally embarrassing.

His mouth found mine for a kiss, smothering the nonsense coming out of it. While I recovered (this was going to take some time), he took care of the condom and then climbed into bed at my side, pulling me against him.

I languidly traced the tattoo on his arm with my finger. I wanted to ask him if the sex was good for him. He'd been so in control the whole time, while I'd been just the opposite. It made my insecurities rear up, so I remained silent.

My eyelids got heavy. "Should I go downstairs?"

His arms pulled tighter around me. "What?" he grunted. "You're not going anywhere."

"But, my suitcase?"

He turned on his side to face me and smiled lazily. "You're not going to need any clothes when you're in this room."

"I thought maybe you didn't want me to sleep in here? That you were a wham bam thank you, ma'am, no cuddles, here's the door type of guy?" I glanced quickly at him.

He stuck out his lower lip. "That's kind of insulting, Angel. First of all, wham bam thank you, ma'am? That wasn't exactly a quickie you just got. I could have gone longer, but if I recall, you were absolutely begging for an orgasm. And I didn't want to tire you out, because second of all, it's not even 11:00 yet. I am so far from being done with you. And when I am, you're not going to have any energy left to walk downstairs, so I'll be forced to cuddle with you all night."

"Ryder, I wasn't trying to insult you." I laughed to downplay my insecurities. "I just wanted to make sure that I didn't ... do anything wrong."

He sighed. "I left the suitcase in the guest room for you. I didn't want to put any expectations on you. But obviously, now that I know you can't keep your hands off me, I'm going to take full advantage of that. I'll move your shit up here tomorrow if you want."

I giggled. "This pillow talk is so romantic."

His smile lit up his entire face. It was irresistible. "You started with your trying to run away bullshit."

I snuggled into him. "I don't want to go anywhere. So, you've got big plans for tonight, huh?"

He started playing with my breasts. "Mmm. I know the time change is going to mess you up, so I'll try to behave tonight, but we have absolutely nowhere to be in the morning. This is just a fair warning."

"Well, I have to warn you, I absolutely hate morning sex."

The face that he made was comical, a blend of horror, shock, and maybe some disgust mixed in. "We shall see, Angel. Now, roll over on your other side, so I can see that tattoo you were hiding." His finger swept over my belly button ring, a tiny sparkly flower. "I saw this the first time I saw you naked, but I missed the tattoo."

Sighing, I rolled onto my other side, and he pulled me back against his body right away. I fit so perfectly against him. He rose on his elbow so that he could inspect the tribal lotus flower that I had inked on my right hip.

The only bad thing about this position was that I couldn't see him. "I had it done when I turned 18. I kept it hidden for two years; my parents didn't discover it until I was 20."

"I like it. It's very girly." His fingers tickled my ribs.

I slapped his hands. "Of course it's girly. Should I have gotten a manly tattoo?"

His hands began sweeping along my body. "Hmmm," was his answer. I wiggled my hips backward when I felt something prodding against my butt cheeks.

"I love your ink. Are you getting any more?"

His fingers began teasing my nipples. "I don't know."

Suddenly, I was pretty chatty. "I'm thinking of getting one on the back of my neck, but I wear my hair up a lot at work, so that might be an issue. I'm not sure what I want yet, so I haven't done it yet."

He lifted the hair from my neck and began kissing right where I wanted the tattoo. He was sucking a bit and damn if that didn't turn me on. His hand slid between my legs and began massaging my clit. A bolt of lust flared through my body. I locked my leg up over his to give him better access.

Ryder growled against my neck. "Do you have anything else hiding from me on this gorgeous body, Talia? Do I have to inspect you?"

I was rendered speechless again. I croaked, "Maybe."

His fingers were working magic, so I groaned in frustration when they left me. Ryder rolled me onto my stomach so that I was face down on the mattress and held in place with one hand. I listened as he pulled another condom out of the table and rolled it on. He nudged my legs open so that he could kneel between them.

"Fuck. Your ass is amazing." He slapped it, only hard enough to give a little sting, but the zing of pure lust that shot to my pussy had me gasping.

I felt his cock sliding around my wetness and I tried to raise my hips up to give him better access, but he held me down firmly with his hand on my back. He found my opening and pushed in with one hard thrust. Oh my God, it felt so good that my eyes were rolling back in my head.

This time, our joining wasn't slow and controlled. It was hard and fast. Animalistic. Earth-shattering.

I screamed things.

I came so hard that I saw stars.

Chapter 22

Ryder

THIS GIRL COULD RUIN me. The first thing I ever knew about her — before I knew her name, before I knew her eye color, before I knew one damn thing — was how her pussy tasted. I think from there on; I had a pretty good idea of what she could do to me.

I knew sex would be amazing with her. Still couldn't believe that her ex-boyfriend, Max, claimed she was a bad lay. He must either have a pencil dick or absolutely no game in bed. Fuck him. He'd never be able to keep a girl like Talia satisfied.

Last night, she'd passed out cold after the second time we had sex and I didn't have the heart to wake her. She was probably exhausted with jet lag and all, but I'd been in a constant state of horniness, having her tucked in my arms all night. She'd fallen asleep at midnight and it was 9 o'clock in the morning now, so she had nine solid hours of sleep. That had to be enough, yet she wasn't even stirring.

It took ten torturous minutes to wake her up. Who knew giving her soft kisses and skimming my fingers down her smooth skin would get me so damn spun up?

She popped open one eye. "I feel something poking me. Ugh. I told you I hate morning sex."

Was she serious? I scoffed. "Morning? Jeez, it's afternoon, sleepyhead." So, it wasn't, but it was past noon in Ohio so that counted for something.

"Makes no difference what time it is. It still feels like morning. And morning always feels shitty." She tried to roll away from me, but I stopped her.

I fingered her pink nipple and was pleased to see it pebbling in response. "What do you have against morning sex, anyway? Hell, it's like the best possible way to start the day."

She covered her eyes with her hand. "Ugh. I hate when the sun's shining bright in the morning."

I laughed. "This room faces the ocean. It's pretty dark in here all morning."

"And I look terrible in the morning. My hair's a rat's nest. I never removed my makeup last night ..."

This one was easy. "You look well fucked. Satisfied. Like my dick gave you amazing orgasms. It's my favorite look on you so far."

Her eyebrows rose. "I probably smell."

"I've been breathing you in all morning. You smell like sex and vanilla, and it's driving me absolutely crazy."

Her mouth fell open. "Jeez, Ryder." She turned her head. "What about morning breath? That's gross."

"I won't kiss your mouth." I put my mouth on her breast, gave it a good suck, and then pulled it off with an audible pop.

"I have to pee." She frowned like it was the ultimate deal breaker.

This girl. I smacked her ass, remembering how she'd liked that last night, and said, "You have 2 minutes. Do your thing and then get that sexy ass back in here with me."

She remained motionless, staring at me like I was crazy. I started counting down, "120 seconds, 119, 118 ..."

She squealed and then jumped out of bed. Vaguely covering her tits with her hands, she ran into my bathroom and shut the door. Thank God she didn't have any clothes up here. I was going to keep her naked for as long as I could. While she was in the bathroom, I rolled on a condom. I'd been so fucking hungry for her for hours, I was already seeping.

She came out of the bathroom looking shy. She crossed the room to the sliding doors and looked out. "The view is amazing."

I slipped off the bed and stared at her ass for a moment. "It is."

She didn't move, so I walked over to her. I slipped my arms under hers so that I could cup her breasts from behind. "Angel, how can I convince you to try morning sex with me? I promise it'll feel good."

Her ass pressed back against my straining dick. "You're already halfway there."

My right hand slid to her pussy like it was a fucking homing pigeon coming home to roost. "You want to go out on the deck? You can watch the ocean while I fuck you from behind?"

She laughed. "Well, that sounds like such a romantic offer, but your neighbor ..."

"Fuck that guy," I growled. I'd forgotten about that. "Yeah, I'm sorry that creeper saw us. He's not here all the time, but when he is, he spends a lot of time on his deck. And the asshole doesn't seem to own a shirt."

"Well, it is his deck, Ryder. He should be able to go on it whenever."

She squirmed a bit and slid her hips forward, pushing her pussy into my hand. Still, I kept my strokes slow and leisurely. Fuck, I could strum her all day.

"Forget about that asshole." I didn't want her thinking about that guy. I was sure he'd be considered 'good-looking' from a woman's point of view and his muscles were definitely ripped — I couldn't help but notice, since he strolled around shirtless all the fucking time.

I focused my attention back on the sexy woman in front of me. She was practically purring. I had a feeling she was going to enjoy morning sex from here on out.

My left hand had been idly playing with her tits while my other hand worked between her legs, but then I gave her nipple a pinch. Just like last night, it made her weak in the knees; I was the only thing keeping her upright at this point.

"Ryder, I need you inside me."

"Already, Talia?" I chuckled. I'd been ready for hours now.

A moan slipped out before she could answer. "Yes. Pleeease."

I stepped us back from the sliding door and let go of her pussy. "Get down on your hands and knees."

She looked over her shoulder at me with a frown but still had that hazy, half-fucked look. "The floor is going to wreck my knees."

"Don't worry. You'll be fine. Promise."

She did as I asked and the sight of her on all fours had my cock begging. I spread out her legs with my foot and stepped between them. My finger skimmed down her ass crack before sinking into her glistening pussy.

"Are you ready for me, Angel?"

"Yes." It was an emphatic response.

I wanted to hear her screaming out my name again. I grabbed her securely by the hips and then hoisted them up toward my straining cock.

She squeaked in surprise, flailing her legs, but I had an ironclad hold on her.

"Wrap your legs around my waist."

"You're going to fuck me upside-down?" Her forearms were still on the ground, and she was awkwardly trying to hook her legs around me.

"Just your hands on the floor like you're going to do some pushups." She wiggled around and I groaned at the sight. "You should see your pussy right now." I wanted to bury my face in there.

I had to slide her down a bit to line up my cock and put the tip in. God, I was already sinking in; she was so wet. Using my arms to pull her hips back, I thrust in deep. Fuck, she felt so good squeezing my cock inside her like a silken clamp.

I pumped a few more times. She was already crying out to God. I knew I was probably hitting her G-spot in this position, which was good because I couldn't do this for long. It was murder on the arms, but it was way better than any arm workout at the gym.

I was pounding into her pretty fiercely. That shit felt so good that I wasn't even thinking about my burning arms. With my next thrust, I realized she was already coming, and it was fantastic. Her heels were digging into my lower back, and her ass was jiggling like crazy. Fuck, I could watch this all day. I filed the wickedly erotic sight to memory.

She was crying out, and her arms were collapsing, but I kept going full speed. Fuck, I felt like I was taking more than I had a right to take, but I couldn't hold back. I was a greedy fucker when it came to this girl. A few more pumps and I blew like a champ. I stood motionless for a few moments, relishing the feeling of her thighs trembling around me, her soft mewling noises as she came down, and her musky scent in the air. I felt sated. Connected. Completed.

But my arms were about to give out. My legs, too. I had to get my upside-down girl off my dick before I dropped her on her face.

The dismount was messy between my weak muscles and her flailing limbs. She remained on my floor, unmoving, while I went into the bathroom to deal with the condom. When I returned, I gave her my hand to help her up and led her back to my bed, where we both collapsed.

Neither of us moved for a couple of minutes. I actually thought I might fall back asleep when I heard her stomach grumble. "Are you hungry?"

"Starving. I can't believe I slept so late."

I chuckled guiltily. "It's only 9:30 ... California time." I gave her a quick kiss. "I'll go make breakfast. Eggs and bacon? Pancakes? Coffee? What do you eat?"

She rolled onto her back. "Usually nothing, but I think I could eat it all right now."

I forced myself out of bed, loving the way her eyes drank me in as I pulled on some clothes. "I'll make it all. I want to keep your stamina up."

I dug around in my drawer until I found a Ghost Parker tour T-shirt. I pulled it out and then tossed it to her. "You can wear this. Remind me to bring up your suitcase later. There's a new toothbrush in the bathroom cabinet you can use."

I left her to some privacy and went in search of my phone. It was still out on the deck from last night. I scanned through my messages and saw one from Talia's roommate.

> **ELLIE:** Talia didn't text that she arrived safely and she's not answering my texts. I'm just going to assume that's because you haven't let her up for air yet?

I fired off a quick reply:

ME: Safe assumption. I'll have her text you.

I flipped on the radio and then began preparing breakfast. When Talia came out of my bedroom in my T-shirt, I froze. She'd tamed her hair and washed her face, but she still looked sexily defiled. She'd knotted the large T-shirt on the side so that it ended near her belly button, showing off her skimpy panties and long, long legs. Fuck, was I getting hard again?

She strolled over to the counter stools. "I like the T-shirt."

It was a black T-shirt with a negative image of the cover art from our first album, one of the promo photos of the five of us standing together in an arc looking down. We looked ghostly already in negative, but the designer had carefully added wisps of smoke to enhance the effect. The back of the shirt listed dates and cities from our tour on it.

Some fans noticed that with the negative image, a strange dark shadow, shaped like a person, showed up in the image. Rumor had it that the shadow was an old band member who died. Before we had a clue about the rumors, a reporter asked Ghost about it in an interview. The look Ghost gave was so strange, and his actual answer to the question was so convoluted that the rumors only grew. Our band was told to ignore all questions regarding it because merchandise sales went absolutely through the roof after that.

"It looks good on you. You can have it."

She got quiet after that, and I wondered if I'd said the wrong thing, but by the end of breakfast, she was back to her normal self.

"I thought we'd take a walk on the beach before it gets too crowded?" I asked.

She sat up straight. "Ooh. I'd love that."

I got up and grabbed her empty plate. "I'll clean up while you get changed." Please tell me she had a scandalously tiny bikini.

She hopped off the counter stool. "I'll go downstairs. I want to jump in the shower and I need my stuff."

"You don't need to shower. You'll get full of sand at the beach, anyway."

Her brow creased. "But I feel dirty."

I was stacking the plates in the dishwasher. "That will just make me more eager to dirty you up again."

She bit her lip as a blush stole over her face, then she laughed. "If you want me to get into a bikini, I'm going to need a shower."

Yes, I definitely wanted to see her in a bikini. "Okay, but you don't want to use either of the showers down there, trust me. I'll go get your bag and bring it up."

She nodded. "Your shower looks heavenly. But promise to give me space to do all my girly stuff."

"Can I watch?" I grinned.

She drew in a breath. "Hell no."

I finished cleaning up and changed into my swimsuit while she was showering. She'd figured out how to turn on the music in the shower and cranked it up. She really couldn't carry a tune to save her life, and I couldn't help but laugh when she mangled the words to nearly every song that came on. Jesus.

I waited on the deck for her to finish whatever she was doing. The jackass neighbor was on his deck when I walked out on mine. For the first time, I saw him with a shirt on. I gave him an angry scowl, and he retreated into his house. Good.

When Talia came out to find me, I seriously had to stop myself from dragging her back into the bedroom. Fuck, my angel looked like sin.

She was in a bikini, not obscenely tiny, but plenty of luscious skin was showing. The fabric was that heavy material stuff that looks like it's knit together and has a bunch of holes in it. Shit, I don't know what it's called. Under her tits, the wide band was made of the same material shaped into a bunch of tiny flowers that linked in a chain. The material was almost the same color as her skin and had a lining under it, thank God, but shit if I didn't think I could see her areola showing through the tiny holes, regardless. The bottom was a strip of the same fabric that joined at both hips, with two ties that hung down on each side. Fuck, those sashes tempted me like a ripcord — only one pull to yank those bottoms down and free fall into nothing.

She looked like a total babe. Her tits weren't huge, but they were a perfect handful and her stomach was toned. Her belly ring sparkled in the sunlight and her flower tattoo gave her a naughty edge. She'd braided her blonde hair into two braids that reminded me of the Swiss Miss chocolate girl. A very naughty Swiss Miss.

I was surprised my mouth was still working. "Do you need some help with sunscreen?"

"Yes, I'd probably burn like crazy if I didn't. I've already lost most of my summer tan." She handed me a bottle of sunscreen that she'd been holding.

Damn, it was the spray kind; I was hoping to rub my hands all over her. It was probably a good thing or we might never leave. After I sprayed her down thoroughly, she flipped a pair of mirrored aviators down over her eyes and then we headed together toward the beach. We walked hand in hand along the surf for quite a while.

This was the first time she'd ever seen the Pacific. She seemed embarrassed to admit that she'd only seen an ocean a handful of times: twice as a young girl on family vacations to Florida and on a trip to Jamaica as an adult.

I told her that my family didn't go on family vacations as a kid unless I counted the once-a-year day trip to the amusement park. I hadn't seen the ocean until I went to college in Georgia.

She was nearly skipping at my side. "You're so lucky to live here. The weather is perfect and you wake up to the sound of the surf every day! And your house is really nice. I was doubtful when we first drove up to it, but you've done such a great job with it. You could use a decorator, though."

I smiled at her assessment. "Yeah, the street-facing sides of the houses are all horrible. You should have seen the place when I first bought it, though. It was a complete dump. I actually got lucky, otherwise, I'd never have been able to afford it."

We stopped to watch a few kiteboarders, and I told her about Tommy's recent efforts to teach me. As we watched the boarders, she took tiny steps into the surf. She surprised me when she said she wanted to go all the way into the water. It was cold. Icy cold. Normally, I never would have gone in at this temperature without a wetsuit on. We got up to our waists before she ran out of the water, screaming. Her lips were looking purple, but she was laughing.

We trudged back to my house. I was almost sad to see the skimpy bikini go as I stripped it off her in front of the shower as the water heated. We stepped under the water when it was warm enough, and I very thoroughly made sure every last grain of sand was washed clean. I unbraided her hair and then washed it with the girly shampoos she'd left in there.

That was about all the restraint I could muster. Between her soapy hands running all over my body, her tight nipples brushing against my chest, and the way her kisses drove all other thoughts from my mind, I had her back up against the tiles in no time.

I broke our kiss. "I have to get a condom."

She had other ideas. Her nails raked into my skin as she slid down to her knees. She took my length in her mouth and went straight to work, bobbing up and down on my cock and fondling my balls just the right amount. But with those lips, she wasn't fooling around or being dainty.

I allowed myself to enjoy the view and within minutes, I had to let her know I was going to come. Fuck, she was giving me puppy-dog eyes while her lips wrapped around my cock. Spank bank deposit.

I wondered if she'd pull off my dick because I knew for sure she'd swallowed the first night I'd met her. As soon as I started spurting, she withdrew her mouth. Her hands squeezed around my dick, milking me while my cum painted her breasts. Ahh, she was so sexy.

When I reached down to help her up, I smeared my cum over her breasts with my fingers. She pressed herself against me, tilting her head up for a kiss, and I obliged.

When the hot water ran out, I couldn't keep her trapped with me any longer. After we dressed, we had a late lunch on the deck, and then she convinced me to take a nap before the party tonight. I never slept during the day and the thought of a nap appealed as much as fingernails scraping a chalkboard. I was planning on waiting until she fell asleep and then sneaking off to the deck to play my guitar.

It turned out that Talia's idea of a nap differed from mine. I thought she would never fall asleep, because she was antsy as fuck. Cuddling next to her was like torture because her every movement was turning me on. Her legs kept sliding between mine, her boobs kept brushing against me, and her hand was too damn close to my cock to ignore. I was getting hard and frustrated, and she didn't even seem close to falling asleep.

When she wiggled again, her ass pushing back into my cock, I could have sworn I heard a soft, smothered laugh. Was she messing with me?

The next time she squirmed, her hand creeping along my thigh, I rolled us both, so that I had her trapped beneath my body in under a second. I captured both her hands and pulled them over her head, pinning her with one hand. My free hand took care of her shorts and panties. Suddenly, she wasn't squirming much anymore.

I proceeded to torture her endlessly, first with my fingers, and then, when I could no longer hold out, with my tongue. I withheld an orgasm from her, keeping her on edge for so long I thought she was going to start speaking in tongues. After way too long, when she was shamelessly begging, I finally made her come so I could chase my own release.

We were both depleted. I couldn't remember a more perfect day. I didn't want it to end. If the party were for anyone but Tommy, I'd skip it with no hesitation and see if I could wring another orgasm from Talia. She was addicting. Dangerous.

We were lying in bed, my finger drifting up and down her shoulder. She'd been talking about the party. "I've never been to a rock star party before. Is it all just going to dissolve into a giant orgy at the end of the night?"

"It's at a fancy restaurant, so I think you're safe." With this crowd, I couldn't be so sure, but I kept that to myself.

When Talia remained silent, my mind drifted back to a few parties that had been notoriously out of control. Drugs, like Ecstasy, willing groupies, and horny guys were a lethal combination that had resulted in what boiled down to wild orgies.

It was gut-check time when I tried to place Talia in that scene. No way did I want to share her with anyone, but I had no claim on her. She wasn't my girlfriend.

"Unless that's on your bucket list or something?"

She shrugged. What the hell was that supposed to mean?

"How rock star is this party going to be?"

Fuck, did she want to participate in an orgy? "It's just going to be a regular party, Talia."

She curled into me, pressing that sweet pussy against my thigh. "But what should I wear? What do the other girls wear?"

Most of them wore dresses that would make a hooker blush. "Dresses."

"Short dresses, no panties, and fuck-me heels?" she asked, so innocently.

"Uh ... something like that." Dammit, was that what she was planning on wearing? I'd be a mess all night.

"On a scale of 1 to 10, how rock star should I go?" She was smiling so sweetly at me.

Fuck. "I'd say about a 4. Maybe a 3, tops."

Her fingers were tracing the tattoo on my chest. "Just a 4? Okay. I guess I'll wear the pants then."

Pants? Fuck, yes. Pants are good. I sighed with relief. "Sounds good."

I tried to pull her in for a naughty tongue-lashing for getting me so worked up about orgies and shit, but she pulled away.

"If you want to make it to the party, let me get ready now."

I was out on the deck playing my guitar when she was finally ready to leave. After I had gotten dressed, she'd taken over my room to get ready, so I hadn't seen her since she'd slipped into my shower and began shouting out the wrong lyrics to the songs that were playing.

"I'm ready." She stepped out onto the deck.

My mouth fell so far open that I thought my jaw unhinged. Oh fuck. Tonight was going to suck. She was going to attract so much attention in that outfit. All the guys would want to fuck her, including my friends, who were a bunch of assholes that knew no boundaries.

And I'm pretty sure most of the girls would hate her because she'd steal the spotlight from them, even if they were wearing their tiniest dresses.

What the fuck was she wearing? She was wearing pants, but like no pants I've ever seen before. They looked painted on her — black, but with a shine — maybe faux leather? Sounds simple, but they had shit all over them: black leather straps, hooks and buckles, silver studs everywhere, metallic red patches with black fishnet overlays. They were completely badass.

Of course, she wore killer black heels and a shiny silver tank top with millions of crisscrossing straps that showed off some cleavage and a dangling belly ring. Her hair was mostly down but had dozens of tiny braids weaved throughout, which somehow perfectly fit the look. I'd never seen her makeup so heavy, but it was stunning. She even somehow pulled off a glittery pink eye shadow.

I seriously considered not going to the party.

"You look nice." She was looking me over.

Holy shit, I was going to have to stop staring and speak at some point. "Angel, I told you to go 4 on your rock and roll scale and you strolled out here a smoking-hot 10."

A smile lit up her face; she was pleased with my compliment.

"I'm not going to leave your side all night." I groaned. "Guys will be all over you."

She laughed. "You'll survive."

I'd never felt so possessive of a girl before. Like I said, it was going to suck. I picked up my phone and canceled the car. I'd rather drive.

The first sign of any orgy-like behavior at this party, and we were so out of there.

Chapter 23

Talia

WE WERE HURTLING, 70MPH, toward the party I no longer wanted to go to. I felt like an imposter sitting in this ridiculous outfit. The pants were from a Halloween costume, for goodness' sake. Why did I let Ellie talk me into wearing them?

I'd bought the crazy-assed homemade pants years ago from some woman on Etsy. They were a shiny spandex material, so they were comfy, but they were skintight and, well, weird. They had crap all over them. I'd worn them with combat boots, a Victorian-looking jacket, and a few accessories to make up a steampunk costume. People loved my costume, but that was for Halloween. Now, I was actually wearing the crazy pants to a real party on not-Halloween.

Not just any party, but a party with a bunch of famous people — rock stars. A party for the drummer of Cold Fusion. A veritable rock god, Tyler Matthews, might even be there. My stomach was churning.

A lot of Ryder's friends would be there. Judging me. Would they discover what an imposter I was? Would Ryder realize it? Everything had been perfect until now. I loved being with Ryder. In my eyes, he shined like a thousand suns. I'd been a little nervous that I could keep up with a rock star in the bedroom, but it had been no problem because I physically craved being with him. He worked my body like I'd never felt before; I'd lost count of the number of orgasms I had in the last 24 hours. Outside of the bedroom, being with him was fun. Exciting. Intoxicating.

I was hopelessly infatuated with him. Let's face it — it was much more than that, but I wasn't ready to admit it to myself yet. The stakes were too high.

Ryder squeezed my hand reassuringly like he could read my tumultuous thoughts.

The scenery was absolutely gorgeous, but I barely noticed it. I chewed at my lip and worked myself into a nervous tizzy.

"You okay?" Ryder glanced my way.

"I'm great," I lied. "So excited!"

By the time we got to the place, I felt like I might puke. Ryder got out of the truck and circled around to my side, opening my door.

I held back. "We're kind of late. What if Tommy sees us walking in and it ruins the surprise?"

Ryder held out his hand to me. "We're not that late and we're not going to ruin the surprise. Let's go."

It was a lame attempt, but I had to try. I swallowed down my nausea. Damn, I hoped like hell I didn't puke on anyone.

Someone, obviously an old friend, spoke to Ryder as we walked in, but he didn't introduce me, so I kept quiet. I was already invisible. A hostess pointed us toward a terrace out back, but Ryder was already leading us forward. We stepped into a party already in full swing on the terrace.

It was loud. People were having a good time. So far, no one was swinging from the proverbial chandeliers. No one was naked, although some of the women were close enough. But overall, I could handle this.

I snagged a passing champagne flute from a waiter's tray and chugged it down. Ryder cocked an eyebrow and smiled, but didn't comment.

We were only a few feet into the party when we were met with the welcoming committee. Rather, Ryder was met. Women broke off from their conversations and gravitated our way. At least four women had seen his arrival and were incoming. I felt my thin scrap of fake confidence slip.

He put his arm around my waist and pulled me close to his side. I could see the calculating glances of the ladies as they approached. They were looking at my outfit. Seeing his hand splayed on my hip. Sizing me up.

Two gave up right away. After they greeted Ryder with kisses to the cheek, which he returned, dammit, they slinked away to greener pastures. He'd introduced me to them, but I wasn't even listening to their names.

The third woman was named Candie, I think. Ugh. She had mounds of cleavage, a nice curvy body, and giggled a lot. She kept touching Ryder's arm and leaning in close to him. Double ugh.

The fourth woman who showed up was a brunette. I didn't think she was that hot, but she was definitely putting up her A-game. Lots of 'Ryder, do you remember when …' comments. They had some kind of history.

Did I mention that not one girl in the whole place was wearing pants? Ellie was so dead. Making me wear steampunk pants to a rock star party. What the hell?

These women were getting on my nerves. They needed to slither off to somewhere else, to someone else. Candie wagged her tits under Ryder's nose again and I snapped.

I slid my hand up Ryder's chest. Slowly. Possessively. "Would you get me a drink, lover?"

Yes, I just called him lover. It was okay. It was all in the enunciation.

Ryder's lips twitched at the corners like he was trying not to laugh, but then he turned his killer smile on me and I had to remember to inhale. "What would you like?"

"You know what I like." I winked suggestively.

Yes, I winked. Ugh. That may have been a tad too much.

Luckily, Ryder didn't laugh in my face. "I'll be right back, Sexy Pants." He smacked my ass as he walked away.

Sexy Pants, hmmm. Let's not mention my pants. As soon as Ryder left, Candie got bored and peeled away. One more to go.

The brunette looked me over. "What was your name again?"

"Talia."

Her eyes lingered on my pants. She sniffed. "I haven't—"

A woman that looked like she just stepped out of a shampoo commercial interrupted us. I definitely had hair envy. She had luscious, loose-flowing curls of a deep auburn color with some lighter highlights that hung down her back in waves. I sighed. Another gorgeous woman in a tiny dress I'd have to contend with.

When she turned her blue eyes to me, they sparkled with mischief. That's when I recognized her; she was the woman in the pictures with Ryder. Tommy's wife. She was even more beautiful in person.

She turned to the brunette. "Marie, I think I just saw Tyler come in."

Marie's head began scanning the crowd. "Ohhh." She began mumbling something and drifted away from us.

The ball of energy next to me chuckled. "Are you Talia?"

"Yes, that's me."

"I thought so!" She smiled, showing off her perfect, white teeth. "I've heard so much about you. I'm Livvy Erikson."

She seemed friendly so I finally relaxed a bit. "It's nice to meet you. Thank you for inviting me tonight."

"No problem. I'm so glad you could come." She took a sip of her drink.

I scanned the room and saw a mob of people near the bar where Ryder had headed. I was pretty sure I could see Tommy in the middle of the crowd. "Was Tommy surprised?"

"Nah." She waved her hand. "I folded like a cheap suit as soon as he got me alone after the whole fiasco. Don't tell anyone, though. He pretended to be surprised."

"I heard a bit about what happened from Ryder."

She snorted, and then words poured from her. "Yeah, I spent a night of hell trapped in a dungeon with your boyfriend. It was as cold as the darkest pits of hell, if hell was like, you know, cold. There were bugs, spiders, rats — I think — and I was hungry the whole time because I skipped lunch. We ended up drinking wine, lots of it, and that ended up being a big problem. I recommend never trying to pee into a wine bottle; it's really difficult."

I chuckled. "Huh, he never mentioned those ... details."

"Yeah, Ryder made a whole fort out of cardboard to protect me from the slithery things. It was so sweet. But he spent the entire night talking about you. And he is absolutely crazy about you! Let me tell you, I am the expert on crazy, so I know." Livvy was talking a mile a minute. "I found out everything about how you two met — I dragged it out of him, so don't be mad at him. I could tell that you and I could be great friends after hearing that story."

"He told you about Operation Limp Dick?" I bit my lip.

"What?" Her eyes bugged out. "Operation what now?"

"Shhh," I shushed her and then whispered. "That's what my roommate and I called it. Ugh, please don't tell Ryder that. The whole thing was supposed to be a surprise fantasy for my boyfriend, ex-boyfriend now, but it kind of went all wrong."

"Hmmm. Lucky Ryder." She smirked.

"Lucky me," I replied with a grin.

"Yes, you are lucky. Ryder's a keeper. You're lucky I have my Tommy or I'd fight you for him." She laughed, "I'm just kidding. He's a good friend of Tommy's and now of mine, too. And I hope you and I can become good friends." She paused for a moment and then added, "And since he is my friend, I just want to say — don't break his heart, Talia. He's one of the good ones."

The only heart on the line right now was my own. I'd hardly even admitted that to myself, so I definitely would not tell Livvy.

My eyebrows knitted. "We're just—"

Luckily, I didn't have to finish my thought, because Ryder returned with my drink, an Alabama Slammer. He greeted Livvy with a hug and said, "I see you've met Talia?"

Livvy winked at me. "Yes, we were just having a very interesting conversation."

"Oh, really?" Ryder looked intrigued.

Thankfully, Livvy made the motion that she was zipping her lips closed. I really did not want to explain to Ryder why Ellie and I called it Operation Limp Dick. How embarrassing!

I took a large sip of my drink to avoid replying. Just then, two guys joined our group. I recognized them from my internet stalking days. They were members of Ghost Parker, but I acted cool. Pretty darn chill, in fact. On the inside, I was freaking out.

One of the guys in the band, Sid, sidled up to my right side, getting between Ryder and me, and the other pressed in on my other side. They were slowly crowding my personal space, but they were Ryder's friends, so I ignored it.

Sid was in the middle of saying something to Ryder when Ryder's eyes narrowed. The two guys on either side of me were getting uncomfortably close to me, rubbing up against me, and trapping me between them.

Ryder stepped around Sid and grabbed my hand, pulling me toward him. "You two fuckers are not going to sandwich my girl. Christ, I'm standing right here! Go find someone else. Keep your hands off Talia, assholes."

Ryder was practically growling, but his friends and Livvy were laughing at his pissed-off expression. I thought his jealous possessiveness was kind of hot. Plus, he'd just called me his girl.

While they were laughing, he turned to me. "These two jokers are part of Ghost Parker." He pointed to the dark-haired guy. "This is Bash. He's our drummer. And this jackass" — he clapped his hand on Sid's shoulder— "is Sid. He's our bassist."

They were saying hi to me and Livvy, who they obviously knew when Tommy came over. After Livvy introduced me to her husband, he started teasing Ryder about something. The group grew as a few more people joined in, including the guy I recognized as Ghost Parker's lead guitarist, Knox. These rock guys were all so intimidatingly hot in their own ways; it left me tongue-tied.

If I wasn't already star-struck with this crowd, Tyler Matthews strolled over with someone that had to be his wife, another glamorous chick. I heard Livvy greet Tyler as 'Cockblocker' under her breath and Tyler just flashed his killer panty-melting smile in return. Livvy hugged

Tyler's wife and then introduced me to her.

Our circle was growing, and everyone was talking and joking with each other. I was getting dizzy with all the introductions. I knew everyone wasn't coming over to meet me, but they were congregating for some reason. A few more people piled into our group. Everyone was talking over each other and I had trouble following any of the conversations, but Ryder kept me tucked close by his side. It felt good.

I was listening to Livvy and Tyler bicker when a procession of waiters marched into our circle. Three men in tuxedos shirts lined up behind an older man dressed to the nines, who had stopped right in front of Ryder. Suddenly, our boisterous group grew suspiciously quiet.

"Mr. Mathis," the older man addressed Ryder, then bowed his head slightly. "My name is George Van Keulen. I am the sommelier here at The Tides."

Ryder shifted his stance nervously.

The man continued, "I have been told that you are a wine connoisseur of the highest caliber. I have selected my finest bottles to present to you for your inspection and selection."

Ryder's hand tightened on my waist. "Uh ..."

A waiter stepped forward and presented a bottle of wine to Ryder, holding it in his white-gloved hands and turning the label forward.

The sommelier gestured to the bottle like a game show hostess. "The first is a red Bordeaux — the 1990 Latour. I'm sure you would appreciate the fruity bouquet with subtle woody undertones that contributes to the bold, full-mouth feel. It beautifully provides a rich and decadent palate."

The waiter holding the bottle of red wine stepped back and the next waiter stepped forward, holding a bottle of white wine out for inspection.

"Next, we have a 2010 Coche Dury Meursault Les Rougeots A.C. A white burgundy with a near-perfect mix of floral blossoms and fresh orchard fruits with a finish that lasts a near eternity for maximum satisfaction."

I felt Ryder's fingers digging into my side as the last man stepped forward with his bottle of wine.

The sommelier rubbed his hands together. "Ah, the pièce de résistance. This is our finest bottle of yellow. It was bottled right here in our humble establishment. This is our most acidic and perhaps our most flamboyant choice. A complex taste for only the most sophisticated of men, such as yourself."

I had no clue what was going on, but Ryder's face had turned bright red. When the sommelier finished presenting the wines, the entire crowd started laughing hysterically. Even the sommelier was wiping tears from his eyes; he was laughing so hard.

Ryder chuckled somewhat reluctantly. "Fuck off, all of you."

Tommy clapped him on the back. "I warned you, bro. Stay away from the Crazy."

"Not only is she crazy, but she's got a big mouth." Ryder stared accusingly at Livvy, who just kept laughing harder.

♫♫♪♪♪

A couple of hours later, I was pleasantly buzzed and having a good time. I'd gotten to know Livvy and Katie, Tyler's wife, pretty well and they were refreshingly normal — not pretentious or fake, as I'd feared everyone here would be. Ryder kept checking in with me but was giving me space to meet people and hang out. I was pretty proud of myself. I wasn't clinging to Ryder, and I was having fun.

For the most part, for a rock star party, this was mild. I'd seen a few people having sex in the back halls near the bathrooms and I'd definitely seen some drug use, but that had also been fairly discreet. There had been some dancing on chairs (the tables were too small), but that had been in the back corner where some girl looked like she was stripping. I stayed away from that area.

I had wandered away from the girls who had taken me under their wing, thinking I'd check out more of the party. Actually, I wanted to see where Ryder had gone; I hadn't seen him in a while. I was milling about when a girl I hadn't met approached me.

She was one of those girls with perfect bone structure, stunning features, and flawless skin with a model's willowy frame.

She held out a shot glass that matched the one in her hand.

I took the glass. "What is it?"

"Liquid cocaine."

My eyes widened in surprise. "What?"

She smirked. "That's just the name of the shot. It's strong though."

"I can handle it." I stuck out my chin.

We clinked glasses and then threw back the shot. Oh hey, it was pretty good.

"You're here with Ryder, right?" She was checking out my pants. The freaking things had been attracting a lot of attention all night.

"Yep. I'm Talia. Thanks for the shot."

"I'm Kaylie, but everyone here knows me as Bash's little sister, AKA, off-limits." Her lips turned down in a frown.

"Oh."

She nodded. "Yeah. It sucks."

Some guy was calling her from across the terrace, but she ignored him. "So, I heard Ryder had a girlfriend, but I couldn't believe it. Now that I see you, I can see why he digs you. I mean, look at that amazing outfit you're rocking. You stand out. Damn, I knew no one would notice me in this stupid dress."

Her dress was fantastic. Dramatic, even. It was a halter dress, completely backless with a plunging neckline. It was very sexy; however, the salmon color didn't work very well with her skin tone and her lipstick shade was way off. The salmon color washed her out too much.

Her shoulders slumped a bit. "You're pursing your lips. The dress doesn't work, does it?"

"It's a beautiful dress!" I denied.

Kaylie shrugged. "I'm terrible with fashion. I'm an actress. Well, just barely an actress. A starving actress, I'll say. When I get work, I don't have to worry about wardrobe or makeup, because that's all done for me. But let me loose on my own, and I'm a disaster."

I looked her over more critically. "You just need to learn what works best with what you've got. Body shape, skin tones — all that stuff is important. You're naturally beautiful — you'd be super easy to style."

"Wait!" She was grinning like she'd just won an Academy Award. "You're a stylist?"

"No. I've just taught myself because I'm interested. I've always loved messing with clothes and hair and makeup. My roommate calls me a chameleon because I like to change my look all the time."

I scanned the terrace and finally found Ryder near the bar. He was talking to Knox, but the brunette woman from earlier was all over him. Touching him. Practically dry-humping him. He wasn't paying any attention to her, but he wasn't pushing her away, either. Gah.

Kaylie followed my gaze. "Marie's relentless in her pursuit. But don't worry, Ryder isn't interested in her."

"Do they have some kind of history?" I asked.

Over in the rowdy corner of the party, some guy was getting a blowjob. Right out in the open. Things were getting a bit more obnoxious as the night wore on.

"Specifically, no," Kaylie answered. "But I bet she's slept with all the guys in the band. She's been around for years. She's just a groupie."

I wrinkled my nose in disgust. "Yuck."

Kaylie shrugged. "Go stake your claim if it's bothering you."

"I don't have a claim to stake. Ryder and I haven't labeled our relationship. I'm just visiting him; I'll go back to Ohio in a few days and that will most likely be the end of it." I tried to sound nonchalant about it. This was Bash's sister, after all. Whatever I said might get back to Ryder.

"Shit, you're just visiting? I thought you lived here!" She looked horrified. Her facial expressions were exaggerated, probably a byproduct of being an actress. "That's awful!"

I shrugged. I had friends back in Ohio, my family, a great job, and my best friend, Ellie, but suddenly it all seemed so dull. Maybe coming to California had been a bad idea. You didn't miss what you didn't know and all that.

"What are you doing while the boys are at practice this week?"

Without a car, I didn't have many options. "I don't know. Hang at the beach, maybe walk around the city one day?"

Kaylie pulled out her phone. "Give me your number. I'll text you mine. I live about 10 minutes from their rehearsal space. I can show you around the city. There's not much that's exciting. I can show you the Walk of Fame, but it's pretty boring. We can do a studio tour if you'd prefer."

"I would love that. Are you free Monday morning?" I gave her my phone number.

She was putting my phone number into her contacts. "Wait! I have a better idea. Have you ever been to Rodeo Drive? We could go shopping. I need to get an outfit for this event that I seriously need to be noticed at. We'll pretend you're my personal stylist at the shops. We'll get preferential treatment. God, I'd love to see those sales snobs falling all over us."

I loved her enthusiasm, but I was no actress. "I'm not sure I could pull it off. And, I love shopping, but I have to warn you I know absolutely nothing about designer labels."

She shook off my concern. "But you know about clothes and what looks good. I can't get over that outfit you're wearing. Every guy here wants to fuck you and all the women are jealous. That's what I need for this party I have to go to. There will be lots of important people there, casting directors and producers. Also, lots of competition. I'm sneaking in through a friend at the catering company. Opportunities like this don't come around that often. I can't blow it. I have to be noticed."

I would love to see Rodeo Drive, and I was sure Ryder wasn't planning on taking me there, but I didn't want Kaylie to think I was some kind of fashion guru. I was more of a sales-rack guru. "Are you sure you want my help? I don't even know which shops are high-end enough for what you need."

"Don't worry. Anything you buy on Rodeo Drive is fancy enough. I just need advice on what looks good on me. I need a style that isn't a cookie-cutter version of what all the other girls will be wearing. I have to stand out and look absolutely fabulous."

I agreed. "Ok, it sounds like fun. I'd love to see Rodeo Drive and I love to go shopping, especially with other people's money."

She started typing on her phone. "I'll text you my address. Have Ryder drop you off before practice Monday morning. Also, dress nicely. Heels if you can stand it. The sales ladies can be complete snobs and will ignore anyone they don't like. There's a hierarchy to shopping there. Part of it is dressing the part."

"Okay. I have some espadrille wedges with me that don't murder my feet." I glanced over to check on Ryder and my God! "Is she caressing his dick?"

Kaylie followed my gaze. "Huh. It doesn't seem like he even notices. He's definitely not into her if that makes you feel better."

I inhaled sharply. "Not really."

She arched her brow. "You better stop her before she puts her hand down his pants."

"What the hell? You'd think Ryder would have shut that down by now?"

"These guys are used to lots of attention. It doesn't even faze them anymore. It's time to channel your inner bitch and go stake your claim." She gave me a little push towards them.

I strode over to them, ready to unleash hell. Well, maybe not hell. At the very least, I thought I could get rid of Marie.

Ryder's face lit up with a cocky grin when I neared. He shoved at Knox's shoulder. "Twenty bucks. Pay up." He shrugged Marie off him like she was an annoying gnat, and then hooked his arm around me, pulling me against his length. "Hey, Sexy Pants. Glad you could finally join me."

Knox was pulling a twenty-dollar bill out of his wallet. "Aw, you're a wanker, Stroke. I was sure it was a good bet. This sexy pants lass hasn't paid any attention to you all night. Using Marie was not fair. I didn't know your girl was the jealous type."

My mouth fell open. "I'm not jealous."

Both guys laughed like they were humoring me. Knox explained, "He had five minutes to get you over here without talking to you. If you had waited another 20 seconds, I would have won the bet, but once you saw Marie, you hustled right on over. That's real cute, sexy pants lass."

They'd made a juvenile bet and I should be irritated, but Knox calling me Sexy Pants in that Scottish accent was a definite distraction. He probably couldn't remember my name.

I turned to Ryder with narrowed eyes. "So, you were letting Marie paw you to win a bet?"

"Well, I had to do something. You've been ignoring me all night. I was feeling neglected." He pouted out his lip with fake sadness.

Knox looked disgusted. "Ach, that's my cue to leave. I'll leave you to it, then."

He headed off and Ryder shifted me so that I was standing between his legs. "Are you having fun?"

"Yeah, I am. Your friends seem really nice. Livvy and Tommy are so ... normal."

He laughed. "I told you."

I noticed two women watching us, ready to pounce on Ryder the moment I left. "Is it always like this? Women falling all over you and the other guys in the band wherever you go?"

"See, you are jealous." He smirked.

I ignored his comment. "Doesn't it get exhausting?"

He tucked a stray piece of hair behind my ear. "It's easier to just ignore it. It doesn't mean anything to me. The fans, the groupies — it's all meaningless."

Just like when I first saw the internet pictures, it really bothered me, but I guess I wasn't used to it. Kaylie and Livvy certainly seemed more jaded. They took it all in stride.

His legs locked around mine and he was subtly drawing me closer in toward him. Abruptly, his gaze was no longer playful. It was heated. His eyes had darkened. God, when he gave me that look, I just melted. It made me think ... pure sex. And, yeah, I was staring at his lips.

That buzz of awareness that I always felt around him seemed to kick up a notch, or a few hundred notches. I wasn't sure if he wanted to kiss me in front of all his friends, but I was drifting dangerously close to his lips. I couldn't help it.

I was almost too far gone when Ryder's focus shifted from me to directly over my shoulder. He stiffened almost imperceptibly.

I pulled back jerkily like I'd just got caught doing something wrong and turned. Ghost, the only member of the band I hadn't met, was standing there. I didn't even know he was at this party.

He tipped his chin up in greeting. "Hey, Ryder."

"Hey, Ghost. This is Talia."

I mumbled my greeting, as he looked me over thoroughly, up and down. I could see why he was the frontman of the group. He looked just like the pictures I'd seen online: bleached-blond choppy hair, eyebrow and lip piercings, tattoos, and clothes that matched my pants, yet looked way cooler. What the camera couldn't capture, though, was his intensity. It was indescribable. He had the kind of charisma that would have people willingly following him to the pits of hell to drink the poisoned Kool-Aid.

Ghost looked me in the eye, and I had to swallow. The intensity burning in his eyes was uncomfortable. "Kaylie told me you're from Ohio."

"Uh, yeah. I'm visiting Ryder." My answer was dumb, but at least I could speak again.

"That's cool." He turned to Ryder. "Would you mind if I talked to Talia for a few minutes?"

Ryder's head jerked backward a few inches as if he was stunned. He didn't answer right away. "If she doesn't mind?"

Why would Ghost want to talk to me?

"Do you mind? Can we talk?" He addressed me directly.

"Sure." I experienced a mix of fangirling giddiness and tipsy trepidation.

Ghost grabbed my hand and started leading me away. I stumbled slightly behind his long stride, looking back wide-eyed over my shoulder at Ryder. His eyes narrowed and his jaw clenched. Was he pissed? He was staring at our clasped hands as Ghost pulled me away. Well, well, well. He looked jealous.

I didn't have long to gloat, because Ghost was leading me through the crowded party, which was literally parting for us. Everyone was watching. It was like Ghost had a flashing neon sign pointing him out; he was that noticeable.

He led us to the edge of the terrace and then down some steps into the dark grounds beyond the party.

"Uh, where are we going?" I didn't know this guy, and this was definitely on the weird side. I didn't think he was about to accost me, but what the hell?

He kept dragging me forward. "There's a gazebo over here where we can sit."

We reached the gazebo that was lit with fairy lights, and he motioned for me to sit. I sat down and breathed a sigh of relief when he sat across from me and not next to me.

He was pulling something out of his jacket pocket. "Do you want some weed?"

I hadn't smoked pot in years and I wasn't sure Ryder would appreciate me smoking with his bandmate in a dark gazebo. What came out of my mouth; however, was the opposite of what my brain was cautioning. "Okay."

He pulled out a lighter, lit the joint, took a big drag, and then passed it to me. I suppressed a giggle and then took a drag.

He took out his phone. "I wanted to talk to you. Get to know you better."

This was weird. I didn't know what to say to that. I watched as he opened the clock app on his phone and started the stopwatch feature. He was timing something. Our conversation?

He put the phone down on the bench, on the other side of his leg where I couldn't see it, and then looked at me. "So, Talia — what's your middle name?"

"Rose."

He nodded his head. "Talia Rose. I like it."

"Natalia. That's my first name." I passed him the joint.

"Natalia Rose. That's even better." He took a drag.

The silence that followed felt awkward. "So, what's your real name? It's not Ghost? Is it?" I knew it wasn't.

"It's Johnny."

He'd asked me, so I was going to ask him. "What's your middle name?"

He looked surprised at my question. "Geronimo."

"Johnny Geronimo. I like it."

He laughed at the way I copied his words. He took another hit and then passed the joint back to me. "Not even the old ladies know that."

I thought the weed was starting to kick in. "Who are the old ladies?"

"I rent my place from them. It's an apartment in their house. They're cool."

"Oh." I took another drag.

He tilted his head to look at his phone. "So, what are your intentions with Ryder?"

"My intentions?" I think the weed was messing with my head. Or maybe this was just a weird conversation with a weird dude.

He nodded. "Yeah."

"Well, we're just getting to know each other. I don't have any evil plans if that's what you're asking."

"Just looking out for him. Ryder's a good guy."

He held his hand out for the joint and I gave it to him. He smoked some more and then looked at his phone. "Tell me something you've done that even your best friend doesn't know about."

Oh shit. I hated those kinds of questions. I didn't do anything super crazy in my life. Operation Limp Dick came to mind, but Ellie knew all about that. I didn't keep secrets from her.

Then I thought of that one night, and I cringed. "There's a reason I didn't tell her, that's because it was fucking embarrassing."

"Tell me." He was watching me like he really wanted to know. The look in his eyes, all that intensity and emotion, had me squirming. The look was devastating. Dangerous. He was seductive.

"I was 18, and I just moved out on my own — out of my parent's house." The story started bubbling out of me. Jeez. I blamed my loose lips on the pot. "One night, I met this guy at a bar. I really liked him. I'd never had a one-night stand before, or since then, but that night I went back to his place with him."

He blew out a puff of smoke. "What happened?"

I leaned my back against the frame of the gazebo. "We got to his apartment and we started going at it. Ripping off each other's clothes like animals. We were pretty into it when suddenly; a woman came out of the bedroom to join us. I mean, it was just kind of sprung on me. Somehow this hot hook-up turned into a threesome. I was uncomfortable as I fumbled through it, but the more it went on, the more I felt like a third wheel. They started going at each other hard-core. And eventually, I got iced out of it altogether."

I frowned as I remembered that night. "I ended up frantically getting dressed while they fucked. They didn't even notice me leaving. I caught a cab home and never told a soul. It was too damn embarrassing

— like the ultimate 'walk of shame' times a thousand. I felt so damn naïve. Yeah, I've never told anyone about that night. So, there you go."

He passed me the joint. "You shouldn't be embarrassed about that night. They should be."

I cringed. "This hot guy rejected me for another woman right in the middle of sex. It massively bruised my pride."

He peeked at his phone and then rubbed his jaw thoughtfully. "You know, Natalia Rose, sometimes we're forced to play roles in life, roles we never asked for."

"Roles?" My mind raced, as I tried to decipher the cryptic meaning behind his words.

He nodded, his eyes haunted by pain. "Some people, they wear masks — not just on stage, but every day of their lives." His gaze met mine, and I shuddered at the despair swirling within those stormy depths.

"Ghost ... what are you trying to tell me?" My voice trembled as the conversation took a dark turn.

"Let's just say ... there were moments when I felt like a puppet, strung up and controlled by someone else." He clenched his fists, knuckles turning white. "And my stepbrother, well, one day he decided to cut himself free from those strings."

A cold dread settled over me, making it hard to breathe. "What happened to him?" I whispered, afraid of the answer.

"Isn't it obvious?" Ghost stared at the fairy lights, his expression unreadable. "He found a way to end his suffering — the only way he thought possible."

Was he talking about suicide? Anguish clawed at my chest, threatening to tear me apart. But I couldn't let go; I needed to understand what had driven Ghost to this dark place. "And you? Did you ever think about ... ending it?"

"More times than I care to admit." There was a hollow, detached quality to his voice that sent shivers down my spine. "But unlike him, I chose to stay — to face the demons that haunt me."

He took the joint from my fingers and took a long drag before handing it back to me. "I've never seen pants like those before."

My head was spinning with the change of topic and the drastic change in his demeanor. He had a playful smile on his face.

I pulled at a dangling buckle on my stupid pants. "Well, they're one of a kind."

"I like that they're different." He leaned closer. "You shouldn't feel bad about that failed threesome. It might not be your thing. Next time you want to try a threesome, try with two males."

I coughed on my inhale. Was that a proposition? Holy shit.

"Just some advice, but Ryder doesn't like to share. And, neither do you, I think." He leaned back on the bench and pinned me with intense scrutiny.

I didn't even know what to say. Ghost checked his phone again and this time he smiled. He picked it up and reset the stopwatch.

"Is my secret safe with you, Natalia Rose?"

I nodded, but thought to myself 'What secret?' I still wasn't sure what he'd been talking about. "Can I call you Johnny Geronimo?"

He thought about it for a few seconds and then said, "Yes." He pulled lightly on one of my hair braids. "Let's get you back before Ryder kills me."

Chapter 24

Ryder

O NE DAY ON TOUR, I was really hungover on the bus, when I watched this documentary about the famous Russian monk, Rasputin. He rose from being an impoverished peasant in Siberia to wielding significant influence over the entire Russian court. Some said, by exerting his unnatural power over the Tsarina, the Emperor's wife, he ruled all of Russia for a time.

Rasputin literally fucked his way through Russia, acquiring a cult of devotees wherever he went. He was a rock star without the music, long before rock and roll was even a thing. Supposedly, none of the ladies could resist him, but damn, this guy was ugly as fuck.

As I watched this show, it reminded me of Ghost. Imagine all the powers of that Svengali dude, but make him really good-looking. That was Ghost.

When he was on, he shined so bright — on stage and in person. He had it, a real star quality that only the biggest leading legends in rock and roll possessed. When you were under Ghost's spell, it was insane.

I don't know how, but sometimes he turned it off. He could disappear. He'd be in the room with you, but you wouldn't notice. He was a ghost.

But when he'd approached Talia and me earlier, he was on. So fucking on. I saw him coming in hot and I'd let him walk away with my girl. Hand in hand. Into the dark grounds outside the party. What the actual fuck?

I wasn't a jealous guy. I'd never been before, but I was pissed right now. Seething. Every minute they were gone, I freaked out a little more. I guess I didn't actually trust the guy that I'd known for 6 years. My bandmate. The guy I called a friend. Fuuuck.

The fifteen minutes they were gone felt like hours. I hadn't left my spot; my eyes fixed on the exact place where I saw Ghost pull my Angel off the terrace into the darkness. Some chick I vaguely recognized was at my side making some overtly suggestive remarks, but I was barely listening. Sid had stopped by to ask me something, but just laughed and walked away. I'm not sure if I answered or not.

I saw them as soon as they stepped back onto the terrace. Ghost still had her by the hand. They were both laughing. That fucker was so intense, he never laughed, but there he was laughing with Talia.

Everyone noticed them as they walked by. Even the girl at my side finally shut up and watched them approach.

Ghost led her over to me, stopping her right in front of me. "Here you are, Natalia Rose."

Did he just call her Natalia Rose? I swallowed down the jealous anger that sparked in my gut.

He turned to her and said softly, "Remember."

Remember what? Fuck. Why were they still holding hands? Why

was she staring at him like she was star-struck?

I growled, pulling her focus to me, and grabbed her hand from him. She giggled. I stepped into her space, needing contact, and immediately smelled the pot. Ghost got her high? I was about to chew him out, but I looked around. He was gone. Fucking Ghost.

"You're high?" Her pupils were unfocused, and she was giggling again.

"Not high," she denied. "Just ... yeah."

I wrapped my arms around her, pulling her against me. She tilted her head up to look at me. A second didn't even pass before I was claiming those lips. My tongue slipped inside her mouth, tasting the SoCo from her drinks, tasting the pot, tasting her.

She was starting to sag against me, but I didn't let up. My possessive display was intentional; I needed to claim her so that everyone knew she was mine.

She was moaning into my mouth and I knew she could feel how hard my cock was because she kept pressing up against it. I loved the way she responded to me, but this was getting raunchy, and I thought I'd proven my point sufficiently. She was mine.

I broke off the heated kiss and gave her a few minutes to compose herself. It gave me a chance to get my dick under control.

"So, why did Ghost want to talk to you?" I tried to sound casual, but I was desperate to know.

She giggled again. It was kind of cute, but she was so high. "He wanted to know what my intentions with you were."

"What the fuck does that mean?" Was he trying to see if he had a chance with her?

My voice may have been too rough because she frowned. "He was looking out for you. He said you were a good guy."

"And he asked about your intentions?" What the fuck was he doing? "I don't know what's wrong with him. Sorry about that. He can be different. Maybe he's on something. Besides pot."

"I don't think he was. He seemed sober." Now she was defending him.

I tried to relax. "Sober Ghost can be worse."

"He was fine, Ryder. Sweet, in fact. He was looking out for you."

I was skeptical. Ghost and I were friends, but it's not like we were going to trade friendship bracelets. I'd known him for years. I just spent nine months straight with the guy. He was still as much of a mystery to me now as he was when I met him.

"He didn't ... hit on you, did he?" I choked it out. That's what I wanted to know the most.

"Not at all." She was pretty emphatic. "He was just ... intense."

My eyes narrowed. "What do you mean by intense?"

Talia laughed. "I talked to him for literally ten minutes and you're jealous?"

"I'm not jealous," I mumbled. "I just don't know why he's talking to my girl."

She slapped my chest playfully. "C'mon. I need another drink."

I'd been stone-cold sober for over an hour now. I'd driven us here because I wanted to make sure Talia and I could leave whenever we wanted to and get back to my place. I wanted to get her back home so badly, but she was having a great time with my friends. Was I fucking jealous again? See, another reason having a girlfriend sucked.

Tommy stopped over to say goodbye to my brooding ass. Even he and Livvy were ready to leave the party.

He looked over to see what I was watching. "What the fuck are they doing?"

Talia was dancing with a bunch of people. Sid and Bash were surrounding her with their sandwich bullshit, but she was good at hamming it up while dancing. Even Knox was dancing with them.

Talia shouted out 'Hot Lava' and they all started hopping around like some demented version of an Irish step-dancing troupe trapped in a mosh pit.

I cringed at the spectacle. "I don't know, man."

Then she shouted out, 'Quicksand' and they all started shimmying around with their feet planted on the ground. They looked like those giant inflatable tube things that flapped around in the wind in front of car dealerships.

Tommy's eyebrows rose as he watched. "Why aren't you out there dancing with her?"

I scoffed. "Do I look drunk enough to do that shit?"

He slapped me on the back and laughed. "You should at least take a video. It might come in handy someday."

Livvy walked up to us while Talia shouted out, 'Slippery Ice' from the dance floor. "Talia is hysterical. You better nail that shit down, Ryder, or you're going to have some competition."

Her words left me feeling edgy. Sure, I could warn my friends off her, but she was going back to Ohio in days. What then? I couldn't do a long-distance relationship. It just wouldn't work. Fuck, I really hadn't thought this whole thing through.

Tommy laughed. "You should see your face, man. I've never seen you so pussy whipped."

My scowl deepened. "Like you should talk."

Livvy pulled on Tommy's arm. "Let's go. If we leave now, we should have an hour before the sitter has to leave. I've got … plans."

Tommy winked. "Oh shit. When Crazy gets plans …"

Livvy hauled Tommy away, and I was back to watching Talia on the dance floor. I didn't hear what she shouted out, but suddenly they looked like they were all humping each other out there like a pack of rabid rabbits. Fuuuck.

Ghost materialized out of nowhere and edged up to my side. I didn't even know he was still at the party.

He was watching the dancers. "She's a firecracker."

I grunted.

A waitress blocked our view. She stepped directly in front of us. "Um, excuse me ..."

I shifted my focus to her and when I saw her face, I realized this wasn't a waitress moment. This was a fan moment. The only way I could describe it was that she was gushing.

Her eyes bounced between Ghost and me. "I was wondering if I could get both of your autographs? I'm a huge fan and I already got Bash and Knox and Sid's, so if I got you both, I'd just die."

"Sure, babe." Ghost took the black marker from her hand.

She fanned herself like she was about to pass out. "I didn't have any paper, so the guys ..." She unbuttoned a few more buttons from her white shirt and we could see the signatures already across the top of her breasts.

I made an effort not to roll my eyes. Ghost scrawled something on her left tit while she squeaked with excitement and then handed the marker to me. There wasn't a lot of unmarked skin left, so she pulled her bra cup down a bit. I managed an 'R' and then just a bunch of scribble.

When I finished, the waitress put her hand to her mouth. "Thanks so much, guys!"

The waitress moved away, and I saw Talia, five feet away from us, hands on hips, staring bloody murder at me. She'd seen the whole thing, and she was pissed. She'd mentioned this whole signing chicks' tits thing before, and I knew it bothered her, but was I supposed to tell that girl no? Fuck.

Talia marched up to me, eyes blazing. "What the hell, Ryder? Did you just sign that chick's tits?"

I heard a little laugh from Ghost. The fucker.

"She got the whole band to sign. She's a big fan. It made her night." My excuses sounded weak.

"Well, fuck." Talia laughed. "That's okay, then."

I blinked. Hopefully, she was going to let this go.

She stepped away from me and moved straight over to Ghost. She slid her hand down his arm. "Johnny Geronimo."

My hands fisted at my sides and I growled. What the fuck was she doing?

"I'm a big fan of yours," she purred at him. "Can I get your autograph on my tits?"

The fucker had a sly smile on his face like he was enjoying this immensely. "I would love to, Natalia Rose, but I don't have a pen."

He better not touch her. And what was with these cutesy names for each other? I didn't like it.

Her fingers curled around his biceps. "Who needs a pen? You could sign them with your tongue."

Neither of them was paying any attention to me. Good thing, because I was about to explode.

"Oh Ryder," she pulled her phone out of a low pocket on the leg of her sexy pants and handed it to me. "Could you take pictures while he signs my tits with his tongue? I want to post it on all my social media."

Ghost looked over to me and he was full on smirking. The bastard.

I grabbed Talia's hand and tried to pull her away from Ghost, but she wasn't budging. I had to insert my body between them. "Angel, when I get you home, I'm going to spank your naughty ass."

"Whatever for?" She had the innocent look down pat.

I sighed. "You made your point. I get it. You win. Now, can we go home?"

Ghost pushed against my back. I'd almost forgotten he was back there. "Yeah, you better get off my dick, Ryder. It's starting to get ideas."

I stepped Talia and me away from him. Jeez. This fucking night.

Talia pouted out her lower lip. "Sid said they were going to the SkyBar after this."

I shook my head. "That's in the city."

"He said we could crash at his place."

That was a terrible idea. "No fucking way. We're going home." I heard Ghost laughing behind me.

I leaned into her ear and nibbled on her lobe. "We're going home, so I can sign my name"—I kissed down her throat and then brushed my lips over her ear again— "with my tongue" —my tongue licked the shell of her ear— "between your legs."

She moaned and thrust her pussy against my thigh. Her eyes were closed, and she was holding onto me tightly. "Okay. I'm ready to go."

Talia fell asleep the minute I started the truck. Good thing we were going straight home because she was out cold. When I parked the truck in my driveway, I gave her a small nudge. "Angel, we're home."

It took some effort to wake her up. She was cranky as I guided her inside. We got in the door and she unclasped her heels.

"My feet are freaking killing me." She pulled off her shoes and kicked them into the room. We made it halfway up the first set of stairs when she stopped.

She yanked at her earrings. "These things are so heavy. Ugh. Why won't they come off?"

It took me way too much time to pull the incredibly tiny backings off the posts. I handed her the earrings after I'd managed to remove them, but she just put them down on the stairs.

We made it to the second floor when she stopped again. She began hopping around on one foot, wrestling with her pants. I think she was trying to take them off. "Ugh. I hate these Halloween pants. I'm gonna burn them."

Halloween pants? I had no idea what she was talking about. "Everyone loved your sexy pants, Angel."

She sat on the ground and lifted her leg up. "Get them off me."

I thought the pants were going to be difficult to remove, considering they were molded to her body, but they slid right off. She grabbed them from my hand and then threw them on the floor and stomped on them. "Dumb pants."

I took her hand and pulled her behind me as we started heading up the stairs to the third floor. If I had to look at those bare legs and that tiny black thong climbing up the stairs in front of me, we'd never make it upstairs.

We were halfway up when she tugged on my hand. "I hate your shirt, too."

"Really?" I lifted a brow in question. "It's just a plain black shirt. What did it ever do to you?"

She started pulling on it, trying to drag it over my head. "It's blocking my view."

She was struggling so hard to rip it off that I shrugged out of it before she tumbled down the stairs. "Anything else bothering you? How about my pants?"

We made it to the third floor before she removed her own shirt and flung it towards the kitchen with a laugh. She pointed at my feet. "Your shoes."

I stepped out of my shoes. Before I could even straighten up, she launched herself at me. I caught her, my hands grabbing onto her ass as she wrapped her legs around my waist.

"How about my bra? It's in the way." Her hands went around my neck and she was pressing her tits up against my chest.

I started carrying her toward my bedroom. "Can't unhook it. I've got my hands full." I squeezed her ass for good measure.

She shifted her weight to unhook her bra, and I almost dropped her. When she got her bra loose, she twirled it over her head like a lasso before tossing it.

I entered my bedroom and then pulled down the covers before putting her gently on the bed.

She closed her eyes. "Come in here and lie next to me. I want to do something very naughty to you."

My fingers hastily worked to unbuckle my belt and unzip my fly, and in a flash, I'd yanked off my jeans and boxer briefs. I'd been waiting for this moment all night — getting her alone and naked and in my bed. I slipped in beside her and she cuddled up against me like a little kitten.

A grin spread across my face as I planted a kiss on her head. Waited a few minutes. Nudged her arm.

"Angel?"

No response.

"You awake?"

She was out cold.

I readjusted our position to something more comfortable for sleeping and then waited for my dick to calm down before I could fall asleep.

Morning sex was so on the menu.

Chapter 25

Talia

I stretched out on the bed like a lazy cat and couldn't keep the dopey Cheshire grin off my face. I was feeling languorous and fully sated. As Ellie would say, I'd been 'properly fucked'. Ryder had left an hour ago, after another round of amazing morning sex, and I'd laid here daydreaming and fantasizing in a post-coital blissful haze.

Sunday, after Tommy's party, we'd spent the morning in bed. Somehow he'd converted me; I was now a big proponent of morning sex. Having an orgasm before even prying an eye open was extremely addictive. Then, when my eyes would finally blink open and the first thing I would see was Ryder — well, it hooked me deeper than the hardest drug. I was always desperate for another hit.

But, eventually, we got out of bed and had lunch. We took a ferry to Catalina Island, where we had a fun day checking out the sights, zip-lining, and having a romantic dinner outdoors by the water. By the time we got back home, I was dying to rip his clothes off. Let's just say that sex with Ryder at any time of the day was immensely satisfying.

We split up Monday morning while Ryder practiced with his band. He dropped me off at Kaylie's apartment so we could go shopping on Rodeo Drive. We found her the perfect dress for her event, a unique creation that highlighted her attributes and made her shine like the superstar she wanted to be. We also picked up the perfect accessories to complete the outfit and a lipstick shade that was seemingly made for her lips alone.

I couldn't afford to buy anything for myself; the price tags were ridiculous, but I bought a present for Ryder. I found a leather cuff bracelet he could totally rock. It was cool in a bad boy/rock star way and would look sexy on his arm with the tattoos. Even though I choked at the preposterous price tag, Kaylie talked me into getting it, telling me Ryder would love it.

I got it engraved on the inside to personalize it. After much discussion with Kaylie, we decided simple was best. The bracelet would say: 'ALWAYS REMEMBER US' with a heart and then signed 'LOVE, ANGEL'. It'd be ready before we left.

After three hours of hardcore shopping, Kaylie and I had lunch together. She told me a little about her fledgling acting career and her long-term crush on Ghost Parker's bassist, Sid, who also happened to be her brother's best friend and roommate. She lamented that when Sid did occasionally notice her; he considered her like a little sister, which was crazy because she was stunning. I'd observed how often she turned heads as we walked down the streets. Guys in obscenely expensive cars had been checking her out on Rodeo Drive, but she didn't even notice.

What stuck with me the most, though, from that day was when we discussed my penchant and love for shopping. Kaylie had noticed how exuberant I'd become when we were shopping for her. She was so impressed with my 'mad skills' that she said I should make a career out of it. She talked about the opportunities I could find in L.A. doing the thing I loved with a passion. Of course, I laughed it off. I had a career already. Well, I was a secretary in Ohio, but I was good at it, dammit. I already had my working life mapped out, even if it didn't excite me. But like the most persistent earworm, her words were stealthily creeping into my brain and trying to take root. What if I could spend my days doing what I loved, using my innate talent to help other people and getting paid to do it?

Ryder met me after the shopping excursion, and instead of the touristy things he had planned, I asked to spend a quiet day with him at his place. Yeah, I needed another hit. We made dinner together, ate on the deck, and walked the beach hand in hand before I got my fix.

Now, as I lay in his bed, clutching his pillow, enveloping myself in his scent and daydreaming about the amazing time we'd spent together, I was floored by how compatible we were. Sure, I knew those crazy sparks that flew between us were not from an everyday attraction, but the sexual stuff — it was too unbelievable.

We had sex whenever we could sneak it in, and I still wanted more. That Ryder was down to fuck all the time wasn't exactly surprising, but I'd never been so horny in my life. His body was an aphrodisiac. I couldn't even keep track of the mind-blowing orgasms anymore, but I knew I was on the plus side of the oral sex reciprocity scale. He never shied away from it, and he left no doubt about how much he enjoyed having sex with me.

When the amazing sex was mixed in with the intimacy of sleeping together in his bed, being around each other doing normal 'couple things', meeting his friends, and just talking about life, I was doomed. It would make being apart from him even harder. I felt the nervousness that I'd held at bay while we were together creep in and take residence.

We'd both been avoiding the conversation about the future. What did it hold for us? What could it hold? Did we have a relationship? Of course, I wasn't going to leave here without discussing it, but it seemed so daunting and so potentially fraught with landmines that I was too chicken to bring it up. I didn't want to ruin our remaining time together.

The more I thought about it, the more I knew I was so screwed. How could I walk away from this with my heart intact? I couldn't deny it; I was falling for him and I wasn't sure what I meant to him. No matter how scared I was, I needed to talk to him like an adult before I fell any further.

My stomach twisted with doubt. Afraid of thinking about the future too hard, I jumped out of bed. I kept myself busy by taking a long shower and then cooking myself a hearty breakfast in Ryder's incredible kitchen.

I was about to go eat on the deck when I remembered the strange encounter I'd had with Ryder's neighbor the day before. I had been outside, standing by Ryder's truck, waiting while he ran back inside to swap out a guitar he was bringing to his band's songwriting session. A car pulled up in front of the neighbor's house and then a noise brought my eyes swinging to the neighbor's front door, which had just opened.

Two guys appeared in the doorway. One was fully dressed, but the neighbor guy was in black boxer briefs and nothing else. I mentally noted what an impressive body he had, trying hard to keep my tongue from hanging out. It was just an observation. A factoid. Then the cute, dressed guy pulled the neighbor into a close hug. Okay, that didn't necessarily mean anything. But then they started making out. Ohhhh. Well, that meant something. I knew I should turn away, but it was kind of hot.

After the intense kissing ended, the cute guy jogged down to the car that was waiting to pick him up. If my purse hadn't slid off my shoulder right that moment and fallen to the ground with a loud plunk, the neighbor guy would never have seen me there, creeping behind Ryder's truck. He looked right at me and scowled.

"Good morning," I tried to sound casual and keep my eyes away from his underwear.

He remained silent, his face twisted in a grimace, while he slammed the door shut.

The scene played out over and over in my mind — mostly the part where we both stood staring at each other because, at that moment, I experienced a flash of recognition. He looked oddly familiar.

Now that I had some time to myself, I worked the problem over in my head. I recognized him, but I didn't know anyone in Los Angeles.

As I was about to head out to the deck, a light bulb went off in my head. I was in Los Angeles. He must be an actor. Something I watched ...

It came to me in a rush. It was on Ellie's show, the ridiculous prime-time soap opera, *Devious*. The show was about 10 seasons in, but I'd been watching for the last four years that I lived with Ellie. She DVR'd every episode, and I'd become a fan by absorption, although I'd never admit it to her.

Neighbor guy was the character, Colton Grimaldi, the oldest son from the main crime family on the show. On the show, he was the epitome of a bad-boy heartbreaker. Stunned by my epiphany, I put down my breakfast plate and pulled out my phone. A mere minute later, I had his real name. Greyson Durant. I clicked on 'images' to double-check that I had the right guy. Hundreds of pictures of this guy popped up. Photos of him alongside his colleagues were out-shadowed by the dozens of pictures of him with beautiful women — actresses, models, and even some Playboy bunnies.

Whoa. He must be a closeted gay guy. His secret was safe with me, but wait until I told Ellie! She would flip that I'd met him. Well, sort of met him. He had scowled at me, personally!

I was on the deck, internet stalking Greyson, when he stepped onto his own deck, fully dressed this time. We made eye contact. He glowered, obviously unhappy to see me. He was about to turn around and head back inside when I stopped him cold in his tracks.

"I know all about how Serena's identical twin tricked you into getting her pregnant, and then, when your amnesia wore off, how she tried to blackmail you."

His mouth dropped open, then he dragged a hand through his hair as he muttered a string of curses.

His eyes were hard as he glared back at me. "What you saw yesterday …"

I was about to assure him I wouldn't expose his secrets, but then a conniving smile crossed my face. I could be a 'devious' blackmailer too; I'd learned from the best in the business, Colton Grimaldi himself.

Raising an eyebrow, I asked, "Why don't you join me over here for breakfast and we can talk about it?" If he didn't want his secret to get out, he didn't have a choice; he had to deal with me.

He fixed me with the notorious Grimaldi death stare, which I had to admit was pretty intimidating, but I stood my ground.

Seemingly unaffected, I smiled. "I have to unlock the front door. I'll meet you down there."

A few seconds of anxiety ran through me when I opened the door and found no one outside. But a moment later, his front door opened. He grunted something unintelligible when he saw me waiting for him.

At the door, I offered him my hand to shake. "Hi. I'm Talia. Talia Bennett. Come on in."

Greyson entered, quietly taking in the shabby condition of the first floor. He followed me up the stairs to the second floor.

"You should get your money back. Place looks like shit."

I laughed as I led him up to the top floor. "This is my friend's house. I'm just visiting."

When we got up to the main floor, Greyson stopped and took it all in. "I take it back. Wow, knocking down walls and raising the ceiling — it looks totally different in here. Much better."

I headed into the kitchen. "Cheese omelet? With veggies and bacon? That okay?"

He was still checking out the open space. "Sure. Put everything you got on it."

I began whipping up a three-egg omelet. "So, Greyson, I just want you to know that I'd never share anything about your personal life with anyone. Even if you didn't come over, I wouldn't. I'm not like that."

Greyson came over to the kitchen island barstools and sat down. "You can call me Grey. So, you watch *Devious*?"

"My roommate's a huge fan and I've become one by default over the years. I guess it's a guilty pleasure of mine."

He nodded. "I'll sign an autograph for your roommate if you'd like."

I poured the egg mixture into the heated frying pan. "She'd love that!"

"I guard my privacy pretty tightly, so I'm sorry if I seemed rude. I come out to this house when I'm not taping. It gives me a chance to escape the 24/7 paparazzi and the fans."

I frowned. "And here I am bothering you. Sorry, I didn't think about how you must get mobbed wherever you go. I was just so excited when I recognized you."

"Well, I haven't eaten yet today, so the omelet will make up for it." He smiled for the first time, showing off his famous dimples and blindingly white teeth.

I carefully flipped over the omelet. "And nobody recognizes you here?"

"Not as much as in Hollywood. The house isn't under my name, so no one knows I live here. I keep it under wraps. I've been out here for years and so far nobody has bothered me here at my house. I get recognized at a few local restaurants and stores, but everyone's been pretty respectful."

I placed the leftover vegetables that I'd chopped up for my omelet onto the hardening egg layer in the frying pan. I sprinkled on some shredded cheddar cheese and then folded the egg layer in half.

"Well, I won't tell anyone. I promise. Except maybe Ryder, but he understands the need for privacy. He won't give anything away."

Grey rested his elbows on the island. "Ryder's your boyfriend?"

I popped my cold omelet into the microwave to heat it up. "Sort of, I guess. It's complicated." I cringed at my answer. "We met each other in Ohio. We haven't known each other for long, and I'm leaving to head back home in two days. So ... yeah."

"And he left you alone here? Where is he, at work?"

I scooped up Grey's omelet and put it on a plate. "Would you like some orange juice or water?"

"Juice is good," he answered.

I pulled out two glasses and began pouring juice for us. "Ryder's in a band called Ghost Parker. Have you ever heard of them?"

Grey cocked an eyebrow in surprise. "Sounds familiar. I guess that explains why he's always playing the guitar on the deck."

"Yeah. They just got back from a tour with Cold Fusion." I slid the juice glass toward Grey.

"And that explains why he's gone so much. Cold Fusion. Wow, his band must be pretty good." His dimples were showing again.

"Let's eat on the deck. I want to experience as much of the ocean as I can while I'm here." I grabbed my plate and led the way outside.

When we were both seated, Grey said, "He doesn't like me."

"Who, Ryder?"

Grey looked at me and nodded in between bites of his omelet.

I blushed as I remembered how Grey had interrupted us on my first night here. "He wasn't too happy about getting caught out here when I was half naked, but that's not your fault."

"I had no idea you two were out here." A glint of amusement sparkled in Grey's eyes. "I was probably more shocked than you. I'd never seen him with a woman here before. To be honest, I was hoping he was into guys."

My hand flew to my mouth as I tried to hold back a laugh. "Oh my God, is that why you always come out here shirtless?"

Grey started to grumble out a denial, but then said, "Don't tell him. He's going to hate me more."

I speared the last bite of my omelet with my fork. "Actually, he'll probably be relieved that you're gay, especially when I tell him you and I had brunch together."

"I'm not gay. Not really."

"But,"—my eyes flew to his face— "I thought ... I'm sorry. I must have misunderstood."

He put down his fork. "I'm bi. I date both women and men. It's just that I need to keep the dating male side of the equation private. It's important for my career to keep that out of the media."

"Wait, what century is this?" I grimaced in disbelief. "I don't get it. Your fans wouldn't care."

He shrugged like it didn't bother him. "My agent is adamant that this doesn't get out. I need to uphold the illusion that I'm a badass playboy like Colton Grimaldi so that my fans stick with me. Also, it's supposedly important for future roles. I need to maintain my popularity. No rocking the boat."

"I don't see how telling the truth would damage your popularity, but I'm not an expert like your agent. But it must be hard keeping a part of yourself hidden away like a dirty secret. That's got to suck."

He nodded his head in agreement. "It's affected my relationships in the past, but just being a TV star, in general, affects relationships. It's hard, but I'm not about to complain about my life. I'm a lucky bastard. I just have to be discreet."

We ended up talking for another hour. We talked a bit about his acting career, but more about what he liked to do outside of work. I wondered if I might be able to connect Kaylie with Greyson. Maybe he had some contacts that could help her get an acting job. In the end, I didn't mention it, because I didn't want to take advantage of our brand-new friendship.

When Greyson asked me how I met Ryder, I told him all about Operation Limp Dick, minus the actual name of the operation. I didn't think Ryder would mind since he had spilled it all to Livvy in the wine cellar. Grayson seemed very interested in the band, so I told him all about the guys I had met at Tommy's party, including the guys from Cold Fusion.

Before we parted, I invited Grey to go out with us the next night. Since it would be my last night there, Ryder and his friends had decided to send me off with a bang. We were going club hopping in Hollywood. All of Ghost Parker and hopefully Tommy and Livvy and maybe even Tyler would join us.

It was more of a typical night out on the town for them, but it seemed like a huge production to me. Even though it was a Wednesday night, we were doing it big with a limousine, VIP rooms, and bottle service. Grey was worried about being identified in WeHo, but once he heard Cold Fusion and their security would be there, he seemed to consider it.

We exchanged phone numbers, and I asked him for a selfie of us that I could send to Ellie. We were parting at Ryder's front door when Ellie called me on the phone, squealing. She'd obviously received the photo of us. Gray was gracious enough to take my phone and chat with her. She asked him endless questions about what was coming up on *Devious*. To her chagrin, he would only give her some minor spoilers.

It was almost noon when Grey left and Ryder wasn't due back for a few hours. I changed into my bathing suit and spent the time absorbing the warmth of the sun's rays and dipping my toes in the frigid ocean while I waited for Ryder to return home.

Chapter 26

Ryder

IT WAS ONLY MID-MORNING, and the day was already turning to shit. I'd never enjoyed it when the band was writing new material, probably because I was bad at it. I could pick up my guitar and jam with the greatest rock bands in the world, no problem, but composing a new song that checked all the right boxes, fit our image, and was marketable and edgy all at the same time? It had never been my talent.

If I could at least support Ghost and Knox, who were the real drivers of creating hit songs in our group, I'd be happy. But today, my fingers weren't translating their ideas into anything of quality. I was dragging the band down.

This was the second time today that we'd rearranged what was supposed to be our lead single on the new album. I tried to ignore Ghost's vocals and focus solely on the rhythm section. Bash's drumming was overpowering the song, and Sid's bass seemed weak. I worked my electric guitar, but it didn't sound cohesive and tight. We were off.

"Fucking stop!" Our manager, Donovan Byrne, was losing patience. When the room grew silent, he continued his angry tirade. "We've got the recording studio booked for next week and we don't even have one song down. You've been at this for two days. What the hell's wrong with you guys? Ryder and Bash, that was shit."

I held back the nasty reply that was on the tip of my tongue. I didn't even want to be here right now. I fought the urge to say fuck it all and storm right out the door.

Donovan stabbed his finger at all of us. "I can't listen to this right now. You're wasting my time with this garbage. I'm leaving. Ghost, get these assholes back on track. Tomorrow, I want you all to show up with your head in the game. If you don't ride this wave of opportunity, Ghost Parker is over. It'll die a slow and painful death. This is it, boys. Don't fuck it up."

He stalked out of the room while Bash crashed his drumstick into a cymbal. I shrugged the strap of my guitar off my shoulder and leaned it against the wall. I needed a break.

Ghost looked at each of us one by one. "What's going on? Donovan was being a dick, but he's right. We're not playing together as a group."

Bash smashed the cymbal again, which set my teeth on edge. "I need a fuckton of more sleep. Getting in here at 8 a.m. is not fucking working. All so Ryder can get pussy."

I wanted to put my fist through his snarling mouth, but I refrained, because I was tired, too. I'd spent most of the last few nights having sex with Talia instead of sleeping. It was heaven on earth, but it was catching up to me. I took a deep breath. "Yeah, well, Talia's leaving Thursday, so tomorrow's the last morning session."

"Good. Maybe you'll be able to concentrate without the distraction."

Anger flared through my blood. It wasn't good that she was going. In fact, I was dreading it. I hadn't gotten nearly enough of her yet, and after this disaster, there was no way I could blow off tomorrow's session as I'd planned. I'd miss even more time with her. "What's your fucking problem, Bash?"

Knox jumped in between us before Bash could respond. "Hey mates, settle down. This isn't just on Ryder. We all need to get back into the groove. Let's take a 10-minute break and then refocus. I want to get this track sewn up before we leave today. We need to have something solid for Donovan tomorrow. I don't think we're too far off with it. Needs a few tweaks. That's all."

"Fine." Bash threw down his sticks and stalked out the door.

Sid gave me a supportive slap on the back before following Bash. I didn't want to face the criticism I was sure was in Ghost and Knox's eyes, so I stalked over to the mini-fridge and pulled out a bottle of water.

Ghost was at my side before I turned around. "Is everything okay with you?"

"Everything's fine."

Ghost motioned me back over to my guitar. "Play it again with Knox; I want to hear it. I was concentrating on the vocals before."

I didn't want to, but Knox was nodding at me, so I picked up my guitar. It was better that I worked out some kinks before Sid and Bash returned. Knox began playing, and I jumped in. We played for less than a minute before Ghost stopped us. He held out his hand for my guitar.

I handed it over and he began playing a few chords. "You're not leaving room for the bass. You're muddying it up too much. Play it thinner, like this."

He began playing our new song, and then Knox joined him. It sounded tight. Much better. I watched for a minute, even though I got the picture right away.

Ghost looked like he was having fun jamming with Knox. He'd played lead guitar in his old band and then for a few months with us before we found Knox. Then he decided he wanted to focus only on being the singer and frontman. He put on a great show, so I couldn't imagine our band any other way now. Besides, Knox was a fantastic lead guitarist. If anything, I worked my ass off adding flavor to our sound, so I wouldn't feel superfluous. That was another reason I had to keep my sour mood in check. They could kick me out and still make it as a band.

I reached for my water bottle as Ghost and Knox transitioned into a new song. Shit, I felt a pang of jealousy. It sounded like these two had been playing together for decades.

As I chugged the water down, I felt my phone vibrating in my pocket. Someone had been trying to reach me for the past couple of hours, but I'd been ignoring it during practice. I pulled it out and frowned when I saw it was my mother. She never called me. If I wanted to keep in touch with her, I had to call her. It'd been that way ever since I'd first moved away from home to go to college.

I answered the phone. "Mom, is everything okay?"

"Hey, boy. It's Stan."

My stomach clenched. "Why the fuck are you calling me?"

"Where's the money, Ryder? I'm running out of time."

I pinched the bridge of my nose. I hadn't had a non-hangover headache in years, but sure as shit, I felt one coming on. "I already told you that I'm not giving you another penny of my money. Your bullshit won't work with me anymore."

I heard his heavy breaths over the phone. "Listen here, boy. And listen real good. The eviction notice is posted on the goddamn door already. Your mama is going to be thrown out on her ass any day now.

But that's not the worst of her problems."

I ground out through my teeth, "What are you talking about?"

Stan chuckled. "I have your attention now, huh, boy? I need a hundred grand to cover a loan your mama took out. The dudes that loaned it to her ain't messing around no more. They won't be put off any longer. And these are bad motherfuckers."

"What the fuck?" I growled at him. "What loan? I don't believe a fucking word you're saying. Put my mother on the phone. Now!"

"I bought you some time, but it's going up five grand a day. I can't stop them. They want their money and if they don't get it, they're gonna go after her. They won't care that she's a helpless old lady. She's fucked unless you pay them."

There was a note of desperation mixed with fear in his voice that had my heart racing. Could he be telling the truth?

"Put her on the phone."

"Are you listening to me, boy?" I heard someone talking in the background, but it didn't sound like my mother. "I've gotta go. Get the money together. I'll call back in a few days to tell you how to get it to them."

Stan hung up. I stared at the phone for a long minute. Ghost and Knox had stopped playing and were watching me. I wasn't sure how much of the conversation they'd heard.

My thoughts were racing. There was no way this was true. Stan knew I wouldn't fork over any more of my money, so he was just trying to scare me. No way the fat fuck was stupid enough to take out a loan with some kind of loan shark. Was he? God, he was dumb. Maybe the jackass thought he could get away with it — somehow leaving my mom caught holding the bag? Fuck.

I had to talk to my mom. I called her phone back, but it went straight to voicemail. When I first got the phone for her, I'd installed a tracking app on it without telling her. I'd hardly ever checked it since then; I'd never found her anywhere other than at home or at work. On a hunch, I opened up the app.

I zoomed in on the tiny pin on the map. Kentucky? She was in Kentucky? Well, Stan was in Kentucky with the phone. I didn't know where the hell my mother was and Stan had taken away my only means of contacting her. She could be sitting at home clueless about the whole thing. I had no idea.

When I tore my eyes away from my phone, Ghost was watching me while Knox fiddled with the frets on his guitar.

"I gotta go."

Ghost frowned. "Let's just play it through a few times with all of us."

"Can't." I shook my head. "I gotta take care of something."

Knox was listening, but pretending not to. Ghost took a step toward me. "Ryder ... if you walk now, the guys will be pissed."

My head was throbbing. "Sorry. I would stay if I could. I've got it though. Tomorrow, I'll play it just like you showed me. No worries. Just have Bash tone it down a bit and we'll be fine."

I unplugged my guitar and left before he could say anything more. Before I even got to my truck, I was calling Brock. I needed someone to check on my mom. I didn't know any of her neighbors, and she didn't have any friends. As much as I didn't want to talk to him, he was the only one I could think of to call.

I couldn't convince him to leave work early to check on her. I guess it was a good thing that he thought Stan's story was total bullshit. Still, I couldn't relax until I knew for sure. My mother had signed papers that Stan had put in front of her without question in the past. She was willfully blind to all his deceits. He'd do just about anything for money, so a shady loan wasn't preposterous.

Slamming my hands on the steering wheel in frustration, I checked the time on my phone. It would be hours before Brock stopped by my mother's house to check on her. I couldn't do anything else until then. I should go back and finish with the band, but my head wasn't in it. I started my truck and headed home to Talia.

Tomorrow was our last day together.

I don't know when it started, maybe yesterday, but there was a mental clock inside my head that was ticking. It was like a bomb, steadily ticking down to the inevitable explosion. Only this clock was ticking down until Talia went back home to Ohio. Every second that ticked off was one second closer to saying goodbye to her. It was making me edgy and moody.

I wanted to savor my remaining time with her, but band shit was getting in the way. And now, I had to figure out this bullshit with Stan and my mother. My gut roiled with apprehension. Fuck.

Chapter 27

Talia

WHEN I RETURNED FROM the beach, Ryder was already home. He got back earlier than expected, so I hopped in the shower right away so we could go out. I half expected him to join me, and I was more than slightly disappointed when he didn't.

We hiked up to the famous Hollywood sign. It was cheesy and touristy, but the day wasn't too hot. In fact, it was gorgeous, and I wanted some photos of the two of us together. I'd been shy in asking him to pose for pictures with me; and now, nearing the end of our time together, I was regretting it.

After searching the internet, I found two terrific spots to take pictures with the sign in the background. While we drove to those spots, I told Ryder all about meeting Greyson. He didn't seem to share my over-the-top enthusiasm. Actually, I caught him a few times not even paying attention to what I'd said.

I second-guessed my choice of activities when we were hiking up the hills to reach the giant letters spelling out 'HOLLYWOOD'. Ryder trailed behind me, and when I glanced back, he was finger-typing something into his phone. He'd barely spoken to me since we'd begun the hike. Was he bored with me already? Ready for me to go home?

"How did practice go this morning?"

He slipped his phone into his pocket and then caught up to me on the trail. "Not the greatest. Donovan, our manager, showed up to hear our new single, but we still haven't figured everything out with it yet, so it sounded like muddled shit. Part of that was my fault, but the others were fucking up too, even if they tried to pin it all on me."

That must be why he was so distracted. Hopefully, it had nothing to do with me. "Why are they blaming it all on you? That doesn't seem fair."

Ryder shrugged it off. "I'm an easy scapegoat. The guys aren't used to working in the morning, so they're still bitching about the schedule change. You'd think they could quit partying until dawn for a lousy couple of days. But Sid and Bash can be fucking morons sometimes."

He was taking heat because I was here, messing up his schedule. "Are they angry that you're skipping tomorrow?"

"Yeah. About that …" Regret flashed over his face. He kept his eyes trained on his feet as we climbed steadily up the hill. "I can't skip tomorrow. We're gonna be working on this new song all morning and then Donovan is checking in on us in the afternoon. We have to have it ready by then. I'm sorry, Angel, but I won't be around tomorrow until late afternoon."

A sickening feeling began churning in my stomach. "But tomorrow's our last day together. What about the Santa Monica pier? And Venice Beach? I was looking forward to going there."

He stopped walking and grabbed my hand, turning me to face him.

"I know. I'm really sorry. Why don't you see if Kaylie can go with you? Or I can see if Livvy is free tomorrow?"

Sure, I wanted to see Muscle Beach and stroll around the famous amusement park on the pier, but I really just wanted to spend time with him. I couldn't keep the disappointment off my face. "It won't be the same. I wanted to go with you."

"I know." He pulled me in for a hug. "I'm tempted to just tell the guys to fuck off, but this is an important time for our band. Besides, everyone's still in for the big celebration tomorrow night. We'll have a great time then."

I couldn't help but wince at his choice of words. My cheek was resting against his chest, so he didn't see my sour reaction when he used the word 'celebration'.

Hurray, everybody! Talia's finally leaving!

How could he call it a celebration? Intellectually, I knew he didn't really mean it that way, but it still hurt. I took a deep breath before I responded irrationally.

"I don't want to bother Kaylie or Livvy tomorrow, especially if they're going to go out with us later in the night. How about I just go to practice with you tomorrow? I'd love to see you guys at work."

"It would be super boring for you." Wow, he didn't even consider it. He began making excuses. "And there's not a lot of extra room in there. Plus, you'd be a big distraction. You'd definitely distract me."

He leaned down to capture my lips, but the kiss felt forced. After a few seconds, I broke away and smiled weakly at him. "I'm sure I'll be able to find something to occupy my time."

He nodded his head and smiled back at me. The look that swept his face was relief. Oh God!

I couldn't deny it to myself; he didn't want me there. I felt the sting of rejection as I swallowed against the lump forming in my throat.

Suddenly, I was terrified. Scared about us. Scared about what I wanted versus what I actually had. Somewhere along the way, I'd let down my guard and now I was getting a sneak peek at just how much that was going to cost me.

My mood plummeted and put a damper on the rest of the afternoon. We hiked to the iconic letters in near silence. I couldn't enjoy the warm sun on my skin, the cheerful chirping of the birds, or the gorgeous scenery. Even the sexiness of Ryder hiking ahead of me couldn't break through my bad mood. I couldn't even enjoy the fine view of his sculpted ass encased in perfectly fitted cargo pants. The sight just made the mantra run through my head even louder.

One more day.

I smiled in all the pictures we took together. Even as we joked around and had to retake multiple pictures to get the perfect shot, my brain was busy scolding my heart: I told you so, dummy.

This was the beginning of the end. I could feel it in my bones. At least I'd have a photo of us together to show my grandkids and to memorialize my time with an honest-to-goodness rock star. It would be the tangible evidence of my time with the guy who'd been able to insidiously penetrate my defenses and steal my closely guarded heart.

On our way back to Ryder's house, we stopped to get some takeout for dinner. Without saying it out loud, we decided to stay in for the night. When we finished eating and cleaning up our dinner, we headed down to the beach for a walk. I was determined to work up the courage to talk about us. I needed to get the answers to some burning questions about our relationship or else I'd forever kick myself for chickening out. I wanted to leave L.A. knowing exactly where I stood, no matter how gut-wrenching.

We walked down the beach hand in hand. Ryder was unusually quiet. I wondered if he was thinking about me leaving or if he was still worried about band stuff. We'd turned around to head back to his house when I summoned the courage to broach the subject that had been plaguing me.

"I can't believe I'm leaving in a couple of days."

He squeezed my hand but remained silent. Just when I thought he wasn't going to say anything, he replied. "I know. It went by so fast."

That was it.

There was no mention of any future together.

No reassuring words.

Nothing that I could hold on to.

All the important words I had planned on speaking to him dried up in my mouth. Numbness started seeping in.

It was safer that way.

♪♪♪♪♪

It was still early when we got back from the beach, but Ryder pulled me straight into his bedroom. There was always a bit of a manic quality when we had sex and this time was no different. Even though I tried to gird my heart, I quickly fell under his spell. Fighting to keep my emotions closed down, I was determined to enjoy this only on a purely physical level.

I expected sex with a guy who was emotionally pulling away to be distant. Maybe cold and clinical. Mechanically going through the steps with one goal in mind: climax.

But, Lord!

It was anything but distant.

This wasn't mindless sex. It wasn't simply the taking of pleasure. It was giving and receiving. Connecting on a deeper level. It was soul-stirring. Reverent.

It felt almost ... loving.

We both fell to our backs after climaxing, trying to catch our breath.

How could my mind betray me so easily? My body, pfft. A few good orgasms and it was devoted to Ryder for life. But, my mind? Good sex did not equal love.

I rolled over to face Ryder and propped myself up on my elbow. "Ryder?"

I needed some answers about us; I was so confused. When I tried to start a conversation, he shushed me with a finger to my lips.

We ended up making love again. It was slow and sensual. He was even more attentive than usual. Selflessly giving me orgasms. Taking care of me. Looking into my eyes. Connecting, soul to soul.

All while my heart was breaking into pieces.

Chapter 28

Ryder

Leaving Talia in bed to go practice with the band was excruciating. Our time together was ticking down, and I felt powerless to stop it.

I debated skipping it, but then I saw the texts that had come in sometime last night. Ghost's texts were more succinct.

> **Ghost:** Be at practice tomorrow
> **Ghost:** We need you

And then Sid texted me later in the night. He was probably drunk when he sent them.

> **Sid:** Hey man. We practiced for hours after you

> left. Think we've figured it out.
> **Sid:** I know you've got your girl with you. I get it. But tomorrow is big. We gotta get the song right. Donovan's getting pressure from Black Vault.

Black Vault was our label. Sid didn't have to tell me. I knew what they expected of us. I knew we had to deliver. There were hundreds of other talented bands lined up and waiting to take our place if we fucked up.

> **Sid:** This is it, man. What we've been working for.
> **Sid:** Be on top of your game.

When Sid, of all people, had to be the one motivating me, it was not a good sign.

I stood on my deck, resting my coffee mug on the top of the deck rail, as I looked out at the ocean. The waves usually had a calming effect on me, but today my mood seemed to swirl and twist as relentlessly as the breakers that crashed onto the shore one after the other.

I had to leave now, or I'd be late. It was only 7 a.m., but the Los Angeles traffic would be brutal, even at this early hour. I chugged down the rest of my coffee, hoping it would erase the fact that I'd only gotten a few hours of solid sleep.

I couldn't keep my lips from curling into a smile. Fuck, it'd been so worth it. I shoved that thought away as I felt my dick stirring just from thinking about it. Jesus, that woman had me all tied up in knots. What the hell was I going to do?

The smile melted from my face as I turned to head back inside. My neighbor, the one Talia was gushing about yesterday, was out on his deck. He was supposedly a TV star. I scowled at him, maybe growled a little in my throat, before I marched into my house.

It was Talia's last day here, and I was leaving her. And that prick was right next door. It pissed me the fuck off.

It took forever to get to our practice space, but it gave me time to think about my mom while I drove through the stop-and-go traffic. Brock had stopped by her house after he got off work yesterday. She was there. She'd had to get a ride home from one of her bookstore colleagues when Stan didn't show up to pick her up. Brock said she was completely clueless that Stan had left her. Permanently. And I guess Brock didn't have the balls to fill her in.

It was going to be a big blow to Mom. She'd be depressed; shit was going to get bad with her. I knew that, but I was so damn relieved Stan was gone. The tracking app I had on his phone revealed he was in Georgia this morning. He was heading south. Away from my mother. Thank God.

It was looking more likely the phone call about the $100,000 loan the other day was all bullshit. Just one more attempt to shake me down before he took off.

Once I was sure that fucker was gone for good, I'd cut service to the phone. For now, it was comforting to know exactly where he was. I'd have to buy my mom a new phone and possibly a car so she could get around, but that was a small price to pay for having Stan out of her life.

Sid and Bash were already there when I got to practice. Sid gave me a head nod as I put down my guitars, but Bash didn't even acknowledge my presence. He was still butt hurt about getting up so early. I headed to the bathroom instead of enduring the awkward silence and when I returned, Ghost had arrived. We started setting up and 15 minutes later, Knox finally arrived.

It was midmorning before we decided to break for a bit before we focused on some of our other new songs. So far, our session was going well. Our lead single was gelling and no more fighting or backstabbing amongst us had broken out.

As I reached for my phone to call Talia, I hesitated. I didn't want the guys to hear me talking to her, so I headed outside to the parking lot where my truck was. I hoped like hell she wasn't hanging out with the Greyson dude, but logically I knew that wasn't fair. It was my fault that our plans were canceled, leaving her to her own devices today.

Just as I was about to hit call on the phone, I noticed a man approaching. He'd been sitting on a motorcycle parked near my truck. I paused for a moment to see if he was actually heading my way because he didn't look like a typical Ghost Parker fan. He looked straight out of motorcycle gang central casting. He was a giant guy with a long unkempt beard, leather jacket with patches, tats, and shitkicker boots.

When he got about 5 feet from me, he stopped. "You all look like a bunch of pussy boy-band pretty fellas. Not like a real rock band."

Here we go. Sometimes dealing with the public sucked. I better get used to it, though. It was only going to get worse the bigger we got. "Can I help you with something?"

His smile was creepily disturbing. "Can I get your autograph?"

"Uh, sure." I'd scribble my name on something and then head back inside. Not to judge a book by its cover, but this guy wasn't throwing off the friendliest of vibes.

He pulled out a wrinkled envelope and a pen from his pocket. "Make it out to Skull Crusher."

Terrific. I tried to think of something to write that wouldn't offend him.

Skull Crusher-
Keep Rolling!

Then I signed my name, followed by the GP for Ghost Parker, which we all added to our signatures when we signed stuff for the band.

I handed the envelope back to him. "Nice talking to you."

I turned to head back inside when he stopped me. "Not so fast. We've got some business to discuss, Mathis."

This guy wasn't a fan of the band, obviously, but he knew my name. Alarm bells began ringing in my head. "What business are you talking about?"

"The $125,000 that you owe us."

My stomach dropped to my feet. "What the fuck are you talking about? I don't owe anyone any money."

Skull Crusher stroked his beard contemplatively. "Your mother borrowed the money. She was a co-signer. And you were her collateral. Her guarantor. You are our insurance. So yeah, I think you do."

"Fuck!" I ran a hand through my hair. "My mother didn't borrow shit. Stan, that absolute asshole, has been scamming her for years. Bleeding her dry. She didn't know shit about any loans."

"Listen, Mathis. I feel for you. I really do." He paused his speech to crack all his knuckles. "I don't know shit about the loan. And I don't care to, either. I'm what you call a Collection Specialist. The Columbus crew aren't my people, but I know of them. And trust me, they don't give a shit about your problems either. They want their money. You've got one week to deliver the $125,000 to me. Not a day longer."

My mind was racing. I could feel beads of sweat sliding down my back. "I don't have that kind of money."

"You better get it fast, then."

"How?" My arms waved with agitation. "I can't get that kind of money in a week! Why am I on the hook for this? This is all Stan. He's the guy you should be after."

"Stan's as good as dead, but we still need our money. That's the way this works. Let me explain it to you. You owe us. You pay us. We go away. Everyone's happy." He took a step closer to me, getting in my space, trying to intimidate me.

He jabbed a finger at my chest as he continued. "You fuck us over? You call the cops? Try to run? That won't work. I'll tell you exactly how that's gonna go. Back in Ohio, the cops, the judges, the district attorneys? They're all compromised by the network. Law enforcement won't give a shit about your little story. If after a week I tell the boys you reneged on the loan, they'll be forced to take action. They let even one person renege, and it's game over for them. Instead, they make an example of you. They hire some desperate meth addict for $500. Maybe your mom will end up at the bottom of the steps with a fractured skull."

He chuckled to himself as he pulled up his phone and flashed me a picture of my mom taken somewhere in front of her apartment complex. My stomach twisted into a thousand knots as dread crept up my spine.

"Or maybe he'll slash her up with a knife. Who knows? Those meth heads are so unpredictable."

What the fuck! Blood was pounding in my head. I clenched my teeth as I tried to remain calm. "Are you threatening me?"

His smile was greasy and vile. "No. I'm just educating you. You don't seem that bright. Maybe this will grab your attention."

He fiddled with his phone for a moment and then turned it toward me. It was a photo of Brock holding little Joey in his arms with a laughing Jenny walking a few steps behind him. They looked like they were in a parking lot somewhere.

My blood turned to ice and a cold sweat broke out on my forehead.

I couldn't even respond.

"That's what they sent in your file. It's not my business, but I'd get the money fast if I were you."

He walked away, and I was frozen to the spot in shock. I still hadn't moved after he started up his bike, revved the engine a few times, and roared away. It was several more minutes that I stood there before Knox came down to find me.

Somehow, I stumbled through the rest of practice. I mechanically played the songs the way I knew the guys wanted me to. When Donovan stopped in to check on our progress, he seemed happy with what he heard.

Before Donovan left, I cornered him by the refrigerator. I kept my voice down so the guys couldn't hear me, but I could see them glancing over at us curiously.

I tried to act casual, but I was a swirling tornado of emotion on the inside. "Hey, Donovan. Now that the new album is shaping up nicely, do you think there's any way that the label would advance me some money?"

He shook his head. "Ghost Parker's still a gamble, as far as they're concerned. There's no way Black Vault's going to fork over any money yet."

I swallowed the panic I felt rising. "Can you just ask them? I'm in a cash crunch right now. I need money quickly."

"No way. I don't want to rock the boat with them." His eyes narrowed. "What the fuck, Ryder? What's going on?"

Glancing over at my bandmates, I made sure they weren't heading our way. "I'm just in a bit of a rough spot right now. I need money. Can you loan me some? Just until we get paid? I'll pay you back with interest."

A scowl darkened his face. "Is this about drugs?"

"No. Fuck no. But it's fucking important."

"How much do you need?"

I debated in my head for a few seconds on how much to tell him. I'd go with a nice even number. If it worked, I'd only need to scrounge up another 25k. Fuck. "A hundred grand."

His eyes flared with surprise. "A hundred grand? What the fuck is going on? I don't have that kind of money to lend. You're insane. If you're in some kind of trouble, you better tell me right now."

Fuck. I clenched my fists at my sides. "I just need some goddamn money. Just check about an advance, okay? I'm desperate."

"I'll ask, but I wouldn't count on it." He stared at me for several moments before heaving an exasperated sigh and shaking his head in disappointment. "I've got a meeting I need to get to, but this conversation isn't over. You've got to tell me what's going on. If this could affect the band, I need to know. Call my secretary and see if I have any lunches available. Maybe next week?"

I nodded numbly to him. I could fucking tell he wasn't going to ask Black Vault. And next week would be way too fucking late, anyway.

When Donovan left, I headed back over to the band. My feet felt like lead. Bash was messing around on the drums, but the rest watched me approach with questions in their eyes. But nobody said a fucking word.

Would I have told them if they asked? I wasn't sure. None of them could help me with the money. They might be able to scrape together a few thousand dollars here and there between them, but it wasn't enough. None of us came from wealthy families. None of us had ever been good at saving money and we were still on the cusp of making the kind of fuck-you money I needed. As a whole, the band was pretty pathetic with money.

I couldn't rely on them to bail me out of this mess. I knew Tommy had lots of money and would probably help me out. The thought of asking him pained me. I didn't want anyone to know about this. It was shameful to be caught in this sick, disgusting mess. I didn't want to tie anyone else up in it, especially when they had the safety of their children to think about.

Only at a last fucking resort would I ask Tommy.

The whole situation twisted in my gut until I thought I might vomit.

As I approached the band, I felt like I was walking underwater.

Ghost slapped me on the back. "You okay?"

I managed to nod.

"You ready to party tonight? Lacey's got us all hooked up. You get her text with the pickup time yet?"

I picked up my guitar and my fingers automatically found some chords. It was a good thing someone had asked Lacey to organize our night out because I certainly hadn't done any planning. I had no idea how the hell I was going to party tonight with this shit hanging over my head. What was I going to do about Talia? How could I keep her from leaving me when I was such a mess?

Where the fuck was I going to get $125,000?

I couldn't concentrate on practice. I only lasted another 15 minutes before I told the guys I had to leave. Even Knox was scowling with disappointment this time as I packed up my guitars.

I paused just outside the door when I heard Sid answering a muffled comment from Bash. It sounded like he said, "Look, it's just one more day. She'll be gone tomorrow, he'll forget about her and then we can get back to normal."

I brainstormed on my drive home about how I could come up with the money. I sank the only money I had into my house. Ignoring the sick feeling in my stomach, I called my real estate agent, Melanie

Rivera. I banged my steering wheel with frustration as I got her voicemail and then left a pleading message for her to call me back as soon as possible.

I needed to tell Brock what was happening, but he was going to flip out. Rightfully so, he'd be primarily worried about the safety of his family. He didn't have any money; he was firmly middle class — $25,000 would be a stretch for him, let alone $125,000. No, I'd wait to tell him tomorrow, after I heard back from my realtor and had a plan of how to get the money.

The turmoil stewing in my head was momentarily interrupted when I got home and saw Talia. She was sitting at the kitchen island wearing one of my Ghost Parker T-shirts and a tiny pair of cut-off shorts showing off her sinfully long legs. She wasn't wearing any makeup and her hair was pulled up in a messy bun; still, she looked gorgeous.

I wrapped my arms around her from behind, and she leaned her head back against my chest and sighed. "How was band practice?"

I kissed the top of her head, inhaling the floral scent of her shampoo. "Fine. What did you do today? Did you go to the pier?"

"No, I didn't want to go without you. I spent most of the day on the beach here, enjoying the sun. I'm going to miss the ocean. It's so soothing."

Having Talia in my arms was soothing. I was feeling centered for the first time since Skull Crusher showed up this morning.

I swiveled her stool around so that she was facing me. "I'm really going to miss—"

My phone rang. I pulled it out of my pocket and glanced at the screen. My realtor was calling me back.

I gave Talia a quick kiss on her lips. "I have to take this, Angel."

My quick strides took me out onto the deck while I answered the call. I slid the deck doors closed for privacy. Fuck me. The last thing I wanted was for Talia to know about this disaster.

"Your message intrigued me, Ryder. What can I do for you?"

I couldn't even remember what I'd said to her. "Melanie, I need some quick cash, and I'm going to need to tap into the equity in my home."

"Oh." She sounded disappointed. "You're looking for a home equity loan? I can get you some reliable names."

I paced back and forth on the deck. "The house already has a second mortgage on it — I needed it for the extensive renovations. I'm not talking about a traditional type of loan. What I need is all the equity in the house liquidated in less than a week."

"A week?" She let out a mirthless laugh. "That's never going to happen."

I squeezed the phone in frustration. "There's got to be a way to get my money out of this place. Fast. C'mon, Melanie."

"Are you trying to buy a new place? You can get a bridge loan—"

I cut her off and ground out, "No. I just need the money."

"Hold on, Ryder." She sighed. "There may be a way, but — just let's say — it's unsavory. You'd take a bloodbath on the deal. I may know of a few people who deal in this kind of thing, but ..."

Her voice trailed off.

I ran my hand through my hair. "Can I get the money in less than a week?"

"Yeah. Maybe. How much equity do you have in the home?"

I sank down into an Adirondack chair. "Fuck, I don't know. I owe about $650,000 on both mortgages. Depends on what the house would sell for now after the renovation I've done."

"Hmm." I heard her typing on a keyboard. "House number 3522, was it?"

"Yeah."

"How much did you spend on renovations? Give me a quick rundown on what you did to renovate while I look up some comps."

While she typed away at the computer, I explained all the work I'd put into the house and what it had cost me.

She was quiet for a few minutes after I'd finished. "The good news is that the house is worth more now than you paid for it." She paused for a moment and then continued, "You sure you're looking for a turnover this quick? Because you'll have sharks circling like they smell blood in the water. They'll have no mercy. You're going to get squeezed badly and lose so much money, Ryder. I can't recommend this. Are you sure you want to do this?"

I let out a huff of breath as the knowledge of what I was doing sat in my stomach like a brick. "I have no choice."

"If this got out that I was a party to it — it could ruin my reputation, so I'll give you a name, but I can't have any part in it. I can't even help negotiate a price for you."

Was I jumping from the frying pan into the fire? Fuck me. What else could I do? Sit back and watch people I loved get hurt or worse? "Yeah. I get it."

"I'll get your information to my contact. Ryder, if they offer you one million, jump on it. That's where I'd start the negotiations if they leave it up to you. They're going to lowball you, big time."

I started doing calculations in my head. "Yeah, that would work."

"You're never going to get that. You'll be lucky if you get $800,000. I wouldn't go too far below that, though. I'm pretty confident that they wouldn't walk away from $800,000. That's an amazing deal for them, but they'll push hard."

Jesus. "That's less than half the actual worth. Fuck. I gotta get way more than $800,000."

"Not if you need it in less than a week. That's the price you're gonna pay."

I closed my eyes. "And I need the profit I make — whatever's left-over for me to take — I'm going to need that in cash. Actual paper money."

She sighed. "Yeah. That's going to cost you, too. I'll get back to you."

"Thanks, Melanie. Remember, I need this to happen really quickly. Like yesterday."

I stared out at the ocean, which always brought me calm. Not this time. I felt a queasy type of panic stirring in my gut.

It was sinking in. I was losing my house. Hopefully, I'd have enough money to pay off the loan sharks and make the threats to my family go away, but I'd have nothing left to my name. I'd be wiped out financially with nowhere to live.

Doing this went against every fiber of my being. I'd always been conservative with my money, and my business degree made me aware of just how financially fucked this deal would leave me, but I was at a dead end and didn't know what to do.

Chapter 29

Talia

My head was spinning so fast, I thought I was going to get whiplash. Between the mixed signals last night and again after his practice, I wasn't sure which way I was headed. First, Ryder had a secret conversation with someone I heard him greet as 'Melanie' before he rushed off to the privacy of the deck, and then he came at me hot and heavy.

He came inside from his phone call and stalked over to me like a predator. Of course, I couldn't resist him for long, and soon he had me naked and mindless.

Now that I was slipping back into my T-shirt, I was second-guessing everything. He had whispered things like 'I need you so fucking much' in my ear. Was his need purely physical?

Before I'd come to L.A., it felt like we were getting to know each other. He'd opened up a lot during our conversations — about his childhood, his strained relationships with his family, and of course, he gave me glimpses into the rock and roll lifestyle that had once seemed alien to me. When I got here and we'd had sex, it had consumed both of us. The sex was so mind-blowingly amazing that our connection could only be cemented by it. Yet, I felt like we'd lost a bit of the intimacy that we'd had before sex.

I was wandering down a dangerous path. There was no use denying it any longer. I wanted so much more with Ryder. I wanted everything. My heart was his.

We met Greyson in the driveway a little before 8 o'clock. Ryder didn't fangirl over Grey as I had; in fact, he acted quite indifferent to him. He had his arm around me, pinning me to his side as he fooled around with his phone. Just like he'd been on our hike to the Hollywood sign, he seemed pretty distracted while Grey and I chatted.

I nudged him in the side. "Are you going to be on that phone all night? You do remember that it's my last night here? I'll be gone tomorrow."

He frowned for a moment and then tucked his phone into his pants pocket. Slowly, he spun me around until I was facing him and then pulled me against him until we were touching from head to toe.

His lips grazed my ear as he leaned in and whispered, "Have I told you how sexy you look in this dress tonight?"

This was exactly what I wanted, his full attention on me, but I was super aware of Grey standing right next to us. My breath hitched as he nipped the sensitive skin behind my ear.

Grey cleared his throat. "Looks like our ride is here. Just in time."

An excited squeal left my throat. The sleek black vehicle heading our way wasn't as long as a charter bus, more like an extended shuttle bus. It pulled up into Ryder's driveway and stopped. I climbed in first, with the boys following me.

Tommy and Livvy were already on the bus. They lived the furthest from Hollywood, so the pickup had started with them. Already, the sound system was blasting and club lighting was flashing all over the leather interior. Even the speckled disco lights were in effect.

Livvy ran over to hug me as we boarded. She was already passing out champagne flutes filled with the bubbly alcohol to everyone.

She pulled me aside as Ryder was introducing Grey to Tommy. "Are you ready to go wild tonight? Your last night, eh?"

I smiled weakly, but my eyes must have given me away.

She cocked an eyebrow. "Let me guess. You two haven't talked about the future? What's going to happen next with the relationship?"

I bit my lip. "It hasn't come up."

"Drink up then! You need some liquid courage because you can't leave tomorrow without knowing where you stand. It's obvious that he's really into you, so stop being such a chicken."

I took a sip of the champagne glass she'd pushed into my hand just as the party bus started moving again.

Livvy took an off-balance step backward and then steadied herself. "Good thing I didn't wear my crazy heels tonight."

She was wearing open-toe 4-inch lace-up stiletto booties. With her black and lacy deep v-neck dress that hugged her body, she looked kickass.

My finger pointed up and down at her outfit. "You look amazing tonight, Livvy."

"Thanks, hon. You do, too. Although you're going to wish you were back in those crazy pants that you wore last time. Don't be too surprised when a stray hand wanders up your dress." She looked over her shoulder. "I'm sure Ryder will be looking out for you, though. Just be careful. These events tend to get insane."

"Don't worry. I know how to deal with handsy men."

Livvy stepped behind me. "Block me for a minute." She began tugging at the waist of her dress. "This Spanx that I'm wearing is killing me."

My eyes widened. "You look amazing. You don't need Spanx."

"Oh honey, please," she deadpanned. "I've still got a baby belly going on."

"How old is your baby?"

Her eyes gleamed with pride. "Her name's Roxy. She's almost five months old." She stopped pulling at her outfit. "If I get drunk enough, I just might slip out of all this Spanx and let it all hang out. Jeez, I remember when I used to ditch the panties to turn Tommy on. Now, it's like I'm wearing a friggin' chastity belt."

I couldn't help but laugh. "C'mon, let's join the boys. I need to introduce you to Grey. Did I mention that he's a TV star?"

Her eyes bugged out in her head. "I knew he looked familiar! And wow, is he lickable!"

Livvy was so funny. Even as a responsible mother, she still lived up to her nickname, Crazy. I could tell this was going to be a memorable night for me. I only wished that Ellie were here to experience it with me.

The first stop our bus made was to pick up Ghost who was with two girls. The only thing smaller than the dresses on these girls were their inhibitions. Everyone cheered when they came on board.

The bleached blonde girl in the knockout red dress headed straight for Livvy and I. "Tonight's going to rock, ladies."

Livvy and the girl exchanged air kisses. "Lacey, this is Talia, Ryder's girlfriend."

Her eyes sparkled. "I hope you're ready to party, Talia." She turned to Livvy. "Did you complete your assignment?"

Livvy nodded. "Yep. We stocked the bar and we even have some backup bottles in the Suburban that's following the bus. That's the security I told you about."

"Right. Three guys?"

"Nope. Tommy thought we'd only need two tonight."

Lacey scanned the bus as she talked; she didn't want to miss any action. "That's no problem. I told the clubs three, but two works. I only booked VIP rooms for two clubs. Remember last time when we went to too many clubs? We didn't get to enjoy the party bus as much."

Livvy waved her hand in dismissal. "I could hang out on the bus all night. I could altogether skip going into the clubs to watch Tommy get groped all night, and it wouldn't bother me."

"True." Lacey agreed. "But I'm running out of men to hook up with from this batch. I need fresh meat. Speaking of, who's that fine specimen over there?"

I answered, "That's Grey. He's a friend of mine."

"Is he single?"

I chuckled. "As far as I know."

"Mmmm. You'll have to introduce me." Her gaze wandered over to Ghost. She yelled across the bus to get his attention. "Ghost! I gave you one job. Get on it!"

Ghost flipped her the bird, but then smiled. He looked relaxed tonight — not displaying his usual blinding intensity. He headed over to the sound system and plugged in his phone. The music went from top 40 popular music to some kind of hardcore electronic dance music. Rap, techno, house ... who knew, but it was something a club DJ would play. I physically felt the beats pounding in my chest.

Lacey whooped. "Thank God! That other music sucked." Then she sauntered off.

Livvy fake pouted at me and then shrugged. "That was my favorite playlist. Oh, well."

I was sitting on Ryder's lap, working on my second drink, when the bus stopped again. This time, Sid and Bash piled on, followed by Kaylie and a bunch of people I didn't know.

After everyone had greeted each other and the bus started rolling on, Lacey turned down the music for a moment.

"Did everyone bring the stuff I assigned?"

Kaylie spotted me and was making her way toward me. She stopped and turned to Lacey, holding up a bag. "Disposable shot glasses. Check."

Lacey clapped twice. "Kaylie, you goddess. Let's get some shots passed around."

Bash pulled a large baggie out of his pocket. "I brought the weed."

Loud cheers went up.

A girl in a tiny dress with thigh-high boots held up a plastic bottle and shook it, rattling the contents. "I brought the party favors."

One guy I didn't know grabbed her around the waist and pulled her onto his lap.

The music went back up, and chaos resumed. Some girl was flashing her ass cheeks as she attempted some seductive moves around the dance pole. Alcohol was passed back and forth. Someone must have lit up the weed because I could smell the pungent scent filling the bus. It was insane.

About 15 minutes later, the bus stopped again. Knox entered to loud cheering with a guy who I thought was a crew member I'd met at Tommy's party. Another girl was with them, this one with bright pink hair.

Lacey turned down the music, and everyone turned their attention to her. "Did you bring the stuff I asked for?"

The roadie held up a glass bong.

Lacey frowned. "I don't remember asking you to bring a bong, Jack."

Knox stepped over to her. "I brought myself, Lacey." He motioned to his dick. "Isn't this enough, lass?"

"Knox, you know—"

Whatever she was going to say was muffled, because Knox grabbed her, tipped her backward, and planted a scorching kiss on her lips. I felt Ryder chuckle behind me as he watched the display.

The girl with the pink hair stepped around the two making out. With all eyes on her, she pulled up her short skirt and bent seductively to stick out her ass. Her thong must have been wedged in her crack because only a tiny triangle of silk was visible that covered maybe an inch of skin.

She wagged her bare ass. "And I brought this!"

She squealed with surprise when a hand flew out and whacked her butt cheeks with a stinging smack.

Just then, I felt fingertips sliding up my leg and yes, I did look down to make sure they were Ryder's.

This.

This was exactly how I'd imagined rock stars partied. And this was only the beginning of the night. Jeez. I could only imagine what was to come.

The bus was already jam-packed with sparkly women sporting impressive cleavage, skyscraper heels, hemlines that showed ass cheeks, visible garters, sequins, and glitter. The men were outnumbered, but not one of them wasn't sexy. Testosterone was on display: fitted shirts showing off manly muscles, tattoos and piercings, effortless hairstyles, and sexy five o'clock shadow.

After another ten minutes, the bus made the last stop before we got to the first club. Six more women got on; the only one I recognized was

Marie. The girls already looked pretty drunk as they stumbled on and were greeted by Lacey.

They also brought stuff with them. More weed. Pills. Plastic cups. A case of water- which got booed. A bucket in case someone needed to puke with Lacey's comment being, 'Ugh, remember last time?'

A girl held up a large plastic container. She dipped her hand into the container and pulled out a bunch of shiny foil packets. Condoms.

"A variety to choose from." She began tossing them around the bus. "Ribbed, ultra-thin, warming, flavored ... something for everyone. Be safe!"

Ryder caught one that headed our way. He looked at the wrapper. "Glow in the dark. Nice."

The bus began moving again, but Lacey turned off the music to get our attention. "We'll be at the first club in about 10 minutes. We're almost at capacity, so nobody brings any guests from the clubs back onto the bus this time. I'm looking at you, Knox. They can meet up with us at the next club, okay? Also, once word goes out that we're heading out, I'm giving everyone ten minutes to get back on the bus. If the bus leaves without you, you'll have to get a cab to the next stop or you're on your own to get home. That would especially suck for you far-away people. This is just a fair warning. We won't be waiting around for everyone this time."

Livvy was standing next to Lacey. "Thanks for organizing this, Lacey." She held up a condom. "Looks like you covered all the bases."

"Yeah, thanks a lot, Lace," Ryder said. "You should think about coming on tour with us. We could use an organized tour manager."

From the laughter that followed, I knew that Ryder meant his statement as a casual joke. It was. I knew that.

But that didn't stop the white-hot bolt of jealousy that ripped through me. I realized that his joke poked right at the heart of my biggest insecurity. I had to swallow that feeling down, but right now, what Ryder said had to be the most insensitive thing he could say while I was sitting on his lap mere hours from leaving California. My heart plummeted.

Chapter 30

Ryder

I DIDN'T WANT TO be here. That realization was kicking in faster than the drinks were.

There were a decent amount of people at the club, considering it was in the middle of the week and still early in the night. Then again, maybe it just seemed that way, because every last one of them had followed our group out to the dance floor.

I'd noticed Greyson getting a lot of attention, even more than Tommy. I hadn't recognized the name of the show that he starred in, but then again, I didn't watch a lot of TV. It was obvious that the public recognized him. Women especially recognized him.

With our band, we usually had a good 30 minutes in public before word started getting around who we were. If Ghost wasn't with us, maybe longer. That's what I'd expected here. Ten minutes on the dance floor and people were already swarming. To add to the mess, the semi-drunk girls in our group had caught the attention of every male at the club.

As vigilant as I'd been in trying to show those fuckers that Talia was my girl, that she was taken — Talia was busy flitting away from me. It was getting so obvious that I was beginning to suspect that she was doing it on purpose. I can be a dumb fuck, but she was up to something. Maybe trying to make me jealous?

Well, it was working. What the fuck? I was driving her to the airport tomorrow morning. Our hours together were counting down.

Into the single digits.

Women were starting to get pushy with Greyson. One of Tommy's security guys motioned it was time for us to leave the dance floor and head to the VIP room.

Sometimes the girls stayed behind to dance. I was prepared to stay with Talia if she did, but once Greyson and Tommy left, the entire group peeled away. Thank God.

I moved to grab her, but she slipped past me and ran ahead to catch up to Greyson. Fuck, this was driving me crazy.

When I got to the VIP lounge section, Talia was wedged on a couch between Greyson and Ghost, lapping up their attention. I was pretty sure the intense anger brewing in my gut was jealousy, and I didn't like the feeling one bit.

Knox slapped me on the back. "You look well-scunnered."

I peeled my eyes away from Talia to glare at him. "What the fuck are you talking about?"

He chuckled. "Aye, yer up to high doh."

I was catching his drift, but I didn't want to acknowledge it, let alone talk about it. "How about you speak fucking English?"

"Ah, mate, she's just having a good time. What? You want her glued to your side the whole night? Clinging to you?"

"No. But she's leaving tomorrow. You'd think maybe she'd want to spend some time with me?" I winced when I heard the whiny note in my voice.

Knox scoffed. "If you're that insecure, then go get her. If not, then come get a drink with me."

I let Knox lead me away. For the next hour, I tried not to watch Talia obsessively. I'd let her have her fun, but I was only so patient. When Lacey signaled it was time for us to head back to the bus, I was done hanging in the background.

Back on the bus, Talia slipped into the seat next to Greyson. Bash was sitting on her right side, attempting to hide some random girl that he'd smuggled onto the bus from Lacey. I strode directly up to Grey and flashed him a gesture to get up. Amusement glinted in his eyes. I was all out of patience for any games, so I was thankful when he got up.

I sat down next to her. When she stood up to follow Greyson, my arm shot out and caught her. I dragged her onto my lap. All patience had expired.

She wiggled on my lap, trying to get up. "Ryder, I want to talk to Greyson."

My arm was like a steel band around her waist, holding her in place. "You're not going anywhere. How come you're spending time with everyone but me? If I didn't know any better, I'd think you were avoiding me, Angel."

She stopped struggling. "I'm surprised you noticed."

I felt her shiver as I whispered into her ear. "Oh, I noticed. I noticed every fucking minute you spent away from me."

I began tracing little circles with my finger on her upper thigh. "Angel, do you remember the first night we met? When I woke up to your sweet pussy grinding against my mouth?"

A soft moan escaped her lips as she wiggled against the steel rod in my pants. She felt so damn good in my arms. I could feel her heart beating wildly against my arm as I held her locked in place against me.

I kept talking dirty in her ear. Reliving that first night in graphic detail. The dirtier I got, the more she squirmed. I told her that I was imagining how wet her pussy was getting and that it made my dick ache for her. When I started describing what I wanted to do to her, in uncensored and absolutely filthy language, she began wilting in my arms. She couldn't hide how much I affected her. Maybe as much as she affected me.

She collapsed against me and her eyes fluttered shut. "Ryder, please …"

I had been whispering in her ear, but her answering moan was breathy and desperate.

Bash shot me a dirty look. "Fuuuuck." He got up from the seat next to us and took his stowaway girl with him.

I was still getting my Angel all hot and bothered when we arrived at the second club. The music cut off, and the others got up to leave. I didn't move. When I got a few questioning looks, I acknowledged them with a head tip. "You guys go on ahead. We'll just be a few minutes. See you soon."

I had to do something about the raging boner in my pants. And I planned on leaving my girl fully satisfied.

Talia turned her head to me. "Why did you say that?"

I shrugged. "I wanted to make sure that they got the message. Now they'll stay away from the bus. I don't want anyone disturbing us."

Talia's eyes grew wide with concern. "Ryder! Now they think we're going to have sex in here!"

"Angel, you've got quite the dirty mind. But, now that you mention it, that's a great idea. I've been aching for you all night."

My hand slid under her skirt. I'd been waiting for the last person to exit the bus before I jumped on her. My fingers slipped inside her panties and then worked her like a guitar. The music she made was even sweeter than my favorite guitar.

"You are so fucking wet for me, Talia. What kind of condom do you want to use? Your pick."

I slid her skirt up around her waist so that I could watch my hand stroking her pussy.

"Fuck. Take off your panties."

She groaned but then wiggled out of her panties when I stopped playing with her.

"Open your legs wider."

She laid her head back against my shoulder and then spread her knees apart. My chin was resting on her shoulder, so I could watch my fingers dipping inside her pussy and fingering her clit.

I wanted to see her tits, too, but I wasn't sure she'd want to take off her dress because someone could walk on the bus and catch us.

"I want you naked, Angel."

She whimpered and pressed her hips into my hand.

"Is your dress difficult to remove?"

That was her one chance to back down.

She leaned forward. "It zippers in the back."

As I unzipped her dress, I caught the scent of her arousal on my fingers and I almost exploded in my pants. Fuck, I needed her so badly.

I slowly opened the back of her dress and placed a few kisses down her spine. She squirmed out of my touch and I had a brief moment of worry when I thought she was running away. But no, she stepped over to what they called the dance floor. She crooked her leg around the pole that looked suspiciously like a stripper's pole.

She wound around it once and then began sliding her arms out of the dress. Another spin, and she stepped out of the dress and flung it onto one of the seats. She was left bare except for her tits spilling out of a black bra and sexy black stilettos. Nothing else.

"Touch yourself, Angel."

She placed her middle finger in her mouth, sucking it sensually, and then slid it down her body, where she began rubbing it along her glistening pussy. Her head rolled back, and she moaned her pleasure.

Fuuuck. I wasn't sure how long I could sit back and watch. "Take off your bra."

She unhooked her bra, slid it off her shoulders, and then flung it toward me. She began pinching her nipples and plumping her breasts suggestively. My cock was throbbing painfully.

I sprang up and stalked over to her. "Turn around and bend over," I rasped.

She was bent forward, leaning against a leather seat, presenting her perfect ass to me.

"Spread those long legs for me, Angel."

I stopped to admire her pretty pink pussy when all I wanted to do was dive right in. "So fucking sexy."

I wanted to remember this sight forever. It was on the tip of my tongue to ask her if I could take a picture, but I inherently realized that wasn't fair. Giving me that gift would take the ultimate trust, and I wasn't sure we were there yet. I'd never do a damn thing to hurt her, but I don't think I'd convinced her of that yet. Shit, I had work to do. She needed to know exactly how I felt about her before she left.

"Ryder, please. I need you."

My hands clasped her hips as I fell to my knees. I licked her sex once, front to back, before I used my tongue and fingers to make her come all over my mouth.

She was panting; her face pressed into the leather seat, while I unzipped my jeans and took out my straining cock.

"Pick that ass up, Angel. Show me that tight pussy. Baby, your long legs are a ten out of ten and your pussy is making my mouth water."

I kept up a stream of talk while I tore the glow-in-the-dark condom out of its wrapper and rolled it on my dick. She was still spasming from her orgasm when I finally pumped into her. I pushed into her maybe only three times before I was spilling into her. It felt like I unloaded forever.

And it wasn't enough.

I could never get enough of her.

♫♪♩♪♪

After we cleaned up, we finally made it into the second nightclub, which looked almost identical to the first club on the inside. We found everybody hanging out in the VIP section.

This time, Talia sat on my lap. She was talking to other people, including Grey, but she remained on my lap. Just where I wanted her to be. Her sweet ass was nestled right into my groin. Her hair tickled my face whenever she turned her head. I was happy just holding her. Content to be touching her soft skin.

I'd quit drinking so I could take care of her. I could tell she was tipsy because she was talking fast and loud and laughing at everything. She looked happy. She looked like my Angel.

My thumb was idly rubbing her wrist while she talked to some of my friends. I was impatient for this night to end. I wanted to get her alone. Get her home with me. Not for sex, but to talk. Would she even be sober enough to talk? Did she even want to talk? Or just fuck again?

Thinking about her leaving spiked my anxiety. I fucking needed her here with me. A long-distance relationship would be so fucking hard. Not after I knew how perfect it would be if we were together.

I remembered when Max, her ex-boyfriend, choked on the idea of fucking the same girl every night. I couldn't ever imagine having a forever with one girl, either. Until I met Talia. The sex had been the best ever. Every single time it seemed to get even better, and I'd felt even closer and more connected to her. Was that what love was? I'd never felt it before. I'd never even wanted to. Was that love? Because it was so scary. I couldn't even think about being separated. Fuck. Fuck. Fuck.

But was it fair to ask her to move to California? She'd have to leave her home, leave her job, leave her family and friends, leave everything she'd ever known behind. If it wasn't for the band, I'd leave California behind and go to Ohio. I'd leave the ocean, my house ...

A house that I'd no longer own in a week. How could I ask Talia to move here? I'd probably be living on Sid's couch until I found a cheap apartment. I'd be broke, homeless, and heading out on a huge tour soon — leaving her behind.

Fuck, it was so complicated. I'd known I wanted her to stay, but it took until the day before she was leaving to find out how much I needed her to stay. None of this was fair. Everything was happening so fast. Asking her stay was coming on too strong and too fast, but I couldn't do a long-distance relationship. It would kill me.

I made up my mind. There really wasn't any choice. I'd convince her to move to California. We'd get a place together. Maybe not on the ocean; I couldn't afford that anymore, but maybe closer to the rest of the band. She could easily get a new job; if not, I'd be able to hold us both over until money from our second album rolled in. She was already making new friends here, fitting in with his life.

I wanted her in my life. I could see my future — it was just like Tommy's — success with the band, dream home on the ocean, perfect girl, and maybe even the kids. The touring part would be more difficult to work out, but she could visit on tour. I saw how Cold Fusion did it with their wives. Ghost Parker wasn't there yet success-wise, and the band wasn't ready for a full-time girlfriend on tour with them yet, but I was ready. The vision of the future pulled at my heart. It made my pulse race. I was ready.

A tall kid from the wait staff tapped on my shoulder. "Mr. Mathis?"

I shook my cloudy head. "What's up?"

"There's a man over there that wants to talk to you. Your security isn't letting him back here."

I could see Tommy's security guys standing by the entrance to the VIP section but didn't see anyone else over there. "Did he say who he was?"

"No. But he said he wasn't leaving until you talked to him."

Damn. I didn't want to leave Talia. We had so little time left. I just wanted to take her home. Be alone. Convince her to stay with me.

"Hey babe." I rubbed Talia's arm to get her attention. "I've got to get up for a minute. Be right back."

Talia got up, a little wobbly on her feet. She'd been sucking down drinks. I was going to slow her down, so she didn't get too drunk to talk later.

I got up and headed over to the security guys. Halfway there, I stopped and turned.

I met her eyes across the room. Everything seemed to stop moving. Sound muted as if there wasn't loud music blasting. It was as if there was no one else in the room, just the two of us. It was a complete moment of clarity.

It was as if I was telling her with my eyes not to leave. Stay with me. You're the one. I felt it deep in my gut.

You're my forever girl.

The tall kid interrupted my moment. "He's still waiting for you. He told me to tell you he's a friend of Stan's."

My blood ran cold. I stalked over to the security guys, scanning the area for this guy. Fuck, what was going on?

That's when I saw him. Skull Crusher. He was grinning like a maniac when I approached, looking completely out of place in his biker gang threads.

"What the fuck are you doing here? Are you following me?"

"Hey there. Nice to see you too." He snarled like a dog, baring his teeth and showing off all the metal in his mouth. He looked past my shoulder and pointed, leering obscenely. "Who's the bitch with the nice tits that was sitting in your lap? Your girlfriend?"

If he'd been looking at me, he might have seen the flash of rage that quickly morphed into panic wash over my face, before I hastily schooled my features. It was dangerous to give this psycho any ammunition. If he thought Talia was important to me, she'd be in danger.

"No. She's not my girlfriend. She means nothing to me. She's just some tits and ass."

"Just some tits and ass? You wouldn't mind if I took her for a ride then, would you?"

I wanted to crush his fucking skull in, but I'd probably die trying. "Whatever. What are you doing here?"

He leaned in so close to me, I could smell his fetid breath. "Just wanted to let you know that I'm watching your every move. Don't try anything stupid and get me the fucking money. This is your last warning."

"I'll have your money by Wednesday. Where do I find you?"

He was staring at Talia again, licking his lips. "You'll get a text Wednesday morning with instructions. Follow them."

He turned and walked away, leaving me shaking with a mixture of rage and fear. The best thing I could do was get Talia on a plane and as far away from me as soon as possible.

Chapter 31

Talia

OF ALL THE PEOPLE here, I was currently bonding with Marie. Just a few days ago, I wanted to impale her with an ice pick when she'd been hitting on Ryder. We were both drunk, so there was that. We'd gotten talking, and she'd opened up a bit about herself, as drunk girls often do, and I found that I kind of liked her.

But now, Lacey was stopping by the clusters of people from our group and telling them we were headed back to the bus.

I glanced at my phone. How the hell was it almost 3 o'clock in the morning? And more importantly, where was Ryder? He'd disappeared more than an hour ago. On my last night here.

Lacey swooped between me and Marie. "Back on the bus, ladies. Where's Ryder? I couldn't find him. We only have the party bus until 4 a.m., so unless you plan on coming to the after-party and crashing at Sid and Bash's place, we've got to head out now if you want to make it back to Ryder's house."

I scanned the area for the hundredth time, looking for Ryder. "Maybe he's with Greyson? I haven't seen him in a while either?"

Lacey shook her head and wrinkled her nose. "Disappointingly, Greyson left with some skank. Apparently, he lives around here somewhere. Tommy and Livvy left with those security dudes about an hour ago, so he's not with him either. Do you think he's passed out somewhere?"

I started to worry. "He didn't seem drunk at all. Where could he be?"

Lacey's expression turned to pity. "Don't worry. I'll have the boys round him up. Why don't you head to the bus with Marie and wait?"

Marie linked arms with me. "Good idea. Let's head to the bus. They'll bring Ryder along."

"What's going on?" I felt my heart racing like a runaway train. "You both think he's hooking up with some girl right now?"

"Hon. Don't freak out. Everyone's heading to the bus. Let's just go. We don't want it to leave without us." She tried to tug me toward the exit. "I'm sure Ryder will explain everything to you."

I didn't believe it. Ryder wouldn't do that to me. If he was sick of me already, he only had to wait one more day and I was gone. Plus, we'd just had amazing sex only hours ago. He'd sworn to me that he wasn't a cheater. In my heart, I didn't believe he'd do that.

"You go ahead, Marie. I'll be there in a few minutes." I walked away before she could reply.

On unsteady feet, I headed toward the restrooms and ran into Kaylie on the way. "Hey. Have you seen Ryder? I've been looking for him."

The smile slid from her face, and she looked down at her feet. "No. Not in a while. I saw him talking to his friend over where the security guys were stationed about an hour ago."

"His friend? Who?"

Please don't say Melanie. Please don't say Melanie.

I guess I wasn't as secure in my convictions about Ryder after all.

"It was some guy I'd never seen before. Not with our group."

Some guy? Relief filled me. Then why did Kaylie look so guilty? "Is there something you're not telling me, Kaylie?"

Her expression told me everything. There was something. She knew something about Ryder.

She pasted on a fake smile. "Since you're leaving tomorrow, I just wanted to tell you that you're a really cool girl. Thanks for shopping with me; I know I'm gonna kick ass in that outfit we picked out. Maybe I'll land a lead role! I'll make sure to give you a shout-out in my acceptance speech at the Oscars. Hope life is good to you, Talia."

Kaylie was a sweet person, and I hoped she made it in the cut-throat Hollywood world. I smiled at her. "I'm sure you're going to be a big star someday, Kaylie. I put in a good word for you with Greyson, too. The next time I'm in L.A., I'll let you know. We can go shopping. That was fun last time."

Her brow wrinkled. "You think you'll be back?"

"I'm sure I'll be back visiting Ryder in not too long. Even though I haven't even left yet, I'm already missing him." I said, punctuating my statement with a chuckle so I didn't sound so pathetic.

She lifted a perfectly sculpted brow. "You really think you'll visit him again? Wasn't this just a lighthearted fling? A one-time thing?"

Was it really that hard to imagine Ryder with a girlfriend? "No. We're together. In a relationship."

She actually cringed. Hard.

"Kaylie, what aren't you telling me? What's going on? Please, tell me."

She looked around to make sure no one was listening to us. "Look. You're a great girl and I don't want to see you get hurt. I was sure I saw something in the way Ryder looked at you. He seemed different this time. I guess he had me fooled. But I don't want you to be misled. This relationship you have — it means nothing to him."

I let out a huff of breath. "That's not true."

She chewed on her bottom lip. "I'm sorry, Talia. I heard him say it."

Dread was pooling in the pit of my stomach. "Are you sure? I don't believe it."

She put her hand on my shoulder. "I'm positive. It shocked me when I heard it, so I stopped to listen. He was talking to that guy with the beard. They were pointing at you and talking. Ryder said that you meant nothing to him."

My head was shaking in denial. "No. You must have misunderstood."

She frowned. "I was so shocked. And disgusted! He said you meant nothing to him; you were just a nice piece of tits and ass. I'm so sorry; I wasn't going to tell you, but he's such an asshole for using you like this. It's better that you know before you ... get any deeper with him."

It was like someone pulled the rug out from underneath me. My world shook and rattled with shock for a few moments, before shattering into millions of sharp pieces with deadly, jagged edges.

A moan of misery escaped my lips. Oh my God! How could I have been so dumb? So naïve? I knew this was going to happen, but I'd convinced myself that he was sincere. Ryder had a fear of commitment, but I thought that had changed him. I believed he had genuine feelings for me, yet all along I was being played for a fool.

Kaylie saw the devastation on my face. She gently took my arm. "C'mon. Let's get on the bus. It's going to leave soon."

My limbs were functioning on autopilot. I blindly followed where

Kaylie led. When I got onto the bus, I slumped into the first empty seat. The music was blaring, lights were flashing, and people were partying, but I barely noticed any of it. I was shell-shocked.

More people got on the bus and then it was moving. I tensed when I realized Ryder was sliding into the seat beside me. He was trying to hand me a water bottle, but I ignored him.

"Talia, drink some water." He chuckled. "I've never seen you this drunk."

I didn't want to talk to him. How could I with this golf ball-sized lump in my throat? I leaned my head back against the seat and closed my eyes.

♫♫♪♪♪

I awoke with a start. For a few heavenly seconds, everything was wonderful. I was leaning against Ryder's warm body. His arms were wrapped around me, holding me.

We were still on the party bus, but it was silent and dark. There was no music pounding, no drunken people laughing and shouting, and no neon party lights flashing.

I felt a gentle nudge on my arm. "We're home, Angel. Am I going to have to carry you inside?"

Ryder was feathering kisses on my cheek when I remembered.

My heart felt like it cracked in half.

Again.

I pulled out of his deceitful arms and sprang to my feet. I wobbled a bit, feeling dizzy, and then stumbled off the bus.

"Angel, take it easy — you're going to fall. Here, drink some water."

I swatted Ryder's arm away when he tried to stabilize me at the door of his house. Once inside, I swayed up the stairs to the second floor.

"You're feisty when you get drunk." He chuckled behind me.

I reached the first door to the guest room and ducked inside the room. Turning to block Ryder from entering behind me, I said, "I'm sleeping in here tonight. Alone."

Then I slammed the door in his face. Satisfying.

The door opened moments later. Ryder stood on the threshold, looking pissed. "Are you mad at me?"

Ding. Ding. Ding.

"Where did you disappear to tonight, Ryder?" I hissed at him.

His expression softened. "I'm sorry. Something came up that I had to take care of. I didn't mean to leave you alone for so long."

I didn't want to get into it with him. I was drunk and upset, and none of it mattered anymore. My eyes had been opened and there was no going back to that blissful ignorance, no matter how much I wanted to.

"Something came up? Was it your cock? Who was she, Ryder? Melanie?"

"Jesus, Talia." From the look on his face, I knew I'd shocked him. "There was no other woman. I'd never do that to you. Look, let's just talk about this in the morning. You're not thinking clearly right now."

Fuck him. The liar. I was finally thinking clearly. I wasn't buying his bullshit anymore. To think his own brother had warned me about him.

I pushed on his chest. "Get out."

He ran a hand down the dark stubble on his face. "Angel, just come upstairs to bed with me. I won't touch you. I promise. We'll figure this out in the morning."

Tears were threatening to spill. I had to end this now. I spun away from him and yanked at my dress as I stepped out of my heels. It took less than a minute before I was stripped down to my bra and panties. Ignoring him completely, I climbed into the twin-sized bed and closed my eyes.

♪♪♩♪♪

Sun was streaming in the window when I woke up. My head was splitting and my mouth was parched drier than the desert. I snuggled deeper into the comforting arms encircling my body.

Fuck.

I was tangled up with Ryder in this tiny bed. My head rested on his chest, my thigh nuzzled between his legs, and my right hand rested on top of his toned pectoral right over the tribal sun tattoo.

I tried to untangle myself without waking him. He pulled me closer.

"Bathroom," I mumbled.

Ryder loosened my grip and groaned. "Hurry back."

I slipped out of bed, gathered up my clothes and my phone, and headed out the door, closing it quietly behind me. Upstairs in the kitchen, I washed down some aspirin with a bottle of water and then started a cup of coffee brewing.

There was an ache in my chest that was expanding to encompass my whole body. I was hurt.

Devastated.

I didn't want to spend another minute with Ryder. I needed to focus on the physical pain of my hangover to ignore the crippling heartbreak that was threatening to overtake me. More importantly, I needed to focus on the logistics of getting the hell out of there. Once I was home, I could crawl up into a ball and cry. One step at a time.

I pulled out my phone and ordered a cab to the airport. According to the app, I had 20 minutes until it arrived. Luckily, I had packed up most of my stuff yesterday when I was waiting for Ryder to get home.

Ten minutes later, I was stepping out of Ryder's luxury shower. I towel-dried my hair and then combed it out before twisting it into two small side braids that met behind my head, then mixed with the long hair hanging down my back.

Seven more minutes. I could do this.

I stopped short when I left the bathroom. Ryder was sitting on the bed, but he stood up when I came in. He'd been waiting. The only thing covering his perfect body was boxer shorts, and my traitorous eyes couldn't help but soak in every glorious detail. It pissed me off.

If I could channel that anger — feed off it — I might survive these last few minutes without ending up a blubbering mess.

I marched over to the pile of clothes I'd left out on top of my suitcase. I hesitated only for a moment before I threw off my towel and began getting dressed. Speed was more important than modesty, besides it was a little too late for modesty; I'd already stripped myself completely bare for him, right down to my soul.

His voice was still scratchy from sleep. "Are we fighting?"

I ignored him as I pulled on my jeans.

"I wasn't with any girls last night."

My silence was deafening.

"Talia, let's talk about this."

I zippered up my hoodie and then began slipping on sneakers. "I don't want to talk. I'm leaving."

He sighed. "We still have a couple of hours before we have to go."

I began zipping up my suitcase. "My car will be here any minute."

"What?" he sounded incredulous. "No. I'm driving you to the airport."

"No, you're not. I'm leaving now." Tears stung my eyes, but I willed myself not to cry.

"Don't do this," he pleaded with me. "Don't leave like this."

I grabbed my purse and carry-on bag. "Will you carry my suitcase downstairs?"

He made no move to help, so I dragged the heavy suitcase to the floor and began maneuvering it to the door. His hand stopped me as I got to the top of the stairs. He silently took the suitcase and followed me down both levels to the ground floor.

Luckily, the car was waiting for me. He followed me outside even though he was only wearing boxers and it was quite cold outside this early. The driver took the suitcase from him and began loading it into the trunk of the sedan.

I was barely holding it together. I was about to get into the backseat of the car when Ryder's hand on my arm stopped me. "Stop. Talia. Please."

I waited for him to say something. Something that would make this horrible nightmare go away. Some magic words to take away all my pain. 'Don't go' or 'I love you' flashed through my head. If he had said something even remotely like that, my weak, deluded self might have hesitated. I would have clung on to any beacon of hope. But he said nothing.

I was close to crying. No, more like close to ugly crying — falling to my knees and sobbing with nasty snot running out of my nose. And he just stood there gaping. Not saying the words I wanted so desperately to hear.

I wanted to hurt him. Make him feel a sliver of the pain that I felt. I stoked that fire of anger and hate. Of hurt and humiliation. Of loss.

I looked him in the eye and forced a smile. I probably looked demented. "Thanks for a great week, Mr. Rock Star. Thanks for helping me get something checked off my bucket list. Getting fucked by a rock star. And you were a wonderful fuck. Beyond the great orgasms, this week meant nothing to me. But that's over now and I need to get back home to my life. My real life."

I saw the shadow of pain cross over his face. His hand dropped to his side, and I used that opportunity to slip into the car.

"Have a good life, rock star. And do me a favor? Lose my phone number."

I slammed the door shut and told the driver to leave. I got one last glimpse of Ryder's face as we pulled away.

I'd landed a blow. Throwing his words right back in his face had been perfect. You mean nothing to me, Ryder. He looked genuinely upset.

Shattered.

What a hollow victory. I picked up my phone and blocked his number as the first tear slid down my cheek.

Chapter 32

Ryder

I KNEW THAT EVERY single word that spouted out of her pretty little lips was a lie, but I didn't know why. But, holy shit, that didn't stop me from playing them over and over again in my head. They decimated me. I felt like I'd been gutted with a knife and left for dead.

The instant panic I'd felt when her cab drove away started to sink in and settle deep into my bones. I was on the verge of losing my home, losing my girl, losing the future with her I'd only just realized I wanted so desperately.

I had to let her leave. It wasn't safe for her here with me. After the biker dude threatened me at the club, he stayed in the shadows, watching. He'd already seen Talia sitting on my lap; I didn't want to give him any reason to find out who she was. I made sure to stay away from her after that and that led her to believe that I'd hooked up with some other girl. She'd even mentioned the name Melanie, which she must have overheard me say when my realtor called before the party. Fuck. What a mess.

No matter how much I didn't want to, I was going to have to come clean to her about everything. How I was so fucking dumb to let Stan scam money out of me. All my mother's weaknesses and problems. My messed up family. The fucking loan sharks.

The important thing was that she was out of harm's way for now. Getting the money to pay off these animals was already put in motion. I just had to sit tight on that. Now I needed to fill Brock in, so he could make sure his family stayed safe.

It was going to be a brutal phone call. I showered and dressed and then I couldn't put it off any longer.

I called Brock's cell phone.

Not that I expected otherwise, but he didn't sound happy to hear from me. "This better be important. I'm in the middle of work."

"It is." I let out a long breath. "Turns out that the loan Stan took out was real. Mom signed something, I guess. Some guy, he called himself a collection's specialist, showed up to harass me for the money. He was some badass biker guy. Muscle."

Brock was silent for a long time. "Shit. Give me a second. I need to go somewhere more private."

About a minute later, he came back on the phone. "What did this guy say, exactly?"

"Basically, Stan borrowed $125,000 and skipped out. I'm not sure how much he originally borrowed, but it's accruing interest every day. I need to pay this guy $125,000 by next Wednesday. He made threats if I didn't."

"Stan — that motherfucker. He better never show his face around here again." Brock's voice shook with contempt. "How has this become your problem? $125,000 is a ton of money."

I stepped out onto the deck and looked out over the ocean. "No shit. I'm selling my house at a big fucking loss to cover it."

Surprise laced his voice. "You're just going to hand over that much money to some asshole to cover for Stan?"

"I don't have a choice."

"Well, fuck. If you're calling for money — sorry, little brother — you're not getting a dime from me. This isn't my mess."

I hadn't asked; but still, his rejection stung. "That's not why I called. This guy was making threats. Hinted that if I didn't pay, they'd go after Mom. He had a picture of Mom on his phone that he showed me." I took a deep breath. "Then he showed me a picture of you with Jenny and Joey. Said some stuff—"

I grimaced and held the phone away from my ear while Brock roared. Fuck. I knew he was going to explode, and I was right. I patiently waited out the muffled banging sounds and curses coming from the phone.

When he finally calmed down enough to listen, I jumped back on the phone. "Brock, I'll have the money in a few days. If I pay them off, he says it'll be over. It's not in their business model to go after anyone if they get the money they're owed."

Brock growled in my ear. "What the fuck! Start over and tell me the whole thing. I want to know every word he said. I want to know every last detail about him."

Brock made me go over the conversation several times. I told him that the guy called himself Skull Crusher and rode a motorcycle. Brock quizzed me about his clothing and tattoos, trying to see if we could determine some kind of biker affiliation with him. The only helpful detail I could recall was a black patch on his shoulder with a white skull placed in front of an opened flaming gate with the words 'Hell's Gate' stitched underneath.

We went over the threats Skull Crusher made several times. How he said he wasn't a part of the 'Columbus crew', but said they would hire a meth head to do the dirty work to make it untraceable back to them. I explained how he told me that going to the authorities would be useless and dangerous because they were all bought off. Then we talked about the photos that he'd said were sent with my 'file'.

When Brock was satisfied I'd given him all the information I could recall from the meeting, I told him about how Skull Crusher showed up at the nightclub and subtly threatened Talia when he'd seen her with me. This guy was keeping tabs on me.

Brock went quiet for a few minutes, digesting all that I told him. Finally, he spoke, "You've got to pay them off, Ryder. Whatever it takes. If you could get this guy on tape, maybe we could get an extortion conviction for this low-level player, but in the meantime, the big guys would send us a message and it would be fucking devastating. If anything ever happened to Jenny or Joey ..."

"I'm gonna pay them, Brock."

"Yeah. There's no choice. And until we know we're clear — that everyone's safe — I'm going to call in my brothers. Just in case."

"What do you mean?"

"My marine buddies. I just have to make a few calls and I'll have the most lethal fuckers of all protecting my family twenty-four/seven without them the wiser. And I'll get coverage on Mom." He paused and then added, "I can put a guy on Talia, too, if you want."

"She won't know they're there?"

He chuckled. "No fucking way. And she'll be safe from meth heads. Believe me."

"And they'll just do it if you ask?"

"Yeah. That's how it works."

"Okay. Do it. Thanks." I took a deep breath. "What else can I do?"

"Just make sure you get them the money as soon as you can, but don't fucking go past the deadline. No matter what. Get it to them today if you have it."

So far, I hadn't heard back from Melanie. "I'll have it in a few days. I'll get it to them on time."

Frustration ripped from Brock's mouth. "Fuck! I swear, if I ever get my hands on that mother-fucking asshole, Stan, he's dead."

"He's in Georgia."

I had Brock's attention. "How do you know?"

"I put a tracking app on Mom's phone. He took her phone with him. So I know exactly where he is — unless he sold the phone to someone else, but I figure he's too stupid and greedy to do that. I guarantee he's still using it. I was thinking about giving up his location to the Skull Crusher guy. He deserves whatever's coming to him."

"Don't." His response was quick. "You don't want his death on your conscience. Give the tracking app info and password to me. My guys will know what to do with it and make sure you don't turn off the phone just yet."

"Okay."

"And text me Talia's full name and addresses if you have them. Home and work. I'll make sure she stays safe."

"Okay, thanks."

I was about to hang up when he added, "You should talk to Dad."

"Dad?" Frankly, I hadn't even thought once about my dad. He wasn't a part of my life anymore. And Skull Crusher hadn't mentioned him, so I had no reason to believe Dad was in any danger.

"Yeah. Dad. I've gotta make some phone calls. Get that money, Ryder."

He hung up before I could reply.

I sat on the deck for a minute, trying to collect my thoughts. My mind kept circling back to the ugly scene from this morning when Talia left. I wanted to make things right with her, but she probably hadn't even gotten home yet.

Between Talia's leaving, me selling my house, and Skull Crusher's threats looming over my head, I was a wreck.

First things first. I scrolled through my texts to get Talia's work address and then found her home address on my GPS app from when I drove her home. Then I sent her address and all the information Brock had requested to him via text.

Next, I left a message for Melanie to call me back. I still hadn't heard from her and time was ticking.

I nervously paced around my house, waiting for my phone to ring. A crushing weight of loneliness settled around me. My life felt like it was falling apart and I had no one to talk to. No one to turn to. Fuck. And I missed Talia already. The house felt so empty.

About two hours later, Melanie called me back. "We've got a buyer. I gave them your contact information. You should check your email. You should already have a document that you need to sign that allows them to do a title search on your property. If it comes up clean, which it should, they'll send you information about when and where the closing will take place. They expect it to be in two days. That should work for you?"

I sucked in a breath. "Yeah. That works. There's no chance they'll cancel, is there?"

"Not if the title is clear. They would be fools to turn this down. You realize you're about to get absolutely crushed on this deal, right?"

A strangled 'yeah' was my reply.

Melanie sighed. "Bring the property deed with you. Once you settle on a price with the lawyers, you'll sign a bunch of documents —

they'll all be legally binding, so I strongly suggest you bring your own lawyer with you — and then they'll hand over your money in cash as I requested. You'll then be legally obligated to vacate your property, so start packing. I told them that you needed a few days to move out. That was all the time I thought I could buy. They seemed to agree to that."

"Shit. I haven't even thought about moving my stuff out of here yet. Tell me this isn't really happening; this is a complete nightmare." I could be homeless in two days. Where was I going to put my stuff? Where was I going to stay?

"Ryder, are you sure you have to go through with this? Tell me what's going on. Maybe I can help you?"

I went to my fridge and pulled out a beer. "Thanks, Melanie. You've already gone out of your way and done more than you know to help me. I appreciate it."

She hesitated a few moments. "Okay. Well, good luck with everything. Hope it all works out. In a few years, when you're ready for that big house in Malibu, call me. I've seen a few come up for sale that made me think of you."

"You'll be the first person I call. Thanks, Melanie."

I hung up the phone and chugged down half my beer. Dammit. I couldn't even imagine it anymore. The dream was slipping from my grasp. Everything was all fucked up.

Chapter 33

Ryder

I HAD NEVER SLEPT in my truck before. Walmart had closed 40 minutes earlier, but a surprising amount of cars were still coming and going from the parking lot. After searching on the internet for a free and safe place to sleep in a car overnight, I settled on Walmart. There was even an actual term for parking and sleeping there overnight, called wallydocking. Shit, I was wallydocking. I'd sunk pretty low.

I parked in a well-lit section away from the entrance but near the ever-present watchful eyes of security cameras. I chanced running into the store before it closed to use the restrooms and buy some snacks and breakfast for the morning. I said a prayer of thanks when I came back to see that the truck was still there and no one had broken into it.

The bed of my truck contained every last possession to my name.

The Adidas duffle bag stashed behind the seat on the inside of my truck held $96,000 worth of cash — all that I'd netted from the sale of my house.

I rested my head back against the headrest. I needed a plan. I couldn't live in my truck forever. For tonight, though, I felt safer guarding all my remaining worldly possessions and the money by sleeping here amongst them overnight.

I was facing so many problems I couldn't focus long enough on any one of them to brainstorm for solutions. The cutthroat lawyers wouldn't budge on their opening lowball offer; and then on top of that, they added insane transaction fees that gobbled up so much money. After paying off the mortgages I owed to the bank, I was left with much less than what I'd expected. Melanie had been right; I got fucked.

To make matters worse, the lawyers who represented the foreign assholes who bought my house and would never step one foot inside it demanded that I vacate the premises within 24 hours. In between band practices which I couldn't skip because we were about to go into the studio to record, I had to move out of my house.

A few boxes in the back of my truck contained some personal effects and kitchen items: small appliances, cookware, plates — anything I could fit. I stuffed the rest of my belongings, mostly clothing, into hefty-sized garbage bags. My surfboard was resting somewhere beneath all that junk. Inside the cab, I crammed the duffel bag of money, my guitars, a suitcase to live out of, a toiletry bag, and some food from my house that I could fit in the tight space. I'd left behind all the alcohol I had, a decision I regretted now.

I'd had to leave so much behind, including all my furniture and two TVs. It was depressing to think about, especially considering that giving up my house wasn't enough. I was almost $30,000 short on the money. Even if I sold my truck, I couldn't cover it. Maybe I could put the loan sharks off for a bit with the money I had, but they'd just pile on more interest. It felt like I was busy digging my own grave and I didn't know how to stop shoveling.

Sliding back my seat for more legroom, I tried to forget about the money for a moment and relax. I opened up a bottle of water and the bag of trail mix I'd bought in the store. I methodically picked out the raisins before I poured each scoop into my mouth.

Since Talia had left four days ago, this was the first quiet moment I had to think through how to get her back. I'd been running ragged between the long days of band practice, the high-pressure meeting where I sold my house, and then not sleeping last night so I could pack up all my belongings and move out by this morning. I got through today's practice by running on pure caffeine alone.

Even though I'd expected to pass out by now from total exhaustion, physical and mental, strangely, my mind wouldn't shut down. Every free moment I'd gotten in the past four days, I'd tried calling Talia, but she never answered. Dozens of texts, each becoming increasingly more desperate, remained unanswered. Either she'd blocked my number or she'd decided to shut me out for good.

Had she given up on us that easily? Maybe I was deluding myself, but I didn't believe the hurtful words she threw at me when she left.

Getting fucked by a rock star to check off my bucket list.

This week meant nothing to me.

The words repeated in my head. I rejected them. They didn't fit. Talia wasn't like that. She felt something deeper for me; I knew it. I just needed to make her see it.

What was I going to do if she wouldn't even talk to me? I needed advice. Someone to help me figure this out because my head had been spinning in circles for days. Who could help me? There was nothing like being homeless, sleeping in my truck, to make the loneliness feel bone-deep. I felt helpless.

I spun the leather bracelet that was wrapped around my wrist. It had become a comforting talisman for me ever since I'd found it while I was packing up my house. It had been tucked away at the back of a drawer in my bathroom next to the sink that I never used. But Talia had used that sink while she was here, so I'd gone through the drawers hoping she might have left something of hers behind. I needed something of hers to cling to. What I found was so much better.

I opened the square box, wondering what was in it. Had Talia left behind some jewelry by mistake? Inside was a black leather cuff bracelet. Until I read the inscription on the inside of it, I didn't know it was for me. It read, 'ALWAYS REMEMBER US, LOVE ANGEL'.

She'd bought this for me, but then never gave it to me. What did it mean? Sometimes, when I thought about it, it gave me hope. It was proof that she had genuine feelings for me. Other times, like now, it just sounded like goodbye.

I knew I loved her. I'd figured that out before she left but hadn't had the chance to tell her before everything fell to pieces. I would find a way to tell her now. Even if I had to go to Ohio and hire a skywriter. Whatever it took.

I picked up my phone and tried calling her for the hundredth time. Straight to voicemail. I didn't even bother leaving another message. I sent a text begging her to talk to me. It looked like it was sent, but wasn't marked 'delivered', just like with the other texts I'd been leaving.

Without thinking too much, I pulled up Ellie's phone number and called it. Seconds ticked by, excruciatingly slow, as I waited for her to answer. Finally, she did.

She was whispering into the phone. "Is this Ryder? Why are you calling?"

"Ellie, I want to talk to Talia. She's not answering my calls."

She whispered again. "Ryder, she blocked you. She doesn't want to talk to you."

I wanted to punch something. "I need to explain to her. About what happened — I'll explain everything."

Ellie must have moved out of the room because she wasn't whispering anymore. "She doesn't want your explanations. She's done with you."

"I'm not sure exactly what—"

"Ryder, she blocked you for a reason. Why don't you just leave her alone? You've done enough."

"Ellie, you have to listen to me—"

"Sorry, Ryder."

The phone went dead.

♪♫♪♩♫

On Monday, I turned up at band rehearsal unshowered and 45 minutes late. The back seat of my truck was way too small and lumpy for me to get comfortable in. I was tossing and turning until dawn and then, when the sun started coming up, I crashed. I must have turned off my alarm and fallen straight back to sleep.

I couldn't afford to make a misstep with the band at this point in my life — I was fucking homeless and destitute — but I couldn't seem to gather up two shits worth of remorse for being late.

During the first break we took, I left the practice room and wandered down the hall. I wanted to look up the book value of my truck and maybe make a few calls to see if I could get it sold. I stopped at the end of the hall near the stairwell door; I needed to keep the practice room in sight because I'd stashed the duffel bag full of cash in there instead of leaving it in my truck during practice. This section of the city was shady and if the money got stolen, I was totally fucked. I didn't think anyone would mess with all my stuff in the back of the truck because the black bags of clothes made it look like I was hauling a bunch of garbage around.

I kicked angrily at the metal door to the stairwell when I got confirmation from a website that selling my truck was not going to cover the shortfall of money that I needed. That's when I noticed Knox was heading my way.

"You okay?" he asked as he approached.

"Yeah." I kept my focus on my phone, hoping he'd go away.

He didn't take the hint. "What's going on, mate? You're looking a wee bit knackered."

"Just got a lot on my plate right now."

He came and leaned against the wall next to me. "Like what?"

I tried to blow him off. "Lots of shit."

"It can't be that bad. Hit me with what you got."

I looked at the grinning fool and lost it. "How about this — the girl I love won't even talk to me — she's gone, I sold my house to pay off a bad debt so I'm homeless right now and broke, I need even more money to pay off some asshole named Skull Crusher who's threatening my family, so I might sell my truck which is currently filled with everything I own. Man, to top it all off, I fucking wallydocked last night."

Knox's mouth dropped open in shock. "Wallydocked? What the hell? I don't even want to know what that is, mate."

I couldn't help but crack a smile. "No, you really don't."

"Holy fuck, mate!" Knox shook his head. "Why didn't you tell us what was going on? We could've helped with some of it."

"I don't know. It all just started piling on at once."

"You know you can stay on my couch until you get back on your feet. Or any of the other guy's couches — when I get tired of your ass. And maybe, between us all, we can scratch up the money you need."

Despite our recent bickering, these guys were like my brothers and I could count on them when things looked grim. I needed to swallow my pride. "Thanks, it means a lot to me, but I hope it doesn't come to that. I think I'll take you up on your couch offer, though. I was going to ask Sid, but that place is party central and I haven't slept in days."

Knox nodded. "Yeah, follow me back to my place after rehearsal and we'll get you set up. Maybe we can find some room to store some of the crap that's in your truck."

Just having a place to sleep tonight eased some of my immediate pressing worries.

Knox started heading back to the practice room but then turned back. "Your family can't help out with the money?"

"No." I frowned. "It's complicated."

Actually, it was simple. My mother caused this whole mess by turning to Stan, a complete scumbag. My father didn't give a shit about me, and Brock hated my guts. It wasn't complicated, it was just messed up, and I didn't feel like explaining it.

But Knox's question jogged something in my memory — Brock had told me to call Dad. I sat for a moment contemplating that advice. What would my dad say to all of this? How would he react? I wasn't sure. He was a virtual stranger to me now.

I searched my phone for my dad's contact. The number I had was a work number, but I didn't know if it was current. I didn't even know if my dad was still working as a bigwig at the giant insurance company in Connecticut. When a woman answered the phone, I asked for my dad.

"I'm sorry. He's in a meeting right now. May I ask who's calling?"

"This is his son."

"Oh. Hi Brock!" she gushed. "How is your precious little boy doing? He's so adorable!"

I was taken aback. It sounded like my father's secretary was well acquainted with Brock. I had no idea Brock and Dad even spoke with each other. This new information was somehow disconcerting.

"No. This isn't Brock." I decided that calling my father was a mistake. "Never mind. I don't need to leave a message."

"I'm sorry—"

I hung up. Fuck my dad.

I only had two days left. I needed to focus on scrounging up the last bit of money. I went back to researching where I could sell my truck the quickest. Maybe it was time to swallow my pride and beg my friends, including Tommy, to loan me what they could. No matter what, I couldn't miss this deadline.

My phone rang. The number calling was from Connecticut. It couldn't be my father; he was busy in a meeting. Maybe his secretary was calling back from a different line?

I told myself not to answer, but curiosity got the better of me. "Hello?"

"Ryder? It's Dad. Connie told me you called?" The hopeful note I heard in his voice made me recoil.

Dammit, I shouldn't have picked up. I wasn't sure what to say, so I blurted out the first thing that came to mind. "She said you were in a meeting."

"I was, but Connie knows that I'd want to be interrupted for you. Is everything okay?"

This was my chance to unload my problems, so why was I so reluctant to tell him? Maybe my dad would loan me some cash. I'm pretty sure that was why I'd called him, but suddenly, I was reluctant to say anything.

"Everything's fine. I shouldn't have interrupted you. I gotta go…"

"Wait! Ryder, please. Don't go." He sounded frantic to keep me on the phone, but then he switched to the friendly, calm tone that had always made me feel safe as a kid. "Tell me what you've been up to. How is Ghost Parker doing? Are you working on the second album yet?"

I grunted in disbelief. "Dad, this wasn't a social call."

His voice remained even. "Okay. Then tell me why you called. Please."

I needed money. Badly. So I told him.

"Stan left Mom."

He sighed. "And she's not taking it well?"

"She doesn't know he's gone for good yet. I'm glad the fucker is gone, but he left a lot of problems behind."

"Money problems?" he guessed.

"Yeah. Mom is about to be evicted. And even worse, he took out loans with a loan shark and then disappeared, leaving her holding the bag."

"I've been paying your mom's rent and utilities directly to the management company ever since she moved there. She's not going to be evicted."

I leaned back against the wall, feeling nauseous. "I didn't know that."

All the money I'd given to Stan, supposedly to help my mother keep up with the rent, had been a big scam. I'd been so damn stupid to hand over money blindly to that fat bastard. The mortification cut deep. I didn't want my dad or anyone to discover just how gullible I'd been.

Dad prompted me to continue. "The loan shark thing sounds more problematic. What's going on with that?"

He listened closely while I told him about Skull Crusher's visits and the threats he made if I didn't pay the $125,000 by Wednesday.

He was quiet for a few moments. "I'll begin getting the money together, but I'm going to speak with some of my law enforcement contacts to make sure we're doing the right thing by paying these guys off. Sometimes doing that just emboldens them to come back for more, but those threats are serious and not something to ignore, so I'll get the ball rolling with the money. My instinct is to pay it."

Just like that, my father was planning on paying off the whole thing? Skepticism kicked in. "I already have $92,000 and I'm hoping to get another $20,000 from my truck. That leaves $13,000 more. If you could lend me that, I would appreciate it."

"Where did you get the $92,000?"

It was none of his business where I got the money. I almost didn't answer him. "I sold my house."

"Jesus Christ, Ryder. You sold your house? In a matter of days? And you only got $92,000 out of it?" His voice was jagged and raw. "Why didn't you ask me for help sooner?"

My answering laugh was humorless. "I didn't even think about you. You're not exactly at the top of my list of people to rely on, Dad. Frankly, I'm surprised you're helping at all."

I heard the quick intake of air. "We've been strangers to each other for too long." His voice caught with pent-up emotion. "It's not how I want things. I know it's my fault. I want the chance to clear things up between us."

He sounded sincere, but I wasn't interested in our relationship, or lack thereof. "I like the distance in our relationship. The less I hear from you, the better."

He covered a weird gasping sound with a cough. "Right. Back to business — don't sell your truck. I'll cover the money — the $33,000. I'll have it for you in cash by tomorrow. Does Brock know about this?"

"Yeah. He organized his marine buddies to watch out for Jenny, Joey, and Mom. And for my — for Talia."

He cleared his throat. "That's good. Let me get to work on this end. I'll be in touch."

"Okay. Thanks." I spoke into the phone, but he'd already hung up.

Chapter 34

Talia

October in Ohio sucked. What sucked even more were November, December, January, February, and March. Even April was sometimes too damn cold.

I'd only been back from California less than a week and I was already missing the 80-degree weather and bright blue skies I'd left behind. The morning commute had been awful. Sleet and freezing rain had left a sheet of ice everywhere.

The roads were sufficiently salted and sanded for my ride home, but they left the landscape looking grimy. The bitter, stiff wind was sending cascades of shriveled and dried leaves to the ground. I'd missed peak leaf season while I was away. Now, the trees seemed in a hurry to shed every bit of color still remaining in the bleak gray setting.

I parked my car and then carefully made my way over the slippery pavement to my apartment. I hoped Ellie was alone. Her relationship with Eric, the climber/repeller, had developed while I was away. In fact, they were in the sickening 'can't be without each other' stage.

He'd driven Ellie to the airport to pick me up, so when Ellie had asked how my trip had gone, I'd told her it went great. Since then, she'd been shacked up with him every single day. It took three days for her to figure out something was wrong with me. Of course, she'd been supportive when I finally spilled the beans, but it still hurt that it took her so damn long to notice.

I'd given myself one day to wallow in my broken heart. Friday night, when Ellie went out, I stayed in and spent the night crying and blubbering. It should have been enough. Ryder wasn't worth any more sorrow. But it didn't work.

I couldn't sleep.

I couldn't eat.

The world looked gray and uncaring. Work was agonizingly unfulfilling. Food was tasteless. Jokes weren't funny. Ellie's happiness with Eric sent a jolt of jealousy through me. Maybe I'd lose her, too.

Thankfully, the apartment was empty when I got inside. As I had too many times this past week, I scrolled through the handful of pictures that I had of Ryder. Tears welled up in my eyes. We both looked so happy together.

I missed him.

Why couldn't he be the man I needed? Why couldn't he love me the way I loved him?

I heard Ellie at the door, so I wiped away my tears and swallowed down the fresh wave of pain.

Ellie pulled off her jacket and dropped her work bag onto the floor near the entrance. She sounded way too cheerful. "Man, it's nasty outside. It took me forever to get home. I'm making tacos tonight. You want to join us?"

Oh great. 'Us' meant Eric was coming over again. Ugh. "Sure. Sounds good."

She sidled up next to me. "Whatcha looking at? Ryder again?"

I glanced down at my phone. Busted. My screen was displaying a picture of Ryder and me at the Hollywood sign.

"You still mooning over him?"

"Sorry, not all of us are as perfect and nauseatingly happy as you and Eric." I immediately regretted my bitter words.

"Okay. Let's talk." She moved into the kitchen and pulled out some wine glasses. "I know you're still upset about Ryder and I've tried to be supportive, but maybe not enough? And me and Eric—"

Holding up my hand, I cut her off. "I'm sorry, El. I'm just insanely jealous and lashing out at you. I didn't mean it. Really. I've had a bad day at work and sadly, I'm busy throwing myself a huge pity party."

She pulled a half-full bottle of wine from the fridge and filled our glasses. "Am I invited to this pity party? Because I've got the wine and an ear to listen."

"I've got nothing new that you haven't already heard before. It's just …"

"What?"

I took a sip of wine. "I don't want to say it out loud. It seems so damn pathetic."

She pulled up a stool to sit next to me. "Tell me. No judgment here. Promise."

She was my best friend in the world. It felt good to be talking to her, a bottle of wine in between us. "I guess I was still holding out hope that I was mistaken about him hooking up with some girl. There was a tiny little flame burning, just hoping I was wrong, and he had feelings for me. Real feelings. That he'd try to fight for us."

I took a gulp of wine and continued. "Instead, he hasn't done anything. I'm sure he forgot about me the moment I got in that cab. He was probably relieved to have me gone, so he could go back to hooking up with whoever. Go back to his rock and roll life. I guess it's just sinking in that it really is over."

"Do you think that's all it was? Just a fling?"

"It didn't feel like that." I groaned. "When I was there with him, it started to feel like something more. More than just sex. I fell in love with him, yeah, but I thought maybe he was feeling something, too. That I was different from other girls. Special."

I swirled the wine around in the glass as I thought out loud. "Being with him felt so right. We had a connection. He was so tender and giving at times. Always making me laugh. The way he looked at me sometimes ... We felt so close. It's hard to explain."

Ellie looked at me. "It's not that hard. You fell in love with him.

"I was thinking about texting Greyson. See if he's seen Ryder."

Ellie winced. "Why? How would that help?"

"I don't know. I just want to know what he's doing. Did he just forget about me? Move on? I've scoured the gossip pages and there's nothing new about him on any site. It's been pretty quiet for all the guys. It's frustrating. I know that it's stupid."

"It's probably not a good idea."

I wiped a stray tear away. "I'm not over him."

"No kidding."

I could barely speak past the lump in my throat. My voice wobbled. "I'm still in love with him."

"Oh, honey. Didn't he cheat on you?"

"I'm not sure, but I think he did. Who knows?" Confusion washed over me. "I don't think he's ready for a real relationship. He told me that. But, I thought that changed. God, it just feels so shitty to be without him."

The tears started rolling down my cheeks in earnest now.

Ellie frowned at me. "Let me ask you a few questions ..."

I dragged my sleeve over my face, trying to stem the flow, and nodded at Ellie.

"Did you ask him for an explanation about what happened?"

I shook my head. "No, I didn't give him a chance. I was so devastated by what he did I didn't want to hear him try to weasel out of it."

"But he tried to talk to you?"

"Yeah, I guess."

She poured herself some more wine. "If all he was looking for was a quick fling, wouldn't it have been easier for him to just let you go?"

"That's exactly what he did. He's certainly not fighting for me now."

She raised an eyebrow. "How do you know? You blocked him."

"That shouldn't stop him." I huffed. "He could have come to the airport and stopped me from leaving. Or he could have had people contact me for him. I didn't block Kaylie's number. Or Greyson's. Or his sister-in-law, Jenny's. But I've gotten nothing but silence."

"What if I told you he called me?"

My head whipped around to face her. "What?"

"I told him to leave you alone. I didn't want him upsetting you all over again."

My heart was racing. "When did he call?"

"Sunday night."

"That was two days ago. And nothing since?"

She looked unsure. "He sent me a text yesterday."

"Oh, my God!" I slid off the stool and started pacing. "Let me see it."

"Tal, are you sure?"

I stopped myself from pulling out my hair in frustration. "I'm sure.

Let me see it."

Ellie grabbed her phone and pulled up the text. Attached was a picture — a close-up shot of the leather cuff I'd bought him wrapped around his wrist. Under the picture, it said, 'Don't give up on me, Angel.'

Chapter 35

Ryder

"Who destroyed the toilet?" Bash sauntered into the room, throwing out the accusation.

With everything going on, I'd had the nervous shits all week, but it wasn't me. And I sure as hell wasn't dumb enough to say anything.

"Wasn't me." All eyes turned to Knox.

Sid snickered. "Are you denying it? You know ... whoever denied it, supplied it."

"That's dumb." Knox fiddled with his guitar. "Besides, that only applies to farts."

"Knox, man. What the fuck! It was like a crime scene in there." Bash continued to team up against Knox. "My eyes were watering."

Knox scowled and flipped him the middle finger. "I haven't even gone into the bathroom today. It was probably you, Bash. You're just trying to cover up for a massive shite explosion."

Donovan interrupted the juvenile banter. "Jesus Christ, can we drop it already? What are we, 10 years old?"

Heads swiveled in Donovan's direction and laughter erupted, as several voices called out at once.

"Aha. It was you!"

"Big D with the big dump."

"Donovan desecrated the toilet."

I chuckled as I watched Donovan's face turn beet red.

"It wasn't me, you dumb fucks, but whatever." He suddenly became very interested in something on his phone.

Just then, my cell phone vibrated in my pocket. I rested my guitar in my lap and fished the phone out. It was a text message from an unknown phone number from Connecticut.

> **UNK**: This is Dad. The money is ready. Where will you be in about an hour so I can get it to you?

My stomach tightened. Practice might wrap up in an hour — we'd been here all day already — but I'd stay and wait for the money. God, I couldn't wait for this nightmare to be over.

> **ME:** I'll send you the address. I'm at band rehearsal on the third floor. I'll call the front desk, so they'll let your guy come up.

Then I looked up the street address of the building I was currently sitting inside because I didn't remember it offhand and sent it to my dad in a new text.

One of our new songs was coming off flat and lifeless, so Donovan had us run through it several more times, making various changes. It was finally shaping up into something closer to our band's energetic sound when my dad walked in the door.

I almost didn't recognize him. I'd only seen him three or four times in the past five years, and the last time I saw him must have been over two years ago. His hairstyle was edgy — textured and spiky on top with a fade on the sides — yet the salt and pepper color and close-trimmed beard gave him gravitas. He was wearing a business suit and looked healthy and fit. Compared to the shock of seeing my mom looking so haggard and old when I visited her, it surprised me to see my dad looking so well. Surprised and angered me.

We finished our song, and then all eyes turned to my dad.

I stood up from my stool. "Dad, what are you doing here?"

My dad held up his hand. "I'm sorry I interrupted. I know you're busy. Is that one of your new songs? It sounded terrific. I can't wait to hear the rest of the album."

Donovan looked back and forth from me to my father, studying us with interest. "Yeah. It's getting there. I think we're pretty close with that one. Tomorrow, we've got to get *Embers* worked out. The chorus is working, but we have to tidy up the verse. Let's wrap it up for today, boys."

Donovan introduced himself to my dad while we started putting away our equipment. I was moving in slow motion because my mind was in a whirl. Why had my dad come? Did he have the money? What was going on?

Over the years, my dad had come to a few of our shows, so he'd met all the members of Ghost Parker. When Donovan left, one by one, the guys went over to say hello to my dad, until he was chatting amicably with all of them. From the conversation, I could tell that he followed news of our band. All the guys were laughing and joking with him like he was an old pal. I realized the emotions that this evoked within me were childish, but it felt disloyal to me like my friends were siding with the enemy.

When I couldn't find anything else to fiddle with to delay the reunion with my dad, I forced myself over to the circle surrounding him.

His eyes lit up as he stepped toward me. "Ryder, son, it's good to see you."

He gave me a hug, thumping me on my back, while I stood there enduring it, but not returning it.

"I was hoping we could go out somewhere for dinner tonight? Catch up a bit?" The beseeching look he flashed begged me not to decline, but then he swept his arm, gesturing to the rest of the band before adding, "And I'd love for everyone to join us. It's on me."

I was about to mumble out some excuse not to go when Ghost beat me. "Nah, Mr. Mathis. We don't want to get in the way of your time together. You and Ryder go out. We'll catch you later."

The guys all added their agreement, and it was settled.

Dad beamed at me. "Any favorite restaurants you recommend?"

If dinner was the price I'd have to pay to get the loan from my dad, then I'd suck it up. "There's a Mongolian barbecue restaurant near Knox's place that I've been wanting to try, but it's supposedly expensive."

"Perfect. Sounds great. I took a cab here from the airport, so I'm hoping I can ride with you?"

"Yeah." I grabbed my guitars. "I've got to drop off Knox first. It's gonna be crowded in the truck. You might end up with a guitar on your lap."

After we'd chosen the ingredients for our meal and watched the chef grill up our selections, we sat across from each other, ready to enjoy our food. I'd rebuffed most of the breaking-the-ice questions my dad was asking about my life without being overtly rude. If he gave a shit about me, he would already know this stuff.

Getting out from under the loan shark had been weighing on my mind for days. I couldn't care less about the small talk. My dad had a wheeled carry-on and a briefcase with him. I hoped like hell there was cash inside of one of them.

He took a bite of food, so I cut off the stream of questions he was asking me while I had the opportunity. "I'm assuming you have the money for me?"

"I do." He pushed some vegetables around in his bowl. "I talked to some law enforcement contacts that I have. I'm worried that this gang won't leave you alone after you pay them off. If they did their homework, they know you're in a band that's on the cusp of breaking out big. They might see you as their meal ticket."

I nodded in agreement. "Yeah. That's crossed my mind."

"It's important that we shut this down. Make it a no-brainer for them to leave you alone after you make the payment. I have the name of a guy here in L.A. He's an expert on these situations and I'm told he's an intensely scary dude that has lots of street cred. I've hired him to do the money exchange for you. It's what everyone suggested we do."

I lifted a brow in disbelief. "How can this guy keep them from coming back for more? What's he going to do?"

"Nothing illegal." He tapped the table. "In fact, he's working with officials, but I don't know any details. The authorities coordinated with my bank regarding the cash, so I'm assuming they will trace the serial numbers. This is more than a loan shark operation we're dealing with — I'm told it's a criminal gang. My guess is the feds will map the flow of the money for investigational purposes."

I fiddled with my beer bottle. "I don't know about this. They said if I got the police involved, they'd hurt Mom or Brock's family."

"That's the first thing I told the special task force liaison. At first, they suggested we don't pay the money at all — set up a sting, but I emphasized that the main priority in this was to protect my family — you, your mom, and Brock. So, this alternative is what the experts suggested. The feds will be deep in the background. There's no way for the loan sharks to know the money is being tracked and the delivery guy is in a rival gang — he won't be connected to law enforcement at all."

"What about Stan?" Just thinking that the asshole would get away with everything roiled the food in my stomach.

He speared the last few bits of food in his bowl before answering. "The feds don't care about him. They view him as a victim in this, just like you are. I only care that he never goes near your mother again."

I couldn't hold back my disbelief. "Like you really care!"

"I do care." His eyes narrowed as he studied my face. "I always have. I care about all of you."

"You have a funny way of showing it." Bitterness dripped from my voice.

He leaned back in his chair and methodically wiped his mouth with the linen napkin from his lap. "Would I be here right now if I didn't care, Ryder?"

I watched him, contemplating me from across the table, and felt the simmering anger that was lurking just below the surface rise in my chest.

"Just because you're throwing some money at me doesn't magically wipe the slate clean, Dad. What about Mom? What about our family? You abandoned us. You found a new family and just fucking walked away from us."

A shadow fell across his face and I knew I'd hurt him. Good. He deserved it and so much more.

"I did my best to keep you and Brock in my life." He kept his voice low and even. "I never meant to abandon you."

I snickered disdainfully. "You never meant to? It just sort of happened? By mistake? Please. I don't want to hear your bullshit."

His face twisted with sadness. "You're an adult now, Ryder. Let's talk about this like adults. I know you're angry. I didn't handle everything perfectly, but I did the best I could at the time."

My mind raced as I fought the urge to run from this conversation. I didn't want to have it and I didn't want my father to see my pain, but I did have a burning desire to see him suffer for what he'd done. I wanted his remorse, and then I'd throw it back in his face. It was messed up.

"You want to talk about this like adults, Dad? You realize I've been an adult for years now, don't you? Yet, you barely know me. And, you know what? I don't give a shit. Just give me the money and you can get back to your real family." My voice cracked on the last few words. Fuck, I was losing it.

His eyes blinked rapidly like he was struggling to hold back emotion. "I want to know you, Ryder. I've tried. You've got to let me in."

This was all wrong. I didn't want this. I slid back my chair to get up. "That ship has sailed."

"No, wait!" He held up his hand to stop me. "Don't you think you've punished me enough? You don't return my calls, you won't visit, you make up lame excuses so I can't visit you, all my cards get returned unopened ... what do I have to do?"

I tried to maintain steely indifference, but there was a slight wobble in my voice when I answered. "I don't want to have a relationship with you."

He sucked in a sharp breath. "You know, I've been to dozens — maybe even fifty — of your concerts. All the way back to the first band from middle school, Shadow Society. I went to five shows from your last tour with Cold Fusion. Arianna went to two of them with me, but most of them I went to by myself. Just to see you."

Something tightened in my chest. Hurt. Betrayal.

I never realized he'd come to any of my shows, let alone that many. My mother had never been to even one show, though I'd asked her to over and over. Obviously, Brock hadn't either. It was interesting, but that wasn't what caught my attention.

"You still see Arianna? Even after you divorced her mom years ago? She's not even related to you by blood, yet you still see her. Jesus, Dad. That's fucked up."

He studied his plate, not looking me in the eye. "She's going through a rough patch with her father. We've always kept in contact. Did you know that Suzie remarried her first husband after we divorced? He's the reason we ended our marriage. They began ... reconnecting."

I had no idea. My eyebrows rose. "Seems fitting. Karmic retribution?"

"Mmm. Maybe." His sigh sounded melancholy. "Arianna is a huge fan of Ghost Parker. Frankly, I think that's why she keeps connected with me. She tells everyone about her famous step-brother."

I pictured a bright blonde toddler waddling around in a puffy diaper. "I barely remember her. How old is she now?"

"Eighteen."

"How could she be eighteen already?" His answer shocked me. Time was marching by and I'd been studiously ignoring it. "Let me know the next time you're bringing her to a concert. I'll get you backstage passes."

"She'd love that. And by love that, I mean, high-pitched shrieking absolute teen-aged freak-out."

Yeah, I'd experienced that exact reaction at a few of the meet-and-greets. "Uh. Well."

Dad smiled. "Yeah, that's the age — teenage girls. But really, she absolutely adores you and she's madly in love with Knox, so it would make her so happy to meet the band."

"Knox, huh?" I chuckled.

"The first show I ever took her to, Knox had just joined the band."

I took a long pull of my beer. "I never knew you were coming to so many of my shows."

"Didn't you realize?" His smile was subtle. "I'm your number one fan."

It felt like a boulder had settled in my stomach. Number one fan. I'd heard that before.

The waiter swung by the table and Dad spoke to him for a moment, asking for two new beers. It gave me time to think. My brain shuffled through some memories at lightning speed.

There was the time the van broke down on our 'tour' and we'd almost given up doing the whole damn thing because we were so poor and miserable — but then repairs had been mysteriously paid for.

The Christmas card that was full of cash that we received just in time to celebrate our first holiday on the road with a meal from a decent restaurant.

Then there were the countless pieces of equipment we'd had to replace: guitar amp, microphone and stand after Ghost broke it after a drunken performance, bass drum, cables — the list went on and on — that a mysterious gift at just the right time bailed us out.

When we were straight-up broke, just as we thought we couldn't last another day, our secret benefactor would come through. He always signed the letters 'your #1 fan'. We'd all tried to figure out who it was over the years. We'd even wondered if one of the roadies was secretly wealthy and helped us out because he just liked the rock and roll scene and touring with a band. But roadies were always coming and going. Our anonymous fan had stuck around much longer than that.

Was my father the one who'd been giving the band cash infusions just when we needed it most? He'd been coming to my shows all along, but had he been following us that closely? I didn't know what to think. If it was true, did that make all the other shit go away? Fuck.

I picked up my beer and chugged the rest of it. I wiped my mouth with the back of my hand and then stared at my dad for a long minute. "Why did you leave us?"

He was quiet for too long, struggling as emotions flashed over his face. I was sure he wasn't going to answer, but then he shifted in his seat. "There were six years between you and Brock. The first miscarriage knocked us to our knees, but we survived. It was rough, but we both knew there'd be other chances. The second one, after getting our hopes up again, was devastating. I wanted to stop trying; it was just too painful, but your mother wouldn't hear of it. She became obsessed with having another baby."

I listened in silence, the misery of my parent's marriage becoming clearer. I'd never known any of this.

"We suffered through five miscarriages and with each one, your mother sank deeper and deeper into herself. She was depressed. At times, she couldn't even take care of Brock. She lost a piece of herself with each baby that didn't make it; she became this dull, gray version of the vibrant woman she'd once been.

"For years, I begged her to get help. I wanted to stop putting us through the agony of horrific grief over and over again. I suggested we adopt, but she wouldn't hear any of it. We had been so happy together, and suddenly it felt like we were trapped in absolute hell. It was agonizing."

Dad took a sip of beer, staring out into nothing.

"When your mom got pregnant with you, I didn't believe you'd make it. I didn't let myself feel anything until the very end. It was nine months of torture, waiting for what I thought was inevitable. I was so scared."

Dad's eyes began to fill with unshed tears. "I still remember the day you were born. You seemed like a miracle baby. I was giddy with happiness and so relieved. It felt like a thousand pounds had been lifted from my shoulders. I was on cloud nine, but your mom was listless. I figured she was just exhausted after the long labor."

I swallowed past the lump in my throat. No one had told me any of this.

"I thought your mom would be better after she had you," Dad continued. "I thought we were going to go back to the early days of our marriage when we were both so happy. We had the perfect little family. Everything we'd been desperately trying for the past six years.

"She never got better. After you were born, she didn't want to have sex anymore. She was emotionally distant — to everyone. Something was really wrong with her. All the miscarriages and grief and hormones had changed her. She was just ... broken. I tried to get help for her, but she wouldn't go to any doctors. It was a rough time."

The waiter came back with our new beers. I took a long gulp of beer, using the time to digest everything that I was learning.

"You didn't divorce until I was nine."

My dad frowned. "Yeah, I spent nine years trying to coax her out of it. It was a loveless marriage, but I wanted to stay for you boys. I wanted to help your mom."

His words settled over me. I'd been so young, I'd had no clue as to the state of their marriage. No one had ever told me and I'd never asked. This shit was complicated, but I knew my mom. Her undiagnosed mental health problems drove me crazy. Even now, as an adult, I couldn't stand to be around her too much. I loved her, but she was a hard person to be around. If I detached my emotions, I could understand why my father did what he had done now more than I'd ever admit out loud.

"Then I met Suzie." He looked up at me guiltily and agony twisted his face. "Her husband walked out on her when she was pregnant with her third child. She said she needed me. She wanted me — as a man. I was so desperate for female companionship. I was weak, and it was too easy to stray."

With hindsight, I could understand their divorce, but why had he given up on me? "So, you married Suzie and didn't look back."

He pulled at the scruff on his chin. "I thought I could have it all. Suzie's love. My boys. And I'd take care of your mother financially. I was so optimistic. But everything eventually fell apart."

He tilted the beer bottle to his lips and drank. "We had an informal custody arrangement. It worked out for a while. Then, suddenly, you started missing visits. Then I couldn't see you during the holidays. I took your mom to court and got formal visitation, but then she started dodging that, too.

"We fought in the courts for years. It didn't seem fair, but they always seemed to side with her. My lawyers wanted to say she was unfit.

That she had mental health problems, but I wouldn't let them. In the end, I lost when you testified against me in court. You said you wanted to live with your mom and didn't want to see me. That was the nail in the coffin, and your mom dictated our time together after that."

He said the last part rather nonchalantly, but I saw the flash of pain shadow his eyes. Trying to remember, I sat back in my seat and thought. I remembered testifying in court; the stern judge had petrified me. My mom had been coaching me about what to say, but I didn't remember telling the judge I didn't want to see my father. It was all a bit hazy.

"I don't remember saying that."

My dad was watching me intently. "My lawyers have the transcripts if you don't believe me. I'm not telling you this to place any blame on you. You were just a kid, Ryder. You should never have been in that position in the first place."

How could I not remember that? There was a panicky-fluttering feeling in my chest that made me think he was telling the truth. I thought back to all the terrible things my mom had said about him over the years. I'd absorbed all of that without ever hearing his side.

"When I think back, I have so many regrets, son." His words drew my gaze to his face. "We grew apart after that." A tear slid down his cheek and, oh fuck, I was squirming in my seat. I wanted to run away from this. A sharp lump was lodged in my throat.

"I tried to stay as involved as I could. When I found out from the next-door neighbor that your mom wasn't taking you to guitar lessons anymore, I paid him to drive you there instead. I snuck into your high school graduation ceremony and was at your college graduation, too. And I've kept track of your music career." His voice was thick with emotion. "I'm so proud of everything you've accomplished, son."

I thought back to all the times he'd reached out to me and I'd slapped him down. Again and again. I wanted nothing to do with him. I thought he'd abandoned me, yet he'd fought in the courts, paid for my college, kept up with my career, and anonymously supported the band.

My mother's words echoed in my head over and over. He abandoned us.

I had a lot to untangle.

"I wish you'd had this talk with me years ago."

My dad dabbed at his watery eyes with his napkin. "So do I, son. That's one of many regrets I have."

My brow wrinkled. "Does Brock know all about this? The miscarriages? The custody stuff?"

"No."

His relationship with Brock made me curious. "You talk to him, though? See him and his family?"

"Yes. It's a lot easier since he's settled down. Jenny helped a lot there, too."

I nodded, not able to look my father quite in the eye. I still kept hearing my mother's words in my head — he abandoned us. Was that true?

I wish I could say I left the restaurant with everything resolved and a new budding relationship with my dad, but that would take a lot more time and effort. I did have a new understanding of things and certainly a different perspective. And maybe even a little hope for the future.

Now that the money thing was almost settled, my thoughts were drifting back to Talia. I realized I wanted to tell her about this conversation with my dad and that surprised me. I wondered what she would say about it. Her opinion mattered to me. Fuck. I missed her. I needed to win her back.

Knox was playing video games when I made it back to his apartment. I grabbed a beer from the refrigerator and then plopped onto the couch next to him. "I just dropped my dad off at the airport."

His eyes were fixed on the TV screen. "How was dinner?"

I leaned my head back. "It was the most awkward conversation in the world."

Knox laughed. "He seems like a good bloke."

"I guess." I took a sip of beer. "He did just hand me a briefcase full of cash and help me place $125,000 into a locker for some nameless, faceless badass gangster who may secretly be an undercover cop to hand over to the ever-so-lovely Skull Crusher. So there's that. Life's just a little weird right now."

Knox whistled. "That's a lot of fucking cash. I don't even want to know how this all happened. At least you're not wallybobbing anymore. Are ye, mate?"

"It's wallydocking. You still have no idea what that is, do you?"

I watched him decimate a zombie on the screen. I should feel more nervous about dropping off my entire life savings into a random locker and crossing my fingers that my problems all go away. I guess I trusted my dad. At least, I trusted that he'd have my back if it all went to shit. It felt good to rely on him. It was something I would never have imagined just 24 hours ago.

Tomorrow I'd forward the drop-off information to the number my dad gave me, then I just had to wait for the all-clear text from the nameless guy. It was finally out of my hands. It was a huge relief.

I took a big swig of beer. "I found out that my ex-stepsister is in love with you."

"Me?" A zombie head splattered on the screen.

I laughed. "Yeah."

"Is she hot?"

I smacked him on the shoulder. "Dude, she's 18."

"So?" he glanced my way. "She's legal."

I cringed. "C'mon, man. Gross."

The screen turned all red with splattered blood when a zombie killed him from behind. Knox put down his controller and sat back on the couch. "This loan shark thing is over now?"

"Yeah, I think it's over. I hope so. Now, I'm just broke and homeless. At least I still have my truck."

"You've got the couch." He pointed to the garbage bags stuffed in every corner of the room. "Your shit fits in here, so you don't have to worry about anyone stealing it out of the truck."

I looked around at the bags, my only possessions. "My dad mentioned he'd pay for a deposit and a few months' rent on an apartment. I'll start looking so I can get out of your hair."

He leaned down and pulled his beer off the floor. "No rush, mate. Are you looking in the city or at the beach?"

"City for now. It's closer to you clowns. We'll be touring soon, so I'm not looking for anything permanent. Plus, I can't afford anything by the beach. Oh, man. I don't want to even think about it. I can't believe my house is gone."

We were both lost in thought for a few minutes and then asked, "How's your girlie?"

"Talia?"

"The sexy pants lass."

I ran a hand through my hair and expelled a breath. "She won't talk to me. I'm still trying to figure out how to get her back. We start in the studio Thursday and then I won't be able to see her for at least three weeks. I feel like that might be too late. I need to go to Ohio and make her talk to me."

"Maybe it just wasn't meant to be."

"What?" I scowled at him. "No. You don't understand. I love—" Did I just blurt out that I loved her? Jesus. "I mean — I'm really into her. I can't just let her go." I shook my head in disgust. "Forget it, you wouldn't understand."

Knox frowned back at me. "Why? I'm capable of feelings."

"I've never seen you with the same girl twice. You're almost as big a slut as Vicious and Bash." I laughed to ease the sting of my words.

"Did you know I was engaged once?" His face flashed with pain. "Yeah, I know all the feelings."

The look in his eye was intense. "Fuck. I'm sorry. What happened?"

He took a long drink from his bottle and then leaned his elbows on his knees dropping his head into his hands. "I accused her of cheating on me. It was an ugly scene. She didn't deny it but stormed out of our cottage. I found out later that she drove off the road, down a gulley, and crashed into a tree. She died on the scene."

The air was so thick it was hard to breathe. "Oh, fuck. I didn't know," I said softly.

He wound his fingers through his hair and tugged on the roots. "It hurt so fucking bad. Her family never knew about the fight. I never told anyone. I was so ashamed. I did that. I caused that."

"No!" I denied. "You could never have anticipated all of that. It was just a terrible accident."

"I couldn't take it anymore. The whole thing royally fucked me up. I left Scotland to try to forget it. I miss her so bad sometimes." The last bit came out in a strangled whisper.

I didn't know what to say. He'd blindsided me. I'd never have guessed that was dealing with such a horrible tragedy. He always seemed so carefree.

He lifted his head up and looked at me. "We're in the studio Thursday, so that means you have one day to get your ass to Ohio and get your girl back."

"I can't. We have practice."

Knox waved his hand. "Fuck that. Just go. I'll cover for you. You know I can do your job."

"Yeah, you can. You'd probably do it even better than me."

A big smile lit up his face. "Damn right I would, but Ghost Parker wouldn't be the same without you, so get your lass back so we can get back to taking over the world."

It felt good to know that Knox had my back. Deep down I knew I could always count on my brothers in the band, but I wanted them to know they could count on me, too. How had I never known what happened to Knox in Scotland? Maybe I needed to stop judging people all the time and start listening to them. I wanted to be a better friend. A better son and brother. And, of course, a better man for Talia.

"Knox, about the other thing — your fiancée ... I'm here to talk to if you ever need me."

His face morphed into an impassive mask. "Quit blethering. You need to book a flight and I need to kill some more zombies."

He turned back to his video games, so I got on my phone to book a flight to Ohio. After more than an hour on the phone arguing with multiple airlines, I hung up defeated. "Just fucking great!"

Knox paused his game. "They couldn't get you on any flights, mate?"

All the optimism had drained from me in the last hour of haggling with the airline representatives. "They're all backed up. There's some kind of ice storm in Ohio. I won't be able to get there tomorrow and we're in the studio Thursday. Fuck! Why is this happening?"

He shrugged like it was no big deal. "You'll just have to convince her to take you back from here."

"How do I do that? She won't talk to me. She fucking blocked me!" I tossed my phone onto the coffee table.

"You've got to woo her. Flowers and shit." He turned in his seat. "'You've got to woo before you screw.' Haven't you ever heard that?"

"No. That sounds like some beta male bullshit. Is that a Scottish thing?"

He chuckled. "What the fuck, Stroke. You've got no game. I'll help you romance the hell out of her until she takes your sorry arse back, but you're going to owe me."

I had my doubts about Knox's expertise in the matter, but I was tragically unschooled in romancing women. "If it works, you can name your price. So, what am I gonna need to do?"

He held up a finger. "First, you're going to need money. And since you have none, I hope you have a credit card. With a big limit on it. Also, we might need a helper in Ohio. Maybe your mom? It would be better if it was someone with access to Talia."

"Credit card, check." It would take me a while to dig out of the financial hole I was putting myself in, but some things were worth it. "I have her roommate's number, and I think I can get her to help me. So, now what?"

"Grab a pen and paper. You're gonna want to take notes."

Chapter 36

Talia

Ellie had a far shorter commute, so it didn't surprise me she'd beat me home on a Friday evening.

She yelled out to me from the kitchen. "Hey, Tal. Eric and I are meeting some of his work colleagues out at Grooves. Please say you'll come out with us. I've never met any of them before. I need my BFF."

"Yeah. Maybe." I slipped off my heels and then headed into the kitchen. The last thing I wanted to do was head out to a crowded club. Sitting at home and sulking seemed far preferable right now.

She finished pouring some pasta into a boiling pot of water and then looked up as I entered. "How was work?"

"Sucktastic. I don't know if my job suddenly got a hundred times more hellish since I've been back from vacation or if it's just me. But I can't stand it anymore, and my boss is a raging asshole."

Really, my boss wasn't acting much differently than usual, yet every little thing was setting me off. I was miserable there. My job seemed so pointless. No matter how hard I tried to impress my boss, nothing I did was recognized or even appreciated. I was just another cog in the wheel.

I was unfulfilled. There was that thought again. Ugh. I didn't want to go down that rabbit hole. It led to bad things. All week, I kept thinking about quitting. But then what would I do? And brain — don't answer something to do with fashion, because who needs a fashion consultant or stylist in Ohio? Please. Don't be dumb.

Thank goodness Ellie interrupted my mental ramblings. "You're just in a funk. It'll pass."

A nasty reply formed in my head, but I bit my tongue. Ellie was just trying to help. Yeah, for sure, my mood was black. There was no way I'd have any kind of fun if I went out tonight.

"I think I'm going to stay in tonight. I'd only be a black cloud bringing down everyone's mood."

Ellie gave me the look — the 'I pity you / I'm worried about you' look combined with a scrunch of her nose. "Still thinking about Ryder?"

My shoulders slumped. "How can I not? The jerk leaves that text on Tuesday, telling me not to give up on him, and then, nothing. Radio silence. I even unblocked him."

"You unblocked him?"

My cheeks heated. "Yeah. I'm that dumb. I mean, the words came straight from his own mouth — 'I meant nothing to him', so why am I letting him get in my head? Believe me, I'm embarrassed enough for myself."

Ellie stirred the pasta. "Are you sure he said that, Tal? It doesn't make any sense. Why is he still trying to contact you if you meant nothing? He could just move on. Be with other girls."

I rolled my eyes. "Maybe he's just stringing me along for the fun of it."

She glanced my way. "Is it possible that Kaylie was lying about what he said?"

"Why would she do that?" I scoffed.

Ellie was watching me closely, judging my reaction. "Maybe she loves him? Maybe she was jealous?"

"No," I denied. "She's actually secretly in love with Sidney. Plus, she's really sweet. I really doubt she would lie."

Ellie shrugged. "Maybe she has other motives? She's Bash's sister, right? Maybe the band doesn't want him to have a serious girlfriend?"

"That's really convoluted, El. And I really believe Kaylie was telling the truth." I grew suspicious. "Why are you suddenly sticking up for Ryder?"

"He may have been in contact with me again." She said it so nonchalantly.

"Ellie!" I gasped. "When?" I didn't like the breathless excitement in my voice.

"Calm down," she chided. "I got something from him today."

"First of all,"—I planted my hand on my hip—"shouldn't that have been the first thing out of your mouth when I walked in the door? What kind of BFF are you?"

"I wanted to make sure that I'm doing the right thing here. I don't want you to get hurt by this guy anymore." She paused and then added, "But this seems so sincere."

My eyes widened. "What exactly is 'this'?"

"I've been given my instructions, and I've decided I'm going to play it the way he wants. So, let me start by showing you these ..."

Ellie left the room and came back holding a gorgeous bouquet of red roses.

I felt the stirrings of excitement but tamped it down. "Seriously? How cliché! If he thinks flowers are going to make everything better, he's sorely mistaken."

I walked over to Ellie and took the flowers from her, burying my nose in the petals. "Wow, are these two dozen roses?"

Ellie's smirk told me I wasn't fooling her. "He actually has a plan to win you back, and don't you dare deny how badly you want to be won back. You're not fooling me, Tal. So you might as well sit back and enjoy it. That's what I'm going to do."

I couldn't deny what she said; I wanted to be with Ryder.

She handed me an envelope. "It comes with this."

I tore it open, devouring the words.

```
Dear Talia,

I've never written a letter to
anyone before, so I hope this ends
up making sense. Putting words on
paper has never seemed more diffi-
cult, but I'm hoping I can share
some things with you that I haven't
been able to do before.

By the time you get this, my band
and I will have already been in the
studio recording for a few days. If
everything runs smoothly, we'll be
tied up for 2-3 weeks solid.

What I really want is to be there
```

with you, in person, to explain everything I'm feeling and to clear up any misunderstandings. I'm not sure that will work as well on paper, but I'll try. I'd do anything to give us another chance.

For now, I want you to know that I'm thinking about you. Actually, that's a colossal understatement. You're always on my mind. You're the first thing I think about when I wake up in the morning and your face is the last sweet image I see before I drift off to sleep. During the day, all day, I worry about how much I screwed things up between us.

I hope you like the flowers I sent. They will be the first of many gifts that I'll send. The gifts aren't meant to 'buy' you back. They are meant to show you that I'm always thinking of you and how much I care about you. (But if it starts feeling creepy, tell Ellie and I will stop.)

I think I'll stop here for today.

```
I know you don't trust me. While
I've never done anything to be-
tray your trust, I realize that
I haven't done anything to really
earn your trust either. I haven't
fully shared myself with you. I've
kept things on a superficial level.
I've been thinking about that a lot
and I've come to some revelations
about myself that I'd like to share
with you, but that's for another
letter.

I really hope you'll read my let-
ters and give me a chance to ex-
plain everything.

I miss you,
Ryder
```

I looked up from the letter. "He wants another chance, El. Should I let him?"

She gave me a soft smile. "Only if he earns it."

Saturday

Today, Ellie handed me another envelope and a cardboard box. I opened the box right away. It was a candle and bubble bath gift set. I'd let her read the first letter, but this time she stopped me.

"You can keep the letters private, Tal. But I want to know about all the gifts unless they're super kinky. Oh, hell, I'll want to know about those, too. I know, I'm nosey."

I read the second letter in the bathtub, making sure the letter didn't get wet.

```
Dear Talia,

I worried all day today that my
first letter wasn't good enough.
This is going to be really hard
with no feedback, but I hope that
you'll give me a chance.

So if this works out right, today
will be Saturday. I hope you like
the gift I sent. After a long week
of work, I thought you would enjoy
something to help you relax.

Whenever I think about your last
night here in L.A., my chest grows
tight. It's a weird feeling. Parts
of that night were wonderful, but
most of it was horrible. What I
didn't tell you before the party
was that I was dreading it. I
didn't want you to leave, and I
```

had no idea what to do with those feelings — they were so foreign to me.

I know you think I cheated on you that night, but I didn't. I haven't been with another woman since the first night we met. (The night you crawled into bed with me while I was sleeping and rocked my world.)

I did avoid you at the end of that night at the club. I avoided you for a reason — your protection and yes, I realize how spectacularly ridiculous that sounds. It's a long story that I really dread telling you. I'm ashamed of the circumstances that I ended up in, but I'll explain all of that in another letter.

Just know that it's only been you since I first set lips on you — that first magical night we met in Ohio.

I miss you,
Ryder

Sunday

Dear Talia,

Today you should have gotten the band T-shirt I sent. It's a bit of a selfish gift in that I'm hoping it reminds you of me when you wear it. It's not the same one you wore at my house — I'm not giving that one up. I've been wearing that one to bed every night to feel closer to you and yeah, I should probably wash it by now.

Speaking of the band, we've finished recording our lead single. It sounds great and everyone is excited, including our record label. That's good news.

Did I tell you I'm living with Knox, sleeping on his couch? I sold my house. Yeah, that's another big story I have to tell — you'll have to keep reading my letters to find out why.

Knox has been a great friend to me this past week when I've been going through so much. I've always felt close to the band — they've been closer to me than my own brother has. But I realize now that I've held back so much from them. I've only shown them my happy / party side. When I finally told them about some stuff that was going on with me — they were all completely supportive.

I recently found out something really personal that one of them has gone through. It was horribly tragic. It made me wonder how I'd known this guy for years and never knew this about him. We just toured together for nine months straight — spending practically every second of the day together — and I never suspected how much pain he was in. I never got beyond the superficial with him.

What kind of friend am I? What kind of person am I? I'm just beginning to unravel some of that and the

```
reasons behind it. It makes the
ground feel shaky beneath my feet
sometimes.

I miss you,
Ryder
```

I didn't expect this from Ryder. This level of introspection. I pulled on the T-shirt, thinking about him. I'd never stopped thinking about him. He was like a drug that pumped through my veins.

Monday

I couldn't wait to get home from work and see if there was another letter from Ryder today. Ellie wouldn't even give me a hint this morning. The package, along with another envelope, was sitting on the kitchen table when I got there.

```
Dear Talia,

In case you're like 99% of the
population that hates Mondays, I
thought I'd try to cheer you up.
I sent you a cocktail kit so you
could start the week with a bang.
The kit should include everything
you need to make Alabama Slammers.
(shot or drink — your choice)
```

```
I remember when you told me it
was your favorite. It seemed funny
because it's so random and old
school. You're not even southern.
I like the quirky things I discover
about you.

Share your drinks with Ellie. She's
a good friend — if she's doing as
I asked and making sure you read
these letters!

I miss you!
Ryder
```

Tuesday

A white bakery box greeted me Tuesday after work. I tore it open before reading the letter. An assortment of gourmet cupcakes stared me in the face: red velvet, salted caramel, chocolate peanut butter cup, raspberry amaretto ...

Ellie groaned over my shoulder. "You better be sharing. This gift is even better than the slammers we had last night."

We stuffed our faces with the most decadent cupcakes I'd ever tasted before I retreated to my bedroom to read Ryder's letter.

Dear Talia,

Gourmet cupcakes? That alone should bring me back into your good graces. Just saying. (I hope you know I'm kidding? Letter writing is hard.)

I sent you a dozen because I just couldn't decide on the different flavor choices. They all sounded so good. I hope they put a smile on your face.

I know I've mentioned in the other letters that I was going to tell you what's been going on with me. To do that, I've got to start back at the beginning. I told you a bit about my family when we were getting to know each other better on the phone before you visited.

When I was nine, my parents divorced. After that, I saw my father somewhat regularly, but that tapered off by the time I was in high school. I told you about me breaking up my brother and his fiancée and how that effectively killed my relationship with him. And now, my mother is married to a complete loser who's been taking advantage of her financially. Yeah, it's a real mess.

What I didn't mention is that my mother has mental health issues. She refuses to get any help, so it's undiagnosed — but it's definitely there. I lived with it growing up. It may be plain old depression, but I'm no expert.

My mother has repeated to me more times than I could count that my father abandoned us. Somewhere along the way, that mantra absorbed into my soul and became a complete truth. It was a truth that affected me to the core. It affected who I was as a person. I'm now finding that things aren't so black and white. It's forced me to do some soul-searching and I don't always like what I find.

I miss you,
Ryder

Wednesday

While work still seemed pointless, it wasn't going nearly as badly this week because I was in a better mood. Ryder hadn't given up on us; I was sure of that now. Reading his letters over and over, I'd dug for insights. I was eager to hear more, but mostly I wanted to be in his arms again.

Returning from lunch, I found another bouquet of roses — this time a mix of red and shades of pink — on my desk. It received a lot of attention from my female co-workers, but I remained mysterious about the sender. I still hadn't heard all I needed to hear from him.

There was a new letter waiting for me when I got home.

```
Dear Talia,

I thought some flowers sent to your
workplace might brighten up your
week.

My Dad came to California last week
to visit. Actually, I needed his
help, and he dropped everything to
come to me, even though I didn't
ask him to. In fact, I've been
pushing him away for years. He
'abandoned' me, so why should I
give him anything?
```

He told me about why he divorced my mom. There was stuff going on that I never knew about. I remember our visits after the divorce diminishing over time, but I didn't realize my mother was withholding my brother and me from seeing him. I was just a little kid.

By the time my parents divorced, my mother was a very damaged person. I could make a million excuses for her — she was sick, she feared losing her kids; she was lonely. Whatever her reason, she coached me into telling the judge that I didn't want anything to do with my father. I needed him desperately, but I was too young to understand that. I'm just figuring all this out now. After that, my dad could only see us at the whims of my mom, which wasn't often. My mind had been poisoned against him and I wanted nothing to do with him, so we drifted apart.

This is getting long, so I'll finish the rest of this story

tomorrow.

I miss you,
Ryder

Thursday

Dear Talia,

Did Ellie give you the mp3 file today? It's a recording of our lead single. I'm not sure when the label's releasing it, but I wanted you to be the first person outside of our group that heard it. Please don't share it with anyone; I could get into big trouble!!

Back to my dad's visit …

Dad explained to me how he struggled to keep contact with Brock and me. As he was telling me about the things he did for me behind the scenes, I realized just how hard I'd pushed him away.

He'd gone through some emotionally rough shit with my mother and then he remarried. I hated my stepmother and her family (3 younger kids) even though she was always pretty nice to me. Dad found happiness with his new family (which I resented), but then a few years later, his new wife left him to go back to her ex-husband and her kids' father. My dad was crushed.

I never knew any of this because I was a selfish kid. I assumed that my dad had abandoned his new family and moved on to something better. My dad remarried again a couple of years ago, so I have a new stepmother and she has some kids that are my step-siblings, I guess. I blew off his wedding and I don't even remember the names of Monica's kids.

I never gave a shit about my dad. Now, I'm thinking — fuck! I'm the bad guy when all along I thought it was my dad. Not that he was perfect in all of this, but …

> You're wondering how all this stuff relates to us. I hope I can get around to that in a way that makes sense. I'm working on it.
>
> I miss you,
> Ryder

I was lying in bed wearing my Ghost Parker T-shirt and rereading Ryder's letters. I had my earbuds in, listening to the band's newly recorded single on a loop. Ryder's words made me feel close to him and understand a lot more about his personality. It still didn't explain why he pushed me away that night.

Friday

> Dear Talia,
>
> Happy Friday! I was told by an adorable lady that the wine and chocolate pairing I sent you was to die for. I hope you enjoy it.
>
> Remember the day we went hiking up to the Hollywood sign? Earlier that day, I got a visit from a scary dude. He told me that my mother's

husband owed his gang a lot of money. Stan skipped town and left my mother holding the bag. They came after me because they knew I could pay them back.

The gang gave me a week to gather the money, or they'd go after my mom and Brock's family. They showed me a candid picture of Brock holding Joey, with Jenny standing right behind them. It was a surveillance picture. I was afraid for them.

So much shit was going on and I should have told you, but I was freaked out. I was ashamed of all the crap going on with my mother and ashamed that Stan had scammed money out of me in the past. All I felt was weak and helpless. The last thing I wanted was for you to see me like that.

More later.

I miss you,
Ryder

A nauseous feeling crept over me. I didn't like the way this was heading. Ryder had been so distracted on that hike and I'd thought he was getting bored with me, but actually, he'd been dealing with something horrible.

I wanted to pick up the phone and call him. I needed to know the rest right now. I needed to know that he was okay, but I'd play it his way.

Instead, I pushed the worry out of my mind and enjoyed his thoughtful gift.

Saturday

Ellie and I were eating lunch. Afterward, we planned to go shopping. She needed a new outfit for a fancy date Eric was taking her on.

She handed me an envelope — Ryder's next letter. "You should read this one now."

> Dear Talia,
>
> I'm sorry I left the last letter so abruptly. My stomach still twists in a knot when I think about everything. I don't want you to hear about my problems today. By now, you may know that earlier in the week I had Ellie ask you to go on a shopping trip with her this afternoon, only to keep your afternoon free for today's gift.

```
She assured me you'd love it.

I've booked for you what I hope
is a relaxing surprise. Jenny will
pick you up at your apartment for
a half-day spa session (4 hours)
at 12:30. You each can choose any
services that they offer. She is
really looking forward to seeing
you again and getting some quiet
time. I'm hoping I can be a better
brother to Brock and Jenny — and
a better uncle. (Brock will take
some work, but I had Jenny at 4
hours of relaxation.)

Go pamper yourself and have a good
time.

I miss you,
Ryder
```

In the end, I did exactly as Ryder asked. I forgot about everything and enjoyed my surprise. Being with Jenny wasn't awkward at all. We immediately picked up where we left off. The first thing she told me was that Ryder told her not to ask anything about our relationship — that she was just to know that he was 'working on it'.

We were both enjoying our organic seaweed leaf wrap when she asked, "How's he doing so far?"

I smiled. "Don't tell him, but pretty damned good."

Sunday

I bit into the intricately decorated chocolate-covered strawberry, almost dripping strawberry juice onto the next letter.

```
Dear Talia,

Back to the hard stuff. I felt I had
no choice but to pay off the loan.
I'm positive that the threats these
guys made to my family were very
real. To get that much money, I had
to sell my house. Before we got on
the party bus, I think you heard
me on the phone with Melanie, my
real estate agent. She set up the
sale. (For the record, I've never
seen Melanie outside of the real
estate business.)

That night, at the last club, I
remember when you were sitting on
my lap. I was worried about the
whole loan shark situation and
feeling very upset that you were
leaving the next day. It was con-
fusing because I wasn't sure what
```

those feelings meant. I'd already figured out that you were someone special, and that I wanted you so badly, but sitting there right then with you — I started to realize how deep my feelings ran. I was admitting something that shocked me to my core and terrified the shit out of me.

I decided right then to talk to you. Beg you not to leave. Beg you to move to California. I didn't know what exactly. I knew what I wanted, but I didn't think it was my right to ask. We were still new, and I'd never had any type of relationship with a woman before. But I knew I wasn't going to let you walk away without asking for more of you.

The revelation was overwhelming. I wish I'd never let you off my lap that night.

Hope you enjoyed the chocolate-covered strawberries.

Miss you,

Ryder

Monday

I was so eager to read Ryder's letter that I ignored the pretty wrapped box that came with the envelope.

> Dear Talia,
>
> I guess I mentioned that I sold my house. I'm going to miss being near the beach. The Saturday after you went back to Ohio, it was sold. I desperately needed the cash, so the sale was fast. Unfortunately, I lost a lot of money on it.
>
> The new owners gave me 24 hours to vacate the property. So after band practice on Saturday, I stayed up all night packing. I was upset that you were gone, crushed that you wouldn't talk to me — it was the lowest point in my life.
>
> When I was packing, I found a box in the bathroom drawer. Inside was

a leather bracelet. I picked it up, wondering if it was yours, and saw the inscription inside. Always remember us. Love, Angel.

This bracelet has given me so much hope this last week I've been without you. I'm not sure if you meant to leave it behind or not, but I'm pretending that you did. It's been on my wrist since that night and I've only ever taken it off to shower.

I picked out the bracelet and all the charms, especially for you. They all have special meanings. The music note represents your awful singing that I miss so much. It has nothing to do with me, so don't rip it off. Haha. The guitar represents me, so … The yin-yang symbol was interesting. It represents harmony and balance — how two opposing forces can be so interconnected. To me, it kind of reminds me of the first sex position we experienced together. I think the rest of the charms are self-explanatory.

```
I miss you,
Ryder
```

Falling back on my bed, I stared at the letter. I couldn't believe his amazing house by the beach was gone. He loved that place. It must have been devastating to lose it. I couldn't help how my heart ached for him.

I opened up the present and pulled out the bracelet. It had a heavy weight to it and came from a fancy jewelry store, so I was pretty sure it was expensive. He shouldn't be getting me expensive gifts when he'd just lost everything.

I fingered the pretty charms that dangled from it. There were some fun ones like a high heel shoe with sparkly rhinestones, a sand dollar, flip-flops, and a cocktail glass. I found the musical note and the guitar and then saw a lotus flower charm that almost perfectly matched my tattoo. Of course, there was a pretty angel that glittered with crystals and I picked out the dangling emerald that was my birthstone, wondering how he knew my birthday. There was an intricate lock and key charm, a pretty heart charm, and an infinity symbol. There were several types of spacer beads, each delicately crafted.

The bracelet as a whole was beautiful, but it was the thought that he'd put into each charm that made me love it even more.

Tuesday

Ellie and I sat at the kitchen table enjoying our adult hot chocolate. The basket Ryder sent contained hot chocolate mix, but also a bottle of Kahlua and a bottle of Baileys, mini marshmallows, chocolate syrup, and a recipe guide.

Ellie made the Kahlua recipe, and I made Bailey's hot chocolate, but we both tasted the others. It was a decadent treat.

After we enjoyed our drinks, Ellie went to her bedroom to call Eric, so I eagerly took Ryder's next letter to my own room.

> Dear Talia,
>
> It should be Tuesday when you get this letter. The weather in Ohio said it'd dip into the 30s today. It's a sunny 70 degrees here in L.A. It saddens me to think that we're so far apart that we're experiencing totally different weather right now. I hope the hot chocolate keeps you warm tonight.
>
> Getting back to the night of the party bus. However scared I was of my completely new and overwhelming feelings towards you, I knew I couldn't let you go back home without talking it over with you. You were on my lap when a waiter tapped me on the arm and said — someone wants to talk to you.
>
> I remember getting up and walking across the VIP room. I stopped

```
and turned back to look at you
for a moment. Our eyes met for a
few seconds. I felt our connection
as clearly as if we were still
touching. In that instant of time,
I realized that you were the one
for me. My forever girl. It just
all fell into place.

I miss you,
Ryder
```

Maybe I was too darn easy, but I had tears in my eyes. I missed him. I believed him. And I wanted him back.

Wednesday

Surprise flitted across my face as I opened the box from Ryder. It was perfume. I removed the wrappings from the bottle and spritzed some on my wrist. It wasn't what I expected. I had expected some kind of flowery smell, but this was really different. I sniffed it again. I'd never smelled a perfume like it. Thank goodness it wasn't too heavy, but I wasn't sure if I liked it.

```
Dear Talia,

It's been almost 3 weeks since I've
seen you. I miss you. Did I mention
```

that I've been sleeping on Knox's couch? I brought my pillows from home and realized that they've lost the subtle scent of your perfume that they used to have on them. If I close my eyes, I can see your hair — with all the different shimmering shades in it — spread out across my pillow and I can catch the faint scent that reminds me of you.

The gift I give to you today might be a dud. I created a custom perfume for you. I chose scents that reminded me of you. The online tool offered tips and guidance, but who knows if I blended the top, middle, and base note percentages correctly or even if the scents I chose go together well. You'll have to let me know.

I miss you,
Ryder

He sent me a custom perfume. I smiled as I sniffed at it again. It wasn't so bad.

Thursday

After dinner, Ellie pulled out my next gift. It was my favorite ice cream. I groaned. By the time this was over, I was going to gain 50 pounds.

```
Dear Talia,

I don't know how someone could
choose strawberry ice cream as
their favorite when there exist
things like Rocky Road or Moose
Tracks. It's a travesty. But, since
it's your favorite, I sent you a
gallon and a bunch of toppings so
that you can make sundaes. Do you
even put toppings on strawberry ice
cream?

So — party bus night. I went to see
who wanted to talk to me at the
club. It was Skull Crusher. Yes,
that's his name. He was the gang
guy that was threatening my family
if I didn't pay the money.

He'd noticed you sitting on my
```

lap and asked about you. It would put a target on your back if he knew what you meant to me, so I pretended I didn't even know who you were — just some random girl — completely meaningless. He was watching me that night, so I kept away from you until we left. I made myself scarce so that he wouldn't associate anyone with me. No one deserved to be in the crosshairs of some psycho because of me.

When I got back on the bus, you were so angry, but I just figured it was because you were so drunk and upset that I'd disappeared on you. It took me a while to realize something was seriously wrong. Before I knew it, you were gone. I let you go because I didn't want you around while Skull Crusher was threatening everyone around me. It was a big mistake.

I miss you,
Ryder

I sat stunned as I stared at the letter. I finally had my explanation. The conversation with the guy called Skull Crusher must have been what Kaylie had overheard that night. I had based all my rotten assumptions about Ryder on that one thing; I had jumped to all the wrong conclusions.

I dashed into Ellie's room to tell her I was ready to talk to Ryder. My mind was made up.

No matter how hard I tried to convince her, she told me I had to wait.

Friday

Ellie handed me my next letter as soon as I got home from work.

```
Dear Talia,

I was devastated when you got into
that cab. The words you left me
with were worse than a kick to the
gut. They took my breath away. It
was brutal. I know I hurt you. I'm
praying you were just lashing out
at me.

I've done some lashing out at
people that have hurt me and I'm
only just starting to realize it.
With all the hurt, I didn't see
things clearly.
```

```
I'm hoping you give me a chance to
make everything right. I've still
got a lot to figure out, but other
things have become crystal clear
to me.

So, this should be Friday night.
Another week has gone by. I sched-
uled an at-home massage for you
to let out the end-of-the-week
stress. I hope my letters are not
upsetting you. I'm just trying to
be as honest as I can be with you
and myself.

I miss you,
Ryder
```

I didn't want to do this anymore. I wanted to talk to Ryder. Instead, I let the woman who showed up at our apartment with her portable massage table work her magic and remove some of the anxiety I felt.

Saturday

```
Dear Talia,

I hope you like today's gift.
```

First, the picture frame — I found it in a local shop near Knox's place. I have never seen one quite like this before. Black leather with square rivets and buckles. It's one of a kind (like you) and reminded me of those sexy rock star pants.

After Tommy's party, one of my friends texted me this picture they took of us. I didn't show it to you, because it made me uncomfortable at the time. We're standing looking at each other, and you look so amazing. You were rocking those sexy pants and that entire outfit like nobody's business. I couldn't take my eyes off you as you were smiling and laughing the entire night. God, you were breathtakingly beautiful. I wondered how I'd gotten so damn lucky.

But the look on my face in the photo is what made me nervous. I didn't know a picture was being taken, but I remember that moment. My hands resting on your hips — not wanting you to pull away ever. The ache

```
in my chest thinking how beautiful
you were. Staring into your eyes
and feeling that tug in my chest.
I was feeling a lot of emotions I
wasn't ready to admit.

The picture broadcasts that. I saw
it immediately when my friend sent
it. It bared my soul without words.
The truth of my feelings shone
through loud and clear.

For the past few weeks, I've been
looking at that picture a lot. Now,
I'm ready to share it with you.

I miss you,
Ryder
```

So far, this was my favorite present. I stared at the photo of us and swallowed past the lump in my throat. I loved him so much.

Sunday

Ellie told me to listen to the recording Ryder sent before reading the next letter. I headed to my bedroom and popped in my earbuds.

The recording was Ryder playing an acoustic guitar and singing the Counting Crows song, *Accidentally In Love*.

I listened to him singing the words with my heart pounding. Was he telling me that he loved me? No, I must be reading too much into it. It's just a cute song. I listened to it a few more times, my head spinning, before I read the note.

```
Dear Talia,

Did you like the recording I sent
you? I hope it puts a smile on your
pretty face.

I chose this song because I thought
it was the perfect description of
the start of our story. The night
we met was a big mix-up. I was sound
asleep after nine long months on
the road when, suddenly, my world
was turned upside down. It'll never
be the same.

I found myself Accidentally In
Love.

I love you,
Ryder
```

Tears were streaming down my face when I finished his letter. It was a moment I'll never forget.

Monday

A picture fluttered out of the envelope. I picked it up and stared at it, tears stinging my eyes. I was crying again.

> Dear Talia,
>
> Are you still reading these? I really hope you haven't gone running for the hills yet. Ellie won't tell me anything, believe me, I've tried to crack her.
>
> Today, I'm not giving you a present, but I wanted to show you something. I got a new tattoo. Angels symbolize hope. Today, I'm filled with a lot of hope. And of course, every time I look at it, I think of my very own angel. My feisty angel.
>
> It's hard to see in the picture, but the angel's body and halo are on the side of my wrist where I can always see it. One wing wraps to the back of my wrist and the other

to the inside, so the whole thing
can only be seen from one angle. It
came out great. I watch it while
I play guitar. It sits right below
the leather bracelet you bought for
me. My angel is always with me.

I love you,
Ryder

Tuesday

Dear Talia,

I'm not sure if I explained everything properly. I have so much more
to say to you. Things about my
life to share with you. New things
I'm discovering about myself every
day.

It took my entire life to realize
just how guarded my emotions had
become. Until I met you, I'd never
let myself experience the highs
in life — all just to protect

myself from the lows. I lived life in the muted, dull grays in the middle. That protective mechanism bled into all my relationships — with my family, friends, my brothers in the band, and with women. I didn't even realize it was a problem until you broke down my barriers and showed me the rainbow of colors that existed in the world. You have made me face myself and it's been liberating.

No matter what you choose about the two of us, you will always be in my heart.

I love you,
Ryder

Wednesday

Dear Talia,

This is my last letter to you. Obviously, I want to see you again,

```
but the choice is yours. If you
never want to talk to me again,
I'll respect your wishes. Before
you make your decision, I ask one
thing from you. Please unblock me
on your phone. I plan on calling
you tomorrow at 7 p.m. your time.
(Tomorrow should be Thursday if I
didn't screw this up.) I can't wait
to hear your voice, Angel.

I love you,
Ryder
```

The first line of his letter panicked me for a moment. Then as I read on, I realized I would be talking to him tomorrow. Finally! I had unblocked him weeks ago, but I double-checked my phone — just to be sure.

God, I needed him. I needed to tell him how much I loved him. I never wanted to feel apart from him again. Twenty-four hours was going to be an excruciatingly long time to wait.

Chapter 37

Ryder

I put my heart on the line. I'd never done anything remotely like that before, and it was scary as shit. Ellie had given me no clues as to how Talia was taking my letters and gifts. She could have been ripping them up and tossing them for all I knew. Maybe she hadn't even read them. Fuck, I was nervous.

It was almost 7 p.m. I'd been sitting in a rental car outside her apartment for two hours. I'd driven straight from the airport when I should have gotten some dinner first. Nah, I was too nervous to eat, anyway. Still, it would have distracted me from the thoughts racing through my head. The past two hours had felt like two days.

I watched as the time on my phone changed to 7:00. It was time. To say there were butterflies in my stomach was an understatement. There was a fucking stampede of elephants in there. Even though it was cold enough in the car to see my breath, I wiped the sweat from my brow. Here goes.

The phone rang too many times for my liking. When I realized she might still be blocking me, I felt like I might vomit.

Then she picked up. "Ryder?"

My voice stuck in my throat.

Finally, I croaked some words out. "I thought you might not pick up."

"I've been waiting for your call." Her voice sounded so sweet to my ears.

"Did you read my letters?" I closed my eyes.

"Yes."

"Did you enjoy your gifts?"

"Yes. I loved them."

That was a good sign. I took a deep breath and silently blew out a sigh of relief.

I hopped out of my car and hurried across the street. Ellie was waiting to let me into the building. "I still have more I want to tell you, Talia. But I'd like to do that in person."

Talia spoke softly. "I want to see you, too."

I followed Ellie as she led me to the door of their apartment. "We just got done recording our new album, so I'm going to be tied up for the next few weeks doing all the PR stuff that comes along with that. I can't get out of it."

"I understand." She sounded disappointed.

I stepped in front of Talia's door. "I've got to go, but before I do, I wanted to tell you that I've got one more surprise for you, Angel. It should be sitting right outside your door. I hope you like it."

"Another one? Ryder, you've already given me too much."

"I think you'll like this one. Text me tomorrow and let me know if you like it."

"All right." I smiled to myself as I heard the sadness in her voice. I was pretty sure she wasn't too impressed with this phone call. After all the buildup I'd created, we'd only been on a few minutes and I told her I had to go. I felt bad, but I couldn't wait to see the look on her face when she saw her surprise.

I stood at the door like a damn fool for at least 15 minutes. I thought she'd go look at her present right away. Ellie had gone to visit a neighbor down the hall, so I was standing here alone, just waiting. And waiting.

She wasn't going to come. Jesus.

Five minutes later, I texted her. "Did you like the surprise?"

Nothing. No answer.

I was ready to pull out my hair with frustration. I pulled up Ellie's name to text her for help when I heard the door opening.

Her mouth fell open when she saw me. I was grinning like a fool until I saw how red and puffy her eyes were. "You're crying? Shit!"

She expelled a shaky breath. "Oh, my God. Ryder!"

I was rooted to the spot. "Fuck. I didn't mean to make you cry, Angel."

My heart skipped seeing the tears spill over her eyes. I'd upset her. I didn't know what to do. Then, I noticed that she was wearing my T-shirt. And she was wearing the charm bracelet.

I opened my arms, and she didn't hesitate. She jumped into them.

Her body shuddered against me as she held back one last sob, and then she melted into my hold. Feeling her in my arms righted my world. It had been tilted off its axis without her. The love I felt for her slammed into me.

I managed to get us inside the apartment and over to her couch.

She snuggled up against me. "Are you really here?"

This part was going to suck. "I'm here, but I can't stay for long.

Someone took forever to answer the door, and it ate into our time."

She groaned.

I positioned myself so that I could look into her eyes. "In case I haven't made it clear, I'm crazy in love with you."

Some new tears leaked out of her eyes. She opened her mouth to speak, but I stopped her.

"You don't have to say anything right now. I just wanted you to know that. I wanted you to know exactly how I felt about you. I love you, Talia."

Pulling her close to my body, I stole a quick kiss. I had to stick to my plan, but keeping my hands off her was impossible.

"I came here tonight because I needed to see you. Being separated these past few weeks killed me. But I also came to ask you something."

I took a deep breath and then continued. "I've thought about this and the way I see it, our relationship could go one of three ways — Number one: If you want, I'll go away and leave you alone. If that's your decision, I'll accept it and I'll try to act like a mature adult about it."

She frowned and bit her lip.

"Number two: We do the long-distance thing. I'll move mountains to keep you in my life, so we'll figure it out together. I'll visit whenever I can and you can visit me in L.A. We'll work on our relationship, make it stronger, but we'll be exclusive. A couple. I promise that I'll wait for you forever until we can be together."

She lifted her gaze to meet mine with a curious expression. "And what's the third option?"

"Number three: You move to California. I'm not sure of the living arrangements — I'd love for us to find a place together, but our relationship might be too new for that. I know you'd have to get a new job and leave behind your whole life here. It'd be a big sacrifice. It's what

I want, Talia, but it would have to be your decision."

"I think I know what I want, Ryder." Her finger was tracing the new tattoo on my wrist.

"I don't want your answer now. I want you to really think about it. It's a big decision." I reached into my pocket and pulled out the plane ticket I purchased for her. "This is a plane ticket to L.A. I want you to come and see me in three weeks ... unless you choose the first option. Someone will be waiting for you at the airport. If you come, I'll know that we have a future."

I placed a kiss on her forehead and then got up. It was killing me to walk away. Killing me not to touch her more.

"That's it? You're leaving now?" Her lips turned down into a frown.

"I have to."

I headed to the door. This was the toughest thing I ever had to do. I looked back one last time. "I love you, Talia."

Then I was out the door.

Chapter 38

Talia

I DIDN'T NEED TIME to think. I already knew what I wanted. Three weeks with no communication from Ryder made it impossible not to think, though. I thought non-stop going over every permutation of every possibility my choice might bring, and ultimately; I was satisfied with my decision. My only regret was with leaving Ellie, but even she conceded that this was the right thing for me to do.

I was moving to California.

Three weeks and I hadn't spoken to Ryder, but I'd stalked the hell out of him and his band. The hype surrounding Ghost Parker's new album was ramping up. The band had been absorbed in a whirlwind of radio spots, interviews, print articles, a few shows, and even a live performance on a late, late-night show. Their new single was released and was getting a lot of radio time.

When I stepped off the airplane at LAX, I made my way to baggage claim. Not knowing what to expect, I'd only packed for a small visit. I didn't have any checked baggage, but assumed someone would meet me there. Would it be Ryder? Nervous excitement coursed through me.

The person holding up the sign that read 'Talia Bennett' was definitely not Ryder. He was a tall man in a ball cap, wearing scruffy shorts and T-shirt — not a professional driver. He had inked arms, and yeah, I recognized those tats. Freaking Tommy Erikson, from Cold Fusion, was picking me up at the airport.

He gave me a big smile as I approached. "Thank God you showed up! Otherwise, I'd have to put him down like a dog if you hadn't."

I returned his smile. "It's that bad?"

"Yeah." He swiped at his face. "He's been a fucking mess."

I followed as Tommy began leading me toward the exit to the outside. "So, why are you picking me up exactly? Not that I don't appreciate it. Where's Ryder?"

Tommy chuckled. "You're staying at our house tonight. You'll see Ryder tomorrow — we're having a big party at our house. Right now, he's with Livvy. They're scheming — probably something crazy. I'm sorry in advance for whatever Livvy thinks up, but it comes from a good place."

I had to wait another day to see him. Lord, this was torture.

The wait seemed to drag on forever, but Livvy and Tommy did their best to keep me entertained. Finally, it was time to see Ryder. I was just finishing up my makeup, waiting the last few minutes for the exact time when Livvy told me I should come downstairs.

I'd packed one party dress for this trip just in case, but at the last minute, I decided not to wear it. Instead, I was wearing a denim mini-skirt and one of my favorite shirts — a beautifully patterned long-sleeved shirt that molded to my chest and then flared outward at the hips. The front tie exposed just a tantalizing peek of cleavage and midriff. The gauzy material and trumpet sleeves completed a fun and flirty look. I had slipped on some gold heels — they looked a bit like gladiator sandals — except they had a 3-inch heel.

I skipped the usual braids or twists in my hair and left it simple — flowing down my back. My makeup was natural, with no eyelash extensions or pink glitter eye shadow this time.

This was just me, a simple girl from Ohio.

When I made it downstairs, the party was in full swing, but there was no sign of Ryder. I had watched earlier in the day as some guys set up a spot in Tommy's house for a band to play. Some of the equipment was labeled 'Ghost Parker' so I had an idea that the band would perform at the party. One by one, I'd run into everyone from the band: Sid, Knox, Bash, and Ghost. They'd all made a point to talk to me and make me feel included. So where was Ryder?

Kaylie tracked me down when I first ventured out from the guest room to attend the party. I was immensely relieved that there was no awkwardness between us. She hugged me and then pulled me aside to whisper that she was glad Ryder and I were working things out, that she always saw something deeper between us, and that she wanted to hear the entire story someday.

It was only 4:00 in the afternoon, so I was nursing my first drink of the day. When Knox brought over a round of shots for everyone in the group I was standing in, Livvy swooped in and swept me away before I could do one.

"Trust me, you don't want to be sloppy drunk when you see Ryder," she chirped.

"Which will be when?" I raised an eyebrow questioningly.

"Soon. Patience!" Then she laughed devilishly.

She guided me over to a handsome older man who was talking to a teenage girl. The blonde girl wore a cropped dark denim jacket over a floral skater dress with brown boots. She looked adorable and slightly out of place.

Livvy smiled at the man. "Mr. Mathis, I'd like you to meet Talia." She turned to me. "Talia, this is Ryder's dad and his step-sister, Arianna."

I was nervous as I greeted the pair. "It's nice to meet you both."

Arianna's eyes shined. "Talia! It's great to meet you. Ryder wouldn't stop talking about you last night at dinner." She ended her sentence with an eye roll.

"Oh really," I smirked, basking in the knowledge. "Do you, by any chance, know where he's hiding?"

Mr. Mathis smiled warmly. "He'll be here. I'm hoping that we can all go out to dinner one night while you're in town, Talia."

"That would be nice." It was great to see that Ryder and his dad were making progress on patching up their relationship.

Arianna was scanning the crowd, but then she grinned. "The band is supposed to start around six o'clock." She grabbed my arm and leaned into me conspiratorially. "Roger's being overly protective. He won't let me talk to anyone. Will you introduce me to Ghost Parker? I saw you talking to them."

"Sure."

We worked our way around the party. In between talking to each of the guys, I heard a running commentary on how hot each of them was from Arianna. I thought she might swoon when she met Knox.

Livvy rescued me from Arianna after I'd paraded her around for close to an hour. I was talking to her husband, Tommy, and Tyler, a veritable rock god, from the band Cold Fusion when a pair of hands covered my eyes from behind.

I had been waiting for so long, but finally, I was going to see Ryder.

My heart skipped a beat. I ached to be in his arms.

I was spun around and the hands lifted. I opened my eyes. It wasn't Ryder, but I wasn't too disappointed because …

"Oh my God," I squealed. "Ellie! What are you doing here?" I pulled her into a hug.

"Surprise!" She was beaming.

Was she wearing a black leather halter top? Holy shit, as she would say. She looked hot.

"And, there's someone else here to surprise you. My car stopped by and picked him up on the way up here from the airport." Her eyes sparkled.

Someone tapped me on the shoulder. I spun and locked eyes with Greyson Durant. "Greyson! I can't believe you're here. It's so good to see you again."

"Welcome back to California, Talia. I hope you don't disappear on me this time." Greyson did the European kiss on both cheeks thing. So classy.

Ellie was bubbling over at my side, frothing like a 4th-grade volcano project about to blow. I pulled her aside.

She squeezed my hand hard and her words ran together in her excitement. "I just sat next to Greyson in a car for over an hour. Our legs touched! And I just saw Tommy and his delicious tats in the flesh. He's talking to freaking Tyler Matthews. And I want to meet all of Ghost Parker. Holy shit, Tal, I don't know if my heart can take it."

I looked her over. She was vibrating with excitement. "What about Eric?"

"He knows Greyson is my free pass." She bit her lip. "I should have demanded more free passes. There are just too many hot guys here …"

I had to laugh at the agitated look on her face. I didn't have long to think about it, because Sid joined us and was introducing himself to a very interested Ellie. And no surprise. Suddenly, Bash appeared on her other side. My friend was about to experience a Sidney/Bash sex sandwich in the making.

Luckily, Ellie was spared. Knox came over to gather up the guys. "C'mon, mates. Leave the bonnie lass alone. We're gonna start now."

Bash winked at Ellie. "We'll find you later."

The three of them headed over to the makeshift stage where Ghost was already setting up. I looked all around for Ryder. I couldn't wait to catch a glimpse of him.

Grey, Ellie, and I shifted closer to the stage. Ellie was busy star-gazing. I saw her eyes land on Tyler, who was standing over by the drinks. She turned to us. "I'm going to get a drink. Do you guys want anything?"

We both declined, so she left with a little hand wave.

Grey turned to me. "So, Ryder sold his house?"

Ryder's money problems weren't my story to tell, so I just confirmed his question with a head nod.

"And you're moving back to California?"

I chuckled. "I see you got the whole scoop." Ellie was a blabbermouth when she got nervous. Poor Greyson had to suffer through all my drama.

Grey watched me closely. "Where are you going to live?"

"I'm not sure." I shrugged. "I don't know L.A. at all, but I'm sure Ryder will help me." So far, we hadn't discussed anything. I'd been here a full day, and I hadn't even seen him yet.

"You should move into my beach house."

His statement was so simple, but it floored me. Move into Greyson Durant's house? Whoa.

He continued, "I'm hardly ever there. I've got rooms on the second floor that I never touch, and they're much nicer than the ones at Ryder's old house. And I'm thinking about hiring the contractor Ryder used on his house to do the same thing to mine. Blow out the roof on the top floor and expand the deck. It would be great if someone were there to keep an eye on things. You'd be doing me a favor, so I'd discount the rent. Maybe, say, $500 a month?"

I gasped. That would be amazing. I wanted to jump on the offer right away, but I didn't know exactly where things stood with Ryder yet. "That sounds great. Can I have a few days to think it over?"

He smiled. "Of course."

The sound of a guitar turned all eyes toward the band. The guys were set to play, but there was still no Ryder. Ghost stepped up to the microphone, and the room grew silent with anticipation. "Alright. Is everyone behaving tonight?"

There were some hoots and hollers, and a few 'yeahs' shouted out.

"That's too bad." Ghost shook his head. "Well, the night's still young."

Someone let out a shrill scream.

Ghost took a drag from a joint that was in his hand and then leaned into the mic. "Crazy, get over here and take care of this for me."

Livvy took the joint and then Ghost picked up the guitar that was leaning against his leg and slid the strap over his head. He strummed a few chords.

"We're gonna play a song from our new album. Maybe you've heard it? It's called *Day of Fire*."

The crowd went wild, but there was only one thing on my mind — where was Ryder?

Bash counted them in and then the band began to play their new hit single. Ghost was playing Ryder's part on guitar and doing the singing. Even though he didn't move around the stage as he usually did, every eye was on him. He had a commanding presence that couldn't be denied. That had come through in all the videos of the band I'd watched, but seeing Ghost perform live was absolutely mesmerizing.

They ended *Day of Fire* to tremendous applause but then segued right into another song from their new album. The third song wasn't new, but one of the band's most popular.

Ghost tucked the guitar around his hip and then leaned into the microphone stand. "We're going to take a quick break, so don't go anywhere. You're not going to want to miss what's next."

I was still watching Ghost as he set down his guitar and took a bottle of beer that was offered to him. He turned and offered me a quick lift of his chin when he caught me watching. He joined me a few seconds later.

"Natalia Rose."

Up close, Ghost's allure was ten times stronger. "Johnny Geronimo. That was incredible. I love your new songs."

"Thanks." Already people were moving closer to him. He was a human magnet. "It's good to see you back in California. Ryder was moping around like a sick puppy without you."

"It's nice to be back, although I haven't seen Ryder yet. I'm getting a bit impatient." I raised a questioning brow.

One side of his mouth lifted in a half-smile. "Get ready to be blown away then."

An arm draped across his shoulder casually. The arm belonged to Tommy. My brain was almost short-circuited from the overload of eye candy in front of me.

I watched them banter back and forth for a moment. Ryder had told me that Ghost left a trail of broken hearts behind. He didn't let anyone close to him, but just standing next to him, I could feel the pull of his charisma. I felt sorry for the poor girls that fell in love with him. It would be devastating.

Livvy came over and handed me a shot. I'd ditched my drink long ago without finishing it, so I tossed this back without worrying. It was my first real taste of alcohol all night.

She took my hand. Her eyes sparkled with mischief. "Let's go girl. You need to be front and center for the show."

Forget fluttering, butterflies started rioting in my stomach. It was finally time. I was going to see Ryder again.

Knox strummed a few chords, flexing his muscles, while Arianna panted, stationed a few feet in front of him, never peeling her eyes away. Bash was back behind his drum kit and Sid paced around with his bass guitar. Where the hell was Ryder?

The anticipation grew more and more unbearable. I glanced around, searching for Ryder, my heart pounding wildly. Just then, he stepped into the room and the entire audience of his friends erupted in cheers and applause.

When he stepped in front of the microphone, I truly felt weak-kneed for a moment. He looked so different. His gorgeous thick hair was now bleached very blond and standing up in spikes all over in a very 80s punk hairstyle. He was wearing a black leather jacket, but was shirtless underneath, giving me a delectable glimpse of those washboard abs. He had on his own version of sexy pants, black leather that looked like it was painted on. A wide studded belt with a huge buckle wrapped around his waist and drew my eyes to ... yep, there was a bulge right below. His pants were so skin-tight that I could see a freaking bulge.

Every cell in my body tingled as our eyes met. And, heavens. Was that guyliner? The heat that built between my thighs told me how much I liked what I saw. So very much.

My God, he looked sexy. I couldn't take my eyes off him.

Ryder smirked like the cocky bastard that he was.

He pulled his eyes from me and scanned the crowd. "Hope everyone is having a good time." He glanced back at me and pinned me with a stare. "I know I am."

I willed my knees not to buckle.

"Are you ready to bring the house down?"

The cheer was huge. Everyone was excited. The noise sounded like it was coming from a crowded stadium, not a hundred or so people.

Ryder nodded and then smoothly pulled off his jacket and tossed it to the ground. Girls were screaming, but he only had eyes for me. Someone tossed a pair of panties that landed right in front of him. Mine were soaked through.

Luckily, it was so loud that nobody heard the moan that escaped me. He looked sexy as sin. His toned and tatted body was on display. He was wearing his leather bracelet, and I could see just one angel's wing inked around his right wrist.

I watched the muscles work beneath his skin as he picked up his guitar. He settled it against his body and played a lick. I immediately recognized the sounds. It was unmistakable. Billy Idol. *Rebel Yell*. My favorite song.

He saw the recognition light in my eyes and gave me a little lip curl. My mouth dropped open. Now, everything made sense. The bleached blond hair. All the leather. Not many men could pull off Billy Idol as Ryder did. Even hot-as-hell Tyler — a major rock god with all that attitude, couldn't do it — it just wouldn't fit, he was too Tyler. Possibly Ghost could, he already had the hair color and crazy charisma. Maybe that's why Ghost had stepped aside and given the spotlight entirely to Ryder. And, boy, did Ryder know what to do with a spotlight.

He gave me another lazy half-smile and then started working his guitar like crazy, playing the intro to *Rebel Yell*. I already knew Ryder was an excellent singer. I had listened to the recordings he'd sent me hundreds of times by now, but when he started crooning my favorite song in his deep, raspy voice, I almost forgot to breathe.

The crowd was going wild. When he got to the chorus, he had the entire audience fist-pumping and shouting, "More, more, more". He kept up the intensity level the whole song; I could see a sheen of sweat on his torso and it made me want to do very naughty things with my tongue.

Before the last chorus, he crooked his finger at me. Not one to be in the spotlight myself, I was surprised when my feet brought me right to him. I don't think I could refuse him anything right now. I was totally under his spell.

At his prompt, I shouted "more, more, more" into the microphone, sharing the chorus with him. The magic of the moment took over my body, and I was even dancing and pumping my fist like a goddamned rock star. It was a moment I'd never forget.

After he strummed the last few notes from his guitar, he raised his fist to acknowledge the cheering crowd and then pulled off his guitar. I was about to melt back into the crowd, but he stopped me with a hand on my elbow. The look he gave me melted my insides. The adrenaline of hearing him perform my favorite kick-ass song with him looking like sex on a stick that I'd like to lick overwhelmed me, and I jumped into his arms. Literally. Clinging to him, legs wrapped around his waist.

The kiss he planted on me was so scorching hot, I was surprised the room didn't catch on fire. It ratcheted up so quickly that it verged on being not suitable for minors or adults. Ryder was smart enough to pull it back a bit because I was too busy sinking into bliss to care.

Chapter 39

Ryder

ALL WAS RIGHT IN the world. My girl was wrapped around my waist, right where I wanted her. I wasn't sure what the future held for us, but I was sure going to do everything in my power to make sure she was always by my side in that future.

The weeks away from her had been excruciating. I wasn't sure if my letters were getting through to her or if she'd even want to bother to give me a second chance. I was pretty certain she wouldn't walk away from me after my surprise visit that day in Ohio. That didn't stop the nerves from taking over the closer today's date got. Thank God that we were kept so busy prepping for the album's launch.

Now that it looked like my life was straightening out, I could concentrate all my attention on Talia. I'd invited Dad to visit, and he brought my step-sister, Arianna, with him. We'd spent a few days getting to know each other as a family. We couldn't be absolutely positive, but it looked like the loan sharks were satisfied with the payment and would no longer bother us. I was still sleeping on Knox's couch. I didn't want to do anything until I found out what Talia wanted. Whatever she chose, I was so thankful to be a part of it.

I slid her to her feet and then whispered in her ear, "Let's get out of here, Angel. I want you all to myself."

She lifted her head from my shoulder and looked at me. "Yes."

I took her hand and led her through the crowd. Friends slapped me on the back and were complimenting my performance, but I was single-mindedly focused on one thing only.

Livvy caught my eye as we passed by. She gave me a thumb's up, and I smiled my thanks to her. She'd been the one who took my performance up a notch. I'd balked at her idea, but she'd insisted that I get my hair dyed blonde and cut in this crazy style. She found the leather get-up for me and laughed her ass off as I struggled to worm my way into the pants. They were so damn tight I had to walk like a wooden board; I could barely bend my knees. And stripping off my jacket like a Chippendale dancer? Not my idea. Thank God Talia seemed to like the whole thing.

We got to the back end of the crowd when Tommy and Tyler stopped us. Fuck, I was never going to hear the end of this.

Tommy bit on his fist to keep from laughing at me. "Fuck. Look at you."

Tyler laughed outright, but then he smiled, showing his perfect white teeth. "You know how to work a crowd, Stroke. Ghost should share a bit of the limelight with you."

"Like you share with any of us?" Tommy scoffed.

Tyler turned his attention to Talia, and I automatically gripped her hand tighter. I knew Tyler was happily married, but how could anyone resist my Angel?

"How about you, Talia? Ever think of becoming a rock star? You were rocking it up there."

I let an incredulous chuckle slip out.

Talia glanced at me and then answered. "Um, no. I'm surprised Ryder hasn't banned me from singing in the shower yet."

I raised my eyebrows. "If you call that singing."

Talia was fighting her own grin. "It's not that bad."

I couldn't help but tease her. "You just scream a bunch of words. You don't even know the lyrics."

She planted her free hand on her hip. "I improve the lyrics."

Tommy and Tyler were following our conversation with amusement.

I snorted. "You make shit up because you don't know any of the words."

She sniffed her disagreement. "I'd make a terrific songwriter."

That had me barking out laughter. "Like when you were belting out, 'like a virgin, touched for the 31st time'?"

Tyler cringed.

Talia huffed, but I could tell she didn't mind the teasing. "Well, it kind of makes sense if you think about it — in a weird way."

"What about, 'living on a prayer ... it doesn't matter if we're naked or not'?" I asked.

She jutted out her jaw stubbornly. "Aren't those the words? Anyway, that's definitely an improvement."

"How about I'm a believer?" I sang out the way she mangled the song, "Then I saw her face, now I'm gonna leave her."

"Holy shit," Tommy mumbled.

Her bottom lip pulled out in a fake pout. "I figured she must have been super ugly or something."

"I like big butts in a can of limes?"

Talia shrugged. "I have no explanation for that one ..."

"Sweet dreams are made of cheese?"

Her eyes widened. "I was joking. Clearly."

She wasn't fooling anyone. "Might as well face it, you're a dick with a glove?"

Tommy and Tyler were both snickering by now.

She scowled. "Okay. I get it. I may have been slightly off a few times. My motto is close enough ..."

Tyler held up his hand. "Forget I said anything. Sorry, Talia. You're song lyric kryptonite. I'm surprised Ryder dared to pull you on stage with him. He's one brave dude."

Tommy nodded. "That's true love right there."

Before I could answer, Livvy stepped into our circle, flashing warning eyes at Tommy. "Tommy, leave them alone. They have better things to do than talk to you."

Livvy was jerking her head, attempting to give me subtle signals to leave. When we didn't move right away, she started shooing us away.

I intertwined my fingers around Talia's and pulled her away with me. "C'mon, Angel. Let's go."

"Where are we going?"

I led her out to the back of Tommy's house. "You'll see."

It was dark outside, but the temperature was still mild. I led her down the deck stairs to the back of Tommy's house. As Livvy had instructed me, we made our way along the pathway, which was lit by landscape lighting, to the bluff's edge. A wooden staircase led down to the beach below. I kept a solid hold on Talia as I led her down the uneven steps, knowing she would have difficulty in her heels. How women managed to get anywhere strapped on top of a spike the width of a toothpick, I'd never know. But, damn, Talia sure looked sexy doing it.

When we reached the bottom of the staircase, we could see the shimmering candlelight about 20 feet ahead down the beach. Livvy had set up everything for a romantic 'tryst' on the beach, as she called it. I told Talia to hop up on my back and then I walked her over to the blanket laid out in the sand, surrounded by dozens of flickering candles.

Beyond the candles, it was so dark that I could only just see the whitecaps breaking in the ocean. The beach was narrow here; I hadn't realized the ocean would be so close, but the sand was soft and Livvy had said this spot would be ideal to romance Talia.

Talia was peering at the scene over my shoulder. "This is beautiful, Ryder."

I lowered her to the blanket and sat down beside her. An ice bucket with a bottle of champagne rested next to a picnic basket. I opened the basket and pulled out two champagne flutes and a corkscrew. I opened the champagne while Talia set some food out on fancy linen napkins: strawberries, grapes, cheese and crackers, a baguette, and some chocolates. Livvy had outdone herself.

"I've missed being with you." I caught her eye as I filled the glasses with champagne.

She took the glass I offered her. "I did too."

I picked up a strawberry and held it to her lips. "I missed your awful singing in the shower."

She smiled and then took a bite of the strawberry.

"I missed all the crazy made-up lyrics. Coming home from band practice and having you there. Having the smell of your perfume imprinted on my bedsheets. Eating dinner with you on the deck. Walking on the beach with you. All your girly stuff taking over my bathroom."

She took a sip of champagne and looked out toward the ocean.

I slid in closer to her on the blanket. My hand brushed the side of her cheek. "I missed waking up in the morning with you in my bed."

Her eyes burned into mine. "I did too. That's why I've made the decision that I have. I'm going to move to California to be with you. I don't want to be apart from you any longer. It was horrible."

I set down my glass in the sand and then pulled her close to me so that she was fitted against me. "Sometimes two people have to fall apart to realize how much they need to be together."

"Now that we realize it, let's not do that again." She turned her head and our lips locked.

This woman turned me on like no other. The snugness of my pants just got a hundred times snugger. Without breaking our lip lock, I took her champagne glass and tossed it somewhere near my own. I lowered our bodies to the blanket. She was lying on top of me, her hands running over my chest and through my hair.

My hand had made its way up her skirt and into her panties and she was moaning in answer to the delicious things I was doing to her. My other hand had untied the knot on her shirt and snapped open her bra, freeing her gorgeous tits.

I was in heaven. With my Angel. I never wanted to be anywhere else.

A cold sensation on my foot registered briefly in my brain, but with the sexy woman squirming on top of me, it was soon forgotten.

I flipped us over so that I was on top. My tongue needed to taste her. I left her mouth and trailed kisses down the cheek, into her neck, to her collarbone. I was mindless with lust.

The shock was instantaneous. Jolting. Icy.

A rogue wave washed up, completely engulfing us, leaving us sputtering and frozen in disbelief.

Talia scrambled to sit up. "Oh, my God! The champagne! The blanket's soaked."

I don't know how she could see anything. Every single candle had gone out. "Don't worry about the damn blanket. Are you okay?"

Instead of freaking out, she just laughed. "I'm fine. Just freezing. That was ice-cold water."

She scrambled to her feet. "You think another wave is coming?"

Talk about a bucket of cold water squelching our passion. "Yes, if the tide's coming in."

"I can't find the champagne bottle. Ugh. I'm freezing." I heard her teeth chattering.

"Forget about the stuff. It's swept away and we'll never find it all in the dark. You're freezing. Take off your shoes, so we can get back to the house. There's someone I need to find so I can wring her neck right now."

We stumbled back to the stairs and up to the house. During our journey, I discovered something. Leather and water didn't go well together. My pants felt like they had swollen until I could hardly move my legs. They were so stiff and heavy; it felt like my legs had been poured into concrete tubes.

We tried to sneak unnoticed into the house. But two drowned rats seemed to draw a lot of attention.

Livvy rushed over to us. "Oh, my God! What happened?"

Tommy was right behind her. "Did you guys decide to take a swim in the ocean?"

By now, most of the party was watching the scene unfold. I held my breath praying that Talia wasn't going to be too upset. I wouldn't blame her if she wanted to kill me.

Talia shook her head and spoke through chattering teeth. "A tsunami interrupted our romantic moment."

"Down on the beach?" Tommy was looking at us like we were complete idiots.

"Yes." I glanced at Livvy. I spoke through clenched teeth. "Someone set up a romantic love nest — I think she called it, for us."

"Oops." Livvy looked between Tommy and me, guilt written on her face. "That's never happened when, um, you know. We've been down there."

Tommy barked out a laugh. "There's a reason for that, Crazy. I've never taken you down there at 7 o'clock at night. It's called high tide."

I stared at them for a second. How many times had I been warned not to trust Livvy?

Livvy turned to Talia. "You need a hot shower and some new clothes. C'mon."

Either my legs were numb from the cold or I was losing circulation. "Um, I think my pants are shrinking. I can't feel my legs anymore."

In the end, they had to cut me out of my pants.

Chapter 40

Talia

I'D BEEN IN THE shower for ten minutes. The hot water had stopped my uncontrollable shivers and my teeth had stopped chattering. I had rinsed off all the sand and washed my hair.

And I was about to scream.

Ryder pushed my hand away from its destination once again. "Let me finish taking care of you."

Ryder's hands had already soaped over every inch of my body. Our slippery bodies had rubbed together over and over until I was crazed for him. He began rubbing slow circles around my clit.

"Ryder," I moaned. "I need your cock inside me right now."

He didn't even speed up his slow torture. "Patience."

"I'm tired of waiting. I've been waiting for weeks. And then, just when — ugh ... the beach happened." I pressed against his relentless hand, looking for more, but he kept a steady pace.

His free hand slid up to play with my breasts. "Sorry, but I don't have a condom in here. I was so focused on getting you warmed up that I forgot to get one."

I almost told him to forget the damn condom, but he was right. Being responsible sometimes sucked. "Let's get out of the shower, then. There's a perfectly good bed just outside this door. I need your cock."

He slid a finger inside me and I gasped. "I want to make you come first."

I tried to reach for his cock again if only to make him see reason. "That'll take far too long."

Famous last words. He took that up as a challenge and I swear he had me coming in less than a minute. As I came back to earth, I realized that he was the only thing holding me up. I'd slumped against him.

After we got out of the shower, I let him towel me dry and then he led me back into my bedroom. I slid into the bed as he pulled the covers back. Then, he was crawling in between my legs, his mouth leading the way straight to my pussy.

"Ryder, your cock. Inside me. You promised." I sounded so needy.

He was kissing closer and closer to my center. "Let me taste you first."

His mouth began doing very wicked things and before long, another orgasm ripped through me.

The third orgasm was the one that I'd been waiting for. We moaned together as he pressed into me. The crazy connection that felt like an electric charge in the atmosphere between us whenever he was near me seemed to grow ten times stronger. Sex without the emotional insecurity that had plagued me only made our bond grow deeper. I was all in for this.

I was wrapped up in his arms and feeling so content that I was getting sleepy. Maybe it was the remnants of jetlag. I didn't want to fall asleep; I wanted this night to last forever.

"Should we go back downstairs and join the party?" I sat up a bit to wake myself.

"No."

His answer was so quick, I giggled. "All our friends are down there."

He kissed my forehead. "They'll understand."

His cock thickened against my thigh as I pressed against him. "I know what you want."

He shifted so he could see my face. "Actually, I want to talk."

"About what?"

He swallowed. "Us. The future."

Even though I thought we were now on the same page, it made me a little nervous. "What kind of future do you see for us?"

Ryder smiled and began tracing patterns on my skin with his fingertips. "I see the future so clearly it's kind of scary. I see us living in a big house right on the beach, just like this one. You're by my side, coming with me when the band tours. You'll have a career that you're passionate about — something that involves fashion. How does that sound so far?"

My head was resting on his chest. I could hear the steady beat of his heart. "It sounds perfect."

He smiled. "Are you ready to hear more?"

I nodded.

"We're married. We've got a few little princesses running around. You like to dress them up all girly, but they just want to surf with their daddy. We have a son, too. I think he's going to be all trouble, that one. He takes after me, but we've got all our friends around us to help."

My throat was clogged with tears. I couldn't speak.

He nudged me gently. "You still with me, Angel?"

"I am." My voice came out wobbly. "I want that future, Ryder."

"Someday, I know we're going to get that. It's the near future that's harder. I'm broke and homeless. You live in Ohio. I just want to make sure — what you said at the beach — you'd move to California? You wouldn't resent leaving everything behind?"

Gazing into his eyes, I smiled. "Yes, I'm positive, Ryder. I've never been more certain about anything. The thought of leaving my job and starting something new is exciting to me."

His hand cupped my cheek. "This feels so good. I don't ever want this feeling to stop. I love you so much, Angel. You're moving to California ... I just can't believe how lucky I am. I'm so fucking happy. When you left that morning — I was so scared ..."

Putting my finger to his lips to quiet him, I said, "I thought I didn't mean anything to you and I was just so heartbroken and crushed that I said some horrible things." I shuddered. "Ryder, I'm so sorry." A shudder ran through me. "Oh, let's not talk about it right now. Not when I'm so happy."

His arms tightened around me. "You were wrong, Talia. You mean everything to me. I want you to know that. I love you. I was so dumb that I didn't even know what those crazy feelings were. It happened so fast that my head was spinning. I've never been in love before. It's fucking terrifying, but so damn amazing."

"I love you, too. I figured it out soon after I got here, but I didn't think you could reciprocate those kinds of feelings, especially with the whole rock star thing you have going on. I tried telling myself that we could have a casual fling — that I should just enjoy the orgasms while I could, but the more I saw the real you, the harder I ended up falling."

It felt so good to share everything with him — to share what was in my heart, my hopes and dreams, even my fears.

I intertwined our fingers together and pulled his hand to my lips for a kiss. Mostly, I wanted to see his angel tattoo. "Do you miss living on the beach?"

"Yeah, I do." He sighed. "I'm gonna get that back someday for us, Angel. I promise."

I traced the delicate wings of the angel on his wrist. "You mentioned you didn't think we should live together right away. That we should give our relationship more time to grow. I agree. I want to spend all my time with you, but I also want to go on dates. I don't want to skip any of the fun parts."

"Go on dates, hmm. Will any of these dates involve sleepovers?" He rolled me underneath him.

I grinned. "God, I hope most of them do. You still owe me a date at the Santa Monica Pier, by the way."

"Done."

His lips were moving in to kiss me. Before he could, I blurted out, "I got an offer to live at Grey's house."

Ryder stiffened above me.

"You know he's just a friend. He spends most of his time at his home in Hollywood, anyway. I'd love to live at the beach. I kind of got hooked on it when I stayed at your house. Plus, he offered me cheap rent in exchange for keeping an eye on it while he makes renovations. It makes sense."

Chewing on my lip, I waited for his response.

"If I'm being honest; I'm jealous as fuck. But it sounds ideal and I trust you. Him, I'm not too sure. Will I be able to stay overnight there?"

"Whenever you want." I laughed as I thought about Ryder's misplaced jealousy. "By the way, Grey confessed to me that the reason he was always strutting around shirtless before was because he was into you."

Ryder's mouth dropped open. "What? So he's gay?"

"Well, to be fair, I think he's attracted to women, too. But we're not interested in each other that way. We're just friends. I've only got eyes for you."

"Damn right." He smacked a kiss on my lips. "As long as we're honest with each other. But this relationship stuff is all new to me. You might have to remind me from time to time that we need to talk things through."

Ryder nudged his thigh between my legs. "Now let's stop talking and start making up for all the time we lost. That's the one thing I regret."

"I regret the loss of those leather pants you were rocking. Talk about sexy pants! What a shame they got ruined."

"I don't think I'm going to keep this blond hair, but I'll keep the leather just for you, baby. I'll find out where Livvy bought those pants and get another pair."

A few minutes later, when Ryder was pressing his cock deep into me, I opened my eyes to study his face. "Give me the lip curl."

He made a semi-decent approximation of Billy Idol's famous lip curl as he pumped into me. I about died laughing.

Epilogue

---

2 years later ...

Ryder

"You couldn't wait two more days?" I teased.

Talia sat in the truck beside me. We were heading north up the Pacific Coast Highway on a gorgeous spring day. "You know I'm terrible at waiting. I can't wait to see it again."

Our plan had been to wait until we were married before we bought our dream home, but Melanie had found us a house and we knew immediately we had to have it. It was serendipitous; we put a bid on it on the spot. The closing was in two days from now, months before our wedding date.

She squeezed my hand, and I glanced over at our entwined fingers. I loved seeing the diamond on her finger, the promise that she was to be my wife. I proposed to Talia at the top of the Ferris wheel in Pacific Park on the Santa Monica Pier. I had to work fast because the attendant would only stop the ride for three minutes while we were at the top, no matter how much I tried to bribe him. At the top, over 130 feet from the ground, the panoramic view was breathtaking; we could see up and down the coastline for miles. She was so surprised when I popped the question. Her hands were shaking so much that I almost dropped the ring, trying to get it on her finger. It was a moment I'll never forget.

I turned off the highway toward the ocean. Our new house was located just south of Malibu, on the edge of a large promontory loaded with lush tropical vegetation and backed by the rugged coastline. We got to our street, a cul-de-sac, and drove down to the end.

Even when I'd lived in my beach house in Huntington Beach, I'd never thought I could own this, my dream home, so quickly. Ghost Parker had done well in the two years since then. Our album was a success, our tours always sold out, and our merchandise sold exceptionally well. What put us over the top, however, was our smash single *Okay Babe*.

Okay Babe was one of those freak occurrences like lightning striking the same spot twice. It was the one and only song ever written by Sid. It was recorded almost as an afterthought and against our band's wishes, even including Sid's. Despite our efforts to make it sound edgier and harder, it was a quintessential pop song. It never made it onto an album, but it was responsible for our label locking us down and offering us a sweet new record deal.

Black Vault Records promoted the hell out of us after our unexpected hit. *Okay Babe* flew up the charts and stayed there forever. I cringed whenever I heard it — it was way too pop-sounding for Ghost Parker. We couldn't do any shows or make any appearances without playing it. We would be stuck with it for life. But for all the grumbling we did about it, the song catapulted our band into a different stratosphere and it made us a fuck ton of money.

I stopped on the road in front of our new house. The view of the structure was mostly obscured from the street by palm trees and other thick vegetation. It was built on an elevation, so what looked like a two-story home from the front was actually a three-story home whose backside, which was mostly glass, faced the ocean for breathtaking views from almost every room.

"I can't see it. Go down the driveway."

I tapped the steering wheel with my fingers. "What if the owners are home?"

Talia smiled. "They're not. Melanie told me they moved out days ago."

I turned down the driveway and drove toward the house. Talia hopped out even before I turned the engine off. Her cheeks were flushed with happiness.

I smiled at her infectious enthusiasm. "What are we going to do? Peek in the windows?"

"No, silly." She held up and jiggled a set of keys. "I got the keys from Melanie."

We walked through the house hand in hand, seeing the space for the first time in over a month. The house had everything I ever wanted and more. A fabulous master suite with a private balcony, three other bedrooms and a separate guest suite, outdoor decks, a media room, and a giant indoor/outdoor entertainment space on the ground floor which included a pool and spa all surrounded by Palm and Cyprus trees.

As we passed through the bedrooms, I imagined filling them up with our future children. "This would be the perfect room for a little princess."

She slid her hands around my waist. "The surfer princess?"

I pulled her close to me. She remembered the conversation we'd had two years ago, the night of Tommy's party when I imagined our future together. Here we were on the very cusp of that vision.

I had it all. The perfect woman. My dream home. My brothers in the band — true friends that I'd forged deeper relationships with than I'd ever thought possible. A much better relationship with my father and his family. Even a tenuous new connection with Brock that was mostly facilitated by Jenny. And Talia fit seamlessly into all of those pieces. She completed me.

My fears about starting a family were gone, and I was ready to take the next step with the perfect woman by my side. I'd done a lot of growing over the past two years and I was confident that someday I'd make a terrific father. I planned to get started on that dream on our honeymoon.

Talia had sunk into my arms, but now she lifted her eyes to me. "Let's take a walk on the beach before we leave."

"It's getting late. Don't we have to drop off some purple shoes for Kaylie?" She'd dragged me out of our place to run the quick errand for Kaylie, but we'd ended up here on her insistence.

She winked. "We have time."

♫♫♪♪♪

Talia

The purple shoes had merely been an excuse to get Ryder out of the house. I'd purposefully cleared my work schedule, but Ryder didn't know that. It had taken two years of constant hustle to get my fledgling style consultant business to where it was today. My client list was still small, but word was slowly getting out. So far, I've attracted no one glamorous. I assisted mostly the wives of the local elite and a few celebrities' wives. I still hadn't attracted any women who were famous for their own achievements, but I think I liked it that way. My clientele was real. Likable. Warm.

I led Ryder down the narrow pathway to our own private paradise on the beach. The sandy beach was wide on this part of the promontory, but our new house was tucked into a tiny little cove. The surf slapped against the large rocks that jutted out from the ocean in front of us. We loved that the landscape and rocky beach kept this part of the shoreline so secluded. There was no public beach access anywhere nearby, and I'd never seen any neighbors walking the beach near our rocky outcrop any time I'd been here.

Twilight was settling quickly to dusk. I could just make out the flickering candles ahead. Ryder was watching the ocean, so it took him a few minutes to notice as we approached. "What's this?"

I led him to the beach blanket surrounded by lit candles set in mason jars. Only a few had blown out. The bottle of sparkling cider was in place. The picnic basket sat next to it. Melanie, who'd become a friend, had done a great job. I owed her big time for this and for the two clients she'd pushed my way.

"Does it look familiar?" I sat down on the blanket. I was almost giddy with anticipation.

Ryder glanced at the blanket and then back to the ocean — a wary look on his face. "It reminds me of getting my junk crushed by those suffocating pants after almost drowning in ice-cold water."

This time we were much further back from the ocean. "I consulted the tidal charts this time. We're good. Trust me. Tonight, I want to finish what we started before the tsunami struck."

"Ooh. In that case ..." Ryder relaxed and joined me on the blanket.

"I have a surprise for you." A tiny laugh bubbled out of my throat.

Ryder pulled me onto his lap and began nibbling at my ear. "What is it?"

"Mmm. It's hidden somewhere on my body. You'll have to search for it."

Ryder rolled me to the ground, laying me out on my back. "Challenge accepted."

He didn't waste any time in removing my clothing and lavishing every single inch of my body with his mouth. After I was panting from a deliciously languid orgasm caused by his slow inspection of my pussy by his tongue, I sat up on my elbows.

"Ryder, you have to look for your surprise with your eyes, not your tongue. And it's not near my pussy, so you can stop your meticulous search of that area."

He leaned down and flicked my nipple with his tongue. "Is it near here?"

"You're getting closer."

His mouth blazed a trail of fire up my neck and over to my mouth. His kiss was long and sexy. I'd kiss him forever if I could.

"Closer."

He slid his hand under my hair and placed a line of kisses from my shoulder, up the arch of my neck, and over to my ear.

"You're getting very hot."

"Hmmm." He slid my hair over to one shoulder and was about to kiss me again when he stopped. "Angel," his voice was rough and sultry.

"You like?"

I had gotten a tattoo, the same exact angel that was on his wrist, on the nape of my neck.

"I love it. It's perfect. Just like you." He softly fingered the spot, tracing the wings, before kissing it.

His kiss made me shiver.

"Are you cold?" He pulled off his T-shirt and handed it to me. Since I was naked and still had more surprises in store for him that didn't include sex, I slipped it on. Plus, bonus, I got to see his naked chest.

I opened the picnic basket and pulled out a corkscrew and a couple of glasses lying right on top. "This time, I want to actually finish our picnic. Will you open the champagne?"

He pulled the bottle of sparkling cider from the ice bucket, and I handed him the opener. He made quick work of the bottle, never realizing it wasn't actually champagne.

I inched closer to him as he filled both our glasses. He set the bottle aside and then pulled me onto his lap, exactly where I wanted to be.

I was practically purring with contentment. I turned so I could see his face. "Should we make a toast?"

He lifted his glass. "To our new house. To filling it up with lots of babies." He flashed an arrogant smirk. "To the process of filling you up with babies."

"Ryder!" I slapped him playfully.

He continued, "To my angel. My fiancée and soon-to-be wife. I love you. You're my forever girl."

My eyes filled with tears. I loved this man so much. "I love you, too, Mr. Rock Star. Forever."

Our kiss went from sweet to wicked in a flash. I had to force myself from his lips and slide off his lap. "Oh, no. This time, I want to enjoy the strawberries, the chocolate, and all the picnic goodies. Can you get them out of the basket?"

Ryder frowned for a second. He clearly had other activities on his mind, but then he flipped open the lid on the picnic basket. He reached in and pulled out the first item. It was a miniature T-shirt. He looked confused as he held it up. There was a flaming guitar on the front with the words Little Rock Star underneath.

I pulled it from his hands and frowned. "How did that get in there?"

He paused for a long moment but then shrugged. He dug into the basket again. This time, he pulled out a bigger T-shirt. This one had a matching guitar on the front but said Hot Rocking Dad.

His eyes flew to mine. "Does this mean what I think it means?"

Happy tears gathered at the corner of my eyes. I nodded.

"You're pregnant?"

I nodded again. And then I tumbled into his arms.

That night we laughed, we cried, we made love and finally we even enjoyed the food in the picnic basket. We'd found our happily ever after.

The End

Next in Series

Author's Note:

Did you enjoy reading about Tommy from Cold Fusion and his wife, Livvy a.k.a. Crazy? Livvy was my all-time favorite heroine to write! Find out how Crazy got her nickname in this laugh-out-loud rockstar romance: ROCK ME: CRAZY

Bad Boys of Rock

Book 2

(Keep turning the pages for an excerpt!)

How to Tempt a Rockstar
Get ready to toss your panties on stage — it's gonna get wild!

I live my life in a haze of booze, sex, and rock 'n' roll. I have it all — fame, fortune, and an endless parade of women at my beck and call. So the day a tiny bundle shows up at my door, *oh baby!* my life changes overnight. My carefree existence is shattered and I'm catapulted into unchartered territory.

Only one person can help me, but she's always been off-limits — my best friend's little sister. When temptation and the forbidden collide, I know I should resist, but the dangerous embrace of sin and pleasure is too strong to ignore. Surrender has never tasted sweeter, but as the forbidden lures me into its intoxicating embrace, the consequences threaten to destroy everything.

Grab your **backstage pass** to meet the boys of Ghost Parker and get ready for a deliciously scandalous journey through the wild world of rock 'n' roll, where love, lust, and longing collide in a symphony of temptation. Turn up the volume and prepare to be utterly consumed by this rockstar romance — a steamy and erotic tale of forbidden love, unbridled desire, and the search for true love amidst the chaos of stardom.

Keep turning the pages to read an excerpt from
How to Tempt a Rockstar

Arabella Quinn Newsletter

Let's keep in touch!

Sign up for my newsletter and be the first to know about new releases, sales, giveaways, and other exciting news. As an added bonus, you'll receive a FREE ebook as my thank-you for signing up!

Arabella Quinn newsletter
https://subscribepage.io/ArabellaQuinn

Bad Boys of Rock Series

Who doesn't love the tattooed bad boys of rockstar romance? **Get ready to toss your panties on stage — it's gonna get wild!**

Book 1: How to Seduce a Rockstar — A mind-boggling case of mistaken identity sets the stage for a scorching hot romance between Ryder, the sinfully sexy guitarist of a famous rock band, and Talia, the unsuspecting woman who stumbles into his life. After the erotic encounter with the mysterious and sexy stranger in his bed, Ryder's world is rocked.

Book 2: How to Tempt a Rockstar — Forbidden desires ignite in this sizzling romance between Sid, the tattooed bad-boy bass guitarist, and Kaylie, his best friend's little sister. When a tiny bundle shows up at Sid's door, Kaylie reaches out to help as his world turns upside-down. As the lines between love and lust lose focus, they must weather the tempest of forbidden desire and hidden truths to see if their love can survive the ultimate test.

Book 3: How to Date a Rockstar — In this sizzling rockstar romance, enemies become lovers while secrets threaten to tear them apart. Knox, the lead guitarist with the irresistible Scottish accent, becomes entangled in a fake dating scheme with Summer to appease her meddlesome mother. When the lines between fake and real blur, Knox must confront his tragic past and face the truth that he's been battling. Can their budding relationship survive the harsh glare of the spotlight and the ghosts of the past that haunt them? Or will the truth shatter their hearts beyond repair?

Book 4: How to Catch a Rockstar — Passions burn hot when Ghost, the enigmatic lead singer of a popular rock band, becomes ensnared in a tempestuous love triangle between Remi, a woman who ignites his dormant emotions, and her boyfriend, whom he despises. As lust and hatred collide with betrayal, can the three navigate the treacherous waters of a passionate love triangle and find redemption amidst the chaos of stardom, or will their dangerous games leave them shattered? The only question is—who will be left standing when the music stops?

Book 5: How to Marry a Rockstar — Bash, the reckless and carefree drummer of a chart-topping rock band, is busy juggling fame, fortune, and fatherhood. Lacey, the sultry vixen, has been friends with Bash and his band for years. Their lives take an unexpected turn when one reckless night in Vegas changes everything, leaving them entwined in more ways than one. With their secret passions and insatiable cravings unleashed, they embark on a steamy friends-with-benefits arrangement with a side of untamed kinks.

Also By Arabella Quinn

BAD BOYS OF ROCK SERIES

How to Seduce a Rockstar

How to Tempt a Rockstar

How to Date a Rockstar

How to Catch a Rockstar

How to Marry a Rockstar

ROCK ME SERIES

Rock Me: Wicked

Rock Me: Naughty

Rock Me: Crazy

Rock Me: Sexy

ROMANCE NOVELS

My Stepbrother the Dom
Impossible (to Resist) Boss
Being Jane

THE WILDER BROTHERS SERIES
(small town romance)

Fake Marriage to a Baller
Luke – coming soon

About the Author

Arabella Quinn is a *New York Times* and *USA Today* bestselling author of contemporary romance. When she's not busy writing, you can often find her clutching her Kindle and staying up way past her bedtime reading romance novels. Besides contemporary romance, she loves regency, gothic, and erotic romance — the steamier the better. She also loves thrillers, especially psychological thrillers. She saves reading horror for when her husband is away on business but doesn't recommend that. She averages about five hours of sleep per night and does not drink coffee. Also, not recommended!

Arabella Quinn newsletter
https://subscribepage.io/ArabellaQuinn

Excerpt

How to Tempt a Rockstar

Chapter 1

Bash

D<small>EBAUCHERY WAS ON THE</small> menu tonight.

It didn't matter that it was a Monday night; in fact, most nights I partied my ass off. But the knowledge that I didn't have practice at our rehearsal studio tomorrow ramped up the level of this party a hundredfold. There was no doubt in my mind, tonight was going to get very ugly. I'd been drinking steadily for hours, and I'd already done too many bong hits to count. I was in the mood to take a hit of something even wilder, but my little sister was here.

My sister, Kaylie, had an apartment within walking distance of my own. While I loved that I could keep an eye on her in Los Angeles, sometimes, like tonight, she cramped my style. She partied with us a lot, usually bringing her wannabe actress friends with her.

I shouldn't complain too much, because tonight one of those friends pulled me into Sid's bedroom, even though my bedroom was only one door further down, and gave me a blowjob. It was sloppy, but it did the trick. If Sid had walked in, she would have blown him too.

I had to be careful of the wannabe actresses because they were all about social media. They loved nothing more than to be plastered all over it. From experience, I knew that if they could link their name to a rock band, all the better for them. The wilder the scandal, the more these girls benefited, no matter how shitty it could turn out for me and the band. Our label had warned us to keep our image squeaky clean after a bit of malicious gossip about us recently hit social media, so I was extra cautious of them.

When a new group of girls showed up, the party got even wilder. A few hours later, I was stumbling around and slurring my words, almost completely wasted. It was to the point where I knew I should grab a few girls and head to my bedroom so I could fuck them until I passed out. Of course, that's not what I did.

I wasn't exactly clear on how it all started. One of our roadies, Ben, who looked more like a member of a motorcycle gang than a sound engineer, was running his mouth, bragging about how good he was at eating pussy. The next thing I knew, I was being roped into a pussy-eating contest. Two girls volunteered to be the subjects, and Sid and I were pitted against each other. I was confused as to why big-mouth Ben wasn't a contestant considering he was the one making all the ridiculous claims, but I was too wasted to figure it out.

I chugged a beer someone handed me and glanced around the room. It was packed full of outrageously drunk people. The music was blaring, and people were dancing, spilling drinks, and snorting lines off the coffee table. A few couples were fucking in the corners; they knew that if Sid or I found them in our bedrooms, they'd never be allowed back here. That threat seemed to work most of the time.

Sid was saying something to me, but I wasn't listening. He shook my shoulders, and I tried to focus on him. Sid was like a brother to me; we'd been friends since we were 13 years old. Our band, Ghost Parker, was the fourth and hopefully, last band we'd be in together. Our second album was in production and, by all accounts, it was going to be huge.

Sid's lips turned down in a frown. "I'm not doing this, man. You can't either. You're totally wasted."

"I'm fine." My head was spinning wildly, but I felt pretty damn invincible.

"You're not fine. And Kaylie is here. You can't do this in front of her."

I looked around the apartment, searching for Kaylie. I'd forgotten about her. "What the fuck is she still doing here? Tell her to go home."

Sid ran a hand through his hair. "You know she's not going to leave. And I'm not eating some girl out in front of her. You're not either, asshole."

Ben sidled up to us and slapped his meaty hand on Sid's shoulder. His voice boomed above the music, "What the fuck, Vicious? You can't puss out. I have a hundred bucks on you. No way this pretty boy can beat you."

Sid, who was called 'Vicious' by most of the people that worked with the band, shook his head. "It's not happening, Ben. Bash won't do it either."

"What are you? His old lady?" Ben was always instigating trouble. Problem was that I somehow always ended up in the middle of it. The fucker knew how to push my buttons.

Ben turned to me and started trash-talking. "What's the matter, Bash? You afraid you're going to lose? I tell you what; I'll make it easy for you. How about Dylan? You think you can beat Dylan?" He started getting in my face aggressively. "Or are you just a little bitch?"

I scoffed. "Dude, I thought you were the world's greatest pussy eater. Now you're getting Dylan involved? Look who's a little bitch now."

"Oh, shit." Ben laughed. "Is that a challenge? I could beat you with both hands tied behind my back. Let's do it, fucker. A hundred bucks says I can take you."

God, I wanted to wipe that smirk off his face so badly. "There's not a pussy on this planet that doesn't shrivel up in fear when it sees your ugly mug coming at it."

Our trash talk had gathered a lot of attention. The crowd around us began laughing and heckling Ben at my idiotic insult.

Ben shook his head and laughed. "You fucker! Alright, you and me. Let's go. And, let's make it $200."

Everyone was listening now. I was too drunk to even consider that I could lose this bet. "Fine, $200. When I win, you have to pay it to the poor girl who has to put up with having your ugly face between her legs."

Another round of raucous jeering broke out. I vaguely noticed Sid shaking his head in disgust, but then he was gone and I was being dragged over toward the couch.

I'd never been in a pussy-eating contest before. Hell, I'm not sure I'd even heard of one before. Ben was making a big show of getting his hands tied behind his back while another roadie was laying down the rules. I realized I was really drunk when I could barely focus on what was happening. Two girls were reclining on the couch, legs spilling over the front, in the middle of the party. One was sliding her panties off from under a short skirt. The other girl was already bare from the waist down and her legs were boldly parted, giving the crowd an unimpeded look.

Someone had turned off the music and almost everyone had gathered around the couch. The roadie who was acting as the judge — I think his name was Garrett — had everyone's attention. "The rules are simple. The first one to get their girl to cum wins. I'll be the one to verify the orgasm, so ladies, raise your hand when you orgasm, so I can check. Ben, you are only allowed to use your mouth, but Bash, you can use your mouth and your fingers."

Fuck, this should be a piece of cake. I would attack her clit with my mouth and her G-spot with my finger and have her coming in seconds flat. For a split second, I thought about not using my hands — to make the competition even — but then disregarded it. I was drunk, and I wanted to win. I absolutely did not want to lose to this asshole.

Ben held his hands behind his back as they got tied. "Which girl do you want? You pick, Bash."

I looked at the two girls. The girl with the short skirt looked uncomfortable. She couldn't even look me in the eye. When the other girl smiled at me, I pointed to her. "I'll take her."

As we knelt down in front of the girls, the crowd got rowdy, chanting our names and grunting and hollering like a bunch of zoo animals.

Ben smiled at his girl. "Hike your skirt up a bit, honey, so I can get in there real good."

My girl looked unfazed that I was about to dive between her legs in front of a crowd of onlookers. I picked the right girl; she was definitely less uptight.

Before I could form another thought, Garrett began a countdown. "5, 4, 3, 2, 1 ... Go!"

I wasn't concerned about finesse, just speed. I parted this girl with my fingers, secured my lips around her clit and slipped two fingers inside her, immediately searching out her G-Spot. Working hard and fast, I wasn't sober enough to know if anything I was doing was actually turning her on, and I didn't really care.

I was going to town for a while when the crowd suddenly erupted with cheers. I lifted my head for a moment to see that the other girl had raised her hand. Ben was dancing around in celebration, while Garrett was supposedly inspecting the girl's orgasm — however the fuck that worked.

My mouth dropped open in disbelief. "That's bullshit! That was like ... not even a minute."

Ben was wagging his tongue like an insane clown. "That's all it takes when you've got it, brother."

Garrett pulled the girl with the short skirt up from the couch and raised her right arm in the air like a champion prizefighter. "Folks, we have a winner!"

"Pay up, bitch." Ben approached me with his hands still tied behind his back. "That'll be two hundred fucking bucks."

I wiped my mouth with the back of my hand. No way that fucker won. They must have cheated. "You'll have to take an IOU."

I remembered taking a good amount of ribbing after that, which did nothing for my mood because I hated losing. I looked for Sid, but he was nowhere to be found. Suddenly, I wanted everyone out of my apartment.

♫♫♩♪♪

The next thing I knew, I was waking up to an annoying noise. Shit, it was my cell phone. I grabbed the phone off my nightstand and looked at the screen. Kaylie was calling.

I pulled the phone to my ear and croaked out a greeting. "Hey, Kay."

When I rolled onto my back, I realized I wasn't in my bed alone. I suppressed a groan when I caught a glimpse of the girl I was in bed with. Sadie. Fuck.

I hated this girl. Sadie was hot with her pretty eyes, plump lips, shiny black hair, and luscious tits, but I never liked her 'emo' personality. She was always lurking in the periphery, glowering like she was ready to flip tables or frowning as if her puppy had just died. Talking to her was a huge chore because she was always so whiny and negative. Perhaps the creepiest thing about her was that I felt her eyes on me all the time, watching from the shadows like I was her prey. I'd made the mistake of kissing her once before, at a party. It had taken me months to shake her after that.

What the fuck was I doing naked in my bed with Sadie, the girl Sid and I secretly called Satan? She opened her mouth like she was going to talk, so I put my finger over her lips to shush her.

Kaylie's voice came through the phone. "Did I wake you up? I'm not surprised; you were pretty drunk last night. You were gross."

Fuck, I couldn't deal with Kaylie right now, especially not when Satan was naked in my bed. "Did you have a reason for calling?"

I heard her sharp inhale of breath. "I'm pissed at you, Sebastian. You were out of control. Do you even remember what you did last night?"

"Not particularly," I mumbled. But, shit, it was all starting to come back to me.

"Does a certain contest ring a bell? Of all the disgusting things you've ever done, Sebastian, that's probably the grossest. You have no respect for women—"

I could not deal with this now. "Kaylie, we'll talk later. I've got to go. Bye."

She was still speaking when I hung up. Damn, the pussy-eating contest — the memory was really fuzzy. Apparently, Kaylie knew all about it. I hope to God she didn't actually witness it. Could this day get any worse?

I turned to Satan and groaned as I flicked a finger back and forth between us. "Did we?"

She shrugged like she didn't have a single care. "Like bunnies."

I may have winced.

She reached out and stroked my arm. "Want to do it again?"

Chapter 2

Sidney

It was 10 o'clock when I rolled out of bed to use the bathroom. Thank God the girl I'd been with last night had taken off without a word about a half hour ago. I didn't know much about her, but I'd seen her arrive last night with Lacey. She'd just recently started hanging out with some girls who were part of our local groupie gang. Alyssa was her name. She was okay looking, but the sex had been less than stellar. We were both drunk, so maybe that was the problem. At least she hadn't taken part in the pussy-eating contest.

Christ. What was Bash thinking? I clearly recalled the look of absolute disgust and horror that swept over Kaylie's face before she'd run from our apartment. I wanted to chase after her, just to make sure she got home safely, but I was too much of a coward. My stomach twisted with revulsion.

I slipped a pair of sweatpants over my boxers and threw on a T-shirt before I stumbled out of my room and weaved my way into the kitchen. It smelled like a frat house in our apartment. The seedy smell of old weed clung to the fabrics. Beer bottles, containing various amounts of liquid, were scattered everywhere. I hit a few damp spots on the carpet as I crossed the room. A red solo cup that had once contained a mix of beer and cigarette ashes was overturned on the coffee table.

I stopped in my tracks. There was a naked man on our couch. I squinted in an attempt to identify who it was. Probably one of the roadies. And, fuck, there was a spent condom lying on the floor next to him.

I was just sick of everything. Between the pussy-eating contest in my living room, my less than pointless and unsatisfying hook-up last night, a random naked and sweaty ass touching my couch cushions and now a jizz-filled condom lying on my nasty beer-stained rug, I was pretty much done.

It was hard to be philosophical about existential matters when I hadn't even had my first cup of coffee yet, but there had to be more to life than this. Right? My friend and bandmate, Ryder, had been banging the same girl for months now. He was happy as hell now that she'd moved to California to be with him. I guess I just hadn't found the right girl yet, because I couldn't imagine settling down with one chick.

An image of a girl with wavy, dark hair and big green eyes flashed in my head. Scowling at my rogue thoughts, I pushed the image from my mind. No, I definitely hadn't found that sort of girl yet.

I made a cup of coffee and began surveying the damage. I just didn't have the energy to clean anything up right now. Plus, Bash would probably invite people back here again tonight and it would just get trashed all over again. Maybe I should take off and leave the cleanup all to him this time. It would serve him right.

I had a trash bag half filled with empty beer bottles when Bash emerged from his room. I glanced over my shoulder to see who would come out with him and about choked on my tongue when I saw Satan trailing behind him. She was dressed head to toe in black, as usual, and her heavy black makeup was smeared around her eyes.

She was one of those goth-type girls. I'm not sure who she was friends with, but she showed up around here like a bad penny. Bash looked miserable, and it was the funniest thing I'd seen in a while.

"Well, good morning, you two." I snickered. "Did you have a good time last night, Sadie?"

I'd never seen her smile, and she didn't crack one now. Her voice was always monotone. "It was ... underwhelming."

A burst of laughter, which I tried to disguise as a cough, escaped from me.

Bash frowned. "What do you mean by that?"

She shrugged. "Not what I expected."

He grabbed a mug from the cabinet. "Me neither, believe me."

No one spoke after that. Satan just stood in our kitchen watching us. I felt an overwhelming urge to hide the knife block. Why did she have to be so creepy? She was a cute girl, but so weird.

Finally, Bash sighed loudly and turned to her. "Do you need a ride home?"

"No." She didn't move.

Bash caught my eye, but I just shrugged. He was the dumb ass that hooked up with her. She was his problem.

When the atmosphere got too heavy for me in the kitchen, I headed out to the living room and saw the naked guy again.

I yelled into the kitchen. "Bash, come help me get this guy out of here."

I'm sure Bash was eager to escape from the kitchen. He was at my side in seconds, staring down at the naked guy.

"I think his name is Garrett. He's coming on our next tour," he said.

I started looking around for his clothes. "Well, wake his ass up and get him out of here. He better not have pissed on the couch or anything." I toed at a lump of material on the floor and discovered a hoodie. "Bash, it's fucking disgusting in this place. I'm getting sick of it."

"Yeah, yeah. You've told me." Bash shoved at the guy a few times.

"Get up, Garrett."

Garrett finally stirred and then sat up and let out a long groan as he ran his face through his hands. "I feel like hell."

I threw the hoodie at him. "Time to hit the road, Garrett. Maybe you can share a cab with Sadie?"

I turned to the kitchen to look for Sadie as I said the words and jolted. She was right fucking behind me. Standing less than a foot away. I almost had a heart attack.

Satan, I tell you.

Garrett got dressed and then stumbled out the door. At least some people got the hint. Satan was still hovering.

"You want to collect the beer bottles?" I thought I might as well put her to work if she wasn't going to leave.

She looked at Bash for a long moment. "No. I gotta go." With that, she turned on her heel and walked out the door.

Bash let out a pent-up breath. "Thank God."

I studied his pale face. "What the fuck were you thinking? Hooking up with her? Remember after you kissed her?"

He closed his eyes. "I don't remember hooking up with her. She says we fucked, but I don't even remember bringing her to my room."

I shook my head like a disappointed parent. "You were so wasted. Do you even remember the pussy-eating contest?"

I didn't get to hear his answer, because our door opened. Satan returned. She was carrying something big and bulky by its handle. It looked like a baby contraption. With a baby in it.

What. The. Fuck.

Satan put the baby carrier down in the middle of our living room floor. "Someone left this outside your door for you. There's a note."

She left without a backward glance.

Bash and I stared at each other for way too long without talking.

I had no idea what he was thinking because my brain was too busy short-circuiting.

Bash spoke first. "It's a baby."

Okay, we were getting somewhere.

I slowly made my way over to the bundle, my heart beating a mile a minute. The baby's eyes were closed. I imagined it was sleeping. A folded piece of paper rested on top of its small blanket. Bash joined me at my side as I bent down to gently pick up the note. I opened it and read the contents to myself, with Bash reading over my shoulder.

I'm so sorry, but I can't do this anymore.

I'm leaving town. My boyfriend doesn't want us to take the baby.

I should have told you sooner, but I wasn't sure what I was going to do.

You're the father. Please take care of our baby.

There was nothing else.

Bash finally spoke. "Holy fuck! That's so messed up. You're a fucking father!"

My eyes about popped out of my head. "Me? What are you talking about? This can't be mine. I always practice safe sex."

Bash scoffed. "And I don't?"

My voice started rising in consternation. "You can't even remember fucking Satan last night. Give me a fucking break, Bash."

"What about that time when you fucked that chick and the condom broke?" He shot back at me.

"What?" I said incredulously. "That was like a year ago."

Our voices grew louder as our argument grew even more heated. "Exactly. The timing fits, Einstein."

The baby scrunched up its face, let out a strangled gurgle, and then started crying.

We looked at each other.

"Oh fuck. What do we do now?"

HOW TO TEMPT A ROCKSTAR

Printed in Great Britain
by Amazon